T0340486

# THE
# LEGEND
## OF
# MENEKA

ALSO BY KRITIKA H. RAO

THE RAGES TRILOGY
*The Surviving Sky*
*The Unrelenting Earth*

# THE
# LEGEND
## OF
# MENEKA

## KRITIKA H. RAO

HARPER
Voyager

Harper*Voyager*
An imprint of HarperCollins*Publishers* Ltd
1 London Bridge Street
London SE1 9GF

www.harpercollins.co.uk

HarperCollins*Publishers*
Macken House,
39/40 Mayor Street Upper,
Dublin 1
D01 C9W8
Ireland

First published by HarperCollins*Publishers* Ltd 2025
1

A catalogue record for this book is available from the British Library.

ISBN: 978-0-00-865046-9 (HB)
ISBN: 978-0-00-865047-6 (TPB)

Printed and bound in the UK using
100% Renewable Electricity by CPI Group (UK) Ltd

MIX
Paper | Supporting
responsible forestry
FSC™ C007454

*For Tate, because it is about time, and because my love story would not be complete without you.*

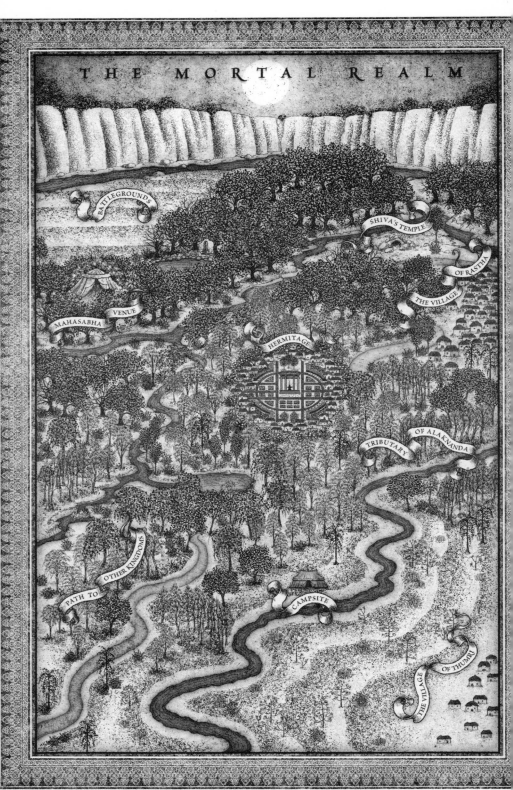

# CHAPTER 1

S eduction is all I've ever known.
I am made for it. I have destroyed lives with it.
I never wanted to.

I CLOSE MY EYES SO I DON'T HAVE TO SEE THE HUNGER IN Queen Tara's face. Instead, I focus on my dance.

My body sways to the music of her singers. The beats of the drum mimic the beating of my heart. Flute strains whisper through my hair, entwining around my thick, coiling braid. The melody makes its way into my body and pulls gently, drawing my movements forward. I bend my arms to beckon to an imaginary lover.

Queen Tara's sharp intake of breath echoes in my ears.

Amaravati's magic fills me from head to toe.

The City of Immortals is my home. It is the cord connecting me to all of heaven's magic. I am in the mortal realm, far from Amaravati now, but the city's power builds behind my navel. It grows over my head like a shimmering halo, expanding around my body in gleams of gold dust. The magic of heaven comes to me in amorphous waves, then in deeper currents. Power pours into and out of me.

My aura starts to pulse. The sari I'm wearing tightens, emphasizing my curves. The necklaces against my collarbone start to tingle. My bangles clink, making music of their own, and the diamond belt around my waist glints brightly, throwing shafts of light across the room. Goose bumps erupt along my skin.

Slowly, languorously, I spin my wrist into a mudra, a dance sigil. The fingers of my right hand touch at the tips, then open into First Blush. A wild red rose blossoms out of thin air onto my palm.

The flower settles its weightless petals on my skin. To Queen Tara, who is avidly watching from her cushioned bed, it will look real. Rambha once told me that the true power of my dance lay not in my beauty but in the strength of my illusions. A smile forms on my lips as I think of her.

First a rose, then a garden, then the stormy cascade of a furious waterfall—the illusion forms rapidly, transforming Queen Tara's bedchamber, burying it in a lush, untamed meadow. My hands move from one mudra into another. Lover's Caress. Dew on Golden Skin. Heart Fire.

My hips undulate. My feet spin in small circles, arms thrown out in release. The music lifts in a crescendo, lilting, teasing, wrapping itself all over me like a beloved's breath.

Dark gray rocks form on the walls, enclosing us in a private recess. Vines twine over the rocks, delicate buds unfurling. The thick perfume of a thousand passionflowers envelops us, heat and spice and musk. Moisture sprays my skin from the waterfall pouring from the high ceiling. In minutes, the illusion is so deep, even I am lost to it.

I *know* the meadow is not real. That I am still in Queen Tara's private quarters. But it is hard to remember when the scents of flowers tickle my nose and sun-warmed moss cushions my bare feet. Sweat beads my forehead, trickles down my throat, pools between my collarbones, before evaporating in mists of heat.

Happiness swells in my heart. I am beautiful. Intoxicating. This gushing waterfall is evidence—I am a creature of joy. Of love.

*A creature of lust*, Indra's voice corrects me in my mind.

I stumble. The joy inside me withers, the honey sweetness curdling to bitterness in my mouth. My eyes snap open, and because I have stopped dancing, the illusion wobbles.

The vines on the walls tremble. The flowers stutter. The fragrance which had overtaken the room softens, then starts to dissipate.

Queen Tara is still staring at me, slack-jawed and heavy-eyed, from her bed, but around us the magical meadow distorts. Rocks liquify into gray sludge. Silver glistens in loud, discordant flashes as the waterfall blinks in and out of existence, reacting to my darkening mood. Slowly the wild garden melts, returning us to her mortal bedchamber. Behind the privacy curtain, I see the shapes of Tara's musicians. I did not cast my illusion for them, and they are not enchanted by my magic, but they will not interrupt us. Tara saw to that. *I* did, with my command of her.

The queen blinks. Concern bleeds through the lust still clouding her eyes. She rises from her gold-threaded cushions.

"My sweet?" she asks, and her voice is throaty, heavy, akin to one speaking through viscous sleep.

It is a timbre I recognize only too well. I have come to associate it with success. With shame.

I say nothing, trying to shake the memory of Lord Indra's voice from my head and sort through my growing chaos. A frown tightens my face, and I attempt to school it, hoping to retain some measure of the peace that I felt through my dance. Tara pulls me into her arms. She strokes my hair, tugging at the strands. Her thumb traces the outline of my lips, pulling at my mouth. Her fingers splay on my neck, holding me captive. My own shallow pulse echoes beneath her touch. An ironic laugh builds behind my mouth, that she—a *mark*—is trying to smooth away my despair, even if it is in a manner *she* desires, not one I need.

"Come," she whispers. "I know what will please you." She tries to lead me, but I shake my head, resisting the movement.

Tara has wanted me in her bed for months, but it is not to please me. It is to please herself. I know this because *I* have created these thoughts in her. *Reveal your lust*, I command silently, and an image blossoms in my mind. Tara seizing my hair, bending me down to her. I am on my knees, naked except for my jewelry. My riches, my body, my mind—all of it belongs to her. Vulnerable and weak, I am to be her greatest jewel.

The image flares, then subsides. I hold my turmoil at bay, watching her and the deep hunger for me that she now feels.

This is the last stage of my seduction. When I first created this spell to discern her lust, I saw her ultimate supremacy over her nation, wrought through fire and sword. It took months to alter that desire. In discreet glances and poisonous whispers, I consolidated it, molding her to want me and me alone. My illusions were subtle and glorious, for her eyes alone. Convinced by them, she imprisoned her brother, exiled her cabinet, shattered age-old rules. Once she had been confident, her gaze imperious, her posture straight. Now she is a ghost of her former self—enraptured with me to the point of forgetting everything else, even food and drink. Her brown skin is waxy, the healthy glow gone.

It is over.

I am the only thing that matters to Queen Tara anymore.

She tugs me again, this time harder. Her eyes dart between me and the cushioned bed. Vaguely, I wonder if I should consummate her desire. Others of my ilk have done so. Tumbled with their marks without regret after those marks have been seduced. Some have done it even before—simply another step in their missions. It would be a kind of reparation—to fulfill the very desire I have created in Tara. I would not be leaving her undone. The corners of her mouth quiver as she notices my contemplation. I lean in—a kiss, what would it hurt? Tara's breathing grows ragged in the space between us.

*No*, I think. Shame grips me, locking my muscles. Self-disgust sinks its nails into my heart, at what I'd been about to justify. Tara does not know her mind. Whatever she thinks she wants, it is not *her* want, not truly. She is enthralled. She is *seduced*.

My face hardens.

I pull her hands away from me.

I step back.

Tara's eyes grow larger, confused, and my shoulders sag, heavy with guilt. I open my mouth, wanting to say something. An apology. An explanation. *Something.*

Yet what is there to say? I've danced for her many times, and my spell will not wear off easily. When I am gone, she will be bereft for years. She will waste away, waiting for me to return. Nothing—not even sleeping with her now—will ever be enough. Even if I were to stay, to live with her as her mate, it would not matter. The lust has taken on a life of its own. Tara will never truly recover from it. My mission has been too successful.

And is any of that wrong? Surely my guilt now is misplaced. Tara deserved this. Lord Indra demanded this. I am his agent, and my missions are a sign of my devotion to him. If I did not do this, what would happen then? Before my arrival, Tara already abolished the public worship of Indra—an act of challenge to heaven itself. Eventually, she would prohibit private prayers too. Once, her dynasty was defined by its devotion to Indra, but Tara and her ministers began traveling a path that would eventually lead to the burning of the lord's temples, the desecration of his rituals, the slaughtering of his devotees. Everything I did was to prevent that terrible future.

I know all of this, yet I wish I could explain that I never meant to hurt her. Never meant to destroy her so completely. The yearning to absolve myself is so acute, spilling nearly out of my lips, that I realize I have lingered in her court too long. What does it make me that I am sympathizing with someone as undevout as Tara?

My eyes slide away from her face. I turn to leave the bedchamber. Though I hear a quiet cry of despair from her, I don't look back.

This is my job. My destiny.

My name is Meneka.

And I am an apsara of Indra's heaven.

THE DOORS TO THE BEDCHAMBER SHUT BEHIND ME, SILENC-ing the music. I can no longer hear Tara, but I move faster as though to distance myself from the anguish of my own heart.

Apsaras have a reputation. Mortal poets whisper we are mistresses of illusion and ultimate control. Lord Indra calls us his snakeskins, ready to shed and birth anew. I think we are cobra venom. Our magical dance is lethal. It has felled kingdoms and tempted saints. It has changed the course of history and taken loved ones away.

Yet when I perform, the world makes sense. I am coated in utter heavenly bliss, my very dance a devotion to Indra and a blessing from him. In some ways, my dance is even more than what Indra allows it to be. It is a secret joy of my own, unspooling the very essence of me. The way my performance is used, however . . .

I am only twenty-three, my time at this early age still measured in mortal years, but I feel older. I have lost count of the number of missions I have gone on, the ways in which I have proved my devotion to my lord. Tara was one of my most sacrilegious marks. One of the hardest. I'm going to make sure she is my last.

I hurry down the palace corridors, turning corners and entering passageways blindly. When I can no longer see any palace guards, I pause. Closing my eyes again, I touch my enchanted necklaces. I invoke Indra's name and request my return to swarga, the lord's heaven.

Permission is granted as a prize for my devotion. The tug behind my navel tightens as Amaravati responds to my call. A gust of wind whistles through the corridors of the palace, bringing with it scents of cinnamon and ghee. My form becomes airy, light and gossamer weaves tingling on my skin. The wind of the celestial city carries me away from the mortal realm.

When I open my eyes next, I am at the gates of the City of Immortals, back home in the heavenly realm. Stars twinkle overhead and under me. Even though it is nighttime, my city is bright and alive, its magical golden dust sparkling on the giant marble gates that form the city's entrance. Darkness itself shimmers with an undertone of luminosity.

No guards prowl here. It is peacetime, and the magic of Amaravati acts as a shield. The gates open on their own, and the underlying rhythms and music of Amaravati greet me as I walk in.

My body immediately relaxes, and a sigh escapes me. The worries of the mortal world shed themselves from my shoulders as the city welcomes me. The magical tether that connects me to Amaravati blooms like a chord struck. In the mortal realm, it was a fragile thing, flat and limp, a faded painting. Here it is a flower, alive, beautiful, golden. I breathe in, and Amaravati's loveliness strikes me like I'm seeing it for the first time. It has been so long since I've been here.

The city hums under my feet as I walk. Every manse I glimpse is more beautiful than all of Queen Tara's palace. The rock-paved pathways glisten under the golden light. Somewhere a bird sings sweetly, holding a single warbling note that strums through my heart. Laughter echoes here and there, though I see no one. The citizens are hidden within glorious buildings, ensconced in fragrant night gardens. The same gentle breeze that brought me back home rustles through the city, this time with scents of lightning and storm, scents that belong to Lord Indra. His magic spirals lazily through the city, tiny sparks that flicker and flash.

I transform as I breathe in the quiet streets. In the mortal realm, I began to question my devotion to Lord Indra. Tara's seduction should have given me joy, each evolution of her lust a testament to my faith, but the mission only pierced my own belief in myself. My very despair was treasonous, and through all the days of my mission, I clutched my reverence for Indra like a beggar clutches alms. Now, with my return to Amaravati, those doubts about my own dedication evaporate like chimerical dreams on wakefulness. I am reminded once again that I am an *apsara*, a creature of the lord's city—yet this time the acknowledgment straightens my spine. My devotion is untainted by turmoil; it is scented with confidence. I am returned to a reality that has burned through a feverish glamour.

The change in me is so sudden, so familiar, that I am shocked. Images burst in my head of Indra studying me when I first began my training as an apsara at seven. Of when I knelt at his feet at fifteen before I embarked on my first mission. Of his kindness and pride as he blessed me before I left the city. His magnanimity, his love, his heroism, all gleam through Amaravati, as though the city itself is singing his praise. Indra is the father of heaven, and though he is no true relation of mine, the same golden blood of swarga runs through our veins. Immortal and celestial, we are one family, all of us beholden to him to succor us.

Slowly, I make my way toward his palace to report on my latest conquest. Rambha waits for me there; I sent a message to her a few hours ago when I knew I had succeeded with Tara, and I can sense her calling to me, her face blossoming behind my eyes. She was the one thing I held on to during my mission, and I ache to see her. Still, my steps grow slower as I contemplate what I am about to do.

Every apsara at the end of a successful mission is granted a boon, whatever her heart desires. All apsaras ask for a chance to continue to serve the lord more faithfully—a blessing that is granted through magical jewelry from his own collection. To wear an ornament that belongs to Indra is akin to carrying a piece of the lord with us. His presence allows us to pull more of Amaravati's magic than we otherwise can, essential to creating the most unwavering illusions, critical to our success in future missions.

Yet my sari belt constricts around my waist. The necklaces tighten, and my hand rises to skim against my collarbone, trying to loosen their leash. What will Rambha say if I tell her this is how the jewels have felt for so long? That wearing them has been no blessing but a prison sentence? The boon I intend to ask of the lord today will surely catch her unaware—but the lord himself will see that it comes from a desire to be more pious. The jewels are wondrous, but they take me away from him each time I leave Amaravati. All I want is to be untainted in my devotion, close to him, worshiping him. Surely he will agree?

*He will rage,* my mind whispers. *You are not asking to be devoted. You are asking for freedom.*

I surge away from the thought. "No," I say aloud, forcefully. "No, I only want to be unsullied. Indra will listen. He is generous and life-giving. He understands true devotion."

There is no reply from my conscience, merely a quiet worry that worms its way into my heart. Only Rambha has dared ask for freedom from future missions, and though Indra granted it to her, her request still shook the kingdom. Time and again, I have thought to ask her why he made such an exception, but it would be a foolish question. Rambha's love for the lord is well known. Heaven's immortal musicians, the gandharvas, sing of her piety at every festival, reminding us of her purity, her virtue, her total dedication.

Will she be shocked that I dare to follow in her footsteps so brazenly? All my life I have wanted to be like her, as unblemished as her, as free. I have performed every mission without complaint. I took no joy in them, but I did them regardless—and isn't that the greatest devotion, to be selfless, believing, compliant? I walked away from Queen Tara without a word of regret. I am Indra's soldier, and—despite the misgivings infesting my mind in the mortal realm—humbled to be one. If I only show this to him, he will relent. Amaravati is sustained through service and prayers to Indra, and Indra will agree that my performance within the city will serve him better than my missions in the mortal realm. And though Rambha might be shocked, she will be delighted. She will see that I do this for her as much as I do this for myself. They will both be proud. They have to be.

I repeat this litany to myself the entire way to the palace, corralling my courage. Before I know it, I am at the crescent-shaped gates.

The guards let me enter unchallenged. Everyone in Amaravati knows what an apsara looks like. We are some of the most beautiful creatures in paradise—we *have* to be. The guards simply nod at me, usher me into the alcove just off Indra's main throne room, where I see Rambha pacing impatiently.

She is stunning. Her long, luscious hair is tied in an intricate braid in the manner of the most elite apsaras. Her skin is a richer brown than mine, nearly onyx in the dim light. Thick, shapely brows arch over large doelike eyes, and her ears resemble delicate shells. Over her gold-threaded green sari, she wears nearly a hundred necklaces studded with emeralds and diamonds. A tiny pin glints on her nose, and even her bindi glows with power. All of these jewels are from the lord's own collection, a sign of her devotion and his favor, and my breath hitches as her power descends over me. Her aura is a luminous gold rising behind her head, so potent I can taste its texture, delicate dewdrops after a sizzling storm. I wet my lips to trap the sensation on my tongue.

A smile breaks across Rambha's worried face as she sees me. She hurries forward to envelop me in her arms.

"Praise Indra," she says, pulling back so her eyes can search mine. "You're here."

My chest rises in a deep breath, and the scent of her sweet star-anise flows into me, hot and seductive. I smile back despite my nervousness.

She is much older than me, but even I don't know by how many years. Like any other immortal, time will never show on her features. Besides, neither of us is a child anymore. What does it matter how old we are? Even as I hug her, I can't help but lightly twist the end of her braid around my fingers. Rambha is my home. Her wisdom is my security. Once she was my mentor, but now she is my handler, one of the best apsaras I know, my closest friend.

In the depths of my foolish heart, I have always wished for more.

The longing must surely show on my features, for she pulls back and brushes her cool hands over my face to examine me in concern. Her fingers hum like butterfly wings, and I can't help but imagine her touch in other places. My cheeks warm. I swallow, trying to ignore the heat pooling in me. But her caress, this intimacy—it is simply another strand of evidence that what I intend to do is right.

I catch her fluttering, featherlight fingers in my own and take a deep breath. "Another successful mission, Rambha. Queen Tara is deterred from her path of impiety. She won't be a threat to Indra anymore."

"Good, that's good," Rambha replies. "The lord is sorely in need of some happy news. Do you know what jewel you will ask of him?" Her smile grows curious, and she touches the crown of my head. A skittering sensation floods through me and I shiver. "I have always loved ornaments in your hair. Perhaps the lord's golden diadem? It changes shape based on the wearer. I would like to see what shape it takes for you."

Her fingers move down the length of my hair to my shoulders. They flicker over my chest, brushing strands off as though to examine my necklaces, but the motion is too slow, too deliberate. I am not imagining it. It is desire. Desire for *me*. Her thumbs skate lightly over the points of my nipples before skimming away.

"I have something else in mind," I say quietly. "Something that will allow me to be closer to you. So we can . . . So you and I can finally . . ."

I stutter to a stop. Her hands still and she tilts her head. Rambha holds my gaze between gold-dusted lashes. Her lips part, perhaps to ask what I mean—and I want to lean in, how badly I want to speak the sweet words that would bring us closer. They burn in me, but my nervousness at Indra's refusal of my boon holds me back. Rambha and I have orbited each other for years now, our touches suggestive, our glances flirtatious, but I have never dared to say anything, not when I feel so unworthy. How could I come to her—this beauty who is famed for her complete devotion to Indra—when every one of my own missions has drowned me in doubts? The boon I will ask of the lord is my only way out, both to wrench out any seeds of impiety I may have collected, and to be with her forevermore.

Rambha tips my chin with a hand. "You look so serious. What are you thinking?"

Now would be the time to speak, to tell her about the boon I want, but explanations form and die in my throat. What if she tells me I am mistaken in my path? It would not merely be a rejection of my dream. It would be a rejection of any future for us. I cannot risk it, not when I am so close. I shake my head wordlessly.

A frown mars her lovely face. "You won't ask him for anything indelicate, will you?" She waits for me to answer, but when I still say nothing, she sighs. "It is your blessing to ask, whatever it is, but do not ask him to part with his favorite jewels. Indra is moody and restless these days. He is in conference, even now."

My brows rise at this, curiosity replacing my worry. The lord of the

devas is not known to take midnight meetings. If anything, Indra famously spends his nights with his most sensual concubines, engaging
in licentious behavior that warms even my apsara ears to think about.

"What has happened?" I say. "What is worrying the lord?"

"A mortal. A man called Kaushika."

The name is familiar. In Queen Tara's court, whispers came of a
prince who deserted his kingdom to practice magic. Rumors said the
prince became so powerful that kings and queens began paying hom-
age to him, to ask him to train their scions. I did not pay attention
then, but my interest piques now.

"Another mortal too big for himself?" I ask dryly. "That isn't new."

Rambha's aura darkens, her star-anise scent growing saccharine.
"He's not just any mortal. He calls himself a sage. Already his influence against Indra has caused royals and nobles to forget the lord in
their rituals. Amaravati is not the same as it used to be. Didn't you
notice? The buildings have lost much of their sheen. Our magic is
depleting without enough prayers from the mortals to replenish it.
It's harder to grasp Amaravati's magic even when *I* dance with all my
jewelry. My own tether lies limp within me when I compare it to the
years past."

I nod slowly. My dance took more effort than usual to create illusions when I was with Queen Tara, but I assumed it was because
my heart wasn't in the mission. Perhaps it was because the city was
in danger. If all this is true, then wouldn't the lord *want* me here, to
sustain Amaravati through my dance from within his court? I could
not be better positioned to ask for my boon.

"The lord has sent one apsara after another to seduce this sage,"
Rambha continues. "Nanda first, and then Sundari and Magadhi.
But . . ." Her voice breaks slightly, the names opening an unhealed
wound.

These three apsaras are so famed for their prowess that even devas, the deities of heaven, are hypnotized by their dance. Only Indra is immune to them. "What happened to them?" I ask, frowning.

"They haven't returned. I fear Kaushika has killed them."

My curiosity turns to horror. Killing an apsara is nearly impossible. We are immortals. Only desperate hate and powerful magic can annihilate us. How has Kaushika done this? *Why?*

Rambha hugs me again. "I am glad to see you safe."

This time I notice how her body shakes. Sundari and Magadhi were Rambha's friends, part of her own cohort. Nanda used to train me, her laughter often raucous when I created a particularly titillating illusion. Rambha must have been their handler, too, on those fateful missions; she often dealt with such elite apsaras. What must it have been like for her to wait and wait for a message, and then finally report to Indra she lost his most prized weapons? No wonder my delay has disconcerted her. A sharp guilt pangs through me. Her worry radiates toward me like a flame's heat.

I straighten and squeeze her hand.

I will make the delay worth it. For her, and for Amaravati.

"Take me to the lord, Rambha. Perhaps news of my success will cheer him up." My voice is more confident than I am, but I do not back down. "It is time for my boon."

# CHAPTER 2

Indra's throne room puts Queen Tara's to shame. It is the heart of his palace, a pulsing that mimics his own rhythm, making me sweat at its alien intimacy. As soon as we enter, the room's aura assaults me. The scents of ghee, jaggery, and camphor ooze through the air, silent reminders of prayer and opulence, power and abundance. Hundreds of glorious artifacts hang on the walls, both from the mortal and immortal realms. Paintings of the lord being worshiped. Murals with dancers in sensuous, alluring poses. Tapestries in fine filigree that change pictures as one moves past them. Intoxication pounds my veins to behold them, like I have drunk too much soma.

Magic here is thick and dense. Shafts of golden dust crisscross like light pouring from the ceiling. The ceiling itself imitates a night sky. Stars shimmer like a million fat gems, yet creeping at the edges are storm clouds, roiling and dark.

A slight coldness permeates the air, making me want to rub away the gooseflesh erupting on my arms. It would be an uncultured move, more suited to a wide-eyed mortal visiting swarga than one of Indra's immortal apsaras. Yet even Rambha, who must surely come to the throne room more often than any other dancer, takes a deep breath. She grits her teeth tight, then relaxes slowly. My contrived confidence from a few minutes ago seems childish. If Rambha herself is so anxious to see Indra, how will I ever make my request to him?

I try to mirror her, but the closer we move toward the throne, the more I become aware of myself in an awkward, clumsy way. Rambha's tactics will not work for me. It is not simply a breath that relaxes her; it is her devotion to Indra. The lord seizes all the grace in this chamber. There is none left for any of us, not unless we reflect to him a piece of his own majesty. Rambha exists in his radiance, separate and secure in her love. I try to hold on to myself, reminding myself that I am just as devoted to Indra in my own way, that his granting of my boon tonight will only cement it for everyone, but I cannot help my nervousness. My eyes dart everywhere. The floor that seems to be moving. The shifting statues. The gleaming pillars. The darkening sky.

Finally, they land on the deva king.

Lord Indra does not lean back in his usual indolent way. Instead, his feet tap the floor, and a scowl mars his handsome, chiseled face. Jewels glitter on him from head to toe, garnets deeper than blood around his neck, sapphires bluer than the ocean clasped on his wrists, moonstone pearls that wreathe his fingers. His dhoti is azure, the delicate weaving on the embroidery resembling violent clouds veering into sudden calm, before glossing back into darkness—a reflection of his tempestuous mood. His ornate gold crown gleams in a splinter of dawn.

All immortals have a recognizable aura, shining like a halo. Indra's aura is so radiant that the auras of the devas surrounding him look dark by comparison. It covers him from head to toe, its incandescent light reaching far beyond his person. Golden dust swirls sensuously around his fingertips like an affectionate pet.

He is so beautiful that I can barely stand to look at him. I glimpse him only in instances, my eyes scurrying to the other devas, benevolent Surya of the sun, burly Vayu of the wind, sharp Agni of the fire.

In one hand, Indra toys with his vajra, the lightning bolt that is his greatest weapon, which crackles with electricity and anger, its glittering edges sharp enough to only be a blur of light. In his other hand, a crystal cup magically refills with ruby-red wine even as he drains it. I can tell at a glance the lord is drunk again. Another pang of anxiety makes my heart jump.

Rambha stiffens and stops in her tracks. Her beautiful eyes go wide, and she whispers, alarmed, "Shachi."

I don't understand immediately; I am too taken with beholding the lord himself. Then my eyes follow Rambha's, and I notice standing among the devas is another figure. Goddess Shachi. Indra's wife and consort, the queen of the devis.

I stumble to a stop. Now that I study her, I cannot imagine how I overlooked her. I have not seen her in years, but she has never looked as resplendent—or as angry.

Her entire being is electrified. Her skin is a golden brown, so shiny that she mirrors the light of her own aura, a seemingly endless spiral of golden glow. Her eyes glint with calculation and intelligence, and she tilts her pointed chin up, staring at Indra down her small, narrow nose. The fiery red sari she wears curls around her luscious curves, sparking with what looks like Agni's fire, except cooler, contained. Like Indra's clothes, Shachi's sari shifts in color, one moment a volcanic orange, then a rosy pink, then the first blush of dawn, until it is a fiery red again. Beside her full bloom, Rambha is merely a budding flower. Compared to her, I am just a seed.

Shachi draws herself up to full height. Her aura sharpens, just for an instant obscuring all the other deities.

"You may be the king of devas," she says tightly to her husband, "but do not forget, lord, that I command the devis. The apsaras are my charge."

Indra scowls. "I cannot give up my greatest weapons, not even for you, Queen. You may care for them, but swarga is *my* heaven. Not yours. As long as I sit on this throne, the dancers are mine."

The goddess's eyes flash. "You invite your own doom," she proclaims. A flash of light—I hear my own shallow gasp—

She is gone.

Lord Indra blinks and sits up. His fingers tighten around his wine cup as silence echoes in the wake of her departure. "It is all because of this damned boy," he says to no one in particular. "The missing apsaras have created this rebellion from the queen."

The devas who are Indra's counselors murmur soothing words, too soft for me to catch, but the lord slams his wine cup on his throne and it shatters.

"We don't *know* anything about him," he snarls. "None of my spies have brought back anything of use. Amaravati is in danger. *I* am in danger. The Vajrayudh is approaching. Don't tell me I have nothing to worry about!"

The devas exchange looks. Agni's fingertips spark with fire. Surya's golden eyes gleam brighter in irritation. Vayu, who loves chaos, allows a brisk smile to flutter across his lips. Yet none of them say anything.

Indra leans back sullenly. He snaps his fingers. The shattered chunks of crystal disappear from around his clothes, and another wine cup appears in its place, filled to the brim. He takes a moody sip from it.

My nervousness pitches higher. Devas get angry. It is their due. They are creatures of the elements, responsible for the fates of the three realms. Indra himself is the lord of sky and storm, volatile in nature, true to his essence. I know this and love this about him. Yet I have never seen the lord and his queen fight in such a public manner.

Is this because of the Vajrayudh? The celestial event occurs once every thousand years, and it is a stark reminder of Indra's limitations. King of heaven he might be, but even he cannot control all the powers of the universe. During the Vajrayudh, all celestials grow weaker. Amaravati shuts her gates, and no souls are allowed in or out. The devas rest, and Indra himself retires to his palace in the comfort of gandharvas and apsaras to lose himself in song and dance until the

event has passed. It is essential that the devas and devis are in harmony, and Amaravati peaceful, during the Vajrayudh. Without that,
heaven itself can implode, eaten up by rising magical chaos.

Next to me, Rambha seems frozen, staring at Indra. I clutch her
hand with my sweaty one and pull her away to the shadow of a pillar,
grateful we have not yet been seen in the hubbub.

"Rambha," I whisper urgently. "What is going on?"

"It's Kaushika," she whispers back, tearing her gaze away from the
lord. She looks stricken but shakes her head to clear herself of the
emotion. "The prince is becoming stronger each day. When first he
declared himself a sage, other sages came to pay him their respects.
Indra too sent gandharvas to treat with him as per tradition. But
Kaushika only laughed at the singers and dismissed them. The lord is
reasonable—he has bent to sages before—but this unprovoked insult?
Indra could not abide it. He sent his followers to challenge Kaushika
in combat, but Kaushika is of warrior stock, and he defeated the
kshatriya devotees with ease, humiliating Indra again. It was then
that the lord sent apsaras to Kaushika—yet those apsaras haven't returned. Shachi is furious they are missing."

Rambha quietens and memories of Shachi flood me. Running in
her garden, chased by her laughing handmaidens. The first jewel I
was given, a thin gold chain the queen removed from her own neck.
Sweetmeats and ambrosia she brought to the apsara girls while we
crowded around her, pawing at her sari. Apsaras are Shachi's daugh-
ters, in a way. The oldest of us were born of the Churning of the
Oceans, from which Shachi herself came—but the younger ones like
me were born from the union of other celestial beings. I have never
known my parents, but I have not needed to. An apsara's birth is a
blessing for all of Amaravati. I grew up with other girls in Shachi's
grove, was sent to train for Indra's army on my maturation. The day
I left the grove, the queen's eyes followed me with sadness. I thought

she was melancholy because I had outgrown the innocence of my childhood. Yet perhaps she did not like turning me over to Indra? Did she fear our missions? Does she fear Kaushika too?

"Can Indra not simply smite this sage with the vajra?" I ask. Not even immortals can survive a strike of celestial lightning from Indra's bolt, after all.

But Rambha shakes her head, anxiety pooling in her eyes. "Indra cannot directly harm Kaushika, not unless the sage performs an unquestioned act of war against heaven first. If we had any evidence of Kaushika killing our sisters, that would be enough for the lord, but the mortal covers his tracks well. He is devoted to Shiva, the Destroyer, and Indra dare not make a careless move. Yet if this sage continues to spread irreverence for the lord . . ."

"All of our magic could vanish," I finish grimly. "Our dance. Our illusions."

The thought turns my stomach, filling my mouth with sourness. I have struggled with how my dance is used, but who will I be without it? Despite my uncertainties, I have always been devoted to the lord—it is why I dare to come here with an agenda of my own. Yet mortals are so shortsighted and fickle. Indra is the lord of rain and water, of storm and sky. Without him, the mortal realm would suffer, crops die, lands grow arid. Shouldn't a sage know this? How can one be a sage yet be so misguided? This ridiculous man is threatening everything I love. The ceiling darkens, the lord's anger pressing beneath my veins, soaking my own resentment.

I am about to speak, to ask my questions, when thunder rolls overhead. "Rambha," Indra's deep voice calls out, and my knees shake without my volition. "Why are you here?"

Rambha falters in front of me, the tiniest of pauses, before she steadies herself. Straightening, she continues toward the throne, and I follow, the lord watching the both of us approach. Nervousness crawls over me in a beelike hum, and I try to repeat my justifications for what I am about to do, but the closer we come, the more my mind scatters. It is all I can do to put one foot in front of the other.

Lord Indra raises his brows, irritated at our intrusion, but sighs when Rambha bows deeply to him. Rambha's hands move in subtle dance mudras. Her necklaces and rings shine brighter. She is using magic, creating a delicate illusion for Indra himself, perhaps to calm him, and Indra must surely understand this. Yet far from being annoyed that she is attempting to manipulate his mood, he looks amused. Distractedly, I wonder what she is showing him. I wonder at their relationship, and the way his divinity coats her.

"Well, Rambha?" he asks.

"Meneka has returned, my lord," she answers quietly. "From another successful mission in the mortal realm. Your devotees are still protected."

Indra's eyes travel to me, noticing me fully for the first time. I am absorbed by his intense scrutiny.

"One of the ones you sent to Kaushika?" he demands. "What did you find, girl?"

"No, my lord," Rambha interjects hurriedly. "A different mission. One to Queen Tara of the nation of Pallava. She who terrorized many, including your devotees. Who was on a crusade to gain power beyond her reach. This has been a difficult journey for Meneka, my lord, but she has done as you commanded. As per tradition, she is here for her boon."

Indra leans back, his expression already bored now that he realizes I'm an ordinary apsara. "You're blessed, daughter. Go take the rest that is your due before you have to prove your devotion to me again."

He plucks a few rings from his own fingers and tosses them toward me. I catch them, feeling their weight. I can tell how powerful the rings are, how much of Amaravati's magic they hold. This is a treasure beyond expectation for any apsara, one the lord has stripped from his own body in front of his devas. I know I should take the gems and leave. That my chance is already lost. But desperation floods me, spilling into panic. How long will it take, how many more missions, until the time is right? I nursed the possibility of my boon through my time with Queen Tara like it were a beloved child. I endured the trials of my wretchedness because of this one faint hope. I cannot take another hollow mission, another disappointment.

I know it is a mistake. I know I am being foolish. Yet I step forward, the careful words I prepared, the strategy I planned, flying from my mind like startled birds.

"Please, my lord," I blurt out, and my voice is a croak. "I don't want these amulets. I would beg you allow me to remain in Amaravati instead. I would ask you allow me relief from any future missions."

Indra is half-turned back toward his devas. One of them has already begun speaking. Echoing in my ears, my words sound so coarse that I can scarcely believe I have uttered them. I think the lord has not heard me. I *hope* he hasn't heard me.

Then Rambha's jaw drops.

Lord Indra turns back to me, his face incredulous.

"What did you say?" he hisses.

So strong is his magic that the very air congeals with his anger, ramming me down to my knees. I thump inelegantly, my breath slammed out of me. Above, the ceiling crackles and the stars disappear. Storm clouds take over fully. The coolness of the chamber is replaced with a horrible, suffocating heat.

All my thoughts twist inside me. The tether connecting me to Amaravati blooms, radiant despite Indra's anger, or perhaps because of it. I want to be diplomatic, but in reaction to his power, truths tumble out of me without my permission.

"All apsaras are granted a boon of their choice, my lord," I whisper. "I only want what is mine."

Indra's disbelieving gaze moves from me to Rambha, but my friend's eyes are wide. It is clear she had not expected this. Guilt pierces my cloud of haze. Maybe I should have told her what I intended, but Rambha would have tried to stop me. Besides, if Indra is going to be angry, at least she won't be punished. It is better this way. She will not be harmed, she will walk away from it, my foolishness will not have endangered her—

Indra stands up.

Lightning crackles around him, fingertips to crown. His entire being shines with outrage. His clothes, his very skin, become so glorious that my eyes blink shut. I can hear thunder start to build beyond the palace walls, all through the city of Amaravati. My heart rattles in my chest in quickening terror as I feel him approaching me. Heat scorches me, seeking to burn the flesh from my bones. I am still on my knees, and suddenly grateful for it. My body would not support my weight right now.

Indra looms over me. His voice is dangerously soft. "Is this treason pouring from your mouth? You wish freedom from your service, daughter?"

I swallow again, and panic makes me incoherent. "N-No, my lord. It is because I wish to serve! P-Please. You allowed this of Rambha. I wish—simply consider it for me too. In the mortal realm, my devotion to you suffers, but here, living in Amaravati—the city needs this, with the magic depleting. I can—if you will allow me—"

Lightning crashes above, silencing me. "How dare you speak to me of devotion as you try to shirk your duty?" he whispers, his quiet voice deadly. "Apsaras are *my* weapons. *My* army. It is an honor to go on these missions. You will never be free from them."

Indra's power is too strong. My eyes water from the pressure his presence is exerting. I smell the cinnamon wine on his breath, and the fumes choke me.

Still, through the viselike grip of his magic, one thought stands clear in my head. If I accept his answer, if I'm made to go on another mission to seduce a mortal, I will forever be lost. Queen Tara's yearning face and the faces of the other mortals I have seduced flash before me, cutting through my panic. I look toward Rambha, though I don't dare meet her eyes.

A terrified whisper escapes me, foolishness unable to be stopped. "Please. P-Please, there must be something I can do. *Something . . .*"

"For such a treasonous demand, for such a special gift?" Indra sneers. "Perhaps if you thwarted a problem like Kaushika, I might consider it. Yet nothing less than that would be a sign of your true devotion. Now, leave my sight, daughter, before I truly get angry."

Rambha's hand closes on my wrist tightly in a warning not to say any more. She yanks me to my feet and gestures curtly with her head for me to follow her. Lord Indra is already turning away, disgusted.

Yet all I can think of is that such a chance will never reappear. If I don't get my boon now, if I don't lock Indra into a promise, I will never be able to escape my destiny, doomed into this cycle for the rest of my immortal life.

Desperation claws at me. The words hurl out of me without any further thought.

"I'll do it," I cry, shaking Rambha off. I am already reaching forward, my hands seeking his grace beseechingly. "Lord Indra, my lord, please, *please*. I'll do it."

He turns to me again, his face filled with surprise.

I force myself to meet his gaze, even as my entire body trembles. My own voice comes to me as though from a distance. "If you promise I never need to leave Amaravati after this deed is complete, I will seduce Kaushika. I will neutralize him so he is never a threat to you again."

OF COURSE, IT ISN'T AS EASY.

Even though my heart pounds loud enough to be heard in all of Amaravati, Indra merely raises his eyebrows and returns to his throne to drink again. He waves his hand carelessly, and suddenly I cannot hear any more of the discussions between him and his devas.

From Rambha's expression, she is under Indra's enchantment too. She fumbles for me and crushes my hand in hers. Her breath comes out in shaky whispers. She doesn't look in my direction, but her skin is too cold, her aura conversely smelling burned. A thousand doubts and questions must surely circle her mind, though she says nothing, perhaps fearing the lord's wrath. Instead, we both stand silently next to each other, trying not to shiver. I attempt to draw comfort from her touch while my heart races with adrenaline.

I cannot believe what I've done. What was I thinking? I've never seduced a sage.

Mortal magic comes in many forms, but the strict meditation of a sage kindles its own rival power to the devas—one that can overthrow Indra, cast the lord into the mortal realm, even render his magic useless *within* Amaravati. Sages use prana, the untainted energy of the universe, to bend the forces of reality. Only apsaras like Rambha are ever sent to seduce them, and even she was terrified when talking of Kaushika.

The sheer scope of this man dazzles me. This is swarga, the heavenly realm of the devas, and it is already suffering because of Kaushika. Very few things can destroy a celestial, but Rambha thinks that the prince-sage has killed some of the most powerful apsaras already. His irreverence for Indra is reducing Amaravati's magic. What chance do I have?

Suddenly, I feel small. Defeated. I think back to how hard my mission with Tara was. How every seduction for her sloughed pieces of my own self away, leaving me naked and wretched. My dance is a drug I do not want to escape, but the agony and ecstasy of performing in a mission, the self-loathing and the doubt I lived in within the mortal realm—these warped my love for my art in irredeemable ways. If the experience with a mortal queen exacerbated the ever-present turmoil within me, what would the seduction of Sage Kaushika do? I want to take my reckless request back, but it is already too late. Indra's charm lifts and all his devas watch me, inscrutable.

The lord leans forward. The anger has completely left his face. Now he looks wary, watchful. "Come forward, the both of you," he commands.

Stumbling, we move. I am aware of Rambha only in pieces. Indra's entire attention is on me. His overwhelming radiance drenches me from head to toe as he examines my beauty.

"How good is she?" he asks, the question directed at Rambha.

I hear a choking sound catch in her throat. "She is not the one I would pick, my lord," Rambha whispers. "She does not even know the most useful mudras yet. She spoke out of turn. She has never challenged any sage, let alone someone as dangerous as Kaushika. For the love you bear me, lord. Please don't let her do this."

Indra studies her for a moment, almost coldly, before turning back to me. "Is she capable?"

It is the second time he has asked. I know Rambha does not dare refuse him a clear answer. Thoughtless though I have been, even *I* understand the look on his face. His eyes narrow slightly in barely veiled irritation that she should think to challenge him in front of his devas, after I myself did with my boon. The corners of his mouth twist in warning; now is not the time to test his patience. It is all a subtle reminder. He is a king. Rambha, though favored, is but a courtesan.

*And I*, I think despairingly, *I am nobody at all.*

Rambha's voice trembles, but her answer this time is unambiguous.

"She is unique. She prides herself on never becoming involved with a mark, a failing I have tried to stamp out, yet it has only made her more creative with her missions. Her wits and resourcefulness cannot be denied, and it is because of those that she accomplishes her missions so successfully. While her illusions are rawer than other apsaras, she has been successful so far because she has learnt not to rely only on her magic and beauty. Instead, she studies her enemy deeply, carving her illusions based on who they are and what they fear. In a few years I would have her seduce more challenging marks, and with more training, she could one day become heaven's greatest weapon. But please listen to me, my lord. She is not yet ready. You would be sacrificing a valuable asset—"

"And you, Meneka," Indra interrupts. "You volunteer for this mission?"

My mind is still whirling from Rambha's words about me. That she should think so highly of me, that she should think so little of me . . . Is she right? Do I have it in me to become swarga's greatest weapon?

"Yes," I whisper, raising my eyes to the lord.

"Then I agree," the lord says simply. A smile alights on his lips. It transforms him and the throne room. The storm clouds clear. Stars rush in with a sublime shimmer. Agni, Surya, Vayu, and all the other lords exchange glances, their own auras becoming resplendent now that Indra's fury no longer overwhelms them.

Indra moves forward in a blur, and then his hands are on my shoulders, straightening my posture, giving me strength. I am dazzled by being touched by him. Colors, sunshine, laughter—all of these spin in me, my own soul reacting to his divinity now that he looks upon me with such favor. I feel intoxicated, invincible. Magics I never knew I was capable of seem within arm's reach. The illusions I can ordinarily do as an apsara are laughable; there is so much more grace I am suddenly gifted. Is this how Rambha feels all the time? An absurd laugh escapes me, and I smile at her with pride and kinship, yet she utters a gasp.

"My lord," she says before I can speak. "I must protest. Meneka spoke in error—let *me* handle her. Let *me* take this mission. I beg you."

"I cannot spare you," Indra says shortly. His eyes glint with the reflection of his hundred jewels as he considers me. "The mission is yours, daughter. Seduce Kaushika in the mortal realm. Find out his true agenda for heaven. Learn his lusts and secrets, and thwart him from his power-seeking ways. You shall get your heart's desire—your freedom from any future missions. You shall be a goddess, a devi, in Amaravati. No one shall question your devotion to me or to swarga."

*Say no*, Rambha's look urges me. *Ask for forgiveness. Please, Meneka. Please.*

*I am doing this for us*, I try to tell her without speaking.

She blinks as though she has heard me, and I glance back at the lord. "I accept," I breathe.

"Then go," Indra says, waving a bejeweled hand. "Do not tarry a minute longer. The Vajrayudh approaches in six turns of the moon lord. You must stop Kaushika well before then."

He turns his back on us to return to his throne. We are already forgotten.

Rambha's body trembles with rage and fear. Her lips part, as though to implore the lord again, but then her hand grips me once more, this time painfully. We bow silently, and she wrenches me out of the chamber.

# CHAPTER 3

I grow lightheaded as we leave the lord. His power retracts from me, and I am suddenly alone with myself, reminded of who I am—a mere apsara, unsure of her place. The familiarity of Amaravati mocks me, whispers and taunts in every turn of the breeze. The golden, shimmering light is abruptly too bright, blinding me. I notice irrelevant details—the curve of a pillar, the etching on a wall, Rambha's lustrous braid. My skin grows hot, then cool by turns, like I am about to take sick. My mind is blurred from the throne room, skipping from my desperation, to Indra's enchantment, to the hot temptation of freedom. I oscillate between feeling powerful and poor, wanting to stand tall then slump in exhaustion. By the time Rambha and I return to the adjoining alcove, I am so lost in myself that my head is hurting and my throat is choked.

Rambha spins on me the moment we enter. She grabs my shoulders and shakes me hard. "How could you do this? That senseless boon to ask, and then to volunteer for this mission. What were you thinking?"

"I—I was thinking of you. T-To be like you. I meant to surprise you."

"Instead, you blindsided me. Did you really think Indra was going to grant you freedom? He did not even know your name until tonight. You have no idea the things I did to prove my devotion to him. You have no idea what he and I share, what we've been through."

I recoil from her sharp words. I have never seen her so upset.

Her cheeks are flushed with anger, and her aura glints crimson, its power lashing at me like a whip. Her scent grows sharp, spicy. I step back from her, alarm clearing my head of its despair, but when she sees the expression on my face, the anger seeps out of her own. Slowly, her aura calms down, back into its usual peaceful state.

"Meneka," she says softly, "what have you done, my love?"

She tugs me down to sit next to her, and I lay my head on her shoulder.

For a while, we remain still. Rambha strokes my hair over and over again. I try to contain my turmoil, but the moments in Indra's throne room play in my mind repeatedly. I think of any other way the situation could have gone. How else I should have reacted to get what I want, and whether my desire for freedom had always been unattainable. I wonder if I could simply beg for forgiveness now, or if Indra would listen if I attempted to seduce Kaushika but said it was too hard.

Such a way of thinking is futile. Apsaras cannot fail missions. Once an apsara goes on a mission, she can only return if she is successful. If she is not, she is left in the mortal realm, exiled until she can prove her devotion to the lord in some other manner.

I shudder against Rambha. A shaky breath falls from my lips. I cannot believe this is how it will end. We were both here in this very alcove minutes ago. I had been contemplating telling her then of my plan, of my *feelings*, but if her words to me since are any indication, she would have simply rejected me, if only to save me. A detached horror grows inside me as I accept the inevitability of my circumstances. This is the only way this could have gone. I try to breathe her in, screwing my eyes shut, attempting to forget what happened and delay the moment when I will be lost to the mortal realm. If she is truly my home, then this is all I have. I attempt to still my trembling shoulders, but wetness trickles into my hair, and my eyes fly open. Rambha is crying.

I immediately straighten, my own self-pity disappearing in the face of her sorrow. "I will be all right," I say.

"You will," she agrees vehemently, wiping her tears. "I am sending you with jewelry that channels more magic than you have ever used before. You will find this mortal man, and you will show him who you are, and you will return to me." Her fingers flutter over my face again, cupping my cheek. "You *will* return to me."

We are so close, her breath mingles with mine.

I want to say something. Make a move. Lean forward.

The emotion whirls in me, *needing*. I can almost taste the honeyed star-anise of her lips. I can almost lick the salt of her tears. I want to show her what she means to me. That it is more than the desire to be like her that compelled me to ask Indra for such a boon; that it is *her*, to be with *her*. Surely now, when I have nothing more to lose, I can be brave?

Yet my own reckless suicide mission casts a shadow over us, over-lapping with the sharpness of Rambha's earlier words. I can never tell her of my yearning for her now; it would only make her pity me more. I pull away and Rambha releases me. Clearing her throat, she says, "If you are to do this, then listen carefully about Kaushika."

She tells me of his hermitage in the forest, and where the other apsaras began. Of whatever little Indra's spies found, and the danger Kaushika poses both to Amaravati and to me. Once more, Rambha becomes my handler, preparing me for my mission. The distance opens between us again.

I cannot deny the relief that lances through me. I have come close to admitting my feelings for her so many times, but what would be the point now? The tension of the mission overshadows whatever mo-ment breathed between the two of us. I try to hear her instructions with a clear mind, but fear interrupts any sense I can make of her words. Rambha must know in her heart that this is far beyond my abilities. Will she mourn me like she has mourned our other sisters? Will she hear this last conversation of ours in her head over and over again, and one day realize how much she has meant to me? A kiss would be sweet, but what would be the point? I won't leave her confused and more upset than she already is. The both of us know I am likely never to return.

Rambha looks like she understands what I am thinking, because she gives me a small smile. "Kaushika might be a powerful sage, but you are more than just a dancer, Meneka. He's cunning and devious, but you are too. I meant what I said to the lord. You are one of the best. Do you understand me?"

I nod, too overwhelmed to speak. She loves me; that is why she says this, but I cannot lie to her. Her belief in me is her own, more than what I deserve, more than what I have in myself.

There is no time for long explanations anyway. The both of us know it is time to go. Rambha stands up, holding my hand. We track a familiar path toward Indra's personal garden, where all apsaras stop before departing on a mission.

The hour before leaving for the mortal realm is sacred. Apsaras are allowed to wander Indra's personal garden to seek his peace and meditate on his glory. To remind ourselves he is our lord and king, and our very magic depends on his well-being. Within this garden, a wish necessary for the success of our missions is granted to each departing apsara.

Rambha stops at the entrance, and I hesitate. Entering the grove is a devotional act. My turbulent emotions will sully it. What if my doubts malign my wish too? I cannot believe I just returned from what I thought would be my final mission. I thought I'd seen the last of this garden. Here I am again, only too soon. I glance at Rambha, wanting to speak, ask her advice, beg her to come with me. My fingers flicker, nearly reaching to her, but Rambha's face is quiet, unreadable.

I enter the grove on my own.

THE FIRST TREES SWALLOW ME INSTANTLY.

Magic lies heavy here, the gleaming gold dust of Amaravati clustered like fruit over the foliage. Luscious red berries appear gilded. Leaves sing, a rustle in the cadence of a hymn. The scent of newly birthed flowers makes me slightly dizzy. Like in the throne room, Indra's power suffuses me again, a pull at my skin, a tug at my attention.

Images come to me in whispers and fragrant scents, contoured with Indra's glory.

The lord resplendent, garlands around his neck, each bud picked by a devotee. Indra plowing fields with his bare hands, helping grain grow. The king protecting the sacred cow Kamadhenu in a battle with envious mortals. Indra churning the oceans, to release amrit and other spectacular blessings. On and on, a hundred images of his heroism, lived and lived again through millennia. I blink and the images fade, but the magic winds itself into my blood, reminding me of my allegiance.

This feeling is familiar from all my previous missions. Back then, I welcomed it. When I left to seduce Queen Tara, I wandered this beautiful garden to pray to Indra and replenish my magic. I reminded myself he is one of the oldest beings in the universe, that he has endured and always will. I believed in the lord.

Now I need more to remind me than simply these memories. Ignoring the fruit orchards and the flower-lined fountains, I make my way straight to the kalpavriksh, the sacred wish-fulfilling tree at the center of the garden.

The tree is massive, a forest in itself. Its gnarled boughs reach deep into the soil. The thick canopy blots out even Indra's sky. I have seen similar banyan trees in the mortal realm that spread across acres. None of them compares to the kalpavriksh.

It is said Indra himself planted the kalpavriksh after it appeared during the Churning of the Oceans, the event that created amrit, the golden nectar. Amrit was drunk by the first celestials of Amaravati, giving them and all their descendants—including me—our immortality. All that happened millennia ago, and Indra himself tells different versions of the story, sometimes relating the Churning as a great war, other times calling it a result of a diplomatic mission with rakshasas and asuras, the creatures of naraka, the hellish realm. The only thing all versions have in common is the power of the gifts that came from the sea, including the kalpavriksh.

That power radiates over me as I wander within the grove.

Golden dust sparkles off everything in Amaravati, but at the tree, there is no visible sign of the city's magic. The tree rivals Indra's own power, even here, in his own garden.

A peace descends on me, filling my lungs with the freshest air. My heartbeat slows and my breath grows deeper. Muscles I was not aware I was clenching relax. For a brief moment, my own life seems childish. I am in the presence of one of the oldest, most magical creatures in the universe—a deva in itself. The very power of the cosmos hums within the tree in the rhythms of the sweetest music.

Leaves rustle as I sit at the base of the kalpavriksh's wide trunk. I brush my fingers over the gnarled wood, counting my slow, deep breaths. The last time I was here, before my mission to Queen Tara, I wished for Tara to be amenable. For my every mudra to be an offering to the lord. It is what most apsaras wish for, an ease in their missions.

This time, I am aware I have taken on an impossible task all to escape my own fears and live in the safety of my home. But what is the point of home if I can never return? What is the point of safety if I am dead? Every mission corrupts my devotion to Indra further, but will I shirk from my duty like he accused me? Will I be weak?

"Help me," I whisper, unable to answer myself. "Help me find devotion. I . . . I don't want to lose myself. Help me find what is true."

It's a vague wish, and I'm not sure if it will work. Yet I don't know how else to put my confusion into words. I repeat the unclear prayer to myself over and over again. When I know I am simply delaying the inevitable, I stand up. It would not do for Rambha to come seeking me here, to drag me to my mission. I will not depart in indignity.

Rambha waits for me where I left her, several precious parcels of dyes, creams, perfumes, and oils resting by her feet within an open beaded bag. She greets me with a watery smile, one I am too distressed to return, so I crouch to feign interest in the parcels. I see saris with the most delicate zari weaving, edged with embroidery that tells obscure stories of swarga. Jewels pull at my power despite their wrappings, more luxurious than anything I've ever worn. Any other day, I would be running my fingers through the silks, marveling at the sparkling gems, trying to understand the tales hidden within the clothes. Today I do not bother. I simply nod forcefully, wrap all of them in an accompanying sack, and rise, heaving the sack over one shoulder.

Rambha embraces me tightly. I want to say goodbye, but emotion clogs my throat. If I say anything, I will be in danger of crying. I can't arrive at the mortal realm being weak. It will only make the seduction harder. Rambha probably understands this, because she doesn't offer to walk me to Amaravati's gates, where the wind will take me back to the mortal realm.

"Come back to me," she whispers. "With the Vajrayudh approaching, your devotion to the lord must be unquestioned. Promise me you won't waver."

"I promise," I say, forcing it out.

She tips my chin to her. Her eyes are luminous moons, liquid with sparkling tears. To my everlasting surprise, she leans forward and brushes her soft lips against mine. Honey scents my mouth, star-anise and burned cinnamon.

"I want you back," she whispers, her voice breaking a little. "You said you did this for me. To become like me. Then truly *become* like me and do whatever it takes to succeed. And when you're back, maybe there are other promises we can make to each other."

I blink. My cheeks warm.

A thousand emotions well in me—hope and excitement and confusion, and beyond it a deep, searing lust. Has she known all along about my feelings? Has she reciprocated all this time, the both of us too unsure about each other to say anything? It is absurd that we are at this inescapable moment, close to what we've wanted for so long, when that future is threatened by my own desperate actions. I want to laugh at the irony. I want to weep in despair. I want to be bold now, *finally*, lean forward, and kiss her, truly kiss her. Thread my fingers in her hair and pull her to me. Taste the sweetness of her skin and strip her down and bite down on her soft flesh. Will she like that? Or would she want me pliant for her, liquid and warm? Would she want me to obey her, take *her* lead? Heat pools in me as images flash in my head. I would let her steer if that's what she wanted. I would let her do anything, as long as we were together.

Yet she is an apsara, purer than any other. Her devotion to the lord guides her every action. It is why I have said nothing to her so far about my intentions. It is why I cannot until I return. If I am to be with her, I have to be worthy of her. I have come so far to be deserving. It would be a mistake to be hasty now.

A new resolve fills me.

Rambha's kiss lingering on my mouth, I turn toward my destiny.

# CHAPTER 4

I return to the mortal realm on a wisp of Amaravati's wind.

Maybe it is that I am pining for my city already. Maybe it is because I never expected to leave home so soon. Perhaps it is the taste of Rambha's lips, reminding me of how I have been taken from her again, how much depends on this mission. Whatever it is, I stare at the silent forest I arrive in with revulsion, immediately seeing it for an enemy.

Unlike Amaravati, the mortal realm does not gleam with magic. Chandra's moonlight provides the only luminosity, streaming from the sky, illuminating a patch of grass here, a clearing there. Small creatures run somewhere, the sound of their feet skittering on dry leaves. A hoot of a night owl sounds close to me, then a swish of wings rustles my hair.

The nakedness of it, without any gilding or reserve, unravels me. My magical tether that bloomed in Amaravati is replaced by a flat line. It happens each time I leave the city, and I clutch my jewels for comfort, pearls running smooth under my touch, trying to absorb the power in them, yet I cannot help but wonder. Will any of it be enough? I do not know what shape Kaushika's seduction will take. All Rambha said is that he is older than me by nearly five years, warning me that although I am an immortal, he has lived longer. He is of royal blood like many of my other marks, but he is practiced enough in his magic to be called a sage. If apsaras like Nanda could not seduce him, if he has challenged *Indra*, without even attempting to be subtle about it, then he is, at best, an atheist, and at worst, a megalomaniac. His cruelty is likely calculated, diabolical. His fantasies, for all I know, could be darker than any other mortal's. What will I have to do to come from this mission unscathed?

I harden myself, pushing aside these questions, and crouch to examine the sack I'm carrying. Slowly, I begin to separate the jewels from the clothes and cosmetics. I take off the jewelry I'm still wearing from my mission to Tara, the bangles, the necklaces, even the rings around my toes and the gems threaded through my hair. Maybe my actions are unlike those of the other apsaras who came on this mission before me, but I know I cannot come to Kaushika looking like this. These treasures will simply warn him of who I am.

Still, my fingers hesitate just for an instant as I undo the clasps of the ornaments. What I am doing is too close to blasphemy. Many of these jewels are gifts from the lord. Wearing them is not only a sign of my devotion, it helps me channel my magic directly from Amaravati. An apsara's magic is tied to the city, which in turn is tied to Indra, who harnesses the prana of the universe itself and distributes it through Amaravati. These jewels are a piece of the lord himself, a reminder of his presence.

Yet even without them, as long as I am pure in thought, I should be able to create illusions, albeit only weak ones. Rambha's words echo to me. *She is unique. She studies her enemy deeply.*

I take strength from that and drop all the jewels into one of the parcels. Surely until I know what I am up against, it is more prudent to protect these reminders of the lord. I pick the first large tree I see, a gnarled oak with wide, sweeping branches, and bend to place the parcels at the base. I curl my wrists into a simple mudra, and the illusion forms; light glimmers in golden streaks before diffusing away. When I look next, the jewels are camouflaged in the grass and the rocks, merged with the forest floor.

I barely have time to wonder whether I should wipe the creamy rose dye from my lips too, when a thrumming reverberates around the forest. Snarls and growls follow, disturbing the night, raising all my hackles.

I straighten at once, my eyes darting everywhere. I clutch the remaining packages of clothes and tinctures to me, spinning on my heel. The growls come again, echoing from every direction in the moonlit forest. Shapes die and form within the trees, and my skin erupts in gooseflesh. I turn this way and that, trying to pierce the gloom, knowing I am surrounded.

My palms start to sweat. I was not warned there would be wild creatures in the forest, but of course Rambha would not have thought to tell me. I cannot die through simple means like the attack of a mortal creature. Yet injury? Some scars do not heal, not even for immortal flesh. Without my beauty, I will be useless.

I back away as a roar sounds closer to me. A shape moves in the darkness, too close. A soft cry escapes me, and my body responds on its own. Before I know it, I am running, tripping over roots, stumbling. I want to stop and carve an illusion, something, anything, to distract the creature, but I still cannot see anything clearly. Regret lances through me for hiding my jewels. Without them, I am limited; am I to be punished already for my audacious action? Even as I think this, I crash into something hard.

Vines close around my shoulders, snaking their way down to my hands. My body twists as I fight and cry out—but then it dawns on me. Those are not vines. I am being held by someone. Those are *hands* gripping my own, trying to still me.

The realization shocks me, enough to know that the snarls have stopped. The shape in front of me resolves into a man. I stare.

He looks to be about my age, perhaps a little older. His hair is in a topknot, and he wears nothing but simple pajamas and a plain kurta. Under the thin cotton, I can tell his chest is muscled like a warrior's, yet his attire is too simple for a kshatriya and he wears no bands of any army. I am speechless at the light of his aura. Heavenly auras resemble halos, and most mortals often don't have any aura to speak of. Yet this man's power shines from within, glowing so strongly that it pools around us like a small sun. Confronted with it, I feel lightheaded. I inhale deeply, trying to steady myself. Camphor and rosewood curl into me, weakening me with their charged potency.

The man's thick, dark eyebrows furrow. His lips purse tightly, revealing a ghost of a dimple in clean-shaven cheeks. The unsettling, piercing gaze of his deep-brown eyes pins me into stillness. Anger burns in that gaze, and beyond that something more chilling. *Hate.*

A panic overtakes me. I am gripped by terror again, this one shriller than the one I felt for those snarling creatures.

Of course I know who he is.

I recognize his power. It is apparent in the way he carries himself.

"Who are you?" Kaushika growls, shaking me. "And what are you doing here?"

ALL I CAN THINK OF IN THE MOMENT IS THIS IS THE MAN WHO killed my sisters. The man who is the cause of so much suffering in Amaravati. The man standing between me and Rambha.

Did he see me cast the illusion on the jewels before? Does he already understand I am an apsara? Is this to be my end—even before I truly begin my mission? In my mind's eye, Indra gives me an assessing look, as though to gauge whether I am up to this task. Rambha says, *She does not even know the most useful mudras.* The lord's smile flickers as he commands me to go on this mission anyway.

I realize my fingers are still caught in Kaushika's large hands. He lets go of me in the same instant but does not step back. He opens his mouth again, perhaps to repeat his question, but I recall the reverberation that shook the forest before the roars of the wild creatures. That was surely a magical chant, a mantra of great power. I speak before he has a chance to utter another one.

"Meneka," I breathe. "M-My name is Meneka."

The sound of my terrified voice gives him pause. "And what are you doing here, *Meneka*?"

"I—I—" Nothing occurs to me. No lie, no excuse, nothing. I desperately realize how ill prepared I am. Even Rambha was unable to tell me anything helpful about this mark. I hoped to learn of him before approaching him, but I never expected to stumble into him moments after arriving in the mortal realm. His face grows more suspicious with my silence, and panicked, I blurt out the truth.

"I—I came to find Sage Kaushika," I say.

"Why?" he snaps.

"To—to—"

Abruptly, anger overtakes my terror. If these are to be my last moments before he kills me, why should I act guilty? *He* is the evil one. Kaushika looks as arrogant as I thought him to be—cruel, dictatorial, despicable. Mortals who challenge Indra are the reason I have to return to this dismal realm time and again. If they did not seek to rise above their station, I wouldn't be sent on missions like this. Power is all they care about, and I am tired of being a pawn in these games. I forget the sheer danger Kaushika poses, the challenge he presents. A raw impulse streaks through me, honest and foolish. My back straightens and I cross my arms over my chest.

My voice is cold. "My business is my own."

"Is it? *I* am Kaushika. Now. Why do you seek me?"

I step back and press my hands together, feigning surprise at the revelation of his identity. I have bought enough time to recover my wits. I remember everything I heard about this man in Tara's country and incline my head warily.

"Forgive me," I say, injecting contriteness into my tone. "I did not mean to anger you. I am here to learn from you, Sage. I have heard rumors of your powers. Of a hermitage where you teach those who come to you."

"I only teach those who have magic in them. Do you?"

Not all mortals can do magic, of course, but it isn't uncommon either, especially for those who have inherited some power from their past lives, or through their lineage, or through rigorous meditation. The magic I can perform is deeply different from mortal magic, but that is not what he is asking.

"Yes," I say, searching for my tether to Amaravati as I speak the word.

Kaushika stares at me silently. His lips part, and a chant emerges from him, deep and somber. A ripple goes through me at his voice, and my bond to Amaravati flares as though Indra himself is standing before me. My eyes widen, but the feeling is already subsiding. Kaushika still looks suspicious, but before I can ask for an explanation, he offers one himself.

"You are strong in magic, but the rumors are wrong. I cannot help you. Leave."

"No—please. You cannot send me away, not when—not when there are wild creatures within the forest."

His face is unreadable. "There are no creatures. That was a conjuring. The forest is warded. You can leave and you will be safe. Find someone else to train you."

I blink. So that was the purpose of the mantra I heard. It must have been placed here by him, to terrify intruders. Did my sisters walk into this as well? He is already turning away, but Rambha's face flashes in my mind.

"Don't send me away," I say. "Please. I'm doing this for my family—for the people I love."

The words are true, hurled out of desperation, and they make him stop. He studies me, intrigued. "What do you mean?"

I remember Tara's kingdom, where I first heard of this man. Swiftly, a story forms. "I belong to a noble house within the nation of Pallava," I say. "My country is in peril, our queen acting irrationally. I know my magic can help my people, but I must learn of it first. Rumors of your power came to my country, and so I am here—but please, you cannot send me away to be useless."

Still, he doesn't reply, though I can see the indecision on his face.

My mouth feels dry. His hesitation indicates he has experience with a conflicted past. Kaushika comes from a royal family, yet none of Indra's spies learned which kingdom he hails from. After all, there are thousands of countries in the mortal realm, with royals and nobles and younger children who routinely leave to find their destinies. Even though swarga keeps track of particularly powerful kings and queens, the mortal realm is always restless and moving. There is only so much that is worth remembering.

Did Kaushika leave his home of his own accord, or was he made to leave? Either way, my story about helping my kingdom has given him pause, and I have already learned something about him. I push my advantage in one final move.

"You are *Sage* Kaushika," I say softly. "All sages have a duty, to teach those who come to them wanting to learn. Or were my teachers wrong?"

His eyebrows rise at that, a sardonic look entering his features. "A sage chooses his own students. Those who are worthy. Those who are pure of heart. Are you?"

I lift my chin, not answering, but it is obvious in my expression. *Find out.*

A tilted smile forms on his face. He cocks his head, considering me. "Very well," he says. "But be warned. Training is hard. Few people have the discipline for the asceticism I require. Even fewer have the purity of heart to know themselves, which I need."

Saying no more, he strides away. My teeth worry at my lip as the darkness deepens. Fireflies blink in the distance, pinpricks of golden beauty that remind me of home. I stare at Kaushika's retreating back, this man whose seduction will take forms I cannot know. Anger pounds through me at how I have debased myself already by begging to enter his hermitage. At how arrogant he is, challenging my lord. Rambha is right; he is not like other marks. There will be no guilt in seducing him. As for the danger . . . my identity is still hidden for now. Although he can sense my magic, he is unable to tell it is celestial. As long as I never create an illusion in front of him, I am safe. Right?

"Changed your mind already?" he calls out, his sneer carrying in the darkness.

The thrill of the hunt rises within me, heating my blood. Twigs snap under my feet as I follow.

# CHAPTER 5

For a while we march silently through the forest. The only sound is the crunch of leaves under our feet and the skittering of night creatures. Moonlight streams through the gaps in the foliage, and the quiet of the forest grows tenfold with Kaushika by my side.

His scent threads through me, sweeping over my skin, curling through my hair, settling at the base of my throat. It beckons me closer, and I glance at him, the angles of his face hidden in shadow, the graceful manner in which he moves. It is clear that though he now refers to himself as a sage, he has forgotten none of his warrior upbringing. I wonder how much of a sage he truly is. He has the power to be one, certainly—it is evident from his aura. Yet sages seek the ultimate truth of enlightenment, the knowledge of the universe. They undertake arduous meditation and mold the same form of prana magic that Indra himself does. It is why Indra seeks to parley with them before trying to thwart them. It is why Indra even bends to their counsel when it suits him.

Kaushika refused the lord's previous attempts at conference. He laughed at the gandharva ambassadors, defeated the devotee warriors, and killed the apsara dancers. Heaven does not know what his true intent is, but his actions have been nothing but degrading and aggressive. With every move, he has only shown that he despises Indra. Why? What does he seek?

In that lies the answer to his seduction, so I clear my throat and begin my work. "Why would you ward the forest in such a terrifying way?" I ask.

"For protection," he says shortly.

"From whom?"

Kaushika's jaw moves, and his stride grows longer. I have to hurry to keep up with his tall frame. Leaves crush under us, and he doesn't reply for a long time. I count five heartbeats and am about to repeat myself when he sighs.

"You might as well know," he relents. "The hermitage is a dangerous place. We practice many kinds of magic there, and our very strength poses a threat to outsiders. The forest is enchanted with a warding of intent. If anyone arrives here to hurt me or my people—" He looks down his aquiline nose at me and his lips part in a dangerous sneer. "I know of it immediately."

My shock must show on my face, for he grins a tight, sharp smile.

This is what must have given away my apsara sisters. Sundari and Magadhi and Nanda were gifted beyond compare with their illusions. They must have come to the forest, ready to spin their magic, armed with all of heaven's shining jewels. But the warding of intent betrayed them. The warding clearly works in two ways—one to inform Kaushika of ill-intentioned intruders, and the other to keep the intruders occupied until he arrives.

I am inexperienced, which is why I reacted with panic. But my sisters would not have been fazed. They would have created illusions of defense against the wild, conjured creatures. Kaushika must have recognized them as Indra's agents at once. He probably executed them before they could charm him. Did they even get as far as I have?

A sick feeling spreads through my chest. I recall the flash of hate I saw on his face when he encountered me. Sundari used to wear flowers in her hair. Magadhi's smile made even my knees weak. Nanda could sing to rival a gandharva. Dead, all of them dead. Through desperate hate and overwhelming magic—and trickery. Because of this man.

I realize that Kaushika is still watching me, reading the horror on my face. I swallow and look around to account for it. "Then there really is danger here in the forest?"

"There might be," he says. "Or it could be the obvious answer. *You* are the danger."

My fingertips tingle. It occurs to me that the warding was only triggered when I created the illusion to hide my jewels. I might not have fooled him about my identity at all.

"I don't mean you any harm," I say quietly.

His answering smile is cold. "We will see, won't we?"

We march alongside each other in silence. Every now and then, Kaushika throws me an inscrutable look, perhaps anticipating more questions, but even though I know I must make use of my time with him, I dare not utter a word, unsure of what I will give away unknowingly. The sense of peril closes around me, shadows that bounce in the darkness, my own tether to Amaravati too thin to give me any confidence.

Before long, we are at the edge of the forest and lights glimmer through the trees. The path we're on widens, smeared footsteps indicating that it is well traveled. Raw, unkempt bushes give way to a flower-lined trail, roses and hibiscus and marigolds in a muted profusion of colors, their petals subdued in the dim light but no less beautiful. I follow Kaushika as he strides into a clearing with nearly a hundred huts.

Though the hour is late, voices carry to us. I hear academic discussions of mantras and the Vedas, ethics and dharma. Chants echo around the hermitage, most of them too quiet to make any sense. I recognize only one, an ancient sound that shakes me. It is a mantra calling on Shiva for wisdom to destroy maya, the illusion that conceals the nature of reality itself. A thrill of fear winds up my spine, locking the muscles of my shoulders.

It is not unusual to hear such chants within a hermitage. Sages, by their very nature, seek to peel through the layers of deception of the body and mind.

Yet with that chant, I know that I have fully entered the wolves' lair. As a mistress of illusions, an apsara, I am the epitome of everything the sages want to destroy. The central courtyard shrinks in my eyes, its dangerous mortal magic pervasive. Kaushika is not the only threat here. All of these people would destroy me if they learned my true identity. I say nothing, following him as we wind our way past the huts to a darkened, straw-covered shed.

We enter a long, narrow corridor with bare walls. Doors lie ajar, leading into empty rooms. Only one door is closed, behind which presumably another student is asleep. Kaushika deposits me into a room that is unadorned except for some straw on the floor. It is so small I can barely walk ten paces before I must turn. A curtainless window looks out into the main courtyard, and shafts of moonlight lie dully on the floor. There is no bedding, no ornamentation, no candle nor food, not even a jug of water. I think of the manses in Amaravati, the ever-present golden dust, the hymns that resonate through heaven. Mudras nearly form at my fingertips, tempting me to erase this barrenness with my illusions. My eyes rise to Kaushika's. I cannot hide the despair in them.

His lips curve into a thin smile. "We'll see tomorrow how well you will fit in. Ensure you arrive at the courtyard, where your teacher will meet you."

I blink. "You won't train me yourself?"

"Last here long enough, and we will see."

He turns away to leave, but annoyance sparks in me. "You will be surprised with what I can do."

"Oh," he drawls. "I know exactly what you can do. We will see how much of it you give away."

The words deepen my chill. The dark, bare room closes around me as he shuts the door behind him. The forest, the chants, the faces of my lost sisters all flash before my eyes. A part of me is still in disbelief that earlier this night I was with Queen Tara. I was *dancing* for her, *seducing* her. Rambha kissed me with the promise of something more. I can still taste the touch of her lips, but I have never felt as far away from swarga as I do now.

Exhaustion washes over me all at once. So much has happened I can barely keep the events straight in my mind.

I turn away from the door and fling myself on the straw. Dreamless sleep overtakes me instantly.

I'M AWAKENED BY A KNOCK IN WHAT SEEMS LIKE MERE MINUTES.

Dawn is breaking past the window, a pink flush chasing the last of the misty stars. Groggy-eyed, I crack open the door to see a young woman around my age. She blinks at me, her smile faltering, then gathers herself visibly. Amused, I smile back.

I am used to such reactions to my beauty. All celestial beings exude charm, but stories are sung of apsaras' exquisiteness. Kaushika was a rare exception to react to me with hostility, but of course, he has seen—and destroyed—more ravishing apsaras than me.

I open the door wider. The woman hesitates, then introduces herself as Kalyani. "Kaushika told me we had a new initiate," she says hesitantly. "I arrived a few weeks ago myself. Your name is Meneka?"

I study her, the round cheeks, the laugh lines by her eyes, the topknot her hair is tied in. She is dressed in a plain kurta and pajamas, and wrapped in her arms is another set for me. My fingers clutch at

the fabric of my sari from heaven. I trace its delicate embroidery. Reluctantly, I nod.

Kalyani leads me to a stall at the end of the shed, where a bucket
of cold water waits. While I disrobe and sluice water down my hair,
untangling my tresses with my fingers, she chats to me, telling me
about the hermitage. I am to receive linen and candles, but all clean-
ing will be up to me. Everything I have brought must be turned over
to a disciple called Romasha, who is in charge of all outside materials
that come here. Even though, for the most part, the hermitage exists
independently, growing its own food, tending its orchards, creating
its own pottery, and weaving its own clothes, she will use what I give
her to trade with the outside world. Any proceeds will be applied toward the collective use of the hermitage.

"I cannot part with my clothes," I protest when Kalyani tells me
this. "They are a part of my heritage, a part of my country. I cannot
give those away to be traded."

"Then you will have to burn them," Kalyani says, her voice apologetic. "The separation from our past is meant to be complete when
we arrive here. It's why Kaushika forbids any questions or discussions
about where each of us comes from. The separation is meant to help
us on our ascetic path. I am sorry. I do not think he will make an
exception for you."

I tuck away the information about Kaushika's edict in my mind.
If he allows people to escape their past, even forces them to forget
it, then this will only help me; I won't need to fabricate anything
further about my own history. Could it be that Kaushika is running
away from his *own* past? If so, I must find out and use it. As for the
clothes . . . Unless someone is to watch over me to ensure I burn my
saris, I will simply hide them in the forest along with the jewelry at
the first opportunity.

"Are you to be my teacher?" I ask.

"Only a guide," Kalyani answers. "And a friend, if you wish it. Knowledge is shared freely here, but Anirudh and Romasha are the ones who lead all the lessons. You'll see. What kind of magic do you perform?"

"I would prefer to demonstrate it," I say evasively. I have no mortal magic in me, but several of my marks performed magic that threatened Indra. I have encountered chants and artifacts, astrology and potion-making. None of them have compared to my own celestial powers.

I finish drying myself and wear the clothes Kalyani has brought for me. I force my hair into a topknot like the sages, then we make our way to the courtyard.

In the breaking dawn, the central courtyard appears much larger. Nearly a hundred students cluster in separate groups, practicing different forms of magic. Mantras echo, rivaling one another in beauty and complexity. Amulets and clothes are consecrated with flicks of wrists that resemble dance mudras. Fires spark in magnificent shapes, air whirlpools in small tornadoes, and water dances between fingers. Here and there are healers burning herbs, studying contours in the smoke. I even notice some disciples practicing yogic forms that look remarkably like dance.

Kalyani leads me through the students to a quiet spot, where we wait silently. A young man, only a little older than us, detaches himself from the closest group. His eyes widen in telltale shock at my beauty, then he smiles at me.

Anirudh's aura is not as strong as Kaushika's, though it still radiates with power, resembling several small jewels tucked in the chakras at his wrists and chest. I notice his straight shoulders, the noble demeanor of his movements, the cadence of his soft speech. I am not allowed to ask, but I know this man was once a royal.

"Your days will be marked with chores and lessons," Anirudh tells me. "Kalyani will help guide you through it. Are you hungry?"

I shake my head. Celestials do not need food. In Amaravati, if we eat at all, we consume wine and nectar, sweetmeats and ambrosia. I've never been fond of mortal food, but I will have to pick at my meals here, enough not to arouse suspicion. My stomach already rebels at the thought, though I am careful to keep the distaste out of my face.

"Just as well," Anirudh says. "We only eat after the morning practice in the courtyard. The first fasting helps us focus. Things will change the closer you get to the Initiation Ceremony, but the ceremony itself is what all the training here is aimed towards. In approximately two months' time, all of us here—including me—will have to display to Kaushika what we can do with our magic. It is meant to be a demonstration of our power and control, and we get to pick the manner of our demonstration. We are all yogis here, capable of great magic, but the purpose of this hermitage is to turn a yogi into a rishi. You do know what a rishi is, don't you?"

"A sage," I reply, nodding. It is a common mortal term.

"Not just any sage," Anirudh says, shaking his head. "A rishi is a sage who has uncovered the deepest mysteries of the universe. Who has swum in the waters of knowledge that ordinary people like us can only hope to glimpse in our lifetimes. A rishi is a self-proclaimed title, but no one in this hermitage except Kaushika can claim it yet. He alone has demonstrated his power to other sages, to Gautama and Bhardwaj, to Jamadagni and even to ornery Vashishta. If we are to follow in his path, then one day we must do the same, but we will have to begin with convincing Kaushika himself. Understood?"

"Yes," I say cautiously. "Why two months?"

Anirudh smiles. "Because of the Mahasabha. The sages' gathering will occur immediately after the Initiation Ceremony, where Kaushika must present his students to the rest of the enclave. The meeting will not just be a judgment on us but also on him. On everything we are doing here at the hermitage, and the path we take. Kaushika wants us to succeed, so he is giving us as much time as he can before he presents the strongest of us. He will be exacting in his testing of us in the ceremony, but not harsh. He wants us to grow more powerful. That is why we keep to the timeline *and* the training. You have arrived too late, but we will do our best. I will help you every step of the way."

Anxiety pinches my heart. Indra gave me until the Vajrayudh to thwart Kaushika, an event that will arrive in about six months. Yet with the Initiation Ceremony so close, how am I to survive until the Vajrayudh when I cannot do mortal magic at all?

"Do not worry overmuch about what is to come," Anirudh says, reading my expression while Kalyani nods in encouragement. "For now, we will simply see how much your power allows you to do. What form does your magic take?"

"Runes," I reply carefully. "It is what is passed down in my line."

I have had enough time to think about it since Kalyani's inquiry earlier. Of all mortal magics, the creation of runes is most similar to the dance mudras of the apsaras. I even learned the shapes of some of them from one of my marks, a kshatriya warrior called Nirjar.

His tattooed face is burned in my mind, his thick fingers and their brutal strength, and the magic in them that Indra feared. His broad and muscled body was covered with runes that gave him speed, daring, and ferocity. Yet despite his ominous appearance, Nirjar was one of my more likeable marks, gentle in his practice, careful in his words. Indestructible because of his runes, his very existence was a threat to swarga. What purpose did heaven have if Nirjar sought to make an imperishable body? Only souls were supposed to be immortal, moving through heaven or hell in the cycle of karma until it was time to be reborn again. Indra's sacred duty compelled him to thwart Nirjar, and I was sent to accomplish this task.

I can still see the way Nirjar grasped his blades and scraped at his skin, flaying himself. Unlike the illusions I made for so many of my other marks, the ones I created for him were not sexual at all. I simply showed him a life with me, children, and future happiness. His blood ran from his face, lost in this simple vision, and I returned from the mortal realm sickened with myself. Yet the lord was so ecstatic, he rewarded not just me but Rambha, too, with jewels.

I shake myself out of the memory, focusing back on Kaushika's camp. When Nirjar created runes, the very air would crackle with energy and form a fiery shape floating before him. Tentatively, I use my finger to draw the rune for a breeze into the space in front of me—but of course nothing happens.

Anirudh tuts. "That's an easy rune. Try again." He holds my hand, correcting my calligraphy, helping me form the precise strokes.

We continue for what seems like hours. It becomes increasingly clear that though I am mastering the shape, I can produce no magic. Next to us, Kalyani practices her own forms, focusing on her breath as she moves through yogic poses, but from the glances she throws toward me, I know I am shocking her with my incompetence. Anirudh grows frustrated, muttering about how he has never seen such a block to magic.

"Have you *ever* shaped any rune into manifestation?" he asks, exasperated.

I shake my head. Of course not. That is not the form my magic takes.

Anirudh bites the inside of his cheek. "Kaushika let you in. Even I can tell you have magic. But for not even a spark to appear, even though you have a lineage in it . . ."

His face grows anxious. I am about to ask what will happen if I don't succeed when our conversation is interrupted.

"I think you need to start much easier with her," a voice drawls.

Suddenly I am aware that the entire courtyard has fallen silent. Camphor and rosewood swirl around me as Kaushika moves from within the crowd, approaching me like a panther. Disciples separate, making way for him. I watch him approach, and a blaze of fury sharpens in my chest at the arrogant way he walks, the ownership he thinks he has over me simply because I am here, pretending to be his student.

"Runes come after," Kaushika says, his eyes never leaving mine. "Meneka cannot even access her own power yet."

Understanding flickers in Anirudh's eyes. He steps aside and Kaushika takes his place, inches from me. If I raised my hand to make another rune, I would touch him. My world narrows into only him, the danger of him, the relaxed stillness of his body.

Kaushika crosses his arms over his chest. "Close your eyes. Look inside your heart. What do you see?"

Aware with every fragment of my body that he has killed apsaras, I reluctantly obey him. "I see nothing," I mutter. "Merely feel the movement of my breath."

A grunt from him. "Well, there's that at least. Your breath is a sheath moving through your physical body. Within it lies a measure of prana moving through the nadi channels of your subtle body. That prana is your magic. You need to connect with it."

It is absurd that he should explain what prana is to me, when I am a celestial. Prana is so much more than merely *my* magic. It is the magic of the universe, linking and permeating all living and nonliving things. As a celestial, the universe's prana flows to me through Amaravati from Indra. The lord of heaven *manipulates* prana through his divinity to nurture the City of Immortals. Kaushika practices prana magic, the same as Indra, yet he challenges the lord, he who is so skilled in it that he sustains heaven and earth.

I scowl at this incongruity. "How do I connect with my prana?"

"There *is* no 'how,'" Kaushika replies. "There just *is*. You need to learn of yourself. Magic is a conversation with yourself. You need to take some responsibility for your own learning. Did you expect you would simply come here and I would bestow knowledge upon you?"

My scowl deepens at his condescending words. He dares to lecture me on responsibility? This man who challenges the devas in his callousness?

It is so egotistical that I open my eyes and study him, the brooding outlines of his mouth, the sharp intensity of his gaze. A sense of self-righteous recklessness surges in me. I have not dared it thus far, unknowing of the extent of his perception regarding my identity, but I cannot help myself. *Reveal your lust*, I murmur in my mind.

I expect an image to blossom. Kaushika seeking power over all these people he has gathered. Kaushika seeking to unravel the powers of the universe. Kaushika giving me a glimpse into his past.

Yet my whisper slams against a powerful oblivion. Shocked, my mouth falls open.

A blank wall mocks me, as though he has no desire whatsoever. The feeling is so unnatural, so alien, so *profane* to the vitality I live in as an apsara, that I stagger back, my eyes widening.

I stare at him, not understanding at first—then comprehension floods me. It is not lack of desire that creates a block to Kaushika's lust. He has *shielded* himself deliberately so I cannot look in.

Is this because of the other apsaras? Did he build this shield after experiencing them? Or does he know *I* am an apsara? If he knows, surely he would have killed me already. My chest rises and falls as I continue to stare at him. My bottom lip catches between my teeth in worry. Kaushika's eyes track the movement and his own frown deepens. I rally myself, aware we are being watched.

"Maybe," I say softly, "I can learn what I'm capable of based on what *you* can do?"

His gaze grows wary at my change in tone. "What do you mean?"

"You said magic is a conversation with myself. You could show me how you do that. What do *you* do when you are most truthful with yourself?"

Someone gasps. Kalyani utters a half-startled laugh. Anirudh mutters that I am already achieving what it took him a lifetime to do. I do not know what he means, but I see the way Kaushika's eyes glint on hearing it.

I am aware I am pushing, yet urgency races through my veins, like heaven's chariots. What do I care for learning mortal magic? The sun beats down on us, and I imagine Lord Surya watching me and reporting to Indra—but of course, the camp is probably warded against prying eyes, even the eyes of a deva. It is why Indra has not learned anything significant yet. I am alone here, surrounded by enemies. Perhaps I should be more careful, but the realization only angers me further. This man has cut me off from everything I love. If I do not succeed, he will destroy it all.

Kaushika's lips turn into a thin smile, like he can read my thoughts. Like he *agrees*. "Careful, Meneka," he murmurs. "You should not ask questions you would not understand the answers to."

I do not drop my gaze. "I am only here to learn."

"Are you? Let's see how willing you are."

A chant flows from him, the very same one he used last night before declaring I could do magic. My bond to Amaravati flares, yet this time instead of subsiding immediately, it continues to grow. My skin grows hot, burning. My body lights from within, and I feel myself float though my feet still touch the ground.

My voice grows high-pitched. "What are you doing?"

"Showing you how much magic you contain." Kaushika stops chanting, but the mantra takes over, consuming me. I am radiant, golden, bursting with power.

Suddenly I know that everyone can see how much magic I have.

It is more than any one of them, short only of Kaushika. Gasps echo from the crowd. Kalyani looks awed. Even Anirudh's eyes are wide. Are they threatened by my power? Is this what Kaushika intends with such a display—to make me a target, to alienate me? All of these people aim to destroy maya. They will attempt to kill me now simply because I am more powerful. They will see that Indra is my lord, that my magic is celestial. My panicked breath reverberates in my ears. My eyes dart between their faces. I try to move, but I cannot, held by terrible fear.

"Do you see yourself?" Kaushika whispers. "Can you reach inside of you?"

Amaravati's tether blooms in me, luminous, and Kaushika's warmth engulfs me. I try to ease my heart, but it only beats more rapidly. I have trapped myself here with him. This is what destroyed my sisters.

Slowly, painfully, I raise my arms against his magic. He is close enough for me to touch his chest, and I feel the solid muscle of it, the unyielding pressure.

Then I push, *hard*. He raises his brows.

His enchantment comes to a stop.

He steps back, opening more distance between us.

All around us is silence, the solemn looks of the other students, the amazement and disbelief. Kaushika smiles, and his eyes glint in vindication. My hands drop as we stare at each other.

"You are afraid of yourself," he says. "Powerful though you are, you are no use to us here in the hermitage." He looks around, and his next words are louder, carrying into the crowd. "Consider this a lesson. Magical strength is secondary. Self-knowledge comes first. If I were you, I would not get used to her." Kaushika's eyes cut toward me, and his voice is hard. "Meneka will not last a month."

# CHAPTER 6

T he power of a yogi comes from arduous meditation," Romasha says. "Tapasya, as it is known."

Seated on a pedestal circling the massive bael tree, Romasha is as beautiful as to rival many an apsara. Her thick hair is tied
into a topknot, but tendrils escape to frame her heart-shaped face.
Her eyes are focused on a small ball of fire sparking between her
fingers. The fire flickers from between her hands, then races up her
arms to her shoulders, curling around her neck like a snake. It coils
and uncoils around her chest before coalescing into a contained ball
of flames again.

I kneel on the grass in front of her, along with Anirudh and
Kalyani. A soft breeze blows through the hermitage, carrying with
it the scents of rain. We are gathered with the other hundred or so
students of the hermitage, seated in the garden. Beyond are sheds
where the horses and cows are stabled; behind, the open-pillared
pavilion.

The three of us are the only ones to sit in a group, a concession
shown to me because I am new. Fire flickers everywhere as students
follow Romasha's instructions. Some of these disciples use runes, others mantras. Parasara's flames look like a dark eclipsed sun with a
golden corona around it. Eka bounces playful blue sparks from one
finger to another. Kalyani creates wispy embers, more like air than
fire, but no less hot for it. Anirudh, who is more practiced, easily balances a lavalike orb with golden waves on its surface.

I alone hold nothing. Vacuum tingles between my fingers.

"Focus," Kalyani whispers beside me, sensing my frustration. "Visualize the fire inside you. Aim that into the rune you're attempting."

I nod stiffly, but my fingers twitch, wanting to curl into the mudra of Agni's Laughter. With it, I can create an illusion of flames so powerful, it would rival any of these yogis' magic. Would these people know it is not true fire?

The golden tether tempts me to try, but I do not have my jewels to augment my magic. An illusion to fool this many people would tax me too much. I dare not deplete myself. I will need my magic once I break through Kaushika's shield, even if my efforts to do so have been futile thus far. Besides, the mortals have not been able to tell my magic is celestial; power is simply power to them. An illusion of this size could expose me.

"Tapasya is no ordinary meditation," Romasha continues. "It is the ember that kindles a spiritual fire, connecting a yogi to the prana magic of the universe. With it, we access the very same cosmic power the devas in swarga do. Devas rely on prayers to sustain their magic, but with intense tapasya, we yogis take the universe's infinite power into ourselves. We are vessels of the universe, a part of it and the whole of it. Infinity both contains and does not contain parts."

Since that first training session, I have fallen into a prescribed routine, similar to the other disciples. I am up before dawn—milking cows, collecting firewood, kneading dough, and washing floors. Then it is practicing in the courtyard, sessions that so far have resulted in nothing but frustration. Afterward, I break fast within a large communal shed, a meal of almonds and ghee-filled kichdi, or spiced millets with a tall glass of sanjeevani, which I pretend to relish, all the while missing the soma and wines of Amaravati. Then it is more lessons, either in a shed or the pavilion, or right here in the garden under a tree, each of them useless to me.

Romasha's gaze shifts to me like she can hear that thought. "Look inside yourself," she says. "Accept that you belong here, that you have a place here. Feel your breath flowing through you and know that it is simply a sheath for the universe's magic. Access it."

I return her look, trying not to laugh rudely.

It is absurd, this instruction. If I really did accept who I am, an apsara, would I even be here? Would these people *allow* me to be here?

For a week now, I have attended treatises on philosophy and history, on dharma and niyama, on religion and ethics. All of them speak of the same *wisdom*. To burn maya and find the path into true knowledge. Enemies of illusion, any of these yogis would reduce me to cinders given half a chance. Kaushika himself would lead the charge, even though he has completely ignored me since the first day. I have seen him attend the very same classes I have, as if he were not the master of the hermitage but an ordinary yogi.

Even now he sits a few rows behind me. A prickle goes through my scalp at presenting my back to a predator. I resist the urge to turn and look at him. As it is, his scent filters toward me, clouding my mind. I inhale, trying to capture the scent of rain instead.

The way he runs his hermitage bewilders me. At home, reverence is a matter of seniority. Only the most elite apsaras teach mudras to younger ones, and that knowledge is guarded zealously, released through acts of devotion. I have argued often with Rambha because she is my friend, but were she Sundari or Magadhi, I would not have dared. Subtle but clear rivalry has always lingered between the apsaras—to be the most beautiful, the most ardent. To create the best illusions and take on the hardest missions. Lord Indra himself encourages the competition, considering it a sign of our love for him.

Here in the hermitage, Kaushika does not seem to care about such things. Though it is clear his word is law, he rarely interferes with how Anirudh and Romasha run things. I have seen him listen to other students with seriousness in the pavilion, even agree with their perspectives as they challenge his own thinking. Everyone has his regard, and he is clearly not afraid of being questioned, yet my own defiance of him has left him hostile instead of curious. Remembering the first day of training, I have moved around him carefully, even being subservient instead of challenging. I have endured his indifference for a week. It has gotten me nowhere. My body shifts in place, uncomfortable, as Romasha's gaze moves away from me.

"There is only one being who personifies the complete power of the universe," she drones on. "Shiva alone is so united with the power of the universe that he is indistinguishable from the infinite. Even the devas bow to his supremacy, humbled time and again by him. Yet, though he is powerful beyond measure, Shiva does not concern himself with the politicking of heaven and earth. That withdrawal from worldly interactions to learn of oneself is essential to pursuing your own magic here at the hermitage."

Kalyani raises her brow at me. I realize I am frowning. I give her a halfhearted shrug and pretend to return to my magic, though I cannot help the revulsion that streaks through me at Romasha's words.

The yogis in the hermitage often compare themselves to the Great Lord Shiva, claiming to follow his path, but they act more like the devas they hate than Shiva himself. The Lord of Destruction might have broken the cycle of karma, but that is because he turns the heat of tapasya inward instead of manifesting it into the world. Even his once-thriving abode at Mount Kailash is now icy, leached of life as he pulls the radiant power of the universe into himself. *That* is why he is the Lord of Destruction. Because life itself is breakable around him.

The yogis of the hermitage have no such power. Like Indra, who channels prana to wield lightning and storm, the yogis channel their own magic into the world through mantras and runes and consecrated herbs, all in order to effect change on reality. They do not retain their magic for greater enlightenment. Indra is right to be apprehensive of them. In their naïveté and power, they could callously diminish him, not knowing the damage they do to their own kind in the process.

Romasha stands up from the tree. She nods to someone behind me, and I turn in my seat to see Kaushika rise.

His aura is so strong, it calls to me. I can discern the chakras of prana heavy with magic inside his body, the discs shining in rainbow colors. A sapphire blue at his throat, glowing through his dark skin. The one in his heart emerald green. The one right above his head a purple so royal it takes my breath away. I clutch my tether to Amaravati with my mind, limp though it is, holding on to Indra even though Shiva resounds through the hermitage. *Reveal your lust*, I think, aiming my power at Kaushika.

I slam against his shield again. It is intoxicating to know that behind it lies the secret to his seduction. That if I only find the right path into him, I will receive a taste of victory. Like others here, surely his own knowledge of himself is flawed; he is, after all, their true teacher. My eyes move over his body, tracing the shape of his aura, looking for a way inside.

He and Romasha begin to walk from student to student, helping them unblock their energies. Fire rises from fingertips in beautiful, swirling shapes that merge with one another. Kaushika mutters appreciatively before moving to the next student. I know that he will not make his way to me.

Indra's voice echoes in my head. *Thwart him.* How can I when he does not even acknowledge my presence? I keep my eyes on Kaushika's sharp profile, the angles of his shoulders, the strength in his biceps. The tether from Amaravati coils around my heart. My fingers carve the rune for fire, a blossoming sun, and an idea strikes me. I hold on to the tether as I would if I were to create an illusion, but this time I direct it toward the rune.

Sharp pain squeezes my lungs. I gasp, dropping my tether.

It is a reminder. A warning.

I can only use Amaravati's magic to do what Indra has allowed me—to dance and create illusions. I am not allowed to use Indra's magic this way. A frustrated sound builds in my throat. That I will learn none of this mortal method is obvious. Yet I must endure this training, a waste of everyone's time.

It is the one thing Kaushika and I agree on.

I turn my attention to Anirudh and Kalyani. The two have been taking turns at teaching me privately, beyond the classes we all attend. "Is it true?" I ask quietly. "Did Kaushika tell you not to help me?"

Kalyani bites her lip. She glances at Anirudh, clearly unsure of what to say, deferential to his seniority.

Anirudh in turn gazes toward Kaushika. When he speaks, his voice is tired. "He told us not to help you *excessively*. He cautioned us not to do so at the cost of our own training."

"Are you?"

Anirudh sighs. "We all saw how strong you are. How much magic you contain. You will be an asset here, even if he is reluctant to say it. Do not give up yet. We have not."

Kalyani nods emphatically. Their support has more to do with making Kaushika proud of them than unleashing my own magic; for all I know, for their own Initiation Ceremony they might wish to claim teaching me—the incompetent student—as their great talent. Still, their confidence in my potential warms me.

"If I am an asset, then why doesn't he help me?" I ask.

"He doesn't trust you," Anirudh says. "He can only trust people who have complete devotion."

"Devotion to him?"

"To Shiva," Anirudh says flatly. "Our meditation, our yogic practices, our very magic—all of those are offerings to the Lord. For you to deny yourself, Kaushika sees it as a denial of Shiva himself." He shrugs, helpless. "We've tried mantras and herbs, asanas and the wisdom of the Vedas. By now we should have seen something. You are presenting a challenge."

"Maybe only Kaushika can teach me," I say. I glance again toward where the sage helps Yamortri. "This is *his* hermitage. He let me in here."

"To allow you an opportunity," Anirudh says. "He did not make any promises. Everyone here gets the same treatment. He did not even make promises to *me*, Meneka, and I am his oldest friend."

"Really?" I sit up straighter. I imagine the two of them younger, growing up around each other's secrets. I feel such excitement at this little nugget of information that my mind buzzes with possibilities and questions, and I don't know where to begin. Before I can assemble my thoughts, however, a cry ripples through the air.

I turn in its direction and jump to my feet. Other disciples rise as well, all of us crowding around each other to see. A young, pale-skinned girl trembles not far from the bael tree's trunk. Her eyes are closed, her lips parted in a scream. Leaves crackle, then the tree begins to smoke.

Romasha utters a mantra before anyone else can. Next to me, Anirudh draws a rune of moisture as well. Both their spells hit at the same instant, and streams of water rush over the tree in a small, contained storm, stopping the fire from spreading. Yet, though all of us are standing, no one touches the girl. Everyone keeps their distance from her, their gazes grim, clearly following a protocol I'm unaware of.

Then Kaushika is there, kneeling by the girl, his hand on her forehead. He closes his eyes, and I notice what I did not before. It is not just the tree that kindled with fire. It is the girl herself. Under her pale skin flicker orange embers. The embers flash, from her forehead to her throat. She cries out, a tiny whimper, and my heart catches at the sound.

"What is he doing?" I whisper.

"Healing her," Anirudh answers. "Every act of magic we do depletes how much we store inside us, yet healing does it most of all. Kaushika will need to meditate again to refill himself with what he is pouring into Navyashree now. He is generous with how much he's giving her, and it is sure to have an effect on him, tiring him."

"A lesson," Romasha adds, hearing us. Her voice carries to everyone else as well. "Celestials do not burn from holding their magic because they channel prana through their deva king. They are protected, separated from the direct dangers of uncontrolled prana, because Indra forms a barrier to such powerful magic. But they can never have the kind of power we yoke either. Tapasya is fire. Prana is fire. If you do not contain it properly . . ." She lets her words hang as all of us watch the girl pulsing with sparks.

We back away as Kaushika picks her up in his arms, murmuring under his breath. The unearthly light under the disciple's skin slowly flows from her into him. He does not look perturbed, but a serious line forms on his forehead, heavy with concentration. If anything, the combination of the fiery glow within him only highlights the alertness of his body. Even with my limited knowledge, I know this is a feat no one else in the hermitage is capable of.

My mission is churned in me by his unseen danger, by his quiet prowess. By how his senseless vendetta against my king, fueled by a self-assured prejudice, threatens heaven itself. *Reveal your lust*, I whisper desperately, but no image returns to me.

The girl still in his arms, Kaushika marches out of the gathering, Romasha on his heels.

# CHAPTER 7

L ater that night, I knock on his door.

His hut is by the perimeter of the hermitage, the largest of the settlements within the compound. A window points toward the gardens where the bael tree is. The hut itself overlooks the dark, brooding forest—fitting for this man who keeps one eye on intruders and the other on his disciples. Golden light pools inside, visible from the crack beneath the door. Shadows shift as I raise my fist to knock again.

Kaushika flings open the door, filling up the space with his endless shoulders and impatience. For once, he does not wear the uniform of the hermitage but a night-black kurta and matching pajamas. An old brown scarf drapes around his neck, and on one shoulder he carries a jute bag.

Annoyance grows on his features when he sees me. We are but a handsbreadth away from each other, but I hold my ground, resisting the urge to stagger back as he looms.

He doesn't retreat either, but his frown grows deeper as though he is aware of this childish game of superiority between us, yet still intends to win.

"What do you want?" he asks gruffly.

I answer with my sweetest smile, knowing it will only aggravate him further. "I came to ask if Navyashree is all right. After what happened to her in today's lesson."

Kaushika's eyebrows rise, his scowl replaced by curiosity just for an instant. "I did not know you were such fast friends."

"We are not. I simply wish to know."

"Why?"

"She is a fellow human being. A disciple of the hermitage. Should I not care that she burned?"

Kaushika only snorts.

"Do *you* not care?" I ask, tilting my head. "You saved her and depleted the magic you hold inside of you in the process. She is *your* student."

"I did my duty," he says flatly. "Nothing else. I would not get sentimental about it."

This time *I* quirk an eyebrow. "No sentiments about saving a life? How interesting."

Confusion flickers in his eyes. I let the silence breathe, watching the passage of emotions on his face, doubt and outrage and a fleeting sense of shame. A few choice words, and he has begun doubting himself? I want to laugh because of how easy it is to rile him, and how it is usually the sincerest of my marks who respond like this. He reminds me of Nirjar in his openness—but I cannot think of Kaushika as sincere. It is one step away from pitying him, and then growing fond of him, and then what will become of me and my mission? I mentally shake myself, remembering the hate I first saw on his face.

Kaushika mutters something under his breath, then eyes me with consideration. He shifts his sack from one shoulder to the other, a relenting in the gesture.

"She is all right," he mutters. "Romasha has taken over her healing. You can go ask her for more details if you want."

He makes to push past me, but I stand on tiptoe as the candlelight in his house dies away. The hut swims in shadow, the only light coming from the starlight pouring through the windows. Absently, I wonder about his relationship with Romasha. She is certainly beautiful, and I have seen the way the both of them speak to each other in comfortable companionship. Are they merely friends? Or is there something more potent growing between them? If Kaushika and Romasha have an understanding, even budding feelings of romantic affection buried under their vows of asceticism, I can use it to unravel him. Romasha is hardly my competition, yet if I became more like her, he would pay me some mind. Perhaps *that* is the shape of his seduction hiding behind his shield—an image concealed not because he fears apsaras but because he fears his own desires and what it means for his vows of asceticism. How easy it would be to break him, then; just another mortal afraid of himself, despite his proclamations of self-knowledge. It is such an ironic thought, I cannot help but grin.

"Romasha?" I murmur. "She is so strong, but I would not think you would give over *healing* to her. Navyashree seemed so hurt, and wouldn't it weaken Romasha too? Why would you burden her with such a thing? Are you going somewhere?"

"Yes," he says shortly, and shuts the door behind him. Another murmur, and air shimmers across the doorway and over the house in a warding.

I lift my head to see he has been watching my curious reactions. I clear my throat. His scent coats me, entrancing me in a dangerous way with the hidden notes behind it, but I do not climb down the two short stairs that lead to the veranda. I am blocking his way, and if he stirs he will touch me, but even that will give me more information about him, so I simply drop my lashes, this time infusing my smile with self-effacement.

"I was hoping to speak with you tonight. The Initiation Ceremony is coming closer, and I need you."

"You need me," he repeats flatly.

"To teach me. To give me instruction."

"And what kind of instruction would that be, Meneka?"

I blink. I know what *I* am doing with this conversation—but is he flirting *back*? Am I wrong about him and Romasha? Is this a trap? My heart beats faster. "Why, Sage Kaushika," I murmur, widening my eyes, "it can be any kind of instruction you please."

He does not say anything, but he tilts his head. For an instant, a shade of a smile lurks on his lips, rewarding me. Then it disappears, just as fast as it had come.

"As flattered as I am," he says dryly, "I do not fraternize with my students."

Did he read into my observations about Romasha too? Am I giving too much of my identity away, to move this fast? Either way, I blush prettily. "I only meant that you could teach me. Runes are my preferred form of magic, as you know."

"Oh, I know, but I don't teach either. Not until the Initiation Ceremony."

"In that case, we are hardly *your* students until then, are we?"

This time a surprised laugh escapes him. "Oh, you are amusing, certainly. Much as I am enjoying this, I have no time for such inane conversation right now. Step aside, please. I must be on my way."

"But I need—"

"I don't care what you need. Your learning is your own business."

"But—" I begin, trying not to let my desperation show. I am *so* close. I made him *laugh*. He is *enjoying* this despite himself. "If you only teach me—"

Yet already his laugh is turning into a frown. "Step aside, Meneka," he says again. "I do not have the time for you tonight."

This time, his command is unyielding. I dare not refuse.

I obey silently.

Kaushika moves past me, the ends of his scarf billowing. He makes his way not to the stables or the road that leads outside the hermitage to the closest village, but to the forest. The hermitage still echoes with the quiet chants of practicing students, and I glance behind to see a few disciples weaving between the huts, headed either to the pavilion or the shed, perhaps to discuss their study. No one is watching me.

Keeping my distance, I duck my head and follow Kaushika.

In minutes, I am surrounded by trees, the sounds from the hermitage dying. Kaushika has disappeared from view, but his aura leaves a powerful afterimage and I track it like a hunter, pursuing the swirling colors of his magic. Starlight glints between trees, and petrichor eddies between grass blades. For days, I have expected rain, though there has been nothing but this teasing scent. I wonder what is occurring in Amaravati, if Indra is keeping his rain from the hermitage deliberately as a punishment for Kaushika. I think of Rambha, and what she would say if I told her I buried all my jewels, and then my clothes, into raw earth, that I'm not even using them yet for this mission. The colors of the sage's aura diminish, moving from leaf to branch, and I hurry, rounding trees, ensuring my footsteps are quiet.

Before long, Kaushika's aura begins to strengthen. I slow down, my tread becoming even more careful. I have no explanation for if he catches me; my only plan is to not get caught. I weave my way between the trees and finally see him. His tall frame approaches another man, this one older and smaller, though standing no less erect for his age. A gray beard lies tightly coiled over the man's cheeks, and a kind smile lights up his wizened eyes. Kaushika drops to his knees and bends his head low to the other man's feet in a gesture of deep respect. Curiosity flames within me. The older man's aura is powerful, but somehow it does not compare to Kaushika's own. Who is he that Kaushika is humbling himself this way? Why are they meeting in such secrecy?

The man murmurs and Kaushika rises. They begin to walk again, following the path until the canopy of trees gives way to a lake mirroring the starlight. Fed by the River Alaknanda, this lake is the closest body of water to the hermitage, spanning several meters. I have seen it on one of Anirudh's maps, and a pang of homecoming sharpens in my chest. This is a mortal lake, no different from any other, but all water belongs to Lord Indra. Does Kaushika even understand this?

He and his companion walk around the shoreline, shoulders bent toward each other as they discuss something with a feverish intensity. The old man shakes his head, and Kaushika flings out an arm in a gesture of protest, but then nods reluctantly. They settle themselves on a rocky outcropping, and Kaushika moodily listens while the man speaks.

I think fast. The two men are too far to see me, intent on their conversation, yet I am too far to hear them. In order to learn anything, I would have to risk stepping into the clearing, or swim into the water. Well, that's an easy enough choice, then.

I am surrounded by trees, darkness shrouding me. I disrobe swiftly, hiding the clothes from the hermitage under a rock. As quietly as I can, I touch the cold water with my toes. The water recognizes me as a creature of Indra; it responds to my celestial nature. It laps closer, obscuring me in a quiet, rising wave as I crouch and enter the lake. In seconds, I am submerged, swimming toward the two men, knowing the lake will conceal me.

Still, my skin chills instantly. Even though I can breathe underwater indefinitely, the cold will affect me. How amusing that if I could churn the fire of tapasya, I would be able to warm myself. Praying that the men do not intend to linger, I rise unseen and unheard, ensuring I stay just beneath the surface as I come closer to them. From here, Kaushika's voice is blurry, but I sing a hymn to Indra in my mind, and the sounds become sharp at once.

"—is foolhardy," the older man says. "You are training your disciples too fast. Demanding they learn too quickly. You are allowing too many people within your hermitage, and are becoming a concern to the other sages. If you wish to present your students to them—"

"I am *refusing* people," Kaushika interrupts, irritated. In my mind's eye, I can almost see the intensity of his eyes, the frown crinkling his brows. "Fewer will stay after the Initiation Ceremony. I will only allow the ones who are most devoted to the path, the ones who truly know their own souls, to train with me. Agastya—you yourself taught me not to deny seekers of the truth. That this knowledge is meant for everybody. Surely you would not ask me to stop?"

"I also taught you restraint. Are you exercising that choice, my son?"

"To be a sage is to be free. This is *my* hermitage. I must govern it in the way I see fit, precisely like every sage does with their own school. Surely the others cannot object to that?"

"Do you think Vashishta will not?" Agastya asks.

"Vashishta has always hated me," Kaushika snaps. "Before I came to you to train me, I went to him too, but he humiliated me, berating my youth and arrogance, claiming I was drunk with power. He would deny me my place as a sage despite my tapasya, despite what I have done for the knowledge of mantras."

"He values emotional control," the older man replies mildly. "I would ask if your loss of temper has held you back."

A silence breathes with those words. I imagine the passage of emotions on Kaushika's face, frustration and guilt and resignation. *Agastya and Vashishta*, I note. Two of the most powerful rishis in the mortal realm. Songs are sung in Amaravati of Indra treating with them, even inviting them to swarga for conferences and advice. Mortals though the two sages are, they are hundreds of years old. They know the lord intimately, part friends, part rivals. What do they make of Kaushika's irreverence to him? Do they even know of it?

"Forgive me, guruji," Kaushika says formally. "I did not intend to be disrespectful."

"You are powerful, Kaushika. No one can deny you your status as a rishi. Yet in accepting you as one of them, the sages sought to bring you under control. There is an understanding that you will live by their dictates." Agastya sighs, and I almost feel the ripple of air. "Vashishta wants to know if Shiva has seen fit to bless your hermitage. It is the one thing he returns to, always quoting Shiva's absence as an indication of your brazenness. Has the Lord come yet?"

My pulse pounds in my throat, and I have to forcibly remind myself not to breathe out and dispel bubbles. I hold myself very still, my hair swirling around me.

"No," Kaushika says.

Disappointment bleeds from his voice, but all I feel is a mingled sense of horror and relief. Kaushika aims to call Shiva himself to the hermitage, and Shiva has not listened so far, but what if he relents? What would happen to Indra and Amaravati if Kaushika ekes out a boon from the Lord of *Destruction*? Shiva is the Innocent One, unaware and uncaring of the politics of the mortal and immortal realms. Should Kaushika ask him for weapons to take down Indra, he could grant Kaushika's wish without realizing what he is doing. I recall the hymns practiced in the hermitage, mantras recited to empower sages, and those asking for his blessing to annihilate maya. What can occur with such powers unchecked? I shiver, and it is not merely because of the frigid lake.

"We are devoted," Kaushika says, frustrated. "*I* am devoted. The hermitage is a reflection of my own piety to Shiva. Why does the Lord not come?"

"Perhaps," the other man says, "your disciples are not as devoted as you think."

"Those who are not will leave soon enough," Kaushika says darkly.

Coldness creeps into my bones. The impossibility of my mission tightens my throat. I swallow, trying to dislodge the knot of despair. The other sage speaks again, and I strain to listen.

"We have agreed you are a rishi, Kaushika," he says. "However, allow me to offer you some wisdom. You are still bound by the pursuit of power. Your past hangs over you, and you seem unable to rise above it. You create karma, one action into another, but a true rishi breaks the karmic cycle like Shiva himself."

"And I will," Kaushika says forcefully. "You are right, guru, that my past still governs me, but you are wrong too. It is not for mindless power. I do it to satisfy a sacred promise, one I must see fulfilled. That I *need* to see fulfilled. What good am I if I cannot follow what I think is righteous? What good is my tapasya if I do not even keep my word?"

"Only you can decide that, son," the guru replies mildly.

Kaushika grunts, and I remain still. The cold is so terrible that I am burning now with it. I ask for heat from Agni, lord of fire, but even as I pray, I know he will not answer this easily. Agni is tempestuous; he flickers in my mind, the way I saw him last in Indra's throne room, his pointed face glinting with a sharp smile that never reached his eyes.

Kaushika speaks again, and his voice is softer. "What else do the sages require of me at the Mahasabha?"

"A justification for your meadow beyond the reasons of your vow. They will question you on it."

*Meadow?* My ears perk, and I swim closer, trying to fight against the chill.

"They view it as an act of rebellion," the guru continues. "You understand that is why they have called the Mahasabha, do you not? To make you answer for it? Your presentation of your students is only secondary."

"My meadow is not for my benefit alone," Kaushika replies. "It is meant to assist all of the mortal and immortal realms. Surely the sages see that the times are changing. I understand such an act is not tradition, that it has never been done before, but I do not pursue it as a challenge to any being. I do it to fulfill my existing karma. As sages, are we not meant to push the boundaries of knowledge?"

"Yes, but in righteous ways," the guru says quietly. "The meadow is a magnificent display of magic, but Vashishta will not countenance it. The very thought of it infuriates him. It is true that sages push the boundaries of knowledge, but there is a balance to this universe. You must accept this, even if you do not like the balance. The karma you keep building blinds you from this, and all your beautiful words and arguments will not sway the Mahasabha. Vashishta is convinced the meadow is a crime against nature. Even I do not think it is wise. You must consider if there is a different way to achieve what you want."

There is another silence. I imagine Kaushika staring at the lake as he considers this. The two men do not speak again, but they do not move either. My body grows stiff. My mind slows with every instant. I wonder dreamily if I can simply freeze here, aware of my own immortality forever. What would such stillness be like? A slow horror worms within my heart to contemplate it, and I squeeze my eyes shut.

Above me, I hear the two men begin their conversation again, but suddenly, I can no longer focus. The cold attacks me, lulling me toward perilous sleep, sleep I know I will not wake from. I try to move my toes, but it creates a large ripple, one that could expose me if the men were to investigate. I should have swum back into hiding several minutes ago. I am too chilled to do so now, without attracting attention. All I can do is remain here, trapped with knowledge and my recklessness.

Just when it becomes unbearable and I am about to rise, risking discovery, I hear twigs crack above. The two men stand, Kaushika murmuring about accompanying the sage part of the way.

I force myself to count to a hundred. I make it only to fifty before I have to float to the surface, teeth chattering and limbs numb. No one is about, and the night is undisturbed again, but when I find my clothes and dress, I do so quickly, not bothering to dry myself, knowing I cannot be caught here.

My way back to the hermitage is a haze. I rub my skin to warm it, and some of my concentration returns—enough to wonder at what I heard. What is this promise Kaushika made? What did the guru mean when he said Kaushika was caught by his past? Does Kaushika have enemies among the other sages, ones who support Vashishta more? It would not be odd—sages frequently argue about the best way to reach enlightenment, their rival powers a source of conflict among their own kind. Is that something I can use? What is the meadow, and why is it a crime against nature? Does it have anything to do with Indra?

The questions tumble within me, one sparking into another, fleeting embers I cannot catch. I frantically sieve everything I've learned, looking for answers, yet in the end all the questions distill into those from the very beginning, dictating my purpose here, my mission.

What is the shape of Kaushika's seduction?

And how do I get past his shield?

By the time I am back at the hermitage, I am warmer through sheer adrenaline, and I have a plan. There is no one about when I arrive, not even any late-night lingering students. Sleep has overtaken the hermitage, and except for the candlelight by Shiva's altar within the pavilion, all the buildings lie in darkness.

I hesitate only for an instant. Kaushika has warded his house, but this could be my only chance. I open the door and dart inside, aware that I am tripping the ward.

There are others in the hermitage who have their own homes, Romasha and Anirudh, Parasara, and Eka, and even Durvishi, who arrived not too long before I did. All of them have demonstrated excellence in their practice. I have not been in any of their houses, yet I imagine they all look similar on the inside.

The cottage is a single room with a wooden partition that leads to a veranda outside. Night birds twitter in and out of the rafters, and a dry breeze whooshes through cracks in the windows. I dare not light a candle, but I don't need to; there is enough starlight gleaming in to illuminate a cot in the center of the room with a threadbare blanket.

I arch an eyebrow at that. So. The great Sage Kaushika allows himself the comforts of a cot and a blanket, whereas new initiates such as myself must sleep on plain straw. How unsurprising. It is his due, certainly, but it irks me nonetheless. The last few nights have been especially brutal. I have woken with aches in my body, muscles I did not know I had hurting when I move. Only the stretches from my apsara practices have helped remind me that I am, in fact, an immortal.

My eyes wander to the floor, where a dozen books and scrolls lie piled one on top of another near a seating cushion. I approach them and flip through. A few of them are records of yogic poses, depicting the flow of prana. Obscure, half-known mantras cover the rest of them, verses that Kaushika is clearly researching. Petitions from royals flutter in the light breeze, caught between some of the pages. I recognize the names of a few kings and queens heaven has been interested in.

In one of the tomes, something catches my eye, slipped carefully underneath the wooden binding. A piece of yellowed paper, folded and folded again, so small that it is only as large as my thumbnail. Curious, I open it to reveal a faded letter. The calligraphy is too worn. I cannot read the whole of it, though some words jump out at me, *soul* and *rebirth* and *punishment*. I cannot help but feel that this letter and its contents are relevant to my mission somehow.

From the looks of it, it is several years old. Threads of the parchment come apart between my fingers, though my touch is gentle. I imagine Kaushika smoothening this paper out, staring at it, rereading the words he has probably memorized. I imagine his long fingers making the same movements mine are. Who wrote this? What does it say? Why has he preserved it here at the hermitage when he wishes for all of us to forget our pasts? Or is this simply another hypocrisy—like the cot he has allowed himself, which oddly looks so tempting at this very moment?

An owl hoots outside the hut, and I jump. Carefully, I fold the letter back and push it between the bindings of the book. I have been here long enough. I approach the door, attempting to leave, but even as I put a foot over the threshold, a vibration goes through me, stopping me. It is as though something is forcing me back, refusing to let me through.

Frowning, I try again, yet the energy persists, preventing me from leaving.

I have no time to puzzle it out. I hear voices approaching, and I retreat to the closest corner. I clutch Amaravati's tether to me, and my fingers move in a quick mudra, Surya's Eclipse. The illusion forms over me, rendering me invisible, so that when I move my own hand, I see nothing but the thatched wall of the hut. I press my lips together and ensconce myself in stillness.

Two shapes arrive at the threshold. I can tell they both came from different parts of the hermitage, for Romasha whispers, "You heard it too?" Light flickers in her hands, the very same ball of fire I've seen her wield before.

Anirudh does not reply, but he holds a similar ball of flames, his appearing like waves of dark lava. Both of them enter Kaushika's hut, holding their lights up. A sound skitters across the floor, and Romasha starts, almost unleashing her fire at it, but stops when she notices it is only a squirrel.

I squeeze myself back against the wall, knowing I am invisible to them yet breathing hard. I triggered the warding deliberately, to see who would come to Kaushika's hut in his absence. That it is these two should not surprise me; after Kaushika, they are the most learned and powerful in the hermitage, conducting lessons between them. Yet my heart sinks as I see Anirudh prowl through the cottage and check inside the cupboard and under the cot. Romasha I do not know well, but Anirudh has always been kind to me. He has been friendly.

The two of them meet in the center of the hut, looking around. Romasha's shoulders relax. She extinguishes the fire between her fingers and slumps a little.

"Do you think Kaushika made a mistake?" she asks.

"He doesn't make such mistakes," Anirudh replies, frowning. He has still not relinquished his fire.

"Maybe someone came looking for him but didn't enter his home at all," Romasha suggests.

Anirudh nods slowly. "Yes. Yes, of course. If anyone had entered, the ward would trap them, wouldn't it? We would see them. Perhaps they only triggered it unknowingly."

His body relaxes as he accepts this explanation. The fire he conjures finally fizzles out, and all of us are awash in darkness. My heart thumps in my chest, loud enough that I fear they will be able to hear it if they only attune themselves. A dozen thoughts churn within me. Whatever Kaushika is planning, these two must be in on it as well. He deliberately warded his house—perhaps it is common practice, something he does before he leaves each time—yet I saw nothing in here worth hiding or taking. It means the warding itself was meant as a trap to ferret out our true intentions, like the one in the forest that I walked into. Both Anirudh and Romasha came in expecting intruders, and more than that, to mete out punishment with fire. If I hadn't concealed myself, what would have happened? Are they capable of killing too? Is *this* how my sisters died?

I try to still the gibbering of my mind.

When the two leave, I slip out behind them, unnoticed.

## CHAPTER 8

I have no chance to question Romasha, whom I barely see outside of my lessons, and whom I don't know well enough. I cannot be obvious with Anirudh, whom I *do* see all the time and have come to know, because how would I truly begin? I cannot simply spring it in conversation, asking them to divulge the secrets they are undoubtedly keeping for Kaushika. The sage himself does not return to the hermitage, and I feel his absence like a hole carved into my side. My eyes search for him constantly, at the morning practice, at my lessons, even drifting again to his cottage where no candles glimmer in the night.

The conversation I overheard at the lake plays in my mind over and over again. I reassemble the picture of Kaushika incessantly while the Initiation Ceremony looms closer. A part of me blubbers in anxiety at how I am making no progress in my mission nor in the mortal magic I pretend to do. Week after week passes, and everyone but me already knows what they will demonstrate for Kaushika during the test.

Kalyani delves into her breath for physical strength and speed. From one blink to another, she can now circle twice around the hermitage. Anirudh's own skill is even more impressive. When I drop a book, he raises my arm to pick it up. That he can use his magic to influence other people's limbs . . . Even Indra cannot do so—only influence through his potency.

Each yogi is similar in some way, performing astounding feats of magic. While lessons are still conducted, several people no longer attend, focused instead on their personal learning. I am one of the few who is *asked* to attend every class, my inability to form runes now common knowledge. My capacity to hold great magic has become irrelevant. Even though I tell myself I am not here to learn mortal tricks, the prick of humiliation stings me when the other students give me looks. No one is awed by me anymore. They agree with Anirudh; I came too late. They agree with Kaushika; I will be gone by the end of the month.

That end stares at me unblinkingly as the days trickle by. Panic bubbles within my chest with the rush of a waterfall, and I do my best to ignore it. I recall Kaushika saying to the guru how he will ensure unworthy students will leave. I am simultaneously impatient to see him, to carry on with my mission, and terrified he will ask me to go when he learns of my failures. When nearly a month has passed with nothing to show for it, I grow desperate enough to become blunt.

"Doesn't Kaushika do this himself?" I ask.

I am with Anirudh and Kalyani, the three of us on a rare break from our many practices and chores. We are within the pillared pavil- ion, kneeling in the center by the simple cylindrical shaft of Shiva's al- tar, the lingam. Outside, rain has finally begun pattering after weeks of mockery, and I stare at it longingly, wishing to run into it, dance within it with abandon. Instead, I tear my gaze away and glance at my mortal companions.

Anirudh nods. "Ordinarily, yes. But he has not been in the camp for days now. I'm surprised you didn't notice."

Air ripples around him as he chants, a slow, melodious hum that cascades in waves, lifting with the breeze. The lingam, made of black marble, glows with the mantra. Sparkles radiate off it, and I feel its bare power washing over me, settling in my stomach with heat.

I take a few wildflowers from the basket in my hand and arrange them artistically around the lingam. The flowers were my idea; I had to ask Anirudh's permission to be allowed to leave the hermitage to gather them from the forest. I have no great devotion to Shiva beyond what is expected from me as a celestial, but if Anirudh is to report to Kaushika on everyone's devotion to the Destroyer, this act will only help me.

As it is, the flowers are the only ornamentation by the cylindrical lingam. Ascetic as these people are, they deny beauty itself. An unadorned flame burns in front of the altar, held within an earthen lamp and powered by tapasya. Representing the devotion of the hermitage toward Shiva, the flame must never go out. Anirudh closes his eyes, and the mantra becomes a murmur. His magic whistles through the pavilion as the flame rises into a tall, slim pillar of fire. Next to us Kalyani joins her hands and releases her breath in a deep exhale at the same time. Flowers meander up from my basket, swirling around the pillar of flame, then settling on the floor when the flame subsides. She raises an eyebrow at me, as if to say, *This is how you do it.* She has tried to make me use runes for every chore, hoping I will learn, but I have never been less interested in a magic that is not mine.

"It seems so hard to keep the flame burning with your power constantly," I say, still focused on Kaushika. "Does it not tire you?"

Anirudh leans back, satisfied and relieved by the consecration. "Romasha and I take turns in Kaushika's absence, though I admit it will be a relief when he is back."

I make a sympathetic sound in my throat. As casually as I can, I say, "Where did he go?"

Anirudh's tone is as casual as mine. "Why do you want to know?"

I shrug. *Reveal your lust,* I whisper in my mind, and a shape forms behind my eyes, the same one each time I have looked into Anirudh's desires. An image of him, kneeling at Kaushika's feet, asking to be blessed.

The first time I saw it, I was startled. Were Anirudh and Kaushika lovers? Is that why Anirudh followed him from their kingdom? Can it be that Kaushika is not interested in women at all? It would hardly matter to my seduction; instead of showing him my own form, my illusion would simply have taken the presentation of me as a man. It is something I've done many times before with marks.

But I now know it is not lust for Kaushika that guides Anirudh. It is a desire to make Kaushika proud. On my arrival to the hermitage, I mistakenly thought that the revelation of my power would turn the other disciples against me and make me a target. I have learned since then that such competition is hardly something the yogis care about, an antithesis to how matters occur within Amaravati among the apsaras. The yogis here *want* me to succeed in my magic. They want to raise Kaushika's prestige and that of the hermitage. As strange as this way of thinking is, it is something I can use.

"I want to please Kaushika," I say. "If he is back soon, I can show him how I wish to serve the hermitage. Just like the rest of you."

"Pleasing him should not be your concern," Anirudh says, surprising me. "I understand the desire—he is a forceful man, his own power calling to all of us like moths to his flame. But that is not why you are here, is it?"

"I am here to train. I haven't been able to create a single rune, but if he teaches me—"

"If he has not helped you so far, he won't now either, no matter how much you ask him."

"But why?" I drop my pretense as my anguish becomes apparent. "What have I done?"

"Nothing. He is entitled to his decision, however. Do not concern yourself with what he's doing or where he is going, Meneka. He travels often on personal business. He'll return when he wants to. We do not keep track of him, and his rules are his own."

"He is being unreasonable," Kalyani snaps. She turns away from adorning the flowers around the altar, and puts an arm around me. "Why allow her in and then leave her untrained?"

"She isn't untrained," Anirudh replies. "She goes to lessons. She meditates. Kaushika created this hermitage, he brought us together, but he cannot train us personally, not by tradition. He is not allowed to do so according to the dictates of the Mahasabha and the agreement with the other sages. He is only allowed to share secrets he knows to those who are worthy, and the Initiation Ceremony will determine who *is* worthy. Until then he must follow the path of withdrawal, of only observing and not interfering, of guiding and suggesting, but not training. Why do you think he only challenges us instead of providing answers even when we argue philosophy? We are meant to come to an understanding of our own power and path without interference. That is why he does not train any of us yet, not even me or Romasha."

"But Meneka is clearly struggling," Kalyani protests vehemently. "His withdrawal right now amounts to watching an innocent creature drown simply for the sake of noninterference. It is cruel and heartless."

"It is the ascetic method," Anirudh says gently. "What he is doing with her is no different from your own training, Kalyani."

Kalyani scowls deeply. Though the both of them have been helping me, she has gone above and beyond, trying to teach me specific breathing practices. She has shown up at my door late at night, using the power of her own tapasya to facilitate my focus. In the beginning, she was reluctant to disrespect Anirudh by disagreeing with him, but the closer she and I have become, the more she has voiced her displeasure at how I am being treated.

I press her hand in gratitude, knowing that her frustration has to do with me as well as Kaushika. Several times, I have almost let slip in my own aggravation how she *cannot* teach me no matter how much she tries. Only picturing Rambha has helped me hold my tongue. I told Rambha I would return. She said we would make promises to each other. Anirudh's allegiances are clear, but even if Kalyani knows nothing about Kaushika and his secrets, she is a sage in training. No matter her kindness, she is loyal to Kaushika. It is why any of these people are helping me. I cannot forget that.

Sudden tears flood my eyes. Four weeks. Four weeks have passed since I arrived, and I have nothing to show for it. I've barely exchanged two conversations with my mark, his own intention hidden. With any other mark, I would have already been halfway to seducing them, yet Kaushika has already proven too challenging. There is a darkness within him, shadowing his true intents, lurking a nail-scratch away. I can sense it, but I haven't even faced his magic, and he has already thwarted me.

If Kaushika asks me to leave due to my failure at the Initiation Ceremony, I might never get another chance to return to the hermitage to seduce him. I would be in exile until I finished my mission. I can see the events unfolding already. How I would throw caution to the wind, driven by urgency. How I would accost this sage somehow, a vision of blunt surprise, giving myself away instantly instead of completing my mission in a delicate manner.

Were my sisters trapped by desperation as well? Did Nanda begin dancing in the vain hope that Kaushika would simply be seduced by her beauty? Did Sundari create an illusion that worked before, never getting past Kaushika's shields but hoping anxiously that her best entrapments would? Was Magadhi dazzling, her beautiful smile brittle, when she twisted her wrists into mudras?

I can't let myself fall to the same fate. Rambha *kissed* me. We hoped to make promises to each other. All of that will become irrelevant if I am made to leave the hermitage.

Anirudh notices my distressed expression and sighs. "Your problem is that you are not allowing yourself to access the prana that you hold. You are blocking yourself."

I shake my head. Of course that is not my problem. These mortals do not understand. The magic Kaushika revealed to everyone that was stored within me was Amaravati's magic. It was prana, but it was given to me by Indra's grace. I cannot simply perform tapasya like the mortals and access the power that the lord himself does. I have tried. To do such magic is not in my nature. If it were possible, some other celestial would have traveled the path to it by now.

Kalyani's face grows concerned. "What is going through your mind when you meditate?"

My hopelessness rests on my neck like a heavy rope. "I miss home," I whisper.

I know I shouldn't say this, a sure sign of my unsuitability to be here, but I cannot help it. The pattering of the rain, a sound I have sorely missed as a sign of Amaravati, only serves to remind me of how alone I am.

Anirudh and Kalyani exchange another look. Anirudh's face softens. "What we do here is not easy. I am sorry."

"It is not that. I left people behind. Sisters. Friends. A lover." I close my eyes and I can almost believe I am in Rambha's arms again. The honey spice of her lips. The softness of her skin. *Come back*, her voice whispers to me in memory. I open my eyes to see the mortals watching me in sympathy.

Clearing my throat, I nod to the other students. "Does no one here have lovers? Is no one married?"

Kalyani points to two men deep in discussion about the feat of magic they would perform for the Initiation Ceremony. "Shailesh and Daksh are married. They share a home within the hermitage."

My eyebrows rise. "Kaushika allows them the same quarters? Despite his commitment to the ascetic path? Then it means the two men share a bed . . . they . . . they . . ."

I trail off, unsure how to word my question, but Anirudh smiles a small smile. "It is all right to ask, Meneka. It is not an unnatural question.

Daksh and Shailesh are only two of the many married people here within the hermitage. Naren and Abhay, Advik and Sharmisha, all of these people were once lovers, and many of them share a home now. But they transcended the need for sex with their meditation. Now they redirect their sexual energy to a deeper power, Shiva himself. All yogis here have withdrawn from the evanescence of desire. By yoking our desire—even sexual—to true knowledge of ourselves, we feed the process of tapasya and are thus able to access our own magic. Shiva is the Lord of Asceticism. Our own pursuit of it is the greatest form of worship to him."

"Loving one another's body is an act of worship too," I whisper. "Denying it to these people . . . is this Kaushika's decree?"

"He has made no such proclamations, but all of us here follow the ascetic path. It presupposes celibacy." Anirudh frowns. "Kaushika should have warned you about what it means before he allowed you in. It is unlike him to forget something so foundational."

"Could this be why you are magically blocked?" Kalyani ventures. "Homesick for your lover, therefore you stop yourself from accessing your full power?"

"It is possible." Anirudh studies me, tilting his head.

A wrenching tightness cords through my chest. I have no words for them. Who are these people, so austere as to deny themselves the pleasures of the flesh? They are the antithesis of an apsara—passive stillness, when apsaras are sexual movement. Meditative and cold, when apsaras rely on expression and life. Beings of tapasvin fire, when apsaras are creatures of Indra's water. Kaushika is a contradiction to me in every way, an unmoving hermit while I remain an ever-changing nymph. How am I to seduce this man? How deeply will I lose myself in this impossible mission?

I raise my chin to heaven, tears blurring my eyes. I swallow, seeking guidance from Indra, trying to capture the image of his resplendence. Rain patters on the roof and I pretend it touches my skin. This place, this mission—never have I been so vulnerable, so powerless.

Anirudh clears his throat. "If you are finding the path of asceticism hard, I think you need more inspiration than we can give you here."

He utters a chant, and the air above him sparkles into a gleaming, translucent map. The hermitage is a cluster of dots. A dark mass represents the woods I arrived in, and a winding silvery ribbon beyond the forest glistens in the shape of the River Alaknanda.

Anirudh points to a structure away from the river and the forest, leading toward the closest knot of villages. "See this triangle? It is Shiva's temple, the closest one to the hermitage. I want you to go there after your duties here are done this evening. Maybe being closer to the Great Lord will guide you back to his path."

Kalyani arches a brow and waves her hand to the lingam Anirudh just consecrated. "This cannot be done here?"

"The temple is consecrated not through yogis alone but through the devotion of many others. Such a thing has its own potential, one Meneka might respond to." Anirudh makes a balancing motion with his hand. "I wouldn't ordinarily suggest it, but it is worth a try. Everything else has failed."

I stare at him. My voice is cautious. "I thought we were supposed to keep to the hermitage and the forest, our separation from the outside world complete."

"If Kaushika finds out, I will take responsibility," Anirudh answers. "You are not going outside the hermitage to engage in worldly matters. You are going so you may detach even further."

"Keep your heart true," Kalyani urges. "Keep your mind pure."

Misery seeps its tentacles into me, wrapping itself around my body. I understand their words and the risk Anirudh is taking for what they are—a last chance and a desperate attempt to connect with a magic I do not possess. Prayer to Shiva won't help me, but I cannot refuse this instruction. It would be as good as giving up. Perhaps leaving the hermitage briefly will ignite other ideas. Silently, I listen as Anirudh provides me directions to the temple.

# CHAPTER 9

T he rain has become a downpour by the time I reach the small temple a few miles away from the hermitage. My kurta and pajamas stick to me, and my skin is soaked. I shiver, drenched, but I am not truly bothered. Anirudh offered to spin me a shield, but Indra commands the rains. This is but my lord's blessing.

I breathe in the richness of moist earth, the distant sizzle of lightning, the fresh bloom of wild roses. *Home*, I think, and Amaravati shimmers for a second in front of me, golden and magnificent, an undulating mirage. An ache seizes me, a hand clasping my heart. I shake my head, knowing there is no return until I finish with Kaushika.

My gaze runs over the small structure before me. Unlike the finery of Amaravati, Shiva's temple is little more than a cave. Carved into inconspicuous rock by the side of the road, it is bathed in evening shadows. I step inside onto a sandy floor. A quiet, mysterious energy thrums through the cave. Tree roots clamber upon rock walls, their thin, hairy fibers gripping the wide gray stones.

The cave is small, hardly large enough for two people to stand in. I am alone here in the stormy dusk, but some devotee not too long ago brought incense sticks. The air smells like resin and ginger, and tiny embers flicker, throwing dim, wavering light. At the very center of the temple is the power I am to meditate upon—a lingam resting on a yoni. Shiva with his Shakti.

I undo the topknot that holds together my hair like a sage's. Water drips from my locks onto my neck as I squeeze it out. I leave my long, dark hair undone.

My eyes flit to the walls. Shapes blink, reaching for my attention. My fingers brush on jagged rock carvings, and the legends grow alive in my head.

Here is Shiva, a pillar of endless tapasvin fire, with neither a beginning nor an end. Here he is, a warrior beheading Brahma, the Lord of Creation, for Brahma's incestuous longings. Shiva, a forest-dweller, arrives for his own wedding in rags and ashes, innocent of the required decorum. Shiva, a grieving husband, weeps, enraged, setting the universe ablaze when he learns of his wife's death.

Outside, thunder cracks, a long, drawn-out rumble. Rain cascades down a graying sky.

I blink and the legends of Shiva disappear. Indra does not call to me personally, but the thunder is a reminder. I am Indra's creature. Shiva is the Lord of the Universe, but I am too small, too distracted for him. If there is any god who cares for me, who *must* care for me, it is Indra.

Without warning, a sharp grief lances through my heart. The circumstances of my mission crash into me. Slowly, I sink to my knees. A deep homesickness grips me, making my muscles weak. Memories churn—Queen Shachi kneeling, bringing me a golden rattle when I am three. The grove where I watch older apsaras dance, yearning to be as graceful as them. My early illusions, a chubby fist curling into mudras. Lord Indra as he blesses my first mission.

*Make me proud*, the lord of heaven says in memory, his eyes infinitely kind.

*I will, my king*, I whisper before I leave.

Embers dance at the edges of my vision, and tears trickle fast and thick down my cheeks. Amaravati's tether tightens, making me gasp. My fingers open into an unplanned mudra, Sorrow's Shore, a lonely figure on an abandoned beach, revealing to me my own despair. *You are my salvation*, I think. *How could you send me to my doom?*

*Make me proud*, Indra answers, his only reply. His voice twines with Rambha's. *Your devotion unquestioned.*

I thunk my head back to the rock wall. My mind hunts for the lore of Indra. Hero of a thousand battles, tamer of the great elephant Airavat, savior of the mortal realm, lord of rain and fertility, vitality and song— the litany runs through my head without landing on anything meaningful. It should be easy to immerse myself in his greatness, something I seeded and nourished in his garden before my mission. Yet here in the mortal realm, I am bereft, my devotion isolated when I need it the most.

Abruptly, I shake myself.

I rise.

Coming here was a mistake. Anirudh will want to know how I feel after the meditation. I am already lying to him about myself. What is one more fib? I do not need Shiva. I am no sage. I am an *apsara*, and I need Indra. I already have several jewels from him, which I need for my mission. I have not been using the tools I have been sent with, and I move, resolving to find them, to seduce Kaushika like I am meant to. I make my way to the cave's entrance, to drench myself in the rain again, a prayer to Indra forming on my lips.

Before I can leave, lightning flashes again. Two cloaked riders appear in the twilight. A woman speaks, challengingly. A man answers, amused. His cloak falls back for a second, and his aura spills onto the road. Stone, tree, horseshoe, all sparkle with his light before he covers himself again. Kaushika's power ripples toward me, and I draw back, adrenaline coursing through me, suddenly alert.

They ride closer, nearly upon me. From where I am, hidden within the inconspicuous cave temple, I can see and hear them clearly. I breathe, and camphor and rosewood spiral into me.

"—because of them, surely," the woman says. She tips her head up to the rain. Water trickles down the wrinkles in her forehead. "Even you cannot deny that."

"I deny nothing, Rani," Kaushika says. His face is hidden in the hood of his cloak, but I can almost see the smirk. "I'm less interested in what the devas do as an uncontrollable form of nature, more in how their actions interfere in the mortal world. Tell me, which one interests you?"

"Is there a difference? A deva is a deva."

"Would you like me to teach you philosophy?"

The queen snorts. "I would like to know why I should risk angering an immortal, child. My line has prayed to the devas for generations. My people are loyal to swarga. Why should we stop now?"

A chuckle escapes me at this strange queen's quick tongue. Threaded through it is wonder and horror. Here it is, my first true evidence of Kaushika actively conniving to stop mortals from succoring Indra. How many have already joined his cause? According to Rambha, heaven does not know, but this queen does not seem to be the first royal Kaushika has approached. I remember what Anirudh said about Kaushika traveling for personal business. Fomenting irreverence for Indra *is* Kaushika's business. Why?

It is what this queen has asked too. Whoever she is, she is no fool. From the gray in her hair, she is older than both Kaushika and me by several years. For a brief second, Kaushika's lips thin at her reference to his youth. Then he smiles, as though the annoyance never existed.

He cocks his head. "Perhaps the better question is if you would displease a sage."

"You dare threaten me?" the queen begins, turning to him.

Kaushika removes his hood, a movement that silences her from speaking further. He takes off his cloak, then the kurta. The queen watches warily as he drapes his garments over his whickering horse, revealing the holy thread that slashes across his bare chest like a scar. The queen's eyes widen when she sees it, as if she has suddenly remembered he is no ordinary youth but a mortal with great magic. He touches the thread, his gaze contemplative.

My fingers twitch. I have not seen the holy thread on him before, though it is a sage's due. He has not cared for such ritual before—then has he worn it now simply to intimidate the queen? He is as cunning as I have been told, yet he fills up my senses, the water droplets trapped in his eyelashes, the topknot I bizarrely itch to release, the manner in which he sits astride his steed. An unrecognizable aching hunger grows within me, unfurling like warmth from my throat to stomach. I swallow, the movement oddly thick.

"There are devas," Kaushika says quietly, spreading one arm out, indicating the rain. "And then there are sages."

His fingers click, and a rhythmic chant emerges from him. I gasp, an identical response to the queen's.

The rain pauses.

It doesn't stop—it *pauses*, as though Kaushika has frozen the entire world. Globules of water hang motionless in the evening, as far as we can see. Leaves stop swishing, the roar of the downpour silenced. The horses stop whickering, their tails suspended midmotion. Above, lightning freezes too, a jagged golden shard held back from growing into a bolt. The quiet is unearthly, deafening. My breath seizes in terror. Can Indra feel this? Is the lord panicking?

The queen's head snaps from side to side, her face draining of color. Light dances through the suspended gray water droplets, but it is the light of Kaushika's aura, a billion rainbow shimmers visible perhaps only to me.

"Well, Queen?" Kaushika says, smiling guilelessly.

"I—I—" the queen stammers, her eyes wide.

Stories of powerful sages return to me, ones the gandharvas sing only when drunk on soma. Brighu, who made the stars obey his will. Kashyapa, who drained the valleys of the Himalayas, making them uninhabitable. Atri, who tamed the River Ganga to make her flow from the heavens. Though still young, Kaushika is nearly at the level of those great men. *He can do it*, I think. *He can destroy Amaravati. He can end my magic.* Dizziness makes me lightheaded.

"Understand that I do not need weapons, Rani," Kaushika says. "I do not need your soldiers. Consider why a sage is asking you to change who you should offer allegiance to. Consider what we do. What we protect."

"Us," the queen whispers. "Sages protect us."

Her voice is raw, hypnotized. Its cadence is similar to how I have been spellbound by Indra. She turns to Kaushika, and the words seem pulled from her. "Sages give wisdom, their only agenda to increase knowledge in the world. It is how they protect us beyond our years."

Kaushika smiles. "What knowledge can be unleashed when the world is no longer controlled by heaven's tempestuous moods? Will you stand in its way, or be the one who leads the charge for your people?"

The change in the queen's face is startling. She blinks, and a tremor passes through her. Trembling, she lowers her gaze from Kaushika's and joins her palms.

"Forgive me, guruji," she whispers, and my brows rise at the honorific she affords him.

Lazily, Kaushika spins his hand. Some of the motionless rain shimmers, coalescing, creating a shield around the queen and her unmoving horse.

"Go. Return to your people. Confer with your council. I'll await your decision."

The queen bows lower, and Kaushika utters another chant. Sound and movement blast back into the dusk so suddenly it makes me jump. Lightning crashes over and over again, and I imagine Indra raging in his court, the vajra sizzling mercilessly. The queen's suddenly animated horse neighs in terror. She kicks it forward, and they disappear around a bend in the road. Kaushika watches them leave, then the calm expression on his face falls.

His shoulders slump. His eyes close like he is confronting himself. I watch his mask drop, leaving behind true vulnerability. Kaushika breathes hard, lifting his face up to the rain. He clutches the holy thread around him, like he is trying to remind himself of something.

Curiosity fills me about this man, and my mind grasps desperately for the shape of his seduction. Kaushika on his knees, head bowed as I loom over him. Kaushika holding me down, turning me over. Kaushika mesmerized as I dance for him. Kaushika indifferent as I create illusions. The seduction rebounds, one image to another, never settling, and a frantic dread grips me. Who is he? What does he like? What does he seek? Urgency, urgency—these questions must be answered.

The next second, alarm replaces my curiosity as Kaushika looks toward the temple. I suddenly realize why he chose to have this conversation here. Shiva's temple, its power consecrated tenfold by being so close to the hermitage, has helped Kaushika perform the difficult magic he just did. He is a sage, after all, his path that of Shiva's own.

Kaushika nudges his horse toward me.

My shallow gasps echo within the cave. My gaze darts around the rock walls. This won't be like the time I overheard him at the lake. There is nowhere to hide now. No camouflage nor cover. No subterfuge. I have already witnessed the edges of his temper, and it is never wise to rile a sage. What can I do?

A risky idea sparks in my mind, and I spin around and sit down. I face the lingam, my back to the entrance, but my entire body is alert. My palms are joined in prayer, but the lines of my shoulders grow rigid. There is no time to think of anything more subtle. Swallowing hard, I listen to Kaushika dismount and enter the temple.

## CHAPTER 10

He stops the instant he enters. "You!" he spits out. "What are you doing here?"

"Kaushika?"

I turn slightly to see his shape outlined in the doorway. He is impossibly tall, and if it weren't for his aura, the cave would become dimmer with the light he blocks. Instead, a radiance invades the temple. I blink to breathe in, momentarily dizzy from adrenaline and fear.

He does not know I have been eavesdropping. I am still safe. I turn fully to him, making my eyes wide, standing up slowly.

He scowls as he shoulders his way inside. Rain still drips from him, and the tiny cave becomes smaller. His light burns into me, and my skin feels scorched with his potency. It is so intoxicating that I want to lean in and inhale him.

"You're not supposed to be here," he continues, eyes flashing. "How dare you leave the hermitage? If you want to leave, I can make it permanent right now, but do not think you are above the rules simply because you contain raw magic."

"I'm praying to Shiva," I say. "I only wanted to—"

"Like this?" Kaushika gestures at my undone hair, at my wrinkled kurta, at my still-damp skin. "If you are to be a sage, you need to understand there are decrees that disciples must obey, including the manner of their appearance. You come to the Lord like this?"

Despite my terror, my eyes narrow. Pointedly, I run my gaze down his own damp topknot, the warrior chest beaded with raindrops, the low-slung pajamas where I see a sprinkling of dark hair.

"Rich chastisement coming from you," I drawl. "When you are half-naked yourself."

Kaushika's eyes widen in outrage. A quiet oath escapes him, and he ducks back out into the rain. He is back in an instant, pulling his kurta over himself.

A pang of regret goes through me as his chest is covered with cotton, dimming the light of his aura. Perhaps it is my heightened nervousness, but I can't help but giggle at his frustrated expression.

His scowl deepens. "Do not make the mistake of comparing yourself to me. I have been practicing my austerities for years to gain self-control. I can afford to shed them now, but even I had to obey these steps when I was as uninitiated as you are." He takes a deep breath, trying to master himself. "I have proved my devotion to the Great Lord several times. Yours is still under question."

I arch an eyebrow. "And *you* will decide the value of my devotion?"

Kaushika shifts his scowl to the lingam.

The question hangs in the air, sharpening the edges of his own arrogance. He blinks and crouches down to the altar.

The lines of his back are straight, tense, but closing his eyes, Kaushika mutters a chant. His fingers touch the lingam, glowing with power. Silver ash trickles from his fingertips as he draws three horizontal lines, the tripundra, on the black rock. A garland appears from thin air, surrounding the altar. Incense embers flare within the cave with renewed light, and I inhale, stunned by the sudden peace that flows through me. I am too mesmerized, staring at the temple glistening with a rapid golden glimmering, to immediately realize that Kaushika is watching me.

The prayer to Shiva has already calmed his features. He is as unreadable as ever. I open my mouth to speak, but he looks away.

"Will. Knowledge. Action," he says softly, his gaze on the three lines of the tripundra. "The basics of connecting with your prana. Have you learned these yet?"

"No." None of my teachers have ever explained it this way.

"I thought not. Shiva won't listen to you, Meneka. You don't have the restraint needed to silence your mind to pierce through his meditation."

"Shiva is Bholenath," I answer. "He is the Innocent One. Perhaps your path to him is through austerities, but he does not care for devotional politics and rituals. He cares for the trueness of one's heart, the purity of our intention, the sweetness of our love. Or am I wrong?"

"No. You're not wrong. Tell me then, is your heart true? Is your intention pure?" A dark smile cuts Kaushika's face. "Is your love sweet?"

I open my mouth but images flash behind my eyes. Princess Ranjani, my very first successful mission, in my arms. The pleasure in her eyes as I trickled kisses down her belly, as I parted her thighs. The vapid expression as I left her to return to Amaravati. When, sickened, I finally made the rule to never become involved with a mark no matter what my sisters did. Horror, doubt, and distress freeze my body. Sudden tears glint in the corners of my eyes. Kaushika watches my face, and his own grows softer.

"I'm sorry," he says quietly, looking back to the lingam. "That question is never easy. Yet unless you can answer it, you will not be able to call upon Shiva."

Confusion swirls within me, to be given sympathy by *him*, to need it so badly. Even Rambha never fully acknowledged my fears about myself and what we do as apsaras, but here is Kaushika, of all people, attempting in his own detached way.

Thunder cracks outside, and I snap back to myself.

*Enough.*

I will not let Kaushika define me. I will not let my mark dictate this mission. I force myself to remember the resplendence of Amaravati, the real danger of this man, the hate I saw on his face on that first meeting. My tether tightens within me, giving me magic and anger.

"Convenient," I say. "To choose Shiva as the deity for your hermitage."

"What are you talking about?"

I shrug delicately. "Anirudh told me how everyone within the hermitage turns their sexual desire inward to achieve spiritual bliss. He said this is what Shiva needs, in pursuit of austerities."

Kaushika jerks his head toward me. "You have been talking to Anirudh about sexual matters, have you?"

"We talk about many things. Does it bother you?" Kaushika scowls, and my answering smile is poison sweet. "In the hermitage, all I hear about is the path of Shiva sages must follow. Yet it seems to me you yogis repress a lot. Would Shiva condone repression, do you think? The Lord who is freedom incarnate?"

Kaushika's eyes narrow. "Our austerities are not repression. They are a form of ultimate self-control. Shiva is free because he alone controls his mind, perfectly in charge of when and how he reacts. If you do not understand something as simple as this, then you certainly have no place at the hermitage."

"Is that so?" I sigh dramatically. "Tell me, Sage. What does the lingam mean?"

To my surprise, Kaushika utters a raw, amused laugh. "That is your argument? The lingam is an erect phallus, and the yoni a welcoming womb. Every Shiva devotee knows this. Shiva is many things. Lord of Yoga. Lord of Asceticism. The one who performs the greatest austerities, yet the sensual one." His eyes linger over me. "The erotic one."

"Yet he is nothing without the Goddess. Even his representation marks her." I raise my chin, and my own voice hardens. "You follow Shiva's path, but you do not acknowledge that which balances him. You ignore Shakti, who shows him who he is, without whom he cannot enliven his divinity. Shiva would destroy the whole universe with the power of his meditation—destroy his own self. It is the Goddess who anchors him into life, forcing him to react, to give, to participate. It is the Goddess who turns his destruction into creation, into eroticism. Without her, he is incomplete, yet you ignore her in your hermitage, claiming to follow his path. I sit in one lesson after another, Anirudh and Romasha parroting what you have taught them, yet you have not taught them this simple truth. I meditate at the hermitage's lingam, yet though you've built the yoni there too, not a word is spoken about the Goddess. Are you sure *you* have a place in a hermitage that claims to follow Shiva?"

Silence rings within the temple.

Kaushika opens his mouth, then closes it. His gaze moves across the cave, to catch on the carvings of Shakti in her many forms. As violent Kali riding Shiva's body. As benevolent Parvati, rivalling Shiva with her own meditation. As Sati and Durga and Annapurna and Kamakshi—the Goddess always as *Shakti*, power personified, completing Shiva.

Something in Kaushika's eyes shifts. Arrogance is replaced with sudden horror, then humility, and beyond that, a dazzling defenselessness.

It is so unexpected that I am taken aback.

"It is not Shiva alone who is the Lord of the Universe, Sage," I say quietly. "It is Shiva when he is with Shakti. You worship the lingam and the yoni, but your denial of pleasure—your pursuit of asceticism without understanding—rejects love as a force of all creation. It rejects the Goddess, and so it rejects Shiva too. I asked you why you saved Navyashree, and you claimed it was your duty, an ascetic answer if there ever was one, yet your path of austerity does not embrace the beautiful contradictions of Shiva or the eternal shifting permanence of him. You claim to worship him, but how much of Shiva do you truly understand?"

Kaushika's gaze moves from the carvings to me.

I dare not move, pinned by his eyes. I wonder if I have spoken in error. Given too much away. I try to retrieve my anger and indignation, the emotions I started this conversation with. I said the words to trip him up, but the longer Kaushika stares at me, unblinkingly, curiosity in his eyes, the harder it is to remember that I am in control.

He watches me, head tilted, like he is trying to make me out as much as I am him. Like he is truly seeing me for the first time.

Slowly, my breath grows shallow. My eyes dart to the laugh lines on his face. The long, artistic fingers. The fullness of his lips and the ghost of those dimples. What does he see? Why won't he speak? My tether blooms, confusing me. I clutch it, but his perception unmoors me. Rambha, Amaravati, Indra—all of them disappear. Suddenly Kaushika and I are alone, without pretenses, without agendas, here in Shiva's temple.

Kaushika's mouth lifts in a small smile.

"You are right," he says at last. "I have been ignoring the Goddess. Agastya would laugh at me if he knew this is what I've done. Perhaps that is why I have failed to summon Shiva to the hermitage."

My eyes widen in horror. Abruptly, I am brought back to my mission. Did I truly just give him a weapon of knowledge, one that would *help* him? Did Indra see this somehow? Would the lord consider this a betrayal?

"Shiva would not leave Mount Kailash," I breathe, panicked. "He does not simply come when called. You said so yourself."

"He comes when he is convinced of a devotee's love and purity," Kaushika says. "*You* said so yourself. You have given me essential insight into why he has been ignoring me. I should have seen this all along." He rises, surging to his feet. "I will take your knowledge, freely offered. I will use it for the betterment of the hermitage. I thank you for this, Meneka."

I rise to my feet as well, alarmed. "You admit I have knowledge. Then you will allow me to stay in the hermitage?"

"To teach us the path of the Goddess?" he says ironically. "You are unbearably beautiful. No doubt the others would welcome the learning from you." He laughs, a raw, jagged sound, and shakes his head. "I think not. This is still my hermitage. No one stays here without knowing themselves. Without being able to perform the magic that connects them to their deeper self. Grateful as I am, your days are numbered unless you can make runes."

He moves forward to leave the temple, but I block his way.

"Then teach me," I say.

"It is not worth my time."

"Your time?" I mimic his raw laugh. "You have time to leave the hermitage and travel, but not to train me?"

He shrugs callously. "Very well, I have the time. I do not have the desire."

He cannot evict me. Not now. Not when I'm finally advancing in my mission. My desperation makes me bold. "You have not wanted me at the hermitage from the very beginning. Despite my strength. Despite my devotion. Why?"

"That is my business alone—" he begins.

"It is my business too," I say sharply. "You *want* me to fail. You are lying about your intention. Lying about why you don't want me here."

Kaushika's eyes flash. "Do not presume so much," he says. "I thank you for your guidance about Shakti, but gratitude is all you will get from me today."

Anger suffuses me, heating my cheeks. He makes to slide past me again, but I block him again. "Teach me," I demand. "Teach me once, and then decide about my worth."

"No. You debate well enough and you have philosophical knowledge about Shiva, but I sense too much turmoil in your heart. I have no time to treat with it. Linger here and pray, Meneka. Pray that Shiva listens—but I must return to the hermitage."

"So must I. Anirudh is waiting for me. Teach me, Kaushika. One lesson, and if I do not learn, I will leave the hermitage myself. I won't wait for the Initiation Ceremony. I will leave tonight if you wish it."

Interest sparks in his eyes. He inhales sharply, and his gaze travels down to his wrist. I realize I have captured it in my hand. His pulse thunders under my touch, and his eyes darken a fraction in awareness. My throat grows dry, but I refuse to swallow. I blurted the words out without thinking, but I am guaranteed to fail. I cannot do what the others do. My pretense here is over, and so is my mission from Amaravati. Surely he will not agree to my reckless demand? Anirudh told us that Kaushika is not *allowed* to teach by the dictates of the Mahasabha. I stare at him, expecting him to say no, but a roguish smile forms on his lips as though the prospect of having me gone from the hermitage is enough to risk the censure of the other sages. As though he has already won.

"One lesson," Kaushika agrees softly. With his other hand, he gestures to his horse, pawing the grass outside. Air shimmers, rain disassembling over the barrier he conjures. "Let's see how much you can learn from here to the hermitage."

## CHAPTER 11

**M**y body is on fire.

The heat pours from him as he sits behind me on the horse. Above, rain splatters but does not strike us because of his transparent protection. I am alone with the sage, Lord Indra himself removed from witnessing this. Desperately, I hold on to my mission, telling myself that this is my one and only chance to break through his shield. But even as I think this, the images of Kaushika's seduction form and die behind my eyes. I am reminded that I still know nothing about this man.

My muscles grow tense. I sit rigidly, trying to breathe. Behind me, Kaushika is still, too still. A chill clambers up my spine as I sense the hard shape of him. The way his legs press lightly against mine. The way his arms rest inches away from circling me. My hair is still undone, and he has not insisted I tie it back again. I imagine him towering over me now, his gaze lingering over my unbound tresses. I imagine him considering the words I said about Shiva and Shakti, about freedom and sex.

What is he thinking? Did I truly try to teach *him* about Shiva? Lecture him on the divinity of pleasure? I have given too much away. Shown him my true nature. He will know I am an apsara. He will act on it. This ride, this lesson, it is but a performance, one that undoubtedly trapped my sisters too.

Kaushika leans forward to take the reins in one hand. I inhale sharply as his breath tickles my skin. I glance down to his fingers curled around the rope. They are open in offering.

"Take the reins," he says quietly.

My voice is raspy. "You want me to guide the horse to the hermitage?"

"I want you to take control. *I* will guide us back."

His legs move against mine, his knees twitching. My body jerks involuntarily at his touch. Under us the horse begins a slow trot. I remember suddenly Kaushika was once a prince. He has no need of the reins. He has been on horseback since he could walk.

"If you are leading us back, then why am I holding this?" I ask.

I can hear his smile. "Because you need to learn trust in yourself, and this will give you the illusion of that trust until you truly find it."

My heart thuds. *The* illusion *of trust.* He is playing with me. Surely, he knows.

"Maybe we should walk?" I suggest hoarsely.

"Why? Does the horse make you uncomfortable?"

*You do,* I think. My throat is dry. Suddenly, I cannot tell who is the seducer and who the mark.

"No," I reply. "But I think you are trying to trick me."

"I am trying to teach you. That is what you wanted. Here, I will even give you a token of my sincerity. Something I carved myself." His body shifts, and I turn in my place to see him detach his own topknot and remove a comb. I am too arrested by his hair rippling to his shoulders, framing his chiseled face, to fully notice that he is holding the comb out to me.

When I take the ornament, my eyes widen. Shaped like a wooden crescent, it pulses gently with mortal magic. It is almost as powerful as some of the jewels from heaven. How could a mortal create something this potent? How many chants and hours did it take to consecrate this amulet? I pick it up gingerly, and a blaze of power rushes through me. Lights shine behind my eyes, a ringing in my ears, and for the first time I see beyond my breath into an energy pulsing through my body. Prana.

I gasp, and though the blaze subsides, the power still courses through me. Amaravati still connects to this prana, feeding it through the tether behind my navel. Yet I detect another path into the power too. An opening into the world inside me, instead of the one beyond.

I straighten, pulling back from Kaushika. My heart skitters in my throat. I totter on the precipice of something terrible, something beautiful.

"Do you remember what I said about prana?" Kaushika asks.

"A conversation with myself," I whisper.

"Yes." He leans forward and his cheek brushes against mine. His breath washes across my skin. "Close your eyes. Focus on yourself. The will to know who you are. The knowledge to accept it when you see it. The action to transcend what you see and unite it with the greater whole."

"Where do you go when you leave the hermitage?" I blurt out. I would hear it from his lips. The admission that he hates Indra, one that will allow me to probe him further, and force me back to my senses right now.

His voice is impatience sheathed in a whisper. "I might tell you if you end up staying beyond the next few hours. Now, do not make me repeat myself."

His fingers gently nudge my lower back. I hold myself utterly still. Slowly, I close my eyes, clutching his comb with both hands. I forget that I must find the shape of his seduction. I forget this could be my last chance. Instead, I am mesmerized by what I saw inside of me when I clutched the amulet.

"Breathe," he instructs. "Follow your breath. Hold your prana with your mind."

I know this exercise. I have practiced it with Anirudh and Kalyani. Unlike those times, when I only saw the one single tether leading from swarga into my prana, this time I see—

"Dewdrops," I gasp. "Shimmering within me. Trickling into my very soul."

"An unusual image," Kaushika replies softly. "But yours to own. In my hermitage, yogis often view prana as sparks of tapasvin fire, but others have viewed it as air too. I have never encountered someone who views it as water, but prana is simply the universe's magic, more subtle than any imagery we can give it. If this image serves you, follow it."

A dozen thoughts crowd into my mind. The wonderment at the impossibility of what I'm doing. How I am able to view prana directly when my only connection to it should be through the City of Immortals. My mission, and his closeness.

The horse moves rhythmically forward, and the rain feels distant, Indra himself banned behind a shield. Amaravati's magic surges in me, alongside the dewdrops of the prana, two sources that connect me to the universe's power instead of one. My nature asserts itself, clinging to the familiar path of Amaravati. My fingers rise from the comb, curling into a mudra, Moon's Reversal. *Dangerous*, Rambha whispers, and my eyes fly open. My hand drops.

Kaushika leans forward. "Hold on," he says, and his fingers interlace with mine, curling both our hands back around the comb. "Stay focused."

"This was a mistake," I whisper. "I can't do this."

"You can," Kaushika whispers back. "Give yourself the permission you need. Converse with yourself, Meneka. It is the only thing that matters. Feed who you truly are into your devotion."

My eyes flutter shut again, hypnotized.

*Give*, I repeat, and my fingers tingle. The wild prana blooms in me again, radiant, while Kaushika's warmth submerges me. Magic flares inside me. In desperation, I pray to Indra, asking him to intervene somehow. I try to focus on the raindrops I hear beyond the shield. I try to focus on my breath, a deep inhale. The scent of camphor and rosewood. The golden tether of Amaravati. The dewdrops of my own life force.

My focus shifts from Amaravati into my own heart.

My breath transforms.

Power races through my veins, so sharp, so shocking, that I cry out. It is more power than I have ever felt before, as though what I have been receiving from Amaravati has been only a trickle. I am flooded with the universe for a single, terrifying instant.

My back arcs into Kaushika. My head drops back onto his chest. His arms close around my shoulders, keeping me steady, but I am barely aware of him. All I sense is my own self, and my fingers rise to sketch a shape, the rune of delight. It shimmers and undulates like water, not just an imagined construct in the air but a rune, a *true* rune. I am creating that which should be impossible for me as an immortal, yet here it is, sparkling with truth, radiating its strength out to me and Kaushika within the air shield, infusing us.

Kaushika gasps, then laughs, a rich, deep sound. His arms squeeze my own in sudden affection and triumph. I twist in my seat to see the delight in his face. The serious lines on his forehead disappear, and he looks younger, no longer formidable. Dimples pop on his cheeks and I have a sudden hysterical desire to touch them. To taste them.

*Reveal your lust*, I whisper recklessly, pushing. His shield sparkles at me, but I nudge the edges of it, consumed by my own magic. *Reveal your lust.*

My command locks into something. An image pours into my mind. I am straddling him, pushing his muscled chest down. His eyes glitter in anger and satisfaction. *Will you be influenced?* I whisper, trailing kisses up his neck as his pulse grows erratic. *Will you obey?*

*Will* you? he replies. But his eyes shut in ecstasy, his hips bucking as I grind atop him, and it is not in the pleasure I am giving him, not only, but in the pleasure I am giving myself.

I gasp, and the crescent comb falls from my hands into Kaushika's. I release my hold on the dewdrops—on my own prana—and the world steadies, no longer sharpened and awake. The image of his seduction falters, then disappears as I release Amaravati's magic as well.

Stunned, I stare at him. Thoughts circle me, too chaotic to make sense, birds swarming in my mind. Kaushika's eyes meet mine, intrigued, unaware of the apsara magic I've just performed. My breath is erratic, unable to understand what I saw, how I saw it, what it meant.

Trees undulate, and dark shapes grow firmer. Kaushika's gaze lifts from mine, and I am shocked to discover we have stopped. It is fully dark now, and we are back at the hermitage. Lights glimmer from nearby huts, the rain silencing any chants. How did we get here so fast? I closed my eyes only minutes ago. I cannot breathe. I am dizzy, reeling with everything.

Kaushika sweeps off the horse and helps me down. His skin is warm on mine, but too soon, he steps away. A tilted smile forms on his mouth.

"I will admit I didn't really think you could do it," he says. "I may have been wrong about you."

There is a hidden meaning behind his words, but I am too un-moored to make sense of it. I latch on to the most important thing.

"Does this mean I can stay?" I whisper.

"For now. Until the Initiation Ceremony. You will still have to pass that. But your training should go easier. You are stronger than you realize. Your power will only grow now that you've unblocked your path to it." Kaushika nods to me, then leaps back on the horse. He pulls the reins and turns away to return the way we came.

"You're not staying?" I call out.

"No. I have business to attend to."

"What kind of business?"

"Our roads may align," he says, smiling slightly. "You might find out on your own."

"You said you would tell me if I managed to stay," I remind him.

"I said I *might*," he says. "I'm exercising my choice not to."

I make a frustrated sound in my throat. Light from a nearby lamp falls on his face, shadows and darkness, a glint of amusement, laughter in his eyes. He waves his hand, and the air shield over me dissolves. I am drenched in seconds, and so is he, but he does not seem to mind the rain any more than I do. His kurta clings to him and I try not to stare at the shape of his body, still shaken by the image I saw in seeking his seduction.

"Better go inside, Meneka," he says, grinning. "Unless you know the rune to block this downpour?"

I shake my head, and he laughs. Thunder crashes, and the horse turns, the splashing sounds of horse and rider receding.

I stand in the rain for a long time.

# CHAPTER 12

I tell no one about my private lesson with Kaushika. The day after the temple I meet Anirudh and Kalyani again in the courtyard for practice before breakfast, and the anxiety on their faces transforms into wonder and relief when I silently re-create the rune of delight I made for Kaushika.

Without his consecrated amulet, the rune is weak this time. Still, the shape grows for a few seconds, shimmering like dewdrops, reflecting in the mortals' widening eyes. Kalyani begins whooping and clapping even before it fully forms. Anirudh's serious face shines with quiet satisfaction. I release the rune, and it explodes like a silent firecracker, too frail to suffuse me and my two mortal friends with its power.

Even so, startled laughter echoes around us, made not through magic but sincere joy. Suddenly, I am surrounded by others who have watched this. They pat me on the back, congratulate me, embrace me. The usual murmuring silence of the courtyard is broken by elated celebration and laughter. I cannot help but smile back, unable to hide the pride on my face.

"You did it," beautiful Romasha says with a rare smile. "You must tell us what changed in your practice to finally allow this."

I look beyond her to all the listening ears. Burly Jaahnav, who is the tallest disciple in the hermitage, his aura always peaceful, his ideas on dharma always pious; little Durvishi, who is the youngest and most thoughtful, who could argue even Kaushika into rueful acceptance of her philosophy; smiling Parasara, who everyone believes will follow the path of a rishi first because of his utter devotion to Shiva. Dozens and dozens of them, abandoning their practice, eager to listen to my words. Each and every one of them kind and gentle, wanting me to succeed so I can bring honor to the hermitage. Each and every one of them a danger to Lord Indra on their ascetic path to become sages, who would destroy maya, destroy me and my kind, in their pursuit of enlightenment. My moment of pride shatters like broken glass.

My smile is brittle. "I remembered love."

"What do you mean?" Eka asks. She is smaller than I am, though the same age. Her aura is red and gold, scented with cinnamon.

I drop my eyes. "I am not sure Kaushika will like me to speak of it."

As expected, that simply stirs more questions.

Kalyani squeezes my hand. Anirudh cocks his head curiously.

I meet his gaze. "You were right. It was the ascetic path I was failing at. But it was not my failure, it was the failure of the path itself. The power of the universe is that of love, the utter devotion Shiva and Shakti have for each other. This is what I remembered at the temple. This is what a yogi must understand to truly unlock their power."

Next to Anirudh, Romasha stills. Her eyes narrow in thought, a sharp glance thrown at me. The others begin murmuring, Parasara saying how he had considered this too, but did not think to speak it, Jaahnav and Eka debating whether Shiva is angry with the hermitage because of this oversight. I let the mutterings build as others begin to chime in, then when it threatens to become too loud, I flicker my fingers to create another rune, the peaceful aum that connects individual prana to that of the universe.

This time I curve my wrists into a mudra of Light's Dance as well. It is a risk—especially now that Romasha is watching me so intently. I remember how I wondered if Kaushika had feelings for her. I do not believe that anymore, not after witnessing the shape of his seduction—but she is still someone to be wary of, suspicious as she is of me. Yet it is this very suspicion that emboldens me, streaking through me like a lightning bolt of rebellion. I cannot show the yogis any true illusions lest they learn who I really am, but merged in this way with a mortal magic, the rune rises above us with the rainbow power of the cosmos.

The chatter cuts out abruptly as all eyes track it. It is larger than any rune I've seen anyone create, half true and half illusion, growing above the courtyard, over the very hermitage, revolving and shining like a beacon. I hold on to the tether from heaven, feeding the illusion half of it, even as it expands. Then I release it, letting it shower everyone with sparks of light.

"Love," I say softly, "is an understated power. Would you not agree?"

The others stare at me, and I see the seed of doubt grow within their eyes. It rewards me, it shames me, and I greet this blend of emotions like the familiar friend it is.

I am besieged by questions for the rest of the day. Disciples I have never spoken to come to me, making an excuse to assist me with my chores, wanting to know more about the Goddess. Aypan, an androgynous yogi who usually prefers meditation to debate, clutches my hand in theirs, speaking of Shiva as Ardhanareshwar, the form of the Lord that is neither male nor female. I embrace them, stroking their hair, the firewood we're collecting forgotten as we reminisce about past lovers and how we left pieces of ourselves in their souls. I think of Kaushika and his injunction to let the past lie, and Indra smiles in my head from memory. I laugh with Aypan, knowing I am finally succeeding in my mission.

Matronly Shubha confides in me that she left her family behind to learn at the hermitage. Tears glisten in her eyes as the both of us knead dough. "These sugar rotis were her favorite," she says, speaking of her young daughter. "I think of her every day, but I have wondered if doing so was a betrayal of the asceticism Kaushika requires. Is this why my magic suffers?"

"Without love, asceticism is sterile," I say sympathetically. "Thinking of who you love will only enhance your magic for the Initiation Ceremony. It has mine."

She nods, weeping silently, and I pat her shoulder, knowing that another one of these yogis is mine.

Kalyani herself tells me that she left a young man behind in her village. She removes a faded lily from her pocket, preserved through magic, its petals glistening with trapped dew. "He gave this to me on the day I left," she says quietly. "I've burned everything else I brought with me when I came to the hermitage. But this one thing I could not."

"Perhaps you never need to," I reply softly. "If you can channel your affection into your prana, would that not be in service to Shiva too, in a way?"

Kalyani nods contemplatively, and my own prana rushes through my heart, a blazing torrent of water. Lacing this power is a twisting strand of fear. Kaushika will not like any of this. He will be angry, perhaps seeing how I have warped his admission of my knowledge of Shiva into something he would never countenance for the whole hermitage. He might even seek to remove me from here, yet I have gained enough influence. I will not leave easily, and the others will protest. His hermitage will break apart if he tries. Thus, worried though I am, I shine in my own luster, finally embracing that I am worthy of this mission. Have I not accomplished what other apsaras could not? Kaushika is vulnerable, his group of yogis weakened. The sweet poison of my words flows stealthily among them, unseen, unchallenged.

That night the hermitage rings not with hymns and mantras to Shiva but to Shakti—hymns I learned playing by Queen Shachi's knees while she threaded flowers in my hair. A student whose name I don't know sings this song now, and I sit at the back, chanting with the rest of them, attempting to hide my smile.

The next day, Shailesh and his husband, Daksh, openly hold hands, touching each other incessantly during the courtyard practice. Two days later, I see Sagara and Narmada sneak off to the forest, giggling while undoing their topknots. A week after, Sharmisha falls upon Advik in gratitude and triumph after mastering a particularly tricky mantra, brazenly kissing him as though she is in an apsara grove instead of in a communal pavilion within an austere sage's hermitage. Laughter breaks out at this instead of censure, other students clapping and whooping, and this time I have no need to hide my smile. Mantras are hummed, the lingam is adorned in flowers, and once I even see Ineshina and Leela dancing within the pavilion, their forms crude but no less beautiful, as they offer their performance to Shiva.

I expect Anirudh or Romasha to chastise me for my encouragement of these students, but neither of them say a word, even though Romasha's demeanor grows frigid toward me. I wonder if it is because she suspects I am an apsara, but perhaps she is simply a prudish creature. I have encountered many a puritan in my missions, afraid of their own bodies' reactions to me, and if ever there is one to exist, it would be within an ascetic hermitage. I steer clear of her, offering her nothing but the mildest of conversations.

Yet with everyone else, my power grows, an electricity charging through me like currents of Indra's power. Once or twice, I even nudge the disciples toward cleaner forms, knowing that to do so is reckless but feeling the same sense of pride they undoubtedly felt for me when I finally created runes.

All this time, the image of Kaushika's seduction burns behind my eyes. I see myself, hands buried in his hair, his eyes shut in exquisite agony. Each time I relive it, my skin feels on fire, as though I am on the precipice of a revelation. For no other mark has this final image of seduction formed so quickly; it ought to have taken months of dancing and manipulation of his original lust for me to see myself in his mind. How did this form in him without any provocation? Has he been thinking of me all this time? Is he not as indifferent to my beauty as he pretends to be? The thought makes me shiver as I reinterpret my every interaction with him. As I think of how close my mission is to completion.

If I already saw this image—the final image of seduction—I need only to adjust its contours before I charm him completely. I need only to investigate his preferences and create illusions of those over and over again in different forms, so that one day all he can think about is me. Each illusion will need to be more pinpointed, more accurate, the mudras I use a beautiful blend to create the exact vision he sees in his mind. Each revelation of his lust will need to inform the next illusion. Will he like my nails tracing his skin? How should my expression be in those visions? Should I be excited, ashamed, nervous? Each of these are decisions I must make to find the heart of his desire—yet this phase is truly the most enjoyable one of an apsara's mission, even perhaps the easiest.

Eventually, with each illusion an unmissed arrow to weaken him, he will finally become my thrall. Night or day, waking or sleeping, every other thought and concern will abandon him. Just like Tara. Just like any other successful mark. Could it be that this mission, after everything, really is the simplest one?

*I can go home*, I think, my mind dizzy with the implications. *I can be with Rambha, never leaving Amaravati again.* She smiles in my memory, but the images of Kaushika's seduction interrupt the victory the closer I come to achieving it.

I am invited to help lead the prayers, becoming second only to Anirudh and Romasha when it comes to answering philosophical questions. When I conduct the sessions, I imagine Kaushika watching me.

I imagine the hunger in his eyes, the whisper of his fingers and what it would feel like if he should interlace his hands in mine again. The shape of his seduction dances within me, and excitement and adrenaline flow in my veins at how close I am to conquering him. At how I am destroying him though he does not know it.

During practice, I blend my runes with mudras again to entrance the others. We all watch the shapes spark in the air. Each time I wonder how this is possible. Prana is *Indra's* power. If I am able to channel it like him, can other apsaras too? And if so, what does it mean for our service to Amaravati, and to the lord himself? My thoughts are tangled, each of them overrun with memories and hopes. I see Indra on his throne promising me, *You shall be a goddess.* Kaushika's breath burns on my cheek, the way his hands squeezed my fingers. *You're unbearably beautiful.*

I am surrounded one afternoon by a dozen other students, listening to them speak of their families, the longing to return to their homes apparent in their voices, when I finally see Kaushika. The mortals and I are making our way to one of Romasha's lessons to learn yet another powerful mantra, but Renika, a young attractive woman with gaps in her teeth, shakes her head.

"Do we need to listen to Romasha anymore?" she says. "It is clear she does not see the value of love in our paths."

"Her mantras are supposed to help us with the Initiation Ceremony," Kalyani says while others mutter. "Is that not what you want?"

Renika shrugs moodily. I say nothing, but she is only one of the many disciples who no longer care about the ceremony, who might even wish to fail and return home. She is one of those who has taken to dancing in order to offer devotion to Shiva, claiming that he is—after all—the Lord of Dance.

"What about you, Meneka?" Kalyani asks. "Will your demonstration at the ceremony be a confluence of runes? Or do you have a specific powerful rune in mind?"

She pauses, and her gaze shifts beyond me to the bael tree, where the rest of the students are collected. Romasha is not leading the class; it is another disciple called Viraj. The usual crowd is collected under the tree, students settling themselves, chatting in quiet voices, but Kaushika steps through, Romasha and Anirudh on his heels. Two other disciples trail them, Eka with the serious brown eyes and a deep knowledge of nadi channels, and Parasara, with an aura so strong it occasionally rivals Kaushika's own.

There is a strange look on Kaushika's face as he stops in front of my group. His clothes are crumpled, and his hair is in slight disarray. There are bags under his eyes, and he looks haggard beyond recognition.

My palm rises, almost as though to cup his cheek before I arrest the movement, both shocked that my body should think to make it and shocked that he seems to need it.

Where has he been since that night in the temple, and what has made him return in this condition? Will he chastise me for what I have done to his hermitage in his absence? Will he simply ask me to leave?

I brace myself to fight, exchanging a nervous glance with Kalyani, reading the same thought on her mind. The others slink away, reprimanded by Kaushika's very presence. I see them from the corner of my eye, glancing toward me and Kalyani before melting into the crowd. Viraj begins the class, but Kaushika does not seem to notice any of this. He stands there, assessing me and Kalyani.

My anxieties climb with his silence. Romasha must have told him what I've been doing. He is going to expel not just me but Kalyani too. My friend and I laughed about Romasha's primness while trading magical learning, but perhaps we were overheard. Perhaps she has told him about our insolence, about her suspicions of my true nature as an apsara. I take a deep breath, trying to calm myself, and Kalyani squeezes my hand.

"Your help is needed," Anirudh says. His voice is unusually somber, his eyes flat.

"Help for what?" Kalyani says.

"Are you sure?" Kaushika turns to Romasha. His voice is frayed thin. "These two are very new. There are more accomplished yogis here."

She nods. "They are our strongest. Along with Eka and Parasara. The magic they have inside of them, at this very moment, is more than anyone else's. You need raw power, do you not?"

"Power for what?" Kalyani asks. "Help what?"

No one replies, and Kalyani and I exchange another look, this one more disturbed. Parasara and Eka shrug at us. They do not know what is going on either.

A thrill of fear climbs through me, anticipation and nervousness making my muscles tight. I realize that whatever is to come next, it will influence my mission in untold ways.

Kaushika's gaze is grim. "Prepare them. We ride in one hour."

# CHAPTER 13

W e take all the horses. There are six old mares and seven of us. None of the rides look like they can cover long distances, but Kaushika chants a quiet mantra, and all the animals whicker and snort, their ears snapping back. I realize belatedly this is what he must have done on our own return from Shiva's temple to energize the horse. Little wonder then that we reached the hermitage so quickly. He helped me as much as hindered me—giving me sincerity with the offering of his magical comb, yet taking away time I could have used to prove my magic. I study him, this man known to me only in fractured and conflicting pieces in the incomplete lights of a prism. *A mark*, I remind myself. *Nothing more.*

Eka does not know how to ride, so she settles herself behind Anirudh, her gaze nervous. The rest of us climb atop the closest mount we find, our changes of clothes and bedrolls stored within the saddlebags. Kaushika watches us, outlined by the afternoon sun.

"We ride fast," he says. "We ride hard. I know you have questions. Those will have to wait."

Without another word, he begins a canter, and the rest of us follow. Once we are past the hermitage, Kaushika breaks into a fast gallop. My mind whirls with curiosity and dread, but the ride takes all of my attention. It is like being on heaven's steeds—these mortal animals race as though they are flying over the land. Shapes rush by too swiftly for even my eyes to catch, blurred outlines of trees, lights of a village or two, and then the movement of the stars above as the sun begins to set. I lose track of how long we have been riding, or which direction we are going in. All I can think is to hold on to my horse, which follows Kaushika's of its own accord.

Hours pass. Stars grow sharp, pinpointed. We begin to slow down. The land grows arid, dust kicked up by our horses. My throat is parched, and I work some spittle to swallow. Cactus, brittlebush, and saringia dot the landscape, their spiky forms outlined against a dying sun. Wherever we are, we are far from the hermitage. I am astounded that the horses are still alive. Kaushika's magic, of course.

We top a crest, and a small valley lies beneath us, disturbed by a hundred or so shapes. I squint, trying to understand. Statues? No, something else, but I turn my attention to my companions. I do not feel exhaustion, immortal as I am, but around me the others are gasping as we finally stop. Eka's head is slumped on Anirudh's back, and Parasara and Kalyani both rub their faces. Even Kaushika looks weary, his aura no less dim than usual but jagged, casting a sharp scent of unfiltered camphor. I remember suddenly that powerful though he is, he is only mortal.

"Where are we?" I ask, huffing the words to feign tiredness.

"The village of Thumri," Anirudh replies as he passes a waterskin to Eka.

I dismount to study the valley closer. A sour, bitter smell comes to me, carried by a warm, sickly breeze. There is decay in the air, and I focus my sight to see that what I had thought were statues are huts, scattered here and there. It is strange to see not a single light burning in this village, not even at a temple for some local deity.

The others begin descending. Kaushika climbs a small outcropping, which must give him a good view of the entire valley. His back is ramrod straight, his aura shining with serrated edges. He begins to sing, his voice deep and strong, but something about this particular mantra reminds me of the gandharvas, the celestial musicians of Amaravati. A wave of homesickness washes over me, making my knees weak.

The mantra rises, and I think of fresh grass, a stream of golden sunshine, the taste of my own freedom. I think of rain falling, a sweet, honeyed pureness to it. I think of my dance, the only honesty I know. Tears prickle at the corners of my eyes. This chant—it is what my own dance makes me feel. How can his voice be so evocative? How can he plunge me into myself so deeply without even trying?

Kaushika raises his hands gracefully. He touches the tips of his forefingers to his thumbs. It almost looks like a dance mudra, and the air crackles in front of him. We are all of us staring at him, and it is only when the horses whinny that I realize the song has come to an end. I can still feel the reverberations thrumming through me, and Kaushika's eyes are closed, his lips still moving. He is singing, though now under his breath.

All of us turn to Anirudh and Romasha, and the two nod, understanding our unspoken questions.

Anirudh's voice is somber. "Thumri . . ." he begins. "This village needs magic. You've been brought here because, of all the yogis in the hermitage, you are the ones currently holding the most prana within you. We need that power now, but please understand, it could take months, even a few years, of dedicated tapasya to replenish what this task takes. Kaushika would not ask this of you—of *us*—if he did not think it necessary."

Kalyani's gaze darts to Kaushika, who is still chanting. "We've been nurturing and storing our power for the Initiation Ceremony. If we use it up now . . ."

"Then you will likely not be able to do the demonstration you intended," Romasha says. "You might fail the ceremony and be asked to leave the hermitage altogether. That will be Kaushika's decision, but the two things must be separate. This is not a part of hermitage business but a request outside of it."

The rest of us exchange uneasy glances. Kaushika's shoulders tense. He does not stop his mantra to negate her words or give us any assurance. My fingers curl against my will into the mudra of Calm Waters, but I stop from creating the illusion even for myself.

"What do you need from us?" Eka asks.

"Healing," Romasha answers. Her aura shines bright, dipping her in honeyed yellow from head to toe. "Healing for the villagers here, because they have been abandoned by the devas. By heaven itself."

A finger of ice creeps down my back.

"What do you mean?" Parasara asks, frowning. "What have the devas done?"

"Once this land was green and lush," Romasha explains, and even on her usually dispassionate face, there is a sliver of sorrow. "The fields were so ripe that they would drip with harvest. Thumri used to be devout to swarga, Indra its patron deity for thousands of years. It is unclear why, but the village believes it has displeased Indra. Maybe a prayer was performed to another god before invoking Indra, or some ritual where the lord of heaven was not invited to bless the gathering. Perhaps it was deliberate, or perhaps an accident. Whatever the reason, Indra has denied water and rain to this village for several years now. If he brings any, it is meager and sent as mockery, a reminder of what he refuses to give. Drought has come to this land and it only continues to worsen. The effects of such a thing . . . Well, I am sure you can imagine."

Light sparks from the ends of her fingertips, and she shoots a small bloom toward the valley, where it hovers, slicing the darkness. My own gasp of horror is echoed by the others.

A hundred people lie on threadbare rugs, their faces turned to the sky. Two tired-looking women walk among the infirm, carrying a bucket. They stop at each person, offering a small cup of water before moving on to another. Glimpses come to me through Romasha's light. A young man barely older than me, skin taut against his bones, eyes rolled back into his head. An elderly woman sitting listlessly on her rug, holding a young girl in her arms. Cracked earth and parched faces and hopeless desperation.

I don't know what to say. I have heard of this kind of thing happening, of course. Devas will favor or smite mortal villages as they see fit. But in swarga it is easy to neglect the evanescence that is mortal life. Earthly settlements come and go in the great passage of time, turning to dust and smoke. Celestials cannot keep up with such change. Guilt for such negligence sharpens in me for the first time.

"Several times, the villagers tried to appease Indra by praying to him," Anirudh says into our horrified silence. "He sent his lightning instead of rain and killed so many people that the villagers are too afraid now to even think his name. With no water to sustain them, they have taken to drinking mud. To butchering trees and ingesting sap. To killing lizards and vermin and drinking their blood. Death, decay, and disease have overrun this place."

I feel ill. My eyes move over the scorched buildings as I imagine lightning striking them. In the distance, I see charred fields where blight has been burned away. *It is Indra's right*, I tell myself. *He is the lord of rain and storm, the king of heaven. He decides where to share his bounty. He has no obligation. That is the way of the devas. Of kings.*

"I heard about this village on my travels," Kaushika adds grimly. "The epidemic has become worse."

I did not notice but he has joined us again, and his sharp face looks more angular than before, cut by exhaustion.

He glances at me, then looks to the others. "I arrived in Thumri a few hours ago and enlisted the strongest villagers to help everyone out of their houses and collect them on what was once the village green. Hardly anyone has stayed here, only the very old and the infirm. Most have left to find relief elsewhere. I gave the villagers water from my own waterskins. I tried mantras and runes, using all the power of my tapasya to still the decay. But the sickness is too rife, and I cannot heal them, not with my power so reduced, not without conducting more tapasya, a task that will take me months of meditation." Kaushika's face grows withdrawn, but he meets each of our eyes. "I would not ask you to lend your magic if I could think of any other way. But medicine can only go so far now, and it is your choice. You are yogis on your own paths to self-knowledge and enlightenment. You have no debt to pay here."

"You wanted us to see this," Kalyani says, staring at him. "You wanted us to make our choice after bringing us here."

"I wanted you away from the hermitage," Kaushika replies. "The ascetic path demands withdrawal from the world. I did not wish to confuse you, asking you for something within the hermitage that I myself would counsel against while on the ascetic path. But I've recently come to learn that this needn't be the only way to enlightenment—a knowledge you are learning too, is it not? Even so, your own heart must decide what you do. I will not force you."

My heart skips a beat. One by one, all of us nod. Any of these yogis could have—*should* have—refused to get involved. What were they getting from it, if not the loss of their own power, the deviation from their own philosophies? This is because of me.

Yet what am *I* doing—agreeing to help these mortals when Indra himself has denied them? This is heresy against my own lord. Indra has his reasons for all he does. This could merely be another cunning move from Kaushika, something to foment more hate and irreverence against swarga. Something to sow confusion in my own mind.

I have no time to dwell on it. Romasha gestures to us, and the rest of us leave Kaushika to resume his mantra, while we descend into the valley, working in little groups, performing miracles into the long hours of night.

I pair first with Romasha, then with Anirudh, then with Parasara.

My fingers carve the runes of wellness and comfort, the aum and swastik, the lotus, the conch, and a dozen other shapes whose names escape me. They merge with the mantras and the spells cast by the others, augmenting their greater power. Slowly, we ease the breathing of the villagers. We give them water and clear the grayness in their eyes. We lead them back into their houses, our words soft and low, where Kalyani and Eka take their pulses, clarify their nadi channels, and pour their own strength into them.

It is not enough.

*I* am not enough.

Powerful though I am, the magic I hold comes from Amaravati. Whatever wild prana exists within me is only a trickle. The other yogis do not know this; they only see power as power, but I cannot use my enchantments like them. My runes are weak to begin with, and soon they fade into nothing. I begin to work separately from the others to hide this, a hindrance more than help.

The tether from Amaravati coils around my heart, lightly squeezing what is left of my own wild prana. It is a reminder I am Indra's creature. That my very imagery of my own tapasvin magic comes from him, and the only reason I have *any* magic within me in the first place is because Amaravati feeds it. Once, brazenly, I try to use Amaravati's tether to create a true rune—but as before, a sharp pain spikes behind my heart. Understanding pricks me in the limitation of my own power. I am allowed to create an *illusion* of a rune with my celestial power, not a true one. I can fake it, like I did before at the hermitage, but what good will that do here? My illusions cannot help these people. Only true prana can, and I have nothing left to give.

Night climbs, and I drift away from the others. The warm breeze that first ruffled my hair grows cooler. I find myself sitting next to an old mortal. He lies on the ground, his rheumy eyes open to the night sky. His skin is mottled and wrinkled, his white hair sparse. All my tapasvin power is exhausted, so I simply take his hand in mine and pat it over and over again.

Tears trickle from his eyes, down the sides of his face into the parched earth. I am certain he does not know I am here, but perhaps he senses my celestial nature, for his voice comes out cracked, raw with disuse, speaking to a figment of his imagination. "I prayed," he whispers. "I prayed, Sili, for you and our fields, daughter. Why—why—forsake—?"

His tears grow ragged, his breath labored. The man closes his eyes, and alarm goes through me. I scan the shapes nearby, looking for someone to help. I see only Kaushika on the hill above, staring at the skies, chanting.

Perhaps he senses my gaze. His own shifts toward me. I catch the glint of his eyes, and the anger smoldering within them. He does not stop singing, and his mantra takes hold of me, filling my ears as his chant becomes strident. I wonder what magic he is performing, and why my own heart recognizes it beyond waking memory.

Kaushika's aura flares, power bursting within his chakras. He glows iridescent, a blazing torrent of light silhouetted by shadows, and tears flood my eyes to behold him in his glory. Through my blurred vision, I discern the magnetism of his gaze capturing my own, hypnotic, fierce. There is something in the way he watches me, pulling at me, as though he is trying to tell me something. But I cannot think of it now. I wrench myself back to the old mortal, whose breaths have turned into sharp, painful gasps.

*Be comforted*, I think desperately, holding his hand. *Be at ease.*

The mortal's chest flutters rapidly in the throes of death. His eyes shoot open, wide and scared. Desperately, I try a rune one more time, but it does not even form—I am as useless as I have been since my early days at the hermitage.

I do not care if Kaushika is watching. I do not care that this is dangerous.

My hand curls into a fist. The fist opens up into a mudra, Indra's Bounty, and an illusion forms—only for me and this mortal. In front of us, the mirage shimmers—a land green and lush, droplets trickling down plants, a field that blooms golden and heavy with crops. A spasm goes through the old man, a deeply held breath released.

His hand grows limp in mine.

It slips away.

He stills.

A cry rips through me, quiet and unheard, as in the same moment lightning cracks across the sky. Thunder rumbles as the stars disappear. Rain begins to pour, and my teary gaze returns to Kaushika as I finally understand why his chant was familiar. He is silent again, his eyes closed as rain drenches him, but moments ago he was singing. Singing an ancient, obscure prayer, one that has been forgotten even in heaven.

Kaushika called to Indra.

And Indra listened.

Confusion clutches me painfully, shaking my body with its cold fingers. I am weeping, unable to understand what I am seeing, unable to fathom the meaning of my mission, this enigma that is Kaushika, this cruelty of my lord toward Thumri. Have I been mistaken about Kaushika's hate for the lord? Is their feud over?

The others trudge up to me in the downpour. I stare at them, rain mingling with my tears.

"We've done all we can," Romasha says tiredly. "It's time to leave."

# CHAPTER 14

The return is slower. After such an exhausting night, the others need rest. Yogis of immense power though they are, they are mortal, bound by their bodies. Even I feel a bone-deep weariness pressing my shoulders down. Kaushika alone looks like he can go on, but he glances at all of us, the hunched shoulders, the listless expressions, the hanging heads. He stops to make camp by a nameless tributary of the River Alaknanda.

We are silent as we tie our horses in the small copse. Anirudh starts a fire and Romasha begins to distribute rice cakes. Eka and Parasara are already in their bedrolls. For some time, the only sounds are those of quiet chewing and the gentle breathing of the horses.

I bite into my rice cake, surprised to find it still warm. It is stuffed with finely chopped vegetables with a sweet, creamy sauce that bursts in my mouth. This was made hours ago, before we left the hermitage. By rights, it should not be this fresh. Preserved through magic, of course. It is a passing thought, though no less informative for it. Yogis use their magic for significant matters, knowing it can deplete them. They do not waste it on ensuring food remains tasty; food must nourish, that is all. It is the way of the hermitage. That Romasha should make this concession for the rest of us, using her magic this way to keep the food warm, to keep us comforted, while knowing that she would need her tapasya for healing . . . She, Anirudh, and Kaushika anticipated many of the choices the others and I made today. They know far more than they have told us. They always have.

I study the three of them now, their heads bent together, their murmurs quiet. A tendril of hair slips free from Romasha's topknot and she tucks it behind her ear impatiently. Kaushika is deep in conversation with her and Anirudh, and I wonder again if hers is the kind of beauty he prefers. Quiet, unassuming, stealthy, it is so different compared to an apsara's exquisiteness, but powerful nonetheless. I think of my fingers touching his hand instead of Romasha's when she passes him a rice cake. I think of their closeness and the secrets they share, the *trust* that exists in such an unspoken way. It is this trust I need from him.

The last few hours rush through me in a blur. I am still forming the words to ask the right questions when Kalyani leans forward.

"Indra needs to pay for this," she says, her voice hard.

The murmuring stops. Eka and Parasara scramble up from their bedrolls to look at Kalyani. Kaushika does not move, but Anirudh and Romasha exchange a glance. I try to keep my expression neutral, but I cannot help sitting up as well.

"How could he do this to his own devotees?" Kalyani continues, and her eyes blaze in anger. "He is supposed to be the lord of heaven, but all he cares for is to get drunk on soma and be a nuisance for the mortal realm. He meddles in our affairs, his every act only for his own gain. This senseless punishment, these years of callous *violence*. How many deaths did we see today that could have been prevented?"

Eka nods, her expression grave. "The celestials are powerful and manipulative, and mortals are but pawns in their games. Yet the celestials don't understand true power. Or Shiva would not scorn the devas."

"It's because of Indra," Parasara adds, his voice somber. "Heaven is meant to be pure. A reward for mortals after a life well lived. But Indra has corrupted it with his hedonistic pursuits. He is a tyrant. He has always been."

"They know nothing about true enlightenment," Kalyani spits out.

"None of the devas do—whether they control wind or fire or storm. None of the celestials." She makes a disgusted sound in her throat, her face drawing into a scowl.

My heart sinks. I knew Kaushika was swaying others from Indra, but these awful words from people I began foolishly thinking of as friends pierce my heart like thorns. I have not been as successful in my influence at the hermitage as I thought.

I blurt my words out, uncaring of what I am giving away of myself. "The celestials are not all bad. Music comes from the devas, as does dance. The arts, even the magic we do—all of it has roots and foundations in swarga."

"Does one good erase all bad ones?" Kalyani challenges me. She must surely see the shock on my face, to be confronted by *her*, the one person I thought of as a friend, but still she continues, consumed by her own anger. "How much damage has Indra already wrought?" she asks. "How many people have suffered? He does not even respect his own devas—forget respecting mortals. He crushed the chariot of the dawn goddess Ushas, so that dawn itself was delayed for years in the mortal realm. He pursued Sage Agastya's wife, knowing she could not bed him, all because he enjoyed the chase. Indra has been interfering in the affairs of every realm, and look what has happened to Thumri. His inaction—his abdication of his responsibility—Meneka, do you not remember their wasted faces?"

A sharp ache spreads through my chest at her words. How foolish I have been to begin trusting these people. We cannot be friends. We never were.

I turn to Kaushika. "You *prayed* to Indra. I heard you. He listened, did he not?"

Kaushika studies me. He has been silent through the yogis' anger, and from his expression it does not look like he intends to answer me, but I refuse to back down.

"I recognized your chant," I go on, chin lifted. "That is why it rained in Thumri, is it not?"

Kaushika watches me like he is seeing into my depths. Slowly, he nods.

"Then do you think Indra is a tyrant too? That he is evil?" I insist.

"Do *you*?" he asks softly. "After what you saw?"

I frown. He is dissembling. My thoughts on Indra are not what we are discussing here. Still, if that is what will get him to admit his own rancor, I will play the game.

My gaze takes in the other mortals. "In my country, Indra is revered. He brings rain to relieve us. He protects our soldiers. We are told he is the slayer of a hundred asura demons, and his power keeps them within the hell of naraka, unable to run amok in the three realms."

"That's what you have been taught," Kaushika says. "But what do you think? For yourself?"

My frown deepens at his words. The lord glitters in my mind as I saw him last, magnificent on his throne, gloriously powerful. I see him lift me to my feet, his smile benign as he sends me on this suicide mission—yet now his smile changes in my memory, its edges sly, the light of his magic obscuring the hidden pits of darkness in his soul, mesmerizing me so I cannot think clearly. I think of the lord *seducing* me. Indra darkens in my memory, trapping me with my own devotion and naïveté.

I stare at Kaushika. Anger floods through me at his presumption, at his honesty. These are tricks. Kaushika wants something, just like my other mortal marks. *Reveal your lust*, I command, not a whispered persuasion, but a hurled weapon intent on one destination. To cleave through his lies and see the shape of his desire. To see *how* he wants power over me, a vision that will reveal to me his true nature.

The command locks on him without resistance from his shield this time. By piercing it once, I have pierced it forever. I barely register this, because my throat catches. For I see not a vision of *his* power but my own. I see myself naked on the grass, my hands buried in Kaushika's hair. His fingers part my thighs, and his breath is a whisper on the delicate skin just there. *Tell me what you like, Meneka*, he says. *Command me. I am yours.*

*There*, I reply, breathy. *Kiss me there. Lick me softly.*

The sound in my throat becomes a whimper, an echo of the sound the Meneka in the vision makes.

I dispel the vision, but my heart hammers in my chest, so loud I am afraid the mortals can hear me. Confusion rocks me. Kaushika sits there, fully in his mind, yet displaying a vision of seduction only a thrall should display. How can this be? What is happening to me? What has he *done*?

Suddenly, I cannot stand to be around him any longer. How dare he make me doubt myself in this way? How dare he make me question my devotion to my lord and my own magic? It's true I have my problems with Indra—every daughter has issues with her father, and though Indra is not truly my sire, he is the closest I have ever had to one. Indra, for all his faults, has kept me anchored to Amaravati. Knowing that my missions protect the lord and our city is the only way I can endure them. It is he who gives me my magic, and believing in my magic is the only way I have survived this long in the mortal realm. Kaushika is deliberately planting sedition in my head.

Rambha's voice echoes in my mind. *He is cunning and devious.* Now I can see just how devious he is, if with a few words he has made me question everything I know. The ride back from Shiva's temple circles me. How easily he made me forget Indra as I performed mortal magic. Maybe that demonstration of wild prana was a trick too, placed there by Kaushika so my tether to Amaravati would weaken. He is maneuvering me just like he did my sisters. How *dare* he?

I bolt to my feet, seeing the yogis clearly for the first time. All of them removed from me. Each of them an enemy I have forgotten.

Anirudh looks distressed at my reaction, but Romasha watches me indifferently. "You are overreacting," she says, and her voice is cold. "I understand it is unsettling if your kingdom has always worshiped Indra. But we—Anirudh and Kaushika and I—we hear from the outside world. Rumors come to us of kings and queens who have been destroyed by Indra. So many have come to Kaushika too, seeking refuge from Indra's manipulations. King Samar of the Kosala kingdom. Queen Dhriti of Videha. Queen Tara of Pallava. And that's only in the last few months. There are more, many more. Several of them were once Indra's devotees."

My eyes go wide, shifting from her to Kaushika, who is unmoving, still studying me.

Tara.

Queen Tara.

She came to Kaushika. When? Surely after I arrived at the hermitage. I told Kaushika I hailed from her kingdom. Why didn't he tell me of it?

Romasha's eyes are still emotionless, but Kaushika's face softens as though he has heard my question. "Knowing of Queen Tara would have only distracted you from your tapasya," he says. "From the very reason you came to the hermitage. To help your home in Pallava."

Anirudh nods slowly, comprehension flooding him as he understands my defense of Indra. Romasha frowns, throwing Kaushika an irritated look, perhaps curious why a sage of his caliber should debase himself by providing an explanation to a mere disciple. The other yogis exchange sympathetic glances as understanding washes over them. Kalyani reaches out to hug me, her own anger forgotten in the face of my distress, but I flinch back from her.

Chaos takes over my mind. Tara's lovesick face when I last saw her. Indra's charge to complete this mission. Kalyani speaking such hateful words about my kind. And me. The weapon the lord sent to destroy these people.

Is anything they said here a lie? This is who Indra is.

This is who I am.

A part of me has always known this.

I move in a daze, turning away from them all.

"Meneka, wait," Kalyani begins, and Anirudh calls out too.

I walk away from the mortals, making for the banks of the river.

THE TINKLING OF THE QUIET WATER WASHES OVER ME LIKE A hymn.

I sit down, removing the woven slippers we use in the hermitage. My feet sink into the dark, soaked soil by the riverbed. I dig my fingers in too, uncaring of the dirt. My mind buzzes, and Amaravati's tether twists around my heart. I want to take a deep breath, hush the uproar within me, but my thoughts flit like bees in a garden. I don't fight it. I stare into the glistening river and breathe in the calming pattern they've taught me at the hermitage.

Eventually, I hear movement behind me. One of the others comes to call me back, perhaps Romasha, telling me my behavior is unbecoming of a yogi and the dispassion we must feel. Or Kalyani trying to win me over with soothing words and soft-spoken apologies. I prepare to ask them to leave me be, but it isn't either of the women. Kaushika pushes aside a few tall weeds, his frame backlit by the campfire. He moves slowly, as though not to startle me, and when he sits down, he makes sure to give me enough room to move away.

"May I?" he asks quietly, extending his hand.

I stare at it, still in shock that he is here instead of one of the others.

He waits patiently, neither pushing, nor withdrawing.

Slowly, I remove my hand from the moist earth and offer it to him.

Kaushika's touch is tender, careful. As though tending to a small bird, his big hand engulfs mine. He begins to brush the soil from my fingers, his own intertwining briefly between mine, sending tingles spiraling up through my arm into my heart. I can't do anything but stare at the silhouette of his face—the sharp, aquiline nose, the high cheekbones, the lips that look soft enough to bite.

This close, his aura warms me. Scents of camphor and rosewood linger above the scent that is wholly his. I inhale deeply, mesmerized that I should be able to separate the layers of his perfume. The rosewood and camphor come from the rituals he performs, ingredients he clearly favors—but beneath them, that musky scent is simply *him*. It comforts me, reminding me of dawn and dance, of a whispering forest and the taste of salt on fruit. Not even with Rambha have I been able to separate such subtleties. A sigh escapes me as Kaushika's thumb moves over my wrist, rubbing it back and forth. My pulse skitters, and I meet his serious eyes. Some of the tension dissipates from my body. My mind calms enough to tell me, in deep honesty, that I am enjoying his touch and our closeness. That he is bringing me peace.

"I still sense so much power in you," he says. "I'm glad you did not need to use it all."

Gently, he lets go of my hand. My fingers curl as I become bereft of him. Confusion swirls through me again, this time tinged with disappointment, coloring the brief moment of peace. I twist my hands together, brushing off the remaining dirt from them onto my clothes. I try to brush his touch off as well, but it lingers as though it has sunk past my skin into something deeper.

"The others are tired," he continues. "That's why they said those things. Kalyani's temper is frayed and that has always been her challenge to her tapasya, one that I understand only too well. Romasha's path has always been of austerities and dispassion—" Kaushika cuts himself off, aware as I am that the secrets of the two women are their own, not ours, even if it reminds Kaushika of himself. "I will train them," he says, to cover up the moment of indiscretion. "All of the ones who came today, lending their power. But you do not need it. You are already so powerful."

"You did not dispute what they said about Indra," I say quietly.

"No." His answer is just as quiet. Almost wary.

"And what Romasha said about other kings and queens joining your cause?"

"Thumri is the worst I've seen yet," he says, nodding. "But many lands are suffering, whether they are Indra's devotees or not. The lord of heaven is not endearing himself to many at the moment."

His answers are clear, but underneath it, the moment of hesitation burns. He is unsure of how much to tell me. Maybe I should weigh this decision, see how best to draw him out, but I am too exhausted for games now, and unwilling to slowly unfurl him.

I speak bluntly, meeting his gaze. "Romasha mentioned my own country. You knew that is why I came here, but you didn't think to tell me."

"It would not have helped you to know," he says again, but when he notices my hurt expression, his face grows withdrawn. He rubs at his eyes once. "It is your home. I am sorry to have kept this a secret."

"Will you tell me now?"

Kaushika hesitates. My question is not a demand. It is obvious he has a choice, despite his apology and admission. Yet it is obvious that his choice shall have a consequence, even if the only true consequence of staying silent is how I will regard him in the future. Maybe it should not matter to him, but I know instinctively that it does. He would not have come to me otherwise. He would not be explaining himself.

I hold the silence, letting it sharpen until Kaushika finally sighs. "You asked me once where I go when I leave the hermitage," he says at last. "This is where I go, Meneka. To find people who have been wronged by the devas—by the king of devas more than any of the others. Your queen was attacked by Indra. You told me yourself how she was acting erratically when you left. It is because she was seduced. The work of an apsara, if I must guess, though my investigations are limited. Queen Tara is too distraught, and the accounts vague. There is chaos in your homeland. I am truly sorry."

I stare at him. Horror, fear, and guilt crash through me, seizing my heart in their currents. The sympathy in Kaushika's eyes feels like a lie—not because he is insincere but because I am. I want to refute him. Tara *was* Indra's devotee, but I was sent to her because she lost faith in the lord. Her seduction was part punishment and part peace, to dissuade her from her path of violence. Yet the words stick in my throat like bone. Even before Tara, there were other marks—some mine, some heard tell from other apsaras—mortals who had once been Indra's followers. I did not question my missions then, believing in the lord's intentions, but no matter the reasons, the lord has been attacking his own devotees. This even I cannot deny.

I know I should ask questions to preserve my identity. I should ask Kaushika what became of Tara, and try to investigate whether he suspects me of playing a part in it. But all the lies and pretensions die in my throat, unformed.

When I speak, my voice is a croak. "How do you know it was an apsara?"

Kaushika's face darkens. "I've had some experience with them. I am familiar with their methods."

I wrap my arms around my knees. I look away from him, unable to meet his gaze. It is clear he does not suspect *me* of being an apsara, a victory I should exult in, yet I cannot. The question burns in me about what he means by his *experience*. If he will truly admit that he killed my sisters, then it would be an act of war against swarga, and Indra would be able to retaliate. I would finish my mission here and now with such confirmation.

But suddenly I don't want to know. I don't want to know.

"You think heaven is corrupt," I say instead.

"I think *Indra* is," Kaushika replies, still frowning. "The lord of the skies and I have a history."

Shadows shift around us as clouds weave in and out of moonlight. Dread buries its claws into me. Kaushika's jaw moves as though tasting unspoken words, weighing the measure of them. I go very still. I want him to tell me more, but I do not know if it is for the mission or for myself.

"I used to be a prince," he says at last, his voice so soft that I wonder if he is speaking for me or for himself. "I was an only son, heir to the kingdom of Kanyakubja. Ours was not a big kingdom. We were small and peaceful, trading in flowers and perfumes. I remember playing in those flower fields, and the gardeners singing. I remember Anirudh and I getting into trouble. I remember . . . happiness."

Kaushika pauses, and his gaze centers ahead of us, lost in memory. Behind us, I hear the conversation of the others at the camp. Kaushika inhales deeply, and his words grow even softer. I scoot closer, inches away from him, so I don't miss a word, but he doesn't seem to notice.

"A great drought came to our kingdom," he says quietly. "I was young, so very young. Ten? Perhaps eleven? Our flowers dried. My parents grew sick. They died of their illness as did many others. I found myself named king, but what did I truly know of ruling? My ministers and I consulted great gurus. We prayed to Indra in a puja we could not afford, a yagna with the last of our flowers, with whatever magic the kingdom could spare. We called and we called. But Indra did not come."

I remain silent. In my mind, I picture him—a young Kaushika, the laughter of his dimples replaced with sorrow. I must have been a child myself then, running around Shachi's grove. Indra flashes in my head, an image from my childhood, reigning in his court, concerned with petty politics, drunk so often in the company of older apsaras and gandharvas. All while Kaushika and his kingdom starved for rain.

"Indra's indifference to my kingdom made outcasts of us," Kaushika continues. "No one wanted to aid us. What if Indra punished them too? The devas could not be understood, their minds capricious, their wills beyond the ken of simple mortals. The gods abandoned my kingdom and so did our neighbors. Only one king responded to our pleas for help. He would help us with grain and medicines, even protecting us from the wrath of the gods, if I folded my kingdom into his own. I would become a vassal, but my people would be safe. Of course I agreed to his terms. Any king would have taken the same decision. I agreed, but my path became clear then. I needed to become powerful enough that such a thing could not happen again. Kings and queens were just pawns in the great cosmic game. I needed to learn to stand up to the devas. I left when I came of age, traveling from kingdom to kingdom, learning from different sages. It was they who taught me of Shiva's way. Eventually, I began my own tapasya. I have been on the ascetic path since I turned twenty." Kaushika turns to me with a lopsided smile. "I left to help my people, just like you. Somewhere along the way, I found more purpose within my own self. You and I, we are not so different."

Thoughts collide within me, one after another. What spurred him to tell me this now? His sudden confession warms me, shames me, empowers me. I still want to defend Indra, but what can I say after everything Kaushika has told me? I think of the first time I met him in the woods and how he relented when I told him I came to the hermitage to help my people. I think of the warnings Rambha gave me before my mission—of how Kaushika scorned Indra's emissaries when he became a sage. Kaushika's hate for Indra makes too much sense now, but how far will such hate go? Does his wrath for my lord justify the crimes he has committed against my apsara sisters?

"You despise Indra so much," I finally say. "Yet you prayed to him in Thumri?"

His shoulder lifts lightly, an evasion of my question. "We all pray to the deities for our magic. Yogis call to the gods in ancient syllables, constructing the mantras just so. That's how Anirudh made the fire tonight, by asking it of Agni. Romasha's light from before was a gift from Surya."

"Have you forgiven Indra, then?" *Has he forgiven you?* I add silently.

Kaushika shakes his head. "What we do as yogis is not mere prayer. We pray to the natural essence of the devas and devis, their bonding with the creative force that is prakriti. To commonfolk, prakriti simply means nature—rain or sunshine or air. They think that the devas of swarga possess and manipulate these powers. In a way, it is even true, but yogis know the subtle truth. It is prakriti—nature itself— that came first as a primordial force of all reality. The divinities of swarga are simply manifestations of prakriti's own power. In his foundational form, Indra is a natural energy, formless and divine. But he presents himself as a man, with all of a man's follies and pride. We can separate Indra the power from Indra the lord. We pray to Indra, the elemental force. Indra as a lord has much to answer for."

Shock silences me.

*I should know this*, I think.

All I have ever known is Indra, the sire of Amaravati, the owner and keeper of my own celestial magic, but of course, he is so much more than simply that. He is the first of all devas, ancient and impenetrable.

He is a power that formed and became sentient at the dawn of creation. I am dazzled suddenly by the realization of his age.

"*Lord* Indra did not answer my prayer," Kaushika says quietly. "It was Indra in his purest essence. *That* force of the universe had no choice but to answer my prayer, as a simple cause and effect."

I wonder if Indra felt this in his throne room. I imagine his face furious and scared while the vajra trembled in his hand. I imagine Indra on the receiving end of a power he himself wields to make celestials like me bow to him, controlled without his will like he himself has controlled us.

"That's why you did not help us with the healing," I say, understanding. "All your power was used to convince Indra in his essence while Lord Indra resisted the rain."

"It is where I was needed. The rest of you would not have been able to help me, not with this."

Kaushika's eyes are free from any deception. His words are said simply, without arrogance. A deep kinship forms in me in recognition of this. This is how I have felt about my dance, a moment of purity with my own skill and power, which nothing could snatch away. No one else has understood it. Even around Rambha, I have felt lesser, unsure of myself. Yet Kaushika's acceptance of his own power reminds me that even *I* separate Indra and Amaravati and my own missions from the joy my dance gives me. That is how I began down this road. In wanting to dance with freedom.

Kaushika meets my eyes. His fingers move as though to reach for me again, but he stills. "I want to thank you," he says. "Not just for what you did tonight at Thumri, but for what you taught me at Shiva's temple and what you have been teaching the others. Anirudh and Romasha have told me of your assistance. If you had not spoken to these students about the path of the Goddess, I would never have been able to ask them to come to Thumri. You saved lives tonight."

My eyebrows rise. "I thought you'd be angry," I whisper.

"I was," he replies, smiling slightly. "But not at you. This was always the risk. I knew it all along. That night you arrived in the forest, the warding of intent told me you'd be dangerous. I knew you would change the hermitage in some way—it is perhaps why I have been so hostile. You are indeed a threat to the ascetic path, but not all things that threaten us are harmful." He utters a self-deprecating laugh and presses the side of his neck with one hand. The gesture is so boyish that I want to squeeze him in comfort. "I am hoping Romasha will see this too," he adds. "She does not wholly approve of what you are doing at the hermitage, but I think she is starting to understand. Many paths can lead to the same outcome. That is essential knowledge for a yogi. For a sage."

"She does not approve," I repeat quietly. "But *you* do?" I follow the movement of his hands, the way his long fingers steeple on his knees.

"Approve," he repeats slowly, as though measuring my question, trying to see the intention behind it. "I am not sure you need approval. Least of all mine. It has always been about your own."

Slowly, with enough time to allow me to stop him, his fingers reach out to take my hand again. He traces the outline of my palm, and I can do nothing but stare at him, my heart racing. His voice is quiet. It rolls over my body like honey. Excitement and hunger ache within me.

"I am a yogi, Meneka," he says. "A *sage*. You came to the hermitage to learn more about your magic. But I came to this path to devote myself to the pursuit of the one truth, the one universal power. I made oaths to asceticism. I believed it was only through the strict denial of material possessions and sensual pleasures that I could do the kind of tapasya required to grow my own spiritual power. To make my mind strong like a diamond, so that one day the universe would reflect back to me."

Mesmerized, I say nothing. This is what sages pursue. It is one reason Indra fears them so much, for they seek a knowledge even Indra is not capable of fully understanding. I stare at Kaushika, and his breath shudders again. He is close enough to ruffle my hair. I am not sure if he moves or I do. Perhaps it is the both of us, leaning closer, propelled by the intimacy of this moment, the intimacy of his admissions. His eyes glow, and I can make out each individual lash, each groove of a laugh line.

"You opened me up to a part of myself I had been denying," he says. "To a part of *Shiva* I had been neglecting. You reminded me of why I am doing this at all. That enlightenment is love too. If it weren't for you, I might have walked away from Thumri. I would have chosen detachment, in pursuing the ascetic path. But tonight, when even my tapasvin power failed me . . ." His lips lift, and my own feel suddenly dry. I lick them lightly, but it is the taste of his scent I trap. "It was the power of the Goddess that came to my aid. You are making me rethink many, many things."

I do not know what to say. My heart strums a quiet tune, spellbound by this man. I suddenly understand his look when he brought down the rain. It was my wisdom he tapped into then. It was *me* he remembered.

In the back of my mind, I am aware of the danger. Is he saying these words simply to lure me into revealing myself? Is this an elaborate scheme to expose me? I feel strangely excited, to be the hunted rather than the hunter. Heat enters my belly, rising to my chest, tingling over my neck. The challenge floods in me to be with him, a mark who is as powerful as I am, maybe more. I want to seduce him suddenly, not because of Indra, but for myself. I want him to *know* I am seducing him, to know *me* and my danger and want it anyway, in the same way that I want him now.

I squeeze Kaushika's hand. He squeezes back; a quiet smile.

"Should you pass the Initiation Ceremony," he says, "I will introduce you to other sages, as is tradition. You will have a choice to stay with me or go to one of their schools to learn from them. Undoubtedly, Gautama and Bhardwaj and even Vashishta will covet you." Kaushika smiles again, and I understand his words are not to pull away from me. They are to ensure I know I have a choice. He reaches to tuck a stray strand of my hair behind my ear. It is amazing, this understanding that flows between us in this moment, free of small anxieties, drenched with trust. It is as though I have always known this man, a mirror to my own light, a shadow of my own heart.

My fingers tremble. It is all I can do not to touch his face and trace the contours of his jaw with my nails. It is all I can do not to lean in and find the taste of his dimples.

"I know I have not given you much reason for it," Kaushika says softly. "But I hope, Meneka, that you decide to stay with me."

A sigh escapes me, sweet with satisfaction. I fight the urge for closeness no longer. I rest my head on his shoulder, and after a hesitant moment, his own head nestles mine. Kaushika takes a deep breath, warming me and making me tingle at the same time. A silence braided with unspoken words wraps around us, comforting.

## CHAPTER 15

By the next day, that moment has already faded to a dream. We arrive at the hermitage late in the morning, but I leave at once. Throughout the ride, I have been chanting a prayer, an ancient one that works as a call for help when citizens of Amaravati are stranded away from swarga. Once it was used by every celestial, but for years now only apsaras sent on missions use it, and then only rarely. Sometimes assistance is sent, either in the form of Indra's jewelry, or as a gandharva who comes to take a message. Often, there is no response. Once an apsara is sent on a mission, it is understood that she is on her own. It is to protect Indra and Amaravati—if we are caught, Lord Indra can deny he sent us at all. He can claim we acted without his knowledge as rogue agents.

Yet even as we enter the stables, a vision comes to me. Behind my eyes, a clifftop overlooks the River Alaknanda. I recognize the spot as one marked on a map within the hermitage. It is half a day's ride, but it will be safe, far as it is from here. I am not merely getting assistance. An emissary from heaven is arriving to hear me and take my report. As the others pull off their mares, I turn mine back and head toward the road.

Kaushika throws me a thoughtful look but does not challenge me. He can hardly claim I am not allowed to interact with the world outside, not after Thumri. I glimpse his wariness, and guilt gnaws at me, to leave without an explanation after everything he has told me. Still, having a mark pine for you is one of the earliest tricks an apsara learns; I have him exactly where I want him. I offer him a cool nod, ignore the questions from the others, and ride back out of the stables.

The sun is overhead completely by the time I arrive in the woods. The energy here is quieter compared to the forest by the hermitage. There, the trees hum with power, a result of being so close to tapasvin magic. I know this now, aware as I have become of prana, but I am still surprised by how clearly I can tell the difference after only a few weeks at the hermitage.

The celestial vision I received guides me. I weave through the trees, climbing higher, thinking of what I will say to the emissary who has answered my call. My own questions must be careful, discreet. I know I must share what Kaushika has told me about his past, but I feel sick with the thought of relating it when my own mind regarding those truths is not made up.

Did he do it to manipulate me? Even if he did, does it take away the veracity of what I myself have learned at Thumri? How can I make a report now, sharing all of this without context, when the consequences could be so damaging? When Indra will use what I am revealing only to attack Kaushika, without understanding that Kaushika had reasons for his hate?

And if Kaushika killed my sisters because of his hate, does it even matter what his reasons were? Can anything justify such a crime, and can *I* defend it? I have been the one to summon the emissary, but I feel unprepared, each step only increasing my anxiety, my mind going in circles. Yet when I arrive at the cliff, a familiar face greets me and I feel my doubts fly away as though they never existed.

She sits on a rock just ahead of the cliff face. Her expression is thoughtful as she stares at the silver band of the river below. She is so breathtaking that for a moment I can only stare at her, the green sari wrapped sensuously around her waist, the jewelry that glints on her wrists, her arms, her swan neck. Twinkles from her thick braid and her own aura brighten the blades of grass around her. It is her scent that undoes me, star-anise and dewdrops, cracking me open like a ripe fruit.

I utter a soft whimper of relief, dismounting.

Rambha looks up and stands. "Meneka," she says, smiling as she approaches me, but she can't get any other words out. I stagger to her, crushing her to me. We both fall to the grass, our limbs entwined. A laugh escapes her, but it is cut short as she catches my expression. I bury myself in her arms, trying to control my sudden anguish.

"Meneka, what happened?" she asks urgently. "Did he hurt you? Are you in trouble?"

I shake my head, but I cannot answer immediately. A flood of emotions consumes me. I am not just going to make a report to Indra's agent, trying to understand the edges of my own devotion to the lord. This is *Rambha*. Her hair tickles my cheek. Her scent envelops me, full-bloomed roses, honey, and peppery star-anise. I have missed her so *deeply*.

Gently, she sits me down on the grass. "Meneka," she says, putting an arm over my shoulder. "Tell me what happened."

I stare at the ribbon of water beyond. I have so much to relate, and no map for where to begin. The last few weeks flash through me. The disastrous meeting where Kaushika spotted me for the first time. His charm, and my confusion. The fear I have been living in, which has morphed into reason—that Kaushika might truly have a point about Indra's cruelties. His admission of his past, the conversation in Shiva's temple, my performance of prana magic, the lack of any answers regarding my missing sisters. All of these tumble and swirl in me, pulling me toward a different part of the puzzle, never completing the picture. I think of the freedom that awaits me if I can only clear my head. Confusion, pain, and hope bubble to the surface.

Maybe it is that I have been lonely for so long. Maybe it is because the emissary they sent is Rambha. The truth of the last few weeks pours out of me, haphazard and winding. Once I begin talking, I cannot stop, and Rambha does not interrupt. I even come to telling her about Kaushika's past—the most important thing that I have to share—yet something holds me back. I trip over my words, telling her about Thumri instead to cover my lapse. Shadows change around us, the afternoon growing warm. My voice becomes hoarse, and when I finish, there is a small silence.

Leaves swish, and wind ruffles my hair—hair that is still bound in a sage's topknot. Rambha stares beyond the cliff, lost in thought. Slowly, she extracts herself from me. She stands and begins to pace back and forth, never once looking at me.

I watch her, but do not disturb. I know this expression well. I have told her so much. She is trying to sort through everything, alternating between Rambha my friend and Rambha my handler. Anything more I say now will only hinder her honesty and will.

She nods decisively once to herself, then comes back to sit next to me. She takes my hand, and I squeeze it. Her voice is soft and kind, and I interlace my fingers with hers, relieved even though I cannot tell why.

"Kaushika does not know you are an apsara," she begins. "That is good. Very good. You have already been successful where Nanda and Sundari and Magadhi were not."

I bow my chin in acknowledgment of her compliment, but I cannot lie to her. "When I first arrived . . . the things he said, the way he acted . . . I thought he must surely suspect what I am."

"Yet everything you have done since then has allayed his suspicion. You have been devious. The words you said about the Goddess—that was inspired, my love." Rambha utters a rich laugh, and even though it is as melodious as ever, something within me chills. The memory of my conversation within Shiva's temple grows sullied. I spoke those words in purity and grace, even if my actions to sabotage the rest of the hermitage since then have been deceptive. Yet that moment with Kaushika was real. Surely, I related as much to Rambha?

My disturbed gaze meets hers. "How did I do prana magic, Rambha? How is this possible?"

There is true confusion in her eyes, but it flickers only for an instant. "Indra must have allowed it so you could succeed in your mission. That is the only way. It is unheard-of for an immortal to do this, but your mission is the most important one any apsara can undertake. Indra made an exception for you—he temporarily gave you the powers of a *deva*. It is something to be celebrated, Meneka. I do not think it has happened before."

I consider her explanation. I *did* pray to Indra to intervene on that ride with Kaushika. Perhaps the lord sensed my desperation. Perhaps he understood it as his own. Yet why is it that if he gave me this power, he would allow me to make a rune using my wild prana but not using the golden power of Amaravati? I open my mouth to ask this, but Rambha forestalls me, reading the doubt in my face.

"*All* our power comes from Indra," she says. "You know this. Think of the blessing he gave to you before you left. Do you not remember feeling intoxicated with it? Perhaps he was permitting you more than you could know then."

Her words are sensible, and I recall the way Indra pulled me from my knees, bathing me in his radiance. I recall the feeling of possibilities that flooded through me, as though I were suddenly capable of the most arcane of magics. Who am I to deny what the lord can do, and what he has made me capable of? He is *Indra*. He is the lord of heaven.

Still . . . Still . . .

"You doubt it was him," Rambha says, seeing my hesitation. "Surely you do not think that you have discovered that which no other immortal has ever been able to do, Meneka? That you are like the devas themselves? Has Kaushika and his arrogance affected you so much that you've forgotten your own true nature as a celestial? Mortal wisdom is not something to pay too much attention to, my love—" Rambha cuts herself off and pauses.

She tilts her head, studying me.

"Of course," she says softly in understanding. "It is not Kaushika. You're disturbed by what you saw in Thumri. You think the lord cruel for what he did to that village. You doubt him now, his intent, his power." Her face grows colder, her eyes narrowing. "Perhaps you even doubt his divine nature. After all, if you can do such magic yourself, then surely he is not any more divine than you? Surely you have as much power as him?"

I do not speak. To utter any confirmation of these things, even to Rambha, could get me exiled. I lower my eyes, unwilling to challenge her but unable to lie and deny her either.

Yet I do not need to reply. Rambha knows me too well. She watches me for a long moment, then the coldness melts away from her voice. I hear her sigh. "I told you, you must keep your devotion pure," she says.

My body jerks. I look at her, distraught, shrinking away, unable to believe that she should call out my weakness of devotion so blatantly, but she holds my hand tightly, and I realize her words are not said to punish me. Only to remind me.

"Thumri," she says thoughtfully. "I remember it. Those mortals do not know their own history, but that is to be expected. Their memories are short, but in swarga we know the truth. Thumri used to once be a great, thriving kingdom. I remember their prayers, the scents of incense that would drift to Amaravati. The condition that plagues them is not new. It began at the time of the last Vajrayudh, a thousand years ago."

A quiet wonder blooms in me to be reminded of how Rambha truly is so much older than I am, to remember an event so ancient. Her wrists curl effortlessly. An illusion forms from the tips of her fingers, and I see the lord she loves, distraught at his powerlessness to help his devotees. I see Indra in a way I have never seen before—a lord, kind and compassionate, who is driven only by service to mortals so they may live in prosperity. This is an illusion, but it is nevertheless true. Rambha sees the deva king with a gaze I can only aspire to, understanding him like no other. I watch the mirage, transfixed. Lord Indra bleeding golden blood as he breaks his fingernails, trying to squeeze prana from the universe so he may succor the mortal realm. Lord Indra fighting a thousand demons, unseen, unappreciated, while the mortals forget his magnanimity. Lord Indra brokering alliances with the asuras, in order to protect his kingdom and prevent devastation to humanity.

"During the last Vajrayudh, Indra retired to Amaravati to rest," Rambha says gently, still molding the illusion. "Heaven closed its doors, and Indra did not answer prayers. Not because he did not want to, but because he could not, weakened as he is during every Vajrayudh. This was what caused the first drought in Thumri, and in many other places too. Many lives were lost. But Thumri survived, did it not?"

*Survived*, I think, picturing the dying old man and the sickening bodies littered on cracked soil.

"It's been a thousand years," I say quietly. "Why did the lord not help after the Vajrayudh ended?"

Rambha shrugs. She collapses the vision. "Mortals will pray to their gods to receive what they want, but when they do not get it, they turn so easily. When the first draught came, they blamed Indra and cast him aside. And so the droughts continued. You can hardly blame Indra for punishing them for their impiety."

I shake my head. "Those people—they wanted his favor again. Indra could have saved them."

"That is not for us to question. We are mere apsaras. These decisions are for Indra and his council."

"But it is our actions that determine these decisions too," I say. My fists clench into the grass. I cannot believe how Rambha is missing the point. My voice grows stronger, more insistent. "Rambha, in heaven we do not question anything. As apsaras we are told to obey without doubt. I am sent to marks who would be a danger to the lord, but we are never allowed to ask who else might be hurt with our actions. I think you underestimate the lord—if we only told him about all this, it would change his mind, and shouldn't *that* be the form of our devotion, to counsel him when he cannot see—"

"Stop it."

Rambha stands abruptly, and the sharp edge of warning scalds me, the end of her patience with my arguments. My sudden burst of courage dies.

"These are indiscreet thoughts," she says. "The lord asked for Thumri to be faithful to him even when times were hard—and that should have been enough. Just like it should be enough for *you*. Devotion is a twofold path, Meneka. What good is love, what good devotion, if it is only transactional? If it can be taken away so easily, if it has so many *dependencies*, is it even love at all? The lord has granted you great gifts and power, yet you question his intent because a few mortals have told you their tragic stories. Have *you* lost faith?"

I flinch. My words lock in my throat.

My devotion to the lord *has* suffered; it always does in the mortal realm. I was afraid of this very thing occurring. It is why I wanted to remain in Amaravati, never to be sent on another mission. Rambha has reminded me, with nothing but a few choice words, that I can never be like her. She has shown me the impurity of my nature.

Misery sweeps into my heart, and my vision trembles. I drop my gaze.

Rambha's shadow moves. She sits down next to me again and strokes my cheek. Despite myself, I lean into her touch, too distressed to do anything but take the comfort she is offering me.

"You are a celestial, Meneka," she says, and her voice is soft. "You are an apsara of Indra's own court. Do not forget where you come from. Mortals are frail, their faith so often weak. After every Vajra-yudh, Indra must work hard to restore their conviction in him, but the fewer prayers they offer, the less he can do for them in return. People like this Kaushika only ruin the cosmic bond between de-vas and devotees. Indra is growing weaker with each passing day as this Vajrayudh approaches. Should it come and go without Kaushika thwarted, the poison the sage spreads will weaken Indra further even after it passes. All the realms will suffer, and Amaravati will be ir-revocably destroyed. You alone can stop this from happening. You understand this, don't you?"

I nod wretchedly. Rambha pulls me closer, and her breath warms my forehead.

"Please, Meneka," she whispers, and her voice breaks a little on my name. I lift my head to see the pain and fear on her face that she has desperately been trying to hide. "You are so close. Kaushika is grow-ing infatuated with you; you already know this. You are succeeding in shifting him from the ascetic path. All it will take is one more push."

I shake my head. I want to tell her how Kaushika became *more* powerful with the acknowledgment of Shakti. Though he is amena-ble to how I have been conducting myself in the hermitage, his intent and dislike for Indra have only grown tenfold after what I've done. But Rambha's lips linger on my ear, then drift lower, her tongue flashing out to taste the delicate skin on my neck. I shiver, know-ing this is everything I have ever wanted. Everything I can have if I only complete my mission. I cannot bring myself to raise any more objections. My eyes drift, closing, and a soft sigh builds in me as her fingers trace gentle patterns on my back.

"You promised me you would give it your everything," Rambha reminds me, and once again her lips hover over my neck, raising goose pimples. "Fulfill your promise. Now is not the time to worry about your trivial rules. He will give himself over to you if you stop holding back. Kiss him to unlock his secrets. Sleep with him if you need to. I do not care. Just—"

My eyes fly open. I pull away from Rambha, scooting backward, staring at her. "You do not care?" I ask hoarsely.

Rambha studies me, puzzled. "We are apsaras," she says, shrugging. "Sex is merely sex. It does not need to be any more than simple pleasure. You would even be giving Kaushika what he wants. You did say you saw yourself when you looked into his lust, even though you needed no illusions to *create* that lust. It sounds like he has simply fallen for your beauty. Would it be so wrong to fulfill his want?"

I withdraw further away from her. I can still feel her touch, but her words are cold water thrown over our moment together. I stare at her, confused, not knowing why I am confused. Is any of this a surprise at all?

Kaushika's lust did show me my own image, not once but several times. That I did nothing to form that image consciously means only one thing—he desires me. He has always desired me. There is a kind of freedom in that; I am not to blame for what happens to him.

Yet my feelings for Rambha tangle in the roots of duty and the dreams of lust. I *want* her to tell me she desires me for herself. I *want* her to feel upset with the idea of me giving myself over to him, even if it is for the mission. In the depths of my own foolish naïveté, I want her to *care*. Care more about me than her love and duty for Indra.

Yet even beyond that, I want her to understand me. I want her to see why the prospect of sleeping with Kaushika, even if that is what his lust shows, feels abhorrent to me when I have come to him masked by trickery. I have felt this way about all my marks; it is the reason I do not lie with them. It is the one thing that has always bothered me about my own identity as an apsara. The one thing Rambha has never understood.

She tilts her head, searching my silence. "Are you truly so prideful?" she asks, and I am surprised that she can see my thoughts so clearly. "You have always held it in such high esteem, to never involve yourself with a mark, but this is our skill as apsaras, and using it does not take away from your talent as a dancer. How can you hold back the most powerful tool at your disposal? Find that perfect shape he desires and end this mission. Is that not the most important thing?"

I say nothing, doubts choking my throat. Of course she says this. She has always been more an apsara than I have ever been. She has been a true creature of lust, as Indra has decreed us to be. To Rambha, sleeping with a mark is no different from speaking to one, all of it done for the singular intent of serving Indra. Can I do this with Kaushika, after what he has shown me of himself? Is this the true meaning of being an apsara—and why I have never felt I was enough? Am I denying my true nature? One final act . . . Will this finally teach me who I am?

Rambha gazes at me, her eyes beseeching. "You can end this, Meneka," she says. "Once and for all. Find your opportunity. Seduce him before the Vajrayudh arrives. For your sake, and the sake of the world. Promise me you will not back down, not when you are so close."

Her words, Kaushika's scent, Indra's pride, all of them cloud me. I think of Kaushika and the shape of his seduction. The feel of his legs against mine and the image of my own pleasure at his center. He desires me—but what did it mean that I looked into his lust only to find my own? Was that image truly his, or did his warding somehow reflect my magic back toward me? What does any of it even matter, if it is giving me what I need for my mission? Am I not here for one purpose?

The afternoon stifles me, each question a barb burrowing under my skin. I cannot speak, but Rambha still gazes at me expectantly. My mouth feels filled with rocks, but I cannot deny the reason in her words.

Slowly, very slowly, I nod.

# CHAPTER 16

T he day of the Initiation Ceremony dawns with storm clouds wrapping the sky. Kaushika meant to conduct the ceremony in the courtyard, but Anirudh tells me that tapasya cannot be wasted today in creating shields from the rain. Arrangements are made inside the pillared pavilion. A platform is raised in the center, wide enough for each disciple's performance to be viewed. The air is thick with the scent of camphor and woodchips, and Romasha chants in her clear voice, thumping at a hand drum. The rest of us sit cross-legged on the floor, awaiting our turn.

I thread the flower garland I made through my fingers, forcing myself not to crush the petals in my nervousness. Next to me, Kalyani clutches her own offering to the ceremony, a thin gold bracelet she acquired as a blessing for helping the nearby village of Rastha only a few days ago. After Thumri, word spread of our aid, and more yogis were given leave to help. Other disciples hold their own gifts, flowers and fruits, gold coins and small jewels—all of these either acquired personally or given as thanks for pious acts performed. As each disciple steps forward to Kaushika on the platform, they offer these up to him. I watch Kaushika place the gifts at Shiva's altar before anointing the disciple with vibhuti, the sacred ash made of burned wood.

I cannot stop looking at him. Days have passed since my meeting with Rambha, days in which I have not seen Kaushika, though that is hardly surprising. He has been busy preparing for the ceremony. I myself have not come to any conclusion on my feelings, but I know my spiraling questions have no place here. That Rambha is right is indisputable. I am here in the mortal realm, not to learn to be a sage but to complete a sacred task, a heavenly mission. I am here to save my home.

Yet it is hard to remember that now, when the chants to Shiva fill my ears and the air is heavy with spiritual intention. Not even in Amaravati have I felt such depth of connection to my own ineffable soul. Amaravati is gold and glimmer, pomp and pageantry, luxury and ostentation. The hermitage, by contrast, is a searing look into my own heart. The ceremony now, coated in formality, still retains an element of abandon and freedom. We come to give Shiva what we can, surrendering ourselves so we may free ourselves.

Beside me, Kalyani bumps my arm. I tear my eyes away from Kaushika, who is accepting Ananta's offering, and smile at my friend.

We have barely spoken the last few days, the both of us caught up in preparation for the ceremony, but there is no awkwardness between us. I expected her to still be angry with me for my defense of Indra, but she sat next to me this morning, nervously showing me the thin bracelet she brought as an offering.

"Are you sure this will do?" she whispers now.

"Yes," I reply, smiling. "It is quite powerful. You consecrated it, didn't you?"

Kalyani nods mournfully. "Many times. But I don't sense any power in it. Maybe I am not strong enough. Maybe I used too much in Thumri."

I make no reply but squeeze her fingers in comfort. The bracelet does indeed hold power; I can sense it clearly, but it feels deeply buried. Perhaps she attempted to consecrate it using a chant to one of the devas in their natural form. There is something wild about its magic—sharp, dangerous, almost veiled. It reminds me of Amaravati, but of course that is hardly something I can tell her.

I turn my attention back to the platform. One by one, Kaushika calls out the names of different students. Durvishi burns herbs for her demonstration. Outside, storm clouds clear just for an instant, her power forcing Surya's sunshine to glow, forcing a *deva*. Kaushika nods, then bids her return to her seat. Sharmisha and Advik—lovers who opened themselves up to each other's affection after speaking with me of Shakti—perform their magic together. Through a series of yogic postures that resemble part warrior forms, part dance, the two of them move around the gathering, their eyes trained only on each other. Flowers blossom in thin air, showering all of us in petals of roses, tulips, and jasmines. Advik tucks a small bud behind Sharmisha's ear. The two nod at me from the stage, and a thrill shoots through me; this is because of what I said to them. Aypan comes next, chanting the entire time during their presentation. The arrows they unleash pierce through Kaushika's own shield. Everyone can see how powerful they truly are.

One after another, disciples demonstrate their magic, each of their displays impressive. A deep gravity wraps around us all, holding our excitement and nervousness. So far, Kaushika has sent no one away— not even the students I cultivated with my lectures about the Goddess. Even Renika, who was most vocal about returning to her family, has stayed. I am reminded that though my sabotage wormed doubt into their minds, Kaushika still is a rishi, commanding more respect than me. They do not want to disappoint him. Will I be the first one to do so? Despite my own mortal practices, I have only a few runes at my disposal. I cannot fake their power with illusion, not in front of Kaushika. What if I present as the weakest here? Surely he will not send me away, not after the words he spoke to me?

*Not if this vision is true*, I think, unleashing the command toward him once again to reveal his lust. Throughout the morning, I have attempted to probe him, unbeknownst to anyone. The image hasn't changed, not truly. Each time I have seen only a vision of my own pleasure, Kaushika trailing kisses up my belly, his fingers entangled within mine as I show him where to touch me. His eyes blazing in satisfaction as I instruct him to suck and lave, whimpering as he does so.

The images are too distracting. I relinquish them almost as soon as they form. On the pavilion, Kaushika calls out Kalyani's name. I press her hand in reassurance before she weaves past the other disciples to the front. Kalyani trembles and removes the thin gold bracelet from around her wrist. She presents it to Kaushika with both hands, and he nods, accepting the trinket.

What happens next, I cannot make sense of immediately.

The bracelet touches his skin, and I blink as sharp blue light fills my vision, shaped like a massive blade that shoots into the sky. It burns in my eyes, blinding me, silencing every other sense—then crashes down, casting all of us in dimness again.

Romasha's prayer comes to an abrupt halt. The ceiling trembles, then shatters, people around us screaming, rising to their feet, scrambling back. The scent of scorching air fills my nose, and I see Kaushika looking stunned. His form undulates, blurry then sharp, like I am seeing him over a large distance.

I don't realize it, but I am on my feet. I push people out of my way in my rush to get to him, tripping over all the puja samigri, the rice and incense sticks, the dhoop and the havan fire. Every other thought flees me, except to ensure that he is safe. My fingers are already casting the rune of protection, but then I understand what the undulation is. Kaushika has created a shield, one he made instinctively when light ricocheted off the bracelet. He is behind it, protected from whatever occurred.

But Kalyani is not.

She sways where she stands. Her hands are still open in offering. The bracelet she holds is replaced by black fumes that flicker and dance. The fumes are unlike anything I have seen before, dark like midnight, glossy enough that the surrounding students are mirrored in them. I am hypnotized, staring at the way they are held in her palm. Her body does not move, but her mouth drops open, and behind his shield, Kaushika's eyes widen in comprehension.

He breaks his shield, reaching for her in the same moment the fumes are absorbed by her skin.

Kalyani collapses where she stands just as Kaushika catches her. I am there in an instant, kneeling next to them. Silence rings around the pavilion, all of us staring in shock. Kalyani's skin is turning dark, yet it is no natural shade. It is as though the blood inside her is blackening, drying. Her body spasms. Her eyes roll back into her head. Kaushika pulls back her sleeves with his own trembling hands, and I watch as darkness spreads from her palms in waves, each current climbing higher and higher, closer to her heart.

I look up to Kaushika, terror in my eyes. "Please," I say uselessly. "Please."

Kaushika begins chanting.

The mantra is too complex; I can barely keep track of the many syllables. It rises and falls, its words like one long verse. Kaushika's magic blasts the air around us, thick and powerful like an unrestrained volcano. The fumes within Kalyani slow as he sings, and to my great relief, her chest rises in a shuddering breath even though her eyes remain closed.

"Is she all right?" I gasp. "Is she injured?"

"What was that?" Anirudh says, his voice trembling. "The blade . . . it looked like a lightning bolt."

I look up to see that I am not the only one who has rushed to Kalyani. Romasha is here with Anirudh, and Eka and Parasara. Everyone else hovers close enough to help, but not close enough to disturb us, knowing we are the ones who care for Kalyani most.

Kaushika makes no answer to Anirudh. He closes his eyes and joins his palms together. A stream of chants emerges from him, melodious and quick. His voice is as deep and beautiful as ever, but there is something else in it now. A desperate kind of emotion, like he is unsure for the first time whether his chants will work.

The air ripples in front of all of us. I can almost see the letters of the mantra, like the most delicate calligraphy moving around in a swirl. Kalyani gives another shuddering breath then collapses again. Her chest moves, too shallow to mean anything good.

Terror grips my heart like never before. I find myself unable to think clearly. Tears trickle down my cheeks and I make to touch Kalyani, but Anirudh holds me back.

"Kaushika," he says again. "What is it?"

"It's poison," Romasha replies grimly. "He has stopped it from spreading, but it needs to be extracted. Otherwise, Kalyani will die."

Kaushika gives a curt nod but does not break in his singing.

"You know how to extract poisons," Anirudh says, confused. "That's an easy mantra."

"Not this," I whisper, surprising even myself. The understanding floods me at the same time I speak the words. "This is halahala."

Kaushika gives me a piercing, assessing look, then nods. I stare at him, my mind churning.

This is why the magic of the bracelet felt so familiar to me. Why it reminded me of home. This bracelet is from Amaravati. I have seen it before, shining on my lord's own wrist, so long ago the memory feels like a dream.

As for the poison . . . In my mind, I see the kalpavriksh—the holy tree where I prayed before coming to the mortal realm for my mission. The kalpavriksh emerged during the Churning of the Oceans, along with the amrit, the golden nectar that gave the denizens of Amaravati their immortality. Yet before the nectar appeared, the churning

produced halahala—a poison so lethal it killed many devas attempting
to roil the oceans. To stop the poison before it could destroy everything,
the Great Lord Shiva himself swallowed it, an act that turned his throat
blue, earning him the name of Neelkanth—the blue-throated god.

Shiva risked his own life to save all of creation, but small drops of
the poison escaped him. The drops spread through the realms, and
Indra sent his warriors to claim them. The few that were discovered
were placed within a vault in Amaravati that no one but Indra can
access.

I stare at Kaushika now, who lowers Kalyani's limp form to the
ground. The lightning blade . . . the halahala . . . I know what he must
think, yet Indra would never use the halahala for something like this,
not even to attack a dangerous enemy. It would break every tenet of
being a deva. He would be usurped by his own court. Shiva would
descend on Indra with fury and damnation.

I want to utter these protests in any way I can without raising suspicions about my own nature, but Kaushika has not stopped chanting. The air fills with his magic, and Kalyani lies on the floor, her
breathing labored.

I have no opportunity to speak my objections. Kaushika's chanting continues well into the night. Sometimes he places his palms
over Kalyani's forehead, throat, and chest, trying to anchor different chakras. Other times, he moves his fingers in a rhythmic pattern, something I now know are meditative gestures that augment
his power, similar to how the dance mudras augment mine. The heat
of the magic overtakes the cool night, but I know it is because of the
poison. Halahala is fighting Kaushika's chants.

I kneel next to him, creating runes of wellness and strength—for
myself, for him, for Kalyani. Through a blur of the hours, I realize
that someone has cleared the pavilion of the remnants of the ceremony, removing all the puja samigri. Someone else brings us water,

but I ignore it just as Kaushika does. He does not stop singing, but at one time, he takes off his sweat-drenched kurta, and I almost wish I could take mine off too. Rivulets of sweat run down his skin, and the glow of magic suffuses him, from his angular face to the hair on his arms and chest. My body grows warm, half-built images of his seduction dancing in me. It seems so meaningless now, everything I have been sent here to do, the charge to defeat him I have been given.

A desperate appeal echoes in me as I stare at Kalyani's sickening complexion. *Don't die. Please don't die.* When Anirudh gently suggests I get some rest, I cut him off.

"I'm staying," I say, and I look at Kaushika as I speak. Nothing can pull me away from here. Kalyani is my friend, the first one here in the hermitage. My *only* one here, for all I know.

I expect an argument, but Kaushika is too intent on his mantra, and that's the end of it. Hour after hour passes, and true darkness falls in the hermitage, compounded by the storm clouds. The poison moves within Kalyani's body, sometimes climbing higher to her neck, sometimes descending to her very fingertips.

I try not to hover as Kaushika works, but he is too focused on his task to even know I am there. I am amazed at his power. That he can even do this, fight *halahala*, for hours on end is beyond any magic, mortal or immortal. Indra himself cannot do this; I am certain of it. The lord of heaven is right to be terrified of Kaushika—but then my thoughts drift to the lord sending this poison to the hermitage. I shake my head, focusing once more on Kalyani, creating another rune to help Kaushika.

I am not the only one to offer my magic as assistance. Romasha burns herbs in small clay pots, creating a circle around Kaushika, me, and Kalyani. Scents swirl toward us, cinnamon, cloves, camphor. Their healing power rejuvenates me, evaporating my thirst, clearing my mind.

Someone else leads a chant, far enough from Kaushika so as not to disturb him but close enough to affect him. I do not hear the words, but I feel the vibrations in my body. When I look up, a shield hovers over us. The others are warding the hermitage, both to protect us from foes and to protect the outside world from the poison we now have. Shiva's name is called out several times, a plea for the Lord of the Universe to come and take this halahala away, but I know it is futile. Shiva will not hear amidst so much chaos. It takes a clear mind to call Shiva, and though we are all trying, we are struggling.

I am beginning to wonder how long we can last, why Anirudh and Romasha have not sent people away to save themselves should the worst come to pass and the halahala is unable to be contained, when Kaushika shifts next to me.

He gives me a piercing look as though making a decision, then nods. The quality of his mantra changes. A tendril of fume rises from Kalyani's mouth, and even as Kaushika sings, it enters his own mouth.

I don't understand at first.

Then Romasha is there, the herbs abandoned, and Anirudh too, crouching down to the both of us. They stare at Kaushika as if seeing him for the first time.

"You cannot," Romasha gasps. "Please, rishi, please. We need you to guide us. We need you, guruji."

"Kaushika," Anirudh says, his voice pained. It is all he is able to say.

I stare at Kaushika. I remember the disciple who burned herself with her tapasvin magic only a couple of months ago. I recall Kaushika taking the embers within himself, dissipating them. He could do that with raw tapasvin power, but *halahala*?

He is not Shiva.

It will destroy him.

Anirudh and Romasha are still protesting, but Kaushika stands up. The poison has almost entirely left Kalyani's body. She breathes deeply, then stills, falling into a restful sleep.

I am on my feet with my other friends, staring at Kaushika. I don't hear their words of protest. A rushing sound overtakes my ears, blood pounding in my head. Kaushika takes several steps back, distancing himself from us. I do not see the poison flickering in his body in the same way it did for Kalyani. Does it mean he has already absorbed it, unable to pause its attack? He waves a hand, and I react in the same instant his shield snaps toward us. I leap forward, closer to him, my fingers sketching the rune of stability. I pour all my magic into it with the very last of my tapasvin power.

Anirudh and Romasha stagger back, Kalyani between them.

The shield glitters around me and Kaushika—and then I forget everything else. The rest of the hermitage is a blur of shadows outside this circle that Kaushika and I are in. His eyes lock on me, alarmed, terrified, furious. He does not stop chanting, but I face him even as he trembles like he is dying.

His chin drops in exhaustion. His arms grow loose, barely able to hold the shield. I clasp him around his bicep to help keep it up as he shudders. His fingers twitch limply, trying to wave me off, but then his other arm comes to encircle my waist to support himself.

His hair is in total disarray, long strands escaped from its knot and sticking to his sweat-drenched face. His voice becomes raspier. A haunted expression comes into his eyes. He's reaching the end of his power.

I think of him dying. I think of what Rambha would tell me to do now. I think of how I still have so much magic left inside me, a magic tied to Indra. If I looked into Kaushika's lust now, what would I see? A wish to be more powerful than this? A desperate attempt to keep living? Regret for what he has done?

I can defeat him.

I can *destroy* him.

Now is my chance, to strike true, to learn everything about him I need to and undo him entirely. The command almost forms in my mind, to ask him to reveal his lust.

Kaushika stumbles, his shield about to break.

My command dies unformed. Instead, I raise my right hand and sketch the rune of Sri Yantra. I have exhausted all my tapasvin magic already; it is my tether to Amaravati I try to draw from now, knowing it will not work, *knowing* that my celestial magic is from Indra, and Indra has not allowed me to make mortal runes using my tether before. The shape forms sluggishly, wrenching the power with every bit of my strength, and I cry out, pain lancing through me, cutting me with a thousand knives, blinding me.

I expect the rune to do nothing. I expect that we both will perish, my last moments filled with chaos.

Yet something floods me in my desperation. Amaravati's power surges inside me the same way as when I dance. A kind of raw understanding blooms in me as though this rune is simply another way of making a mudra. A tug occurs behind my navel, and for the first time ever, Amaravati's magic connects to the prana in my heart, a clash of two currents in a stormy sea, releasing a wondrous image.

I look within myself into a mirror.

It is a glimpse, a scent, a secret. Dappled light, fresh lotus, endless skies. Power floods me, a wave crashing into me, sweet and fierce at the same time. My eyes widen in shock, but the hand making the rune does not shake. I radiate prana into myself and into Kaushika. Amaravati sings in me, connecting to the wild prana, the two powers mirroring, interlacing, strengthening each other.

Under my other hand, Kaushika's magic soars. The rune affects him as well, and I feel him twitch, then straighten, replenished by my strength. His aura suddenly grows brighter. The rune grows larger, floating up above us, giving us light.

Kaushika's eyes track it, and his chant grows more strident. I pour more of Amaravati's power into the rune, and suddenly I can *see* Kaushika's voice, a riot of blue and indigo and green.

His mantra grows alive.

Letters, song, and symbols swirl and shimmer in the air for a long moment. My ears and my heart are full of Kaushika and his magic, and I know his heart is full of me and my runes. It is an intimacy that brings the blood rushing to my cheeks, and for an instant I see inside him—his passion, his freedom, his strength of purpose. I see my own devotion, my loyalty, my sense of integrity. Rambha surges in my mind, then Nirjar, Queen Tara, and all my other marks. Behind my eyes, I look into Kaushika's mind as well, and the way he used intimidation so callously, turning away those who needed help in the name of enlightenment, all while nurturing his hatred for Indra. We are reflected in each other's souls, and within the both of us is a glorious light that tries to shine, a darkness that eddies and pools. We are both free and imprisoned, soaring with our truths, weighed down by our follies.

I have no time to think of what I am revealing to him. No time to wonder if he can see everything I am seeing. Kaushika's hands tighten around my waist in quiet entreaty, and I feed him my power. He seizes it, and I lean in, his magic coating me, protecting me, releasing me—and he gasps as he sings.

Our powers merge.

Kaushika raises a limp hand, and a weaving appears, a braiding of luminosity.

Before my eyes, a *ripple* tears through the air. Beyond the ripple, a field glistens with tall grass waving in a summer breeze. My hand extends toward it of its own volition. I can almost touch the grass. I am hypnotized; this is unlike any other magic I have encountered. It calls to me like a temptation, but my tether to Amaravati balks.

I watch, stunned, not understanding, as the fumes of halahala pour out of Kaushika's mouth and into the field. Air darkens in bubbles of poison. Sparks sizzle before subsiding, dust bending like it does around the heat of a fire.

The halahala leaves Kaushika rapidly. It shrinks to a pinpoint, roiling into that meadow. I try to watch it, to see what will become of it, but the air crackles once again, and the portal closes without another sound. Kaushika stops chanting and slumps against me. His head thunks on my shoulder, and I hold him close, not caring how it looks, only caring that he is safe. That it is done, and he is *safe*.

Silence rings around us.

A thousand thoughts buzz within me, but I don't have the energy to indulge them. I lean into Kaushika's chest, breathing in his skin, and his exhalations curl around my ear in precious stolen whispers. My hands climb higher, to his neck, my nails grazing his skin. He shivers in a deep sigh. He presses a palm into the small of my back, pulling me closer against his torso. Something stirs in my belly, something familiar, like lust, but deeper, *hungrier*, and I am suddenly aware that he is bare-chested, that his thumbs are reaching below the gaps in my own kurta to skim over my hipbones, that his skin on my skin is scorching hot and glorious and *alive*.

It shakes me—the realization that I've wanted this for so long. It scares me—that I chose to save him instead of destroy him. I pause, stiffening.

Kaushika's eyes snap open, and he staggers back from me.

"Are you all right?" I begin—but his face is not just hardening, it is suddenly furious.

"How dare you?" he says. "How dare you interrupt my magic? What did you do?"

The exhaustion and chaos of the last few hours crash into me. I blink, but then my confusion gives way to anger. I step up to him. "Me?" I hiss. "What was that portal you opened? Where did you send the halahala?"

Kaushika's eyes flash. "You think you can question me? I am *Sage* Kaushika. You are here at my indulgence."

"Sage," I scoff, inserting every bit of contempt I can gather into the word. "You are endangering the entire hermitage. That poison was meant for you, was it not? What actions of yours necessitate this from a foe? You are hiding things from all of us. Don't deny it."

Kaushika surges forward, so fast that I stumble back. "Are you not hiding things?" he counters. "How did you know it was halahala at all, when no one else here could tell? What magic did you just do, in your attempt to *help* me? You have been lying about yourself from the very start, and if you cannot be truthful, you have no place here."

I stare at him, at the fury in his eyes like earth erupting. Anger and hatred throb within me—hatred like I have never felt before.

"I saved your life," I hiss. "This is the thanks I get?"

A growl rolls in his throat, sending a coil of terror through me. Kaushika grabs my shoulders and shakes me hard. "You could have *died*, you foolish woman. Your very soul could have been extinguished had the halahala touched you. If anything had happened to you—"

He cuts himself off, breathing harshly.

I am too shocked to say anything. I stare at him and see lurking under his fury a deep, pained terror.

We both step back from each other. In a corner of my mind, I realize that the shield encasing us has fallen. That there are others in the pavilion, standing in clusters, staring at us. They have seen and heard everything—the magic Kaushika and I did, the portal he opened, the way we stood together, this fight, and his words.

Kaushika's composure slams back into him. His face grows

impassive and cold, and his body straightens, ever the prince, ever the sage. His eyes find Anirudh and Romasha as they hurry toward us. "Await my return," he commands. "I must contain the damage to the meadow before it kills anyone there."

Air ripples again, the same portal opening.

Kaushika steps into the darkness, the doorway sealing behind him.

# CHAPTER 17

I watch over Kalyani.

Vaguely, I am aware that we are taken to Kaushika's own hut. In a corner of my mind, I remember the last time I was here, when I was trapped by his warding. Anirudh and Romasha would have killed me then, or at least detained me until Kaushika did the deed.

I recall all of this, but I cannot work up the interest to ponder the memory any deeper. I sit down on the only stool within the hut and take Kalyani's hand in mine while Anirudh and Romasha murmur to each other.

Neither of them has mentioned my fight with Kaushika, nor the magic I did. I myself cannot get it out of my mind. I should have destroyed him then and there. Instead, I was weak. When I tell Rambha of this—and I know I must—she will be furious. She might even tell Indra, and who knows what the lord will do? He could exile me for this act of betrayal alone. I will never see Amaravati or Rambha again.

The thought chokes me. I try to erase the feel of Kaushika's touch from my skin, erase the memory of his anguished face and those words that seemed so sincere. *If anything had happened to you . . .* Kalyani lies breathing slowly on the cot, and I think of what the poison could have done to her. Did Indra truly send this to the hermitage? Is it because he does not trust in my ability to finish the job? Is the lord becoming desperate enough to resort to such an evil deed? I told Rambha how the hermitage is warded, and she would have been duty-bound to share her information with him. Did Indra hear this news and plan to send the poison here in this form?

"No," I say out loud, vehemently. I cannot believe it. I *will* not.

This is no mere matter of an irreverent village. Halahala could destroy all three realms. Even Indra would not dare. I myself have heard him lament how halahala remains in his care, yet he cannot touch it. But if not he, then who?

Kalyani murmurs in her sleep, and I lay a stilling hand on her.

"I'm sorry," I whisper. "You are my friend, and I know if you could speak, you would tell me Indra is to blame for this. But if so . . ." Tears choke me. "How can everything I've believed be wrong? He is a deva, and loyalty is all I know. That has always been my path, even if I have questioned it. Have I been wrong to be devoted?"

"You have not," Kaushika answers. "But consider who you must give your devotion to. And why."

I stand up slowly. I did not hear him come in. How long has he been there? What did he hear of what I said? I search back to whether I revealed anything dangerous, but Kaushika merely glances at me—a quick, inscrutable look that makes me squirm—and enters his home.

There is no indication of the man who spoke so brazenly to me before. Instead of heat and anger, he looks tired. He crouches next to Kalyani and takes her wrist in his hand, counting her pulse. I notice the shadows under his eyes, the stubble that rakes his cheeks. His hair is no longer in a topknot, but falls in gentle waves to his shoulders. His clothes are different too, no longer ones of a sage or a yogi but of nobility, the pale cream kurta embroidered with delicate gold, the pajamas that are edged with zari. Where has he been that he must dress like this? He looks younger. Softer.

Kaushika counts Kalyani's breaths for a long, silent minute. Finally, he sighs. "She will be all right. The poison was in a dilute form, and we acted quickly. We will use as much of our collective power in the hermitage to heal her as we can spare."

A rush of relief loosens the knots in my shoulders. Kaushika rises and we stare at each other. Memory resurges in me of how we were holding each other. How hot his hands were on my body. The intoxicating scent of his skin.

He must be thinking of the same thing. Pinpoints of color appear on the very tips of his cheekbones. An unrecognizable awkwardness steals over me, as though I am not an apsara at all.

"I want to apologize," he says formally. "For what I said. For the way I said it. You did save my life. Thank you."

I nod. Kalyani stirs, muttering in her sleep again, and Kaushika clicks his fingers. The candle dims. We are plunged in shadow, but at his gesture I follow him past the single room toward the second door that leads out to a tiny veranda. We sit together at the one step to the threshold. From here, I can see the meditation garden, although there is no one there this late in the night. The hymns have become quieter, audible only through the melodic hum of magic. A hundred thousand stars glimmer in the sky. The whispers of the breeze, the scents of rosewood, the sheer solidity of him next to me . . . it is almost peaceful. I want to stay in this companionable silence. Yet there are questions to ask.

I glance at him. "Will you finish the Initiation Ceremony?"

He shakes his head. "It is no longer necessary. I will allow anyone who wishes to stay and train to become a sage."

My brows rise at that. "I thought the ceremony was a matter of great tradition. That as a sage you must weed out those who are impure."

Kaushika shrugs, though the movement looks wooden. "Everyone here has proved their intent already with their actions," he says. "They could have left when the hermitage was attacked. Instead, they chose to stay and help. They have built wards, strengthening the hermitage over and over again. Even now, they are patrolling the forest, looking for possible enemies, all without my say-so. They are devoted, not just to Shiva but to what we do here. Their devotion is undisputed." He glances at me, and his gaze softens. "As is yours."

My mission fills my throat, coating my mouth with the bitter taste of betrayal. I had my chance to end Kaushika and I didn't take it. What does that mean for me now?

"And the other sages?" I ask, to distract myself from my growing anxiety. "They will countenance this break from tradition?"

"The other sages . . ." Kaushika sighs and presses his eyes with the heels of both palms. He looks so vulnerable that I want to peel his hands back, kiss his eyes, comfort him, but I still my body with effort. He sighs deeply. "The other sages are older and far more traditional than I have ever been. They think of me as a rebel, and I have tried to keep to their demands to prove that I am pure of heart. Yet after what occurred yesterday . . ." He shakes his head and meets my eyes. "You were right. I did endanger these people, and I have a duty of care. What is one more transgression against tradition? The Mahasabha was called by the sages so that I may present my students and convince them that I can be trusted to teach wisdom to those who seek it. Yet in reality, the Mahasabha is a political gathering, and they are more concerned with something else."

I hold my breath. "And what is that?"

Kaushika turns to me, and I understand his look. It is here, the secret he would tell me that would destroy him. I can feel it hovering on his lips, wanting to be uttered. A slow kind of horror skims through my blood. I dare not move.

He holds the moment, studying it. I see the point of decision, a shift in the set of his muscles. I know he is going to tell me, and my body freezes. I can neither look away, nor embrace this knowledge I have sought, trapped here in this moment that will inevitably decide my path.

"You asked me before where I sent the halahala," he says quietly. "Where I go when I leave the hermitage."

I nod and say nothing.

"I have—I *created*—a meadow. A place that I go to in order to meditate." Kaushika's words are careful. Slow. "It is a powerful place, Meneka. Years of my meditation have consecrated it beyond any other in this realm. When I meditate there, my power grows tenfold. What would take me years of tapasya, I am able to do in a few hours."

My mind churns with this. I remember what I overheard by the pond a few weeks ago. *A crime against nature,* Sage Agastya called it. Why? Because of the way it rips into the air, the energy it must take? Even Indra cannot simply open a gateway to any place he wishes. Even he must rely on the winds of Amaravati.

Oblivious to the chaos in me, Kaushika sighs again. "The sages at the Mahasabha disapprove of a place this powerful, and of the manner in which I have consecrated it. Yet if I had not, what would have happened to the halahala? We would all of us have been poisoned, every creature burned away from the very cycle of birth and rebirth— not by breaking it and embracing true reality but by never having existed in the first place. Even the sages themselves would have been destroyed by its spread."

I shiver, thinking of how close we all came to destruction. I cannot comprehend it. The power that Kaushika exhibited. The fact that he did it with me.

"Will the poison be safe there?" I ask.

"For now," he replies, though there is frustration in his voice. "But it cannot stay there forever. I have tried to summon Shiva again, but the Lord has not replied. Perhaps he does not believe the sincerity of my intention, but surely he must hear me. Surely he must see who is behind this."

I stare at Kaushika. "I know what you must think, but it cannot be Indra. It simply cannot."

His voice is gentle, and his fingers flicker toward mine lightly as though to give me comfort without touching me. "I am sorry," he says softly. "A betrayal like this is hard to accept. I understand that. Believe me."

"No, you do not understand." My voice grows frantic, and I have to take a deep breath to control it. "How can it be Indra, Kaushika? *How?* I know you despise him for what he did at Thumri and to your own kingdom. He is a deva, and he has behaved irresponsibly, but this? This is unconscionable. Indra could not, not even if drunk on soma."

"Meneka—"

"He is a *hero*," I say, my voice breaking. My desperation spills out rapidly in a half sob. "Do you not remember he saved all of humanity from endless famine and released the waters of the world back into the mortal realm tens of thousands of years ago? That story is still sung in my kingdom. Without him, the dragon-demon Vritra would have destroyed it all. Nothing would have survived. Indra was the only one brave enough to fight the demon. Even you pray to the essence that is Indra. Even you acknowledge his power."

My breath is heavy, filled with silent tears. Kaushika frowns, and I ache for him to see reason in my words. I need him to understand, to *agree*, because if he does not, if Indra truly did send the halahala, I would never be able to live with this knowledge. If the lord is capable of this monstrosity, what else has he done? What else have *I* done, in blindly obeying his orders? I am clinging to my last hope, to Indra's innocence in this heinous crime despite the many mistakes he might have made. I cannot allow Kaushika to strip away my faith in Indra; in my heart, I cannot even allow *Indra* to do so. Who am I if not a creature of heaven? Even at my most despairing, I have always thought to return to his swarga. Am I to live the rest of my life in the knowledge that I have been an agent of *evil*?

Kaushika is still frowning. For a suspended moment he does not say anything, and his gaze flits to the stars, visible in the evening, contemplating Indra and swarga. Weighing my words. Listening.

I know what I am saying is suspicious. If he has ever thought me to be an apsara, I am simply confirming it with my protests. Yet he has already told me so much about himself. Should I not push my advantage? I cannot bear it, to hear such blasphemies from his mouth. I cannot bear what this means for me and for *him*.

If he truly believes all these things about Indra, he will justify any action against my lord. He would kill me now if he knew who I was, and he has probably already killed my apsara sisters without mercy. That thought has never left my mind, since the very beginning of this mission, but in this moment, I know that I have built excuses past it, hoping for it not to be true. This man I have come to understand, even come to like to a certain extent, I cannot reconcile with the sage who would kill apsaras in cold blood. In the twisted corridors of my mind, the two thoughts seem connected. If Kaushika can believe in Indra's innocence with the halahala, he will not hurt me. He will not have hurt my kin.

I know there is no logic behind this—whatever Kaushika and Indra have done, I cannot change the past, yet I cannot bear for either of them to have committed such horrors, not even in the pursuit of their beliefs. Not even if they thought they were justified. I simply know that if any of this is true, it tells me more about myself than about them, because of how I understand them, and sympathize with them. Has this mission ruined me to such an extent already, so stealthily and invisibly, that I am lost to my own good sense? I try to breathe past the thick obstruction in my throat.

"If not Indra," Kaushika says slowly, "then who? You say your kingdom worships him. Then do you know of anyone else who would have access to the poison?"

I try to think. I really do.

I search for another explanation to the halahala, and a hidden memory taps in my mind, a thread I must pull that will lead me to the truth. Yet I cannot sift through it when everything is so blurry. Kaushika is asking me for clarity, but I don't want him to base it on what I say. I want *him* to reassure *me*, to take care of me, to tell me everything I've ever believed has been fine, simply because I am me and he believes me.

I bury my head in my hands, aware of the incongruity of my desire.

Kaushika lets out a deep sigh. "I am sorry," he says again. "Indra *has* been a hero in the past. But please think this through. The bracelet did not reveal itself until I touched it. It was meant for me, and only the lord of heaven has cause. Indra is threatened by me. He knows I do not like him, and he has tried to thwart me many times before. The last many weeks, he sent storms to the hermitage as a warning that he knows where I am. I was able to keep them at bay during the Initiation Ceremony. Otherwise, the hermitage itself would have been flooded away. If there really was someone else behind it . . . well, that might change some matters. But I cannot see another answer, and Indra cannot go unchallenged. This is why the sages and I must meet. The sages must see that Indra is a menace to the entire realm. To send halahala is monstrous by any estimation. Even you agree to this."

I can say nothing. I am to blame for the storms sent to the hermitage. *I* told Rambha of the hermitage's whereabouts. I never expected such a retaliation, but I feel the lord's desperation pressing at my throat like a knife. I feel the urgency of my mission like first blood drawn. Rambha's voice echoes in my head, reminding me to be devoted. I think of how even she did not see fit to tell me everything occurring in Amaravati, of how she told me to do my duty unquestioningly, to be a good little apsara obeying commands blindly.

Yet here is Kaushika, my *enemy*, telling me secrets of his own accord, trying to understand me even though his entire life has been to work against those of my kind. My heart aches so much that I can barely breathe. I think of what I *want* to do, and who owns me. Rambha and Indra and Kaushika and my friends from the hermitage spin in my mind like colors within water. The words almost form on my lips, to blurt out the truth about my identity, simply to see what he will do, but I hold myself close, trembling. I cannot risk it, not even now, *especially* not now. What if I am misreading everything about Kaushika? What if *I* have been seduced by the hermitage and the mortal realm?

Kaushika's voice washes over me in a comforting breeze. "How did you know it was halahala?" he asks.

"I sensed it. I . . . I don't know how." My voice is muffled, my head still buried in my hands. The faint memory tap-taps again in my head. I loosen my topknot, my hair spilling over me, covering whatever of my face Kaushika can see. I do not care about the propriety of appearing like a sage, not anymore. It is enough that the action releases some of the tension in my head. That, just for a moment, I am hidden from him when I am so obscured to myself.

Kaushika shifts beside me. I feel a movement, as though he is about to touch my hair but thinks better of it. "And the magic you did?" he asks softly.

"I—I don't understand it myself."

Everything is confusing. Did Indra allow me to use Amaravati's power for mortal magic? Was it because of him that the two magics combined? Why would he allow me this if he sent the halahala himself and wants Kaushika dead this badly? Despite what Rambha said, I can no longer make sense of how the ability to do tapasvin magic could have been granted by Indra. This magic must be my own. If tapasya truly allows *any* soul to access divinity, then why should I be any different from a yogi? I try to slow myself down, but each stream of thought ends only in more questions and objections. Blooms of sincerity and deception coil inside me, twisting, until I cannot breathe. I have been turned inside out, everything I held within spilled out for all to see and leaving me hollow. I cannot rely on anything, and I float unmoored, a rudderless boat in the roiling waters of chaos.

Kaushika exhales softly. "It is all right, Meneka. I believe you. You have no reason to tell me anything. I have no reason to ask."

I look up at this, surprised. I brush back my curtain of hair.

Irrationally, it is Rambha's voice I hear in my head: *What good is love, what good devotion, if it is only transactional?* A sense of wretchedness steals over me, and I have to breathe hard to contain the sudden sob in my chest. I cannot believe it—that he is offering so much of himself, yet expects nothing in return. That he does not question me further like I have questioned him at every occasion. Is this a trick?

Kaushika smiles slightly, a glint of white teeth in the starlight, as if he has heard me. "I never wanted your secrets, you know. I only wanted for you to be true to yourself. If that knowledge awes you, you are wise. I was awed by you too." His gaze locks on me. "I am awed by you all the time."

My voice is a whisper. "Because of the strength of what I can do?"

"No," Kaushika says. "Because of you. Of what I see in you."

A sound escapes me, half sniffle, half laugh. I am an apsara. My marks see what I allow them to. Yet, I have not shaped myself into his desire—not deliberately.

"What *do* you see?" I ask skeptically.

"I see a vision of beauty, sacred and deep," he says quietly. "I see a woman who is strong, because she has fought terrible battles with herself. Who has won them and lost them and understands the futility of fighting but does it anyway because to not do so would be harder. I see a being, daring and audacious, talented and hungry. I see a power who can challenge the gods themselves. I see you, Meneka, and I see the great Goddess Shakti herself, she who belongs with Shiva. Why do you think that in Thumri I looked to you as I completed my mantra? When the power from my own tapasya started to wane, it was you who gave me strength. Reminded me of another path. Reminded me of love."

My words choke within me. It is too much, the sincerity in his speech, the scent of him, the heated gaze. It is too much, this validation I have never received even from those closest to me, to be seen as something more, to be seen as being capable beyond my own estimation. Whether true or not, I want to believe him. I want to deceive myself, even if all this is an illusion.

I lift my hand to touch the cuff of Kaushika's sleeve, tracing a finger along the embroidery of his kurta. "You met with another royal today," I say inconsequentially. "That is why you are dressed like this."

"A particularly difficult queen," he says, smiling slightly. "Yet I believe she understands what I am trying to do."

"And what *are* you trying to do?" I ask, lifting my gaze to him. "What do you intend to achieve with the irreverence you foment against Indra?"

"An opportunity," Kaushika answers. "An opportunity for justice in the world. How many more must suffer like the villagers in Thumri? Like my own kingdom? I seek wisdom, Meneka, to imagine something different. My meetings with the royals are simply to gauge if they feel similarly. If I take on Indra, we must be united."

I stare at him. I wonder if the queen he met today is the very same one I overheard him speaking with at Shiva's temple. It is significant that he is meeting with a royal so urgently, when so much else is occurring. A part of me knows I must ask about it, but my fingers hover

over his pulse, and his eyes darken. I want to tell him that the clothes are beautiful, that *he* is beautiful. The words catch in my chest, aching.

Kaushika's gaze lingers on my face, watching all this.

I swallow, and the sound is loud. I am drowning, and even though I know it is a losing battle, I call out to Amaravati in a desperate attempt to remember my mission, remember my devotion. *Reveal your lust*, I whisper, and I see my own head thrown back as Kaushika fills me with ecstasy, and this time I accept what I have known all along. That his lust and desire are a mirror to my own, just like the magic we did with the halahala. We are two opposites bound to each other in this game of mark and seducer, each of us taking either role, unknowing, unaware. The lust I saw in him is mine, the empowerment of everything I can be, realized through the mirror he holds up to me.

My fingers skim his wrist again, lightly skating over the kurta, reaching for the strong contours of his bicep. Kaushika exhales, a soft sound that lifts the hair off my forehead. I don't know why I do it, but it is a test of the both of us. I let my touch climb, then hover over his mouth, my thumb tracing the outline of his lips. He licks his lips in the same instant, and his tongue rasps over my finger, tasting it. He gives it a soft nip, catching it between his teeth, and a whimper escapes me.

I stare at him, but he does not touch me any further. I can tell; he is waiting, he is trying not to scare *me* off, when we are hovering here in this moment that will change everything. It is so absurd—that he should care, that *he* should give me the space to retreat when *I* am the creature of lust and he the sage—that my whimper becomes a small laugh, halfway between joy and disbelief.

*Enough*, I think. *No more games.*

Before I can stop myself, I climb into his lap and straddle him.

I have no time to think if I am being too forward or if I have misinterpreted him.

Kaushika's gaze widens, and his arms encircle my waist. I feel his strength beneath me, and the corded muscle of his thighs. We both gasp as I settle and lean into him, eyes closed. All I can smell is *him*, all I feel is his body, so perfectly aligned with mine. His thumbs skim just below the swells of my breasts, and I *feel* the contours of my curves through his touch. I suppress a moan, at how close we are, at what we are about to do. My hands bury themselves in his hair, and it is as soft as his body is hard beneath me.

I force my eyes open. I force myself to draw back and study his face.

I will not come to this now in deception. I will have him understand what this means—no ordinary mark, but Kaushika, *a sage*.

"This will end your asceticism," I whisper.

"I've recently learnt it is not the only way." His eyes are on my mouth.

"This is your choice," I say.

"Agreed. Is it yours?"

I dip my head and graze my teeth on the skin of his neck. "What do you think?"

He laughs, and my heart leaps with that sound. His hand threads through my hair, cupping my scalp. He tugs lightly, bending my head slightly back. I want to close my eyes, but I hold on to myself with a final will. I watch him through my lashes, searching him.

"You cannot blame me for this," I warn.

"Oh," he whispers. "But I am."

And he surges forward, his lips assaulting mine. My mouth is hot, my hands gripping his hair. Under me, he *groans*, his fingers supporting my neck, tangling in my tresses as he pulls me closer. I angle my head, my hunger a hot flame within me. This is madness. It will only end in pain. This man hates my lord, my home. He may have already harmed my sisters. But all those thoughts flitter away like so many seeds in the wind. I cannot stop kissing him, and he devours me like he wouldn't allow me to stop. He tastes of spun sugar and ginger, the camphor of his scent driving me to distraction. I part my lips and pull his tongue along mine, and he groans again, his fingers by my rib cage, thumbs skimming just over my nipples, rubbing them back and forth until they harden through my kurta.

"Meneka." His voice is a tortured whisper, and within it I hear a thousand admissions, a million promises. "I've thought of this for too long."

I shiver against him as the images of his seduction return to me, this time unbidden, golden visions where he pleasures me without asking for anything in return.

A part of me wants to stop. His words make him sound like another successful mark. Yet there is something true within the iron of his voice, something that tells me it is not my influence as an apsara that's brought him here to me, but *me*. Beyond my magic, beyond my power.

I tighten the grip of my legs around his waist. I feel his hardness perched right below my bottom, and his hips rock into mine instinctively. Kaushika hitches me higher, never breaking the kiss, and I kiss harder, rolling my body into his, ragged and breathless, devouring him. A dampness grows between my legs, and his hands cup my backside, kneading, his fingers flickering just there.

Pinpoints of pleasure shoot into my spine, into my head. I moan, biting into his lower lip, sinking my nails into the skin of his throat, unable to get enough. I want more, so much more. I want him on his knees. I want to be on *my* knees, his hand pushing my head while he begs me for sweet release and I give it to him. I want to conquer this man. I want to own him and bend him to me, not because of my mission but because he will be strong enough to take it, to want it, to understand it. Is this truly who I am? Simply another apsara intoxicated with her own power, desiring worship by her thralls? Indra's gleaming court shines in my head again. Rambha says, *Seduce*, and I think of whether I am, whether I have.

I break the kiss, my breathing rough. "I—I don't want to stop," I stammer, but the words are not for him. They are for me, a justification, a plea. Who will I become if I go through with this? There will be no turning back.

"We won't stop," he says firmly. "Not until I give you what you want. Not until you are satiated."

"What if I never am?" I whisper.

"Then we have a long time of discovery, don't we?" he says, and his smile tingles against my skin. "I am certainly not going to complain."

I laugh, and it is a sound torn from me. The thought crosses my mind, that I have seduced him without my knowledge, so much an apsara that I have done this even without *my* permission, let alone his. I want to give into it badly, my control slipping with every kiss he trails across my neck, that I cannot remember why this is wrong. His tongue glides over me in slow patterns, too dizzying to note, and though I am the one being pleasured, a strangled sound escapes him that tells me that he will allow this, that he will let me conquer him, that he will surrender and know it for strength, that he wants this too. I have never been reluctant about sex, and there has certainly been no more meaning to it than pleasure, but knowing what it would mean for him, for *me* to do this with a mark . . . I clutch him, not wanting to leave, not wanting to stop, yet too afraid to continue.

Kaushika rescues me from my own mind. "Let yourself go," he whispers, and his fingers sneak under my trousers, skin on bare skin, kneading the soft flesh of my bottom, reaching. He is inches away from where I need him, and I squirm, trying to get closer, but he holds me tight. I utter a sound of frustration as rapid need courses though me. Dampness is trickling down my thighs, and I press against his hardness, whimpering.

"Do you like this?" he asks quietly.

*Almost too much so*, I think. "Y-Yes," I whisper.

My voice is a rush. His hand slides inward, and I bite my lip to keep from screaming. I try to move my own hand, to feel him in turn, but I am trapped by his hard chest, and he shakes his head. He slides his tongue across my jaw, nips at my ears, a low growl of refusal erupting from him. I can almost hear his words. *Not me. Just you.*

The sound undoes me. It is too intoxicating, that he is both a seduced mark and not. That I am both an apsara and not. We are two raw creatures caught in this whirlpool of identities we have been forced into and embraced.

His knuckles brush over my aching center. Then one thick finger slides through my opening, twisting expertly, and I cannot control it anymore. I cry out, and my back arches. He tugs my head back, his hand in my hair. My eyes are shut in exquisite agony, and I feel the feathery touch of his lips, on my cheeks, my chin, my throat. His breath whispers on my eyelids, the rasp of his tongue as he licks my lips, parting my mouth, stroking it with a skill that I can only compare to lovers I've had in heaven.

I whimper with the dual assault of his fingers and tongue. His mouth ravages me, even as his thumb finds that perfect spot. He moves his hand faster, and my hips grind against his touch. My thighs clamp around him, but he pushes them open again, stroking between my folds with the pad of his thumb. I struggle to touch him, but he has captured my fingers within his free hand, trapped between us, so that I cannot give him pleasure, but finally, *finally*, must take my own instead.

And then all thought flees from me as the apex of my pleasure comes hurtling toward me in showers of gold in my head. I cannot form a single coherent thought. I am reduced to that one sensation.

I cry out, an insensate sound that must surely echo in the night, but Kaushika is there, swallowing it before it escapes. I lose my grip on reality, squeezing his hips between my thighs, riding out my climax. His hands dig into the flesh of my bottom, pressing me to him, bringing us as close as we can be in this position with our clothes still covering us.

Kaushika's mouth continues to stroke mine, his tongue deep with each frantic movement of my sudden climax. I hear his whispered breath, ragged and short, words of endearment in a haze of broken speech. My hands are clenched in his kurta, fists almost painful. Aftershocks of the pleasure still ricochet through me, and we remain entangled, feeling every twitch, every relaxation.

Slowly, my body grows limp. My fists loosen. I open my eyelids and find Kaushika watching me. A smile quirks his lips, half-satisfied, half-curious, the dimple peeking through. What did we just do? Does he regret it? Do *I*?

My hands keep smoothing the cloth on his chest uselessly. I try to pull away but find it impossible to. "You are not bad for a sage," I say ridiculously.

"I was once a prince," he replies, laughing, just as ridiculous an answer. His mouth moves against mine softly, nipping at my lips, kissing my cheeks, brushing over my eyelids. It is like the softest petals, intoxicating and sweet. Heat churns in my belly, and it costs me everything to pull myself back, to make him stop.

Kaushika does not insist. He cocks his head, waiting. I want to say something, but all I can do is tremble, goose bumps erupting on my flesh. Kaushika pulls me into his warmth, tucking me closer in a tight embrace. I drop my head on his chest, letting myself be comforted by this man I am sworn to destroy.

# CHAPTER 18

E ventually we unentangle.

I am suddenly aware of everything, the thunder rolling across the sky, the lightning in the far distance, the hymns radiating across the hermitage, and the disturbance in the air from the wards. I try to extract myself from him, but my movements are too clumsy in the satisfied luxury of my orgasm and the growing nervousness with the man who gave it to me.

Kaushika helps me stand. I step away, embarrassed, but he moves forward, closing the distance between us, tying the drawstrings of my trousers together, settling my kurta, straightening the collar. His fingers tingle on my collarbones. He combs my hair out with his hand, feeling the lush weight of it, before he coils the dark mass up into an expert topknot.

Cautiously, I glance at him, searching for signs of shame on his face. But he simply adjusts his own clothes swiftly and offers me his hand. The same smile from before plays on his face, this time flooded with warmth and satisfaction, and sudden contentment blossoms in my heart. I cannot help but embrace its comfort; the feeling is so unusual. I know I must question this, the act of what we have done, of what *I* have, but for now, it is enough that Kaushika strides next to me more in control of himself than I am of myself. It is enough that he is leading us, and we indulged ourselves in a moment that has plagued both our fantasies for so long.

We walk through the hermitage silently. The hour is late, and I expect most disciples to have retired to their huts, but although lamps flicker at many windows, several yogis still linger within the court-yard and the pavilion, their magic sharp and sparking ready at their fingertips. Several march toward the forest, and I remember Kaushika mentioning patrols. Others are chanting softly, and magic warps the air as wards are strengthened. Durvishi sees me and Kaushika, her eyes traveling to our clasped hands. She giggles and nudges Jaahnav, who utters a loud laugh, which makes Anirudh and Romasha turn.

Anirudh's jaw drops open. I feel my cheeks burn. I told him about a lover I left behind to come to the hermitage. What must he think of me now? Will he tell Kaushika what I said then? As for the lover I mentioned—Rambha herself told me to do this. Her instruction is not why I indulged—no, the moment of intimacy that Kaushika and I shared was pure. But I know I will have to reckon with my tangled love for her regardless.

My gaze travels to Romasha, who stands next to Anirudh. Her eyes are wide, reflecting the moonlight, and even from this distance I see the tears sparkling in them. A look of sorrow and betrayal crosses her face before she stills herself. She abruptly turns away, and the pleasure from my climax recedes in reaction. I have seen that look before. It lingers on the faces of my marks' lovers when I am deep in my seduction. I once suspected Kaushika of being infatuated with Romasha, but the truth is that *she* cares for *him* despite her own path of asceticism. Perhaps one day he would have learned to reciprocate her feelings. Have I taken that possibility away from the two of them unintentionally?

I lower my eyes. This one quenching of my lust has already hurt people.

"Perhaps we should be more discreet," I murmur, edging my hand away from Kaushika.

His grip tightens, his fingers interlacing with mine. He glances at me, curious. "Do you regret it?"

I shake my head. I don't know enough yet to distill my feelings.

"I don't say it for me," I evade, "but for you. You lead this hermitage. You have taught them about asceticism."

"I don't indulge in senseless shame, Meneka. If they have a problem, they will speak with me. Besides, my choices reflect my own understanding of asceticism better, something you yourself have taught all of us." His glance falls over the assembled disciples, some of whom are still smiling, and he sighs. "Let them question me if they will. I will answer in honesty. I have nothing to hide."

"Not even from the sages at the Mahasabha? What if they should find out, bound by tradition as they are?"

Kaushika's shoulders move in dismissal. "Some of them are married. Not all of them have claimed the path of asceticism I have, and even if they did, what I do with my body is not their affair. They understand the path of Shiva, of duality and love and surrender more than I do."

I let my other objections subside. If he does not care about what the sages or the yogis think, why should I? I was sent here from heaven to do precisely this—weaken Kaushika and make him more pliable to me. I am close to my freedom, already making my lord proud; even if I had not meant for this happen for the mission, I am giving Indra what he wants without truly trying. I should take joy in that. Yet all I feel is heartbreak.

Kaushika stops at the entrance of the shed where my quarters are. Kalyani's absence is conspicuous in the darkness within the shed. I can almost see the both of us chatting into the night as she attempts to teach me to connect with my prana, as we speak of her own magic and how she can use love for it. Even in those conversations, my mission had been at the forefront of my mind, but now? I see myself entering this very shed on the first night, trailing Kaushika, wondering about the shape of his seduction. I feel older, and it is the taste of *his* lips that linger on mine instead of Rambha's.

My hand grips his in panic, indecision whirling in me about how to proceed. So much has changed, and yet nothing at all. My allegiances, my very identity, flutter within me as if caught in a fisherman's net. Kaushika looks at me quizzically, and I school my features and utter a half laugh. I release his hand.

"After all that, and I must still stay alone in this little room," I say lightly, trying to distract the both of us.

A smile lifts his lips. "I would offer you my own bed, but even I cannot use it."

"Are you sure that's the reason?" I tease. "Maybe you are afraid of me."

Kaushika laughs. "I *am* afraid of you, but not for the reasons you think. Undoubtedly, there are other more pleasurable things we can both do besides sleep, but I would suggest we get some rest. Bright and early for the Mahasabha, Meneka, I expect you to be on time."

"You are so insistent on taking me. What if I fluster you?"

"You will fluster me even if I do not bring you. This way, I will have you in sight, right next to me. When we travel as a group, you will be but another obedient disciple."

The word makes me arch an eyebrow. "Obedience," I murmur, walking my fingers up his chest. "You enjoy giving commands. The thing is, Sage Kaushika, so do I."

A surprised breath huffs out of him, and his eyes darken. "I would let you command me," he whispers, leaning close. "I would let you teach me, rule me, ruin me. I would let you vanquish me, if that is what you wanted, Meneka. If you asked."

My knees tremble. My teasing falters with his response. I shut my eyes and squeeze my legs together, my core aching in the memory of my pleasure. Kaushika smiles and gives me a light bow before turning away. I watch him leave, still shaking.

Camphor and rosewood light my dreams that night.

I TOSS AND TURN, RELIVING HIS WORDS. THE TASTE OF HIM ON my lips, heat and power and hunger. The way my body reacted, so instinctively and naturally. I cannot lie still, and my hand moves to rest on my legs, fingers dancing, delicate, delicate. I snatch them back, and my cheeks warm, as I see Kaushika in my mind. The curve of his neck. His pulse under his skin. Jeweled beads of sweat on his dark chest.

In my dreams, Indra laughs behind us, as though I am succeeding at the task he set me, yet failing a greater, more important one. I run through the golden passageways of Amaravati's heavenly palace, searching for answers, seeking to understand. I open doors to chambers, and behind each I find Kaushika, his smile merged with Tara's longing, with Nirjar's passion, with Ranjani's innocence. Guilt and desire weave into each other, burning fingers through my body.

It is a relief when dawn streams in through my window. Outside, the storm has passed, and a pink sky blushes through gray clouds. I awaken to bathe and dress, and find a small package outside my door. Kaushika's comb carefully wrapped within a kerchief, a sign as though to wash away the taste of my nightmares. I smile foolishly, my heart swelling.

I meet the others at the stables, arriving at the same time as Eka. Romasha and Parasara are already on their horses, and Anirudh hustles a protesting Eka onto the mare Kalyani rode to Thumri. I leap upon my own, too tired to speak, and Kaushika doesn't say a word either, but I can tell that he has had a difficult night too. His mouth is brooding, and a line creases his forehead. When he sees me watching, he smiles and winks at me as though to reassure me that it has nothing to do with me.

I am not reassured. Kaushika has chosen us to accompany him, not because we are the strongest right now—depleted in our tapasya as we all are—but because he intends to speak about Indra's cavalier attitude toward the mortal realm, and we are his witnesses from Thumri. He expects us to corroborate his words should the need arise; he even *told* me he expects me to be obedient. What will I say if the other sages ask me questions? Was his action last night to make me more docile? If so, he will be disappointed. I am no longer trying to bend the rules of my devotion to Indra for a greater plan. These are *rishis*. Each of them is a threat to Indra already through their sheer power. Each of them—though mortal—is so accomplished in their magic that they have already lived hundreds of years.

We ride in the same formation we rode to Thumri. This time our pace is a slow trot. Kaushika and Romasha take the lead, but Anirudh is next to me, with Eka on his other side.

"What is to happen at the Mahasabha?" I ask. "All I know is that we are to be presented."

Anirudh makes a balancing motion with a hand. "There is not much else to tell. It is impossible to know how many rishis will arrive. It could be only one, or it could be fifty. The numbers do not matter. Whoever arrives, they represent the others. It is to our benefit if there is more than one sage, though. With a single one, we will know the others have made up their minds fully. The more there are, the more room there is to argue and convince them."

*Convince them of Indra's villainy*, I think, but I do not utter the words.

I give Anirudh a sidelong glance. "Last night . . . you saw me with Kaushika . . ."

He nods but doesn't say anything.

"I . . . I don't want you to think," I stammer. "I—I mean, what is between us—"

"Is none of my business," Anirudh completes softly. He reaches over and squeezes my hand. "Kaushika makes his own decisions. He is allowed to. As are you."

"But will it affect the Mahasabha?" I whisper. "Could the other sages act against him? He seems not to care, but what if I have ruined everything for him?"

At that, Anirudh frowns. We ride alongside each other in silence for a time. I myself cannot tell how I want him to react. I cannot bring myself to agree with Kaushika that a confrontation with Lord Indra is the best move. But the halahala . . . everything in Thumri . . . Indra is not innocent either, and my own place in these events is too muddied to distill.

In the east, the pink flush of dawn gives way to a clear day. When Anirudh finally speaks, his voice is thoughtful. "The sages have no cause to question your relationship," he says. "But they have known how devoted Kaushika has been before to the ascetic path. None of us here will tell them of it, if that is what worries you."

"Not even Romasha?" I can't help but ask. I see her ahead of us, the cold lines of her shoulders, the stiff manner in which she speaks to Kaushika. I think of the tears in her eyes and the sorrowful look on her face. Jilted lovers have done much worse than harm the ones they love.

But Anirudh shakes his head. "Romasha reveres Kaushika. She would never do anything to jeopardize his agenda. We won't speak a word, Meneka, as it is not our business—but it does not mean that Kaushika himself will not tell them. He is an honest man. If he thinks they should know, he will not lie."

"He would be a fool to say anything," I murmur, but I cannot keep the fondness out of my voice even though nervousness grips me.

Anirudh utters a short laugh. "Oh, my friend, give him some credit. He is a *sage*. Their questions will be to judge him, and whether he is truly fit for the status he has been granted. If they suspect your relationship, they will only want to understand how you both define it. He should have prepared you for it, but perhaps he was trying to protect you from worrying overmuch."

Anxiety pools in my stomach. Kaushika *was* trying to protect me, but how can he protect me from myself? I asked Kaushika for discretion about what we have done, but it was not just to guard his reputation, it was to shield my true identity too.

I am here pretending to be someone I am not, riding toward more danger than I have ever been in, but the extent of Kaushika's powers is unknown to me, and the sages we are to meet are more accomplished in magics than I can know. Kaushika could not tell the difference between my immortal tether to Amaravati and my mortal tapasvin prana, but these others might not be limited in their vision. What will he do if one of the sages tells him who I am? What will the sages themselves do? My heart beats in tandem with the movement of the horses. I cannot help but feel I am riding toward my own execution.

A little ahead of us, Eka's horse snorts and she utters a panicked squeak. Anirudh turns to her, instructing her how to ride properly. I remain silent the rest of the way. The path we take is the same as the one I took when I met Rambha, and it serves only to remind me of heaven. The way matters are occurring, I expect Kaushika to turn for the very same clifftop I met Rambha at, but fortunately he leads us deeper into the woods, our horses slowing to a walk until we reach a clearing.

A small tent stands amidst the trees. Magic undulates around the cloth, overpowering, moving in waves, confusing my senses. I blink several times to clear my vision, but I can see its tangles as though the tent itself is constructed of white light, shimmering and pure, and the cloth is an illusion.

Kaushika directs us to tie our horses to one of the trees, and we follow him as he leads us into the tent. I am surprised to see no more than three men waiting inside, seated on unadorned rugs. Do these men all have a common opinion? Have the rest of the absent rishis decided about Kaushika already?

I recognize the sages from the discussions of the others in the hermitage. Vashishta is the one with hair as pale as the moon tied into a topknot, a tuft escaping it. His beard reaches all the way down to his chest, and the vibhuti on his forehead is white against his dark skin. Deep in conversation with him is another man, younger by some appearances but no less austere. Sage Agastya is shorter and stockier, his quiet voice gentle. He is the same guru I overheard at the lake by the hermitage, warning Kaushika of this very meeting. His aura shines behind his eyes, contained and relaxed. I expect Kaushika to greet him first, but his attention is taken up by the very last man, Sage Gautama, who is tall and skinny, his bare chest covered with seed necklaces.

Kaushika utters a joyful bark of a laugh and leaps forward to enclose Gautama in a hug. Then, as though remembering himself, he bows low, prostrating himself in front of all of them as they stand. Each of the men bends to pull him up, Agastya patting Kaushika's shoulder and smiling, though I notice Vashishta's frigidity, as though he is being forced to welcome Kaushika.

I take a deep breath to steady myself. The charge I'd felt in the air is tenfold within the tent. Over time, I have become used to Kaushika's magic, but seen here now, in this confluence of auras, a swirl of colors and scents batters me, visible to me and me alone. The strength of all the sages' chakras and the half-moon radiance behind their heads are akin to the auras of the devas. It makes me breathless and lightheaded, and I sway a little. Anirudh wraps an arm around my shoulder, watching me in concern.

We are all of us still standing at the threshold, watching the sages from a distance, and I feel unable to keep my balance, too overwhelmed by the magic here. My knees begin to shake as fear darts through me. What am I doing here? I should have told Kaushika I could not come. Made some sort of excuse. I should have told Kaushika myself that I am an apsara. Controlled the conversation in a moment when he was most pliable. Any one of these sages could reveal me, of course, but some stories say that Vashishta was *born* of an apsara. I have heard in the hermitage how he holds no true love for Kaushika, their difference of opinion often coming to an alarming battle of magics. He will undo the both of us instantly. This is it. The end I have been fearing.

Anirudh squeezes my shoulder. I say nothing, panic making me too nauseous. None of the other yogis look at us, having not noticed my discomfiture.

"Good," Romasha says, her eyes shining as she watches the sages. "This is good."

I glance at her, searching for any signs of deception, but she seems intent on the Mahasabha, her moment of sorrow on seeing Kaushika and me together clearly forgotten. What is going on in her mind?

"What do you mean?" Eka asks, but she glances at Anirudh. "I thought you said the more sages the better, but there are only three rishis who have come."

His hand still supports me, but Anirudh nods. "The others must be intent on their meditation. Had they *all* come, disturbing their tapasya, this would have been a more serious matter. As it is, we could not have picked a better contingent if we wished it."

"These sages never show a united front together," Romasha explains in a low, excited voice. "All of them feel differently about Indra, and that is our true purpose here—to unite them in their thinking. The deva king tried to seduce Gautama's own wife, hundreds of years ago. The guru hates Indra, perhaps more than Kaushika himself. Sage Agastya believes in reconciliation and the peaceful approach. Time and again, he has prayed to Indra, seeking refuge from droughts or inclement weather. He will not be swayed easily, but he *will* listen to reason. Vashishta alone holds neither love nor hate for the deva lord.

He is as likely to support Indra as to thwart Kaushika, but to see one sage of each predilection here is an opportunity, and—"

"So these are your disciples?" Agastya says, and Romasha abruptly quietens.

"Yes," Kaushika replies. "Only a few of many, the ones I believe are most worthy. They will become sages one day, once I am done training them." He steps aside, and the rest of us fall to our knees, prostrating ourselves, foreheads to the floor.

"Oh, get up, get up," one of the sages says impatiently. "Approach us, all of you."

Nervously, my friends and I rise. Agastya gestures to Eka and Parasara, who can barely meet his eyes. Gautama waves a hand to Anirudh and Romasha, smiling. It is Vashishta himself who beckons to me with an imperious crook of his finger.

I can feel Kaushika's gaze burning into me as I approach the rishi, but I dare not look at him. I try to remember what I know of Vashishta. During Kaushika's ascension to sage, it was he who put him through the most arduous trials. He is Kaushika's greatest rival, yet his poetry and wisdom are debated in Kaushika's hermitage, hymns he wrote praising Indra even as he censured the lord. Does he believe in Indra the essence more than Indra the lord too? My body trembles so hard, knowing I am perhaps moments from being exposed, that I stumble as I approach, nearly falling to the floor and back on my knees again.

"Guruji," I murmur, pressing my palms together and dropping my gaze. My shoulders shake in terror.

"Daughter," he intones quietly. He straightens me and tips my chin up. His eyes crinkle in silent mirth, like he can see deep inside me and is amused by what he sees. "Oh," he says quietly. "You *are* unique, aren't you? He has certainly picked a worthy disciple, you who are discovering secrets of magic even without any true training. Would that I could take you to my own hermitage to train you, but that is not your purpose here, is it?"

I cannot hold his gaze. My mind buzzes, unable to understand whether his words are a compliment or a taunt. Can he see the violence of my heart? Does he *know*? I shirk back, laid bare, wondering what his agenda is and what he is about to do, but Vashishta does not elaborate.

He turns from me and raises his voice. "Very well, then. Let us be about it. Rishi Kaushika," he says, and there is amusement in his voice again, the iron edge of it sharp and bitter, "tell us your grievance."

"It is not a grievance," Kaushika answers quietly. "It is a duty."

He gestures to the rest of us from the hermitage, and we retreat. The other sages sit down as well, and Kaushika takes a seat in front of them. Anirudh, Romasha, Parasara, Eka, and I are all but forgotten. A look I have never seen before enters Kaushika's face: part yearning, part hope, part anger. His breathing slows even as I watch his aura become stronger. I understand enough of mortal magic to know what he is doing—silently filling himself with as much of his power as possible, radiating his influence out in waves. The other sages blink. Even Vashishta cocks his head, stroking his beard and listening. The silence is so strong that I can hear the quiet hum of magic emanating from the gathering, like an undercurrent of electricity.

"I will not waste your time, great sages," Kaushika says quietly. "I have already written to you informing you of everything I have found. For years, the three realms have suffered Indra's tyranny. How long ago was it that you yourself cursed him, Rishi Gautama, for what he attempted with your own wife? Nary a few hundred years have passed. You thought to teach the storm lord a lesson, yet even though you stripped him of his manhood, he simply found a way to regrow it."

Gautama nods slowly, fingering one of his bead necklaces. His lined face draws into a frown, and I think with mingled horror and wonder, *One*. One of the rishis at least is persuaded by Kaushika's words.

Kaushika's gaze moves to the next. "And you, Sage Agastya," he says. "When the battle between Indra and the Maruts occurred, you had to break from your own meditation to negotiate peace. Yet the lord of heaven did not listen until you prayed to Shiva to intervene, knowing Indra would destroy the world in his arrogance. Do you truly think he is worthy?"

Agastya's forehead crinkles. It is clear that Kaushika has made this argument to him before, and that is perhaps why the rishi has been so closely allied with Kaushika all along. *Two*, I think. My breathing grows shallow. If Kaushika convinces them all that Indra needs to be punished, it could mean war unlike any the realms have seen in recent times.

"As for you, Sage Vashishta"—Kaushika transfers his gaze to the bearded man, who watches him, eyes cold—"did you not once tell me that my own path to enlightenment was corrupted? Yet where would we be if it weren't for the meadow I created?"

A silence breathes with his words.

Agastya and Gautama turn to look at Vashishta. His face is unreadable. For a long moment, he studies Kaushika, then in a glance so swift that I wonder if I am imagining it, his eyes flicker to me. I inhale sharply.

"The meadow, yes," Vashishta says, inscrutable. "You wrote to us saying that is where you sent the halahala. Then the poison truly was sent to your hermitage?" His question takes in our entire group this time. One by one, we nod.

Agastya and Gautama exchange glances. Vashishta nods and steeples his hands, then places them on his lap. He closes his eyes. I wonder what he is seeing behind his lids. Kaushika can certainly do things with a snap of his fingers. Perhaps the rishi is performing magic even now, unbeknownst to us.

Sage Gautama clears his throat. "If what you say is true," he says, "then Indra has gotten out of hand. It seems like in every age he must be taught a lesson somehow."

Kaushika smiles in satisfaction. He opens his mouth to speak, but Vashishta holds up a hand. "Not so fast," the sage says, eyes still closed. "I would hear from his students. They may agree with Sage Kaushika's summation, but do they know *all* of his reasons?"

His eyes open and rove over us. The other sages look curiously toward us too, and Kaushika watches, unspeaking.

"We have seen Indra's corruption, guruji," Romasha says, bowing. "A yogi who would be here today would tell you herself were she not ill because of Indra's halahala poisoning."

The others murmur their agreement, and I drop my gaze, nodding, but it is not enough.

"You, daughter." Vashishta's voice rings out. "Do you feel the same? I sense turmoil in your heart."

I lift my eyes, but it is not Vashishta I see. It is Kaushika. Younger perhaps by *centuries* when compared to all these men, he nevertheless sits tall, his eyes unfathomable. He does not move, not even a breath, and I think of what he wants me to say. I think of Rambha and her instruction, of the reason I was brought here to this man, of what I have been sent to do. I should defend Indra, but I feel paralyzed by indecision.

*I only wanted for you to be true to yourself,* Kaushika said to me once, and I choke because of how simple that edict is, how hard the demand. He watches me, as do the sages, and I try to clear my troubled mind, my breath coming out painfully shallow.

I do not want to seduce Kaushika. Not in the way I have been sent to do. But I do not want war, either, or the destruction of my home,

the death of my sisters, and the desecration of my kin. I do not want
to betray Lord Indra, he who has been my anchor for all my life. Despite everything I have heard, everything I have seen, how can I wish
harm on the lord when his glory and splendor have surrounded me all
my life? In my mind's eye, I see Amaravati's radiance, the delight and
joy that suffuse it because of *Indra*. Kaushika can dismiss the stories
of the lord's heroism as actions of the past, but I have seen Indra's
kindness too, in the way he attends to the celestials' needs, in healing
injured gandharvas and nurturing the golden horses in the stables, in
tilling Amaravati's lands each year with his own hands to renew the
flow of amrit. I know what Kaushika wants me to say. Can I say those
words, even to escape his wrath?

Vashishta's forehead crinkles at my silence. "Tell me, daughter,"
the sage asks again. "Do *you* believe Indra should be taught a lesson?"

I am shaking like a leaf. My eyes lower in anguish, tears filling my
eyes. "No," I whisper. "I think the lord should be understood."

It is one honest sentence.

It damns everything.

The mortals from the hermitage whip around to face me, their
mouths falling open. Accusation bleeds from their eyes, that I should
say this now when Kalyani lies in a coma, that I should betray
Kaushika when I have been so intimate with him. Romasha looks
furious, rage and suspicion contorting her features. Anirudh's wid-
ened gaze darts between me and Kaushika, horrified and confused.
But Kaushika himself remains unmoving. His eyes do not flicker
from me.

Vashishta smiles. "Interesting strategy, Sage Kaushika. To bring a
disciple here who does not agree with what you are attempting. But
perhaps you bring her here to show that you do indeed have some
wisdom. To not simply surround yourself with lackeys but with those
who would oppose you, too, and bring you to heel."

"I bring her here because she deserves to be here," Kaushika says evenly. "But you are not wrong, rishi. She *does* challenge me, more than any other. I bring her here to show you that I have heard the arguments for Indra. I even respect them to a degree. Yet my mind is made up, and especially after the halahala, I am hopeful your own wisdom shows you the necessity of my actions."

His words are reassuring, but the indifferent tone in which he utters them raises my panic. I cannot read him, but I know that if he begins to hate me, something within me will wither and die.

Vashishta stands up. "The necessity of your actions?" he repeats coldly. He faces Kaushika, and suddenly it is as though there is no one else in the tent but these two men. "The halahala is concerning, and the rest of the sages and I shall plead with Shiva to take it away, since you yourself have failed to do so." Kaushika flinches at that, but Vashishta fixes Kaushika with his gleaming eyes. "Your *meadow*, however, is an abomination."

Kaushika jumps to his feet, and the other sages rise slowly, wariness in their movements.

"How can you say that?" Kaushika challenges. "After what I have told you. After the attack on my own hermitage."

"Precisely," Vashishta says. "Your hermitage. Your past. *Your vow.*" The last words are a whip, and Kaushika recoils.

"My vow has little to do with this."

"Then you have told them about what you intend with the meadow?" Vashishta sneers. "You have told them what they are part of, what they are building karma for instead of seeking enlightenment?"

Kaushika lifts his chin. "They know the meadow is a safe haven."

"Ah, yes, *safe*, because the great Sage Kaushika is defying the evil god Indra." The older rishi laughs, and the sound is like rocks crashing. "You, daughter," he says, glancing at me once again. "You are teaching him about reconciliation, are you not? The path of the God-dess? How well are you teaching him, if he still insists on this?"

I tremble where I stand. How does he know this? Does he also know I said those words only to shatter the ascetic path of the yogis? Or has he guessed at my relationship with Kaushika? Vashishta is so much older than Agastya and Gautama; he is ancient when compared to Kaushika. I am an infant in front of him, and as a sage, he pierces the veil of maya to see beyond into reality. My vision blurs. I tremble so hard that it is as if a chill has overtaken me. He will incinerate me where I stand, and if he doesn't, then Kaushika will, simply to return to the Mahasabha's good graces, simply to save face when I have de-ceived and betrayed him so.

"Leave her out of this," Kaushika snaps. He stalks over to stand next to me. "She has nothing to do with this."

Vashishta simply ignores him. He moves toward me as well, and his hands reach up to my shoulders. I gaze up to him through my ter-rified tears, unable to resist, too dazzled by his aura and power. Even Kaushika feels diminished, though he is standing right next to me.

"I will not spill your secrets," the older man says softly to me. "But think of what role you intend to play in this, child. You are here as a sage-in-training, are you not? Think of who you truly want to be."

He releases me abruptly and steps back. Vashishta nods to the other two sages, who have been silent. "We are finished here," he says to them.

He makes to leave the tent, and I am still too disoriented to accept relief when Kaushika draws himself up to his full height. "You will not dismiss me, Vashishta," he growls coldly. "You *will* hear me."

"You dare—" Vashishta begins.

"Oh, I dare," Kaushika replies, and his eyes blaze with fire and anger. The air warps around him, darkness and shadows that splinter across the cloth of the tent. Light grows between the shadows, like shooting stars ripping the skies. The auras of all of us diminish, and there is only Kaushika, brilliant and beautiful and frightening like a deva himself.

I shrink back, horrified.

Because in that moment I can truly see his fury, his hate, the shadows I have always known lurk within him now erupting with his magic. I see not the sage with control over himself but the prince he once was, bred into power and rule. I see not the man I have come to know but a stranger, with a temper and revulsion so strong that suddenly I realize this is the very same man who likely killed my sisters, a man who would destroy Indra if allowed to. These sages—and I, myself—are the only things standing between him and heaven's total destruction.

My hand flies to my mouth in shock, and even Romasha and Anirudh are stunned. I know from their expressions that they have never seen Kaushika this way. Eka and Parasara cower back, and the other sages watch warily, none of them reacting.

The silence holds a mirror up to Kaushika's temper.

His eyes widen, and suddenly the magic leaves him. His face grows horrified, and without another word, he whips around and leaves the tent, every muscle in his body screaming he be left alone.

The moment breaks. I know it is over. With this display of uncontrolled magic, Kaushika has lost what little support he had at the Mahasabha. He could have perhaps convinced Agastya and Gautama, but provoked by Vashishta, he has lost it all.

Anirudh and Romasha utter soft cries, but instead of following Kaushika, the mortals from the hermitage hover near the other sages, begging for forgiveness for their leader, asking for clemency. I look up to see Vashishta studying me, a world of meaning in his eyes. His words reverberate in my skull. Suddenly I see myself through his calculating gaze—an immortal in disguise, claiming to train as a sage, caught between defending the man who has killed her sisters and is willing to attack her home, and a god-king who has sent her to her death, who expects nothing but obedience.

Are these truly my choices? Am I condemned to protect those who will only hurt me, who are so mistaken in their own way, committed to not listening to reason? And what does that make *me*, to give myself to men like that—whether Kaushika or Lord Indra?

I cannot take this confrontation with myself any longer. I flee the tent behind Kaushika to get away from Vashishta's knowing gaze.

# CHAPTER 19

I do not intend to chase after Kaushika, but my feet track the aura of his magic on their own, following the strong afterimage that burns on the leaves and stones. I weave through birdsong and breeze, wondering at how this forest seems so peaceful even though it has witnessed such fury. My wild prana surges in me, a river of radiance, and I meet it in my mind, trying to capture some of its peace.

It takes me nearly a half hour, but when I finally stumble upon Kaushika, it is within the trees by a small pond. Rocks encircle the pond, a smattering of gleaming sunlight, the tinkling of a nearby brook. I expect to see him by the grass nearby, meditating to calm himself, yet Kaushika contemplates not the beauty in front of him but a strange stone obelisk rising from the forest floor, almost as tall as he is. He glances toward me, hearing my approach, but his eyes are devoid of any expression.

"My greatest shame," he murmurs, nodding at the obelisk. "A reminder of what a loss of my temper can mean."

There is something eerily familiar about this stone column here in the woods like a shrine to a forest deity lost to time. A deep magic strums in it, pulling at my tether, reminding me that immortality can come in many forms, just like magic itself. I do not ask Kaushika to explain what he means, and he doesn't volunteer either. But he turns to me and his face is hard.

He is bare-chested, and I know he has washed himself at the pond, trying to contain his anger. Perhaps he has even prayed for peace of mind. Beads of water linger on him, and his hair is undone from its topknot, still damp. Waves of heat radiate off him, showing how futile this attempt at calm has been.

"I am still angry," he says, confirming this. "You should not be here."

My heart pounds like a battle drum. I want to tell him that his anger does not scare me, but it would be a lie. Still, it is my fear that gives me momentum. I reach out to him and touch his arm. I expect to be scalded, so hot is his aura, but his skin is cooled by the water, and my fingertips trail up his forearm to his bicep, until I feel the pulse on his neck thrumming below my thumb. Slowly I begin to stroke the tense muscles of his neck. Kaushika does not stop me, but neither does he react.

"If you are angry with me for what I said . . ." I begin hesitantly.

"Yes, I am angry with you, though it is not rational," he says, frowning. "I brought you to the Mahasabha knowing I have not convinced you about Indra and his involvement in the halahala. That was my decision, and I stand by it. Nothing you said changed anything anyway. These events were predestined, set on course with my own actions. Vashishta had made his mind up before the gathering, and I worsened it all with my loss of temper. Even Agastya, who has been willing to listen to me so far, will not countenance my audacity now. Yet I cannot waver from my path, even for them."

"Your path, or your *vow*?" I ask slowly.

"My vow," he affirms, lips thinning. "One that Indra obstructs. I have not told you about it."

I shake my head, and he exhales roughly, as though speaking of it is painful. He takes my hand away from his neck and puts some distance between us. His mouth draws into a frown, and he turns to stare at the water. In any other man, I would expect the tension to reveal itself in nervous movements, perhaps pacing the small clearing, perhaps fists slowly clenching.

Yet Kaushika holds himself utterly still, and it is this stillness that mirrors his strain. He is silent for so long that I wonder if he has forgotten my presence, if he intends to tell me any more. I stir, grass crunching under me, and he looks up at the sound. His mouth pinches—but I know him enough now to see it is not for me; it is for what he is about to say.

"You remember what I told you before," he begins, and his words are stiff. "There was only one king who responded to my pleas for help when Lord Indra abandoned my kingdom."

"I remember," I say quietly.

Kaushika nods and looks away again. "His name was Satyavrat. It means one who has taken a vow of truth."

Again he pauses, and I watch the shadows on his face. I imagine him, a child-prince, suddenly faced with defending his people. I think of him and the choices that brought him to this moment now, the choices that brought *me* here to be the one to learn of his story.

Kaushika's eyes glint, reflecting the water. "King Satyavrat knew that in helping me and my people, he invited Indra's wrath. But the king was powerful in his own right. Though he was no sage, he was fueled by his dedication to dharma and the righteous path. He was a man who lived the values of his name, beloved within his kingdom, though he was no less a politician than any other royal. His magic was great, and he knew that should Indra move against him, the other devas would protest. He knew the risks of angering Indra, but he took them—for me and my people, and for the future of his own kingdom. It is why I have never felt resentment for his desire to fold my nation into his own. What use do I have for such petty emotions? He was honorable, and it was only my good fortune that brought him to me."

Each word is taut like a nocked arrow. I raise my hand, trying to ease his anger with my touch again, but magic sparks between his fingertips, molten fire that races over his body. My hand drops. I dare not touch him, not right now.

"For years, there was no retaliation from heaven," Kaushika continues, and a soft scoffing sound huffs out from him. "We all thought that Indra, caught in his drinking and his dancing, simply forgot to enact revenge or chose to ignore us, as gods are wont to do. I left to follow my path to Shiva. I thought Satyavrat would be safe, his dynasty shielded. None of us accounted for the patience of the devas."

Kaushika pauses to withdraw a small parchment from his pocket. He does not show it to me, but I recognize it nevertheless. The very same letter folded over and over again, one that I saw when I broke into his hut what seems like so long ago.

"Satyavrat's sons wrote to me when the king passed." Kaushika's voice is deathly quiet. He tucks the letter back into his pocket, unread. "The missive came to me when I was training in Agastya's hermitage. The king's sons performed the last rites as per their tradition, asking Indra to permit their father's soul to rise to heaven. Yet despite Satyavrat's karma of goodness in this life, despite his piety, Indra denied him his right to a peaceful afterlife. The princes prayed to the other deities; they even prayed to Indra's queen, Shachi, to intervene. Yet Satyavrat's soul still wanders the mortal realm, punished to find no peace, unable to reside in swarga or become part of the cycle of rebirth." Kaushika's eyes flash as he finally looks toward me. "The sages would think that my meadow is a crime against nature, but what about Indra's own conduct? Is that not a crime? How can I rest until Satyavrat does? I vowed that I would see him ascend to heaven, come what may. It is the one thing that defines my tapasya now, the one thing all my magic is aimed towards. Indra needs to be tamed, and I will be the harbinger of his ruin."

The words are so dispassionate, yet so angry, that I recoil. Indra is not perfect, but never before from any mortal or immortal have I heard such venom against my king. Not even from Anirudh and the rest.

"This is unwise," I whisper. "Indra is the lord of heaven. He is the protector of amrit, the very essence of immortal life. He has a sacred duty to protect Amaravati, and it is his *duty* to do what he believes to be right."

"And it is *my* duty as a sage to do what *I* think is right," Kaushika answers. His stillness finally leaves him, and he begins to pace. "What do you think I should do, Meneka? Simply behave like the other sages intent on their impassivity? *You* are the one who told me about participation. About the path of the Goddess. How can you believe that this is not my fight?"

"The other sages are older than you. They have been rishis longer. If all of them counsel that this challenge is wrong, then how can you dismiss them so easily?"

"I am not dismissing them. *They* have dismissed me. I know you are devoted to Indra, but I am asking you to see what you can with your own eyes. I am asking you to think for yourself."

"I *am* thinking for myself, and I know that this path is going to only end in your destruction. Indra has one of the most powerful weapons in the universe. His vajra is stronger than a diamond, sharper than a thunderbolt. Many have come and gone, trying to challenge him on his throne—and what you do here—"

"It is not his throne I am interested in," Kaushika interrupts, and anger fills him again as he paces. "I have no patience to explain all this to you, if you do not already see why this is necessary. I do not deny your importance to me, Meneka; every one of us needs a counselor who would oppose us. It is why I brought you to the Mahasabha today, but perhaps the timing of it was unwise. Advise me a different time. Today, I am fraught, and I have no disposition to listen. I have already demonstrated I have no reserve."

I step closer. "I like you with no reserve."

His eyes gleam. He glances at me over his shoulder, pausing in his stride, and his look is full of heat and promises and fury. "A foolish thing to say, if you only knew what was on my mind. Do not push. Now is not the time."

"Why?" I challenge. "Are you scared?"

"No. But perhaps you should be. Do you understand what you are asking?"

"Do you understand what I am offering? What will you truly look like when you're free? I would like to see that, but your imagined feud with Indra blinds you. Maybe *you* are the one hiding from yourself. How ironic that a lesson you tried to teach me, you yourself have failed. How tragic, a yogi afraid of the idea of liberation."

Laughter erupts from him, grim and raw. "Provocation, Meneka? You'll have to do better than that. If I reacted that easily, do you think I would be called a sage?"

A torrent of curious challenge goes through me that he should call me out on my plot this way. That he should see the obvious manner in which I am trying to distract him. *No easy mark*, Rambha's voice whispers in my head, but instead of fear, I feel excitement that he is *not* a mark, not anymore, that he is here, fully, as am I. A current rushes through me, hot and tempting, and though I turned the conversation this way to diffuse some of his rage, I suddenly want to see him unleashed with me.

"Sage," I say quietly. "Nonreacting, wise, fully in control. That is what it means, does it not?"

"You know what it means," he replies. "Do you think I find your feigned ignorance amusing?"

He turns around fully to face me, his back resting against a tree trunk. His arms cross over his bare chest, and he raises an eyebrow. I utter a small laugh, never taking my gaze off him.

"Feigned?" I say. "We are *all* ignorant, rishi, even the wisest of us in some ways. Who can claim utter knowledge of everything? Even Shiva closes his eyes to the world in order to see beyond the veil of prakriti's illusion. Even he deliberately wraps himself in *one* kind of ignorance."

Kaushika blinks, then his eyes narrow. He doesn't say anything but does not move, either, as I slowly walk up to him, each step emphasizing my curves. A thrill of terror laces through me, to speak so blatantly to him, skirting the line of discovery and danger now when he is angry, now when I have betrayed him in front of the other sages with my defense of Lord Indra. Still, I come closer, and his gaze flickers to my hips just for an instant. That is the only indication of his lust, but it is enough.

A lazy smile forms on my face. I stop when I am a handsbreadth away from him, but I do not touch him. Instead, I lean forward and slowly place one arm by the side of his head, inches from his neck. My other hand curls gently, not quite a mudra but not far off either. Magic rushes through my body, and in this moment I cannot tell if it is Amaravati's golden power or the wild prana of tapasya. I am so close to creating an illusion that my fingers quiver.

A muscle ticks in his jaw, but already I can tell the heat of his anger is cooling into amusement and curiosity. "Are you calling me ignorant?" he asks softly.

"Would you like to choose a different word?" I reply.

My words are barely a whisper and his head dips down, his mouth inches from my own, to capture my breath. The movement brings his skin in contact with my hand, and I startle, not expecting it, but Kaushika's lips curve into a smile. His eyes glint, and suddenly I cannot tell which one of us is in control. My breathing grows faster, my chest rising and falling.

"Oh, there are many words," he says quietly. "I'm not sure *you* should say them, though."

His hand comes up to my own, though he does not touch me. He simply moves his palm back in a smooth, lazy gesture, and the sleeves of my kurta fall back, goose pimples rising on my skin. It is a small thing he does, to control this without making any contact, but my eyes widen.

I lift my chin. We are still not touching, but the air between us *crackles*, the heat of him sizzling with the water of my own power. I feel parched, and my tongue flashes out to wet my lips. Kaushika watches me, and his own tongue mirrors the movement.

My thighs clench and I swallow. I am finding it hard to keep track of the conversation, but I cannot let him win this easily. The both of us know what we're doing, this quiet challenge to see which one of us is going to give in first, which one of us is going to reveal our secrets fully, or relent when it comes to battle. It is dangerous, this game, but I move closer. The fabric of my kurta brushes against his bare, muscled chest. Kaushika inhales deeply, his eyes never leaving me. His pulse quickens as his breathing becomes a beat uneven.

"If you disapprove of what I say," I ask softly, "why do you keep me close to you?"

His other hand rises toward the crown of my head, and of its own accord my topknot unravels, hair cascading down my shoulders. I blink, not understanding, but then as he drops his hand I see the crescent comb—*his* crescent comb—spinning between his fingers. A sudden gust of wind, either natural or created by him, surges around us. Strands of my hair sweep against his cheeks.

His eyes gleam in hot desire, and slowly he brushes my hair back from his face. His fingers twirl around the locks, his touch so gentle that it might as well still be the wind.

"Because I need you," he says quietly. "Except for me, you are the most powerful within the hermitage. Despite how much prana you use, it continues to shine inside you, barely requiring replenishment."

I tilt my head and study him between my lashes. "Then you intend to use me."

"I intend to use you," he agrees. "If I can convince you." He moves slightly, once, and I feel that male part of him stroking my belly, the feeling so very subtle that I cannot tell if it is his movement or the magic still crackling between us.

"Tell me," he whispers. "Are you convinced?"

My mind reels. My legs tremble, and dampness grows between my thighs. The heat from him leaches into me, or perhaps it is my own heat. I do not know; I can't make sense. The pure thrill of our positions reversed rushes through me. That he should ask me this when I am the one trapping him with my body. That he understands me in a manner hardly anyone does and perhaps always has. We are here holding this moment close yet not holding each other. What would giving in to him mean? Would it be so awful, when we have already been intimate? I want him so desperately that all my own rules feel meaningless. I made decisions to never get involved with a mark, but I made them for others, not him. He—*he*—is not any *other*; he is . . . closer.

His mouth forms in a smile, and I know that I am going to break. That I am too enraptured to play like this anymore. The realization torments me, shattering my own bonds with myself, and a rough, outraged sound bursts through me, because of how little I care, and how I know I will have to come to terms with this later—but not now. Not now.

My movement is harsh. With one hand, I capture his chin between my sharpened nails. With the other, I pull him forcefully toward me. My tongue flashes out to lick the hollow of his dimples, and a strangled sound grows in his throat as I begin to strew kisses over his jaw, down his neck, licking the dampness still lingering on his chest, nipping at his skin none too gently. His hand reaches to cup my bottom, but I thrust him back into the tree trunk, and he grunts, anger and shock flashing in his eyes, combined with deep hunger. The look on his face is pure torture, and sweat coats me, surging with his heat.

"I told you I enjoy commanding," I say, my voice clipped.

"Is that what it will take?" he breathes. "To get you to see my point of view?"

"I make no promises."

"I expect none," he says, amusement in his eyes. He leans closer, and his hand drifts to my wrist to stroke it. "Go ahead, Meneka. Command me."

My control slips and I surge up on my toes. Our mouths collide, and another growl escapes him, like relief and frustration. He grips me, fingers tight in my hair, almost painful against my scalp. My hands are everywhere, over his chest, grazing his hard stomach, tugging at his hair. This is unlike the first kiss. This is raw and immediate, and his anger pulses beneath his magic, both of them curling through me, enflaming me.

Power replaces the blood in my veins—and my own magic sings like a hymn. I am certain he can hear it too, the waterfall rush overtaking every other sound, the *chanting* of both our powers braiding.

He lifts me easily, and I wrap my legs around his waist, never breaking the kiss. My back arches and the tips of my breasts press against his chest. Kaushika groans, his tongue skating into mine. I bite his lower lip, and he clutches me harder, moving his body. My nails score the bare skin of his back—so jaggedly that I am certain I have drawn blood. He gasps, then pumps his hips harder, rocking the both of us almost painfully into the tree trunk, and I know that there will be no going back from here, this is it, we will both cross a line, but the hunger in me is too much to ignore, and I do not know which one of us has been seducing the other all this time—

"I beg your pardon," a small voice says.

I freeze, then jerk away immediately, but Kaushika does not release me.

His eyes are heavy, his pupils dilated. His chest rises up and down, and for a long moment he only stares at me, fingers still tight enough to leave marks on my skin. I feel the rumbling in his chest, like he is about to rage at being interrupted, and my eyes widen as I realize I have not truly understood his potential. That this is but a small taste.

I stare at him.

Slowly, taking all the time in the world, he sets me down. He waits until I am steady on my feet, until I have adjusted my clothes and have retrieved the crescent comb to retie my topknot.

Only then does his gaze move to Romasha, who stands amidst the trees, her eyes averted, a blush on her cheeks.

"The sages are leaving," she whispers to no one in particular. "Perhaps you should offer apologies and try to repair some damage of the Mahasabha, guruji."

Kaushika grunts. Glancing at me, he strides over to where his kurta lies. He pulls it on himself and reties his hair in a deft topknot. In an instant, he has returned to being a rishi, but underneath his controlled movements roars the hunger for the release we both seek.

"We will stay the night," he says to Romasha. "I must discuss our plans with you and Anirudh before we head back. Tell the others they can return to the hermitage now if they wish it."

He squeezes my hand, and his mouth opens, on the verge of saying something—but he shakes his head. With a rueful, apologetic glance at me, he leaves the way Romasha came.

She does not follow, not immediately. Her face is withdrawn. I know pining when I see it, but with what I'm doing kissing him, feeling his hands on my body, the impressions of him still stamped on my skin . . . Who am I doing this for? I wonder again about her feelings for Kaushika and their relationship. Guilt swallows all my excuses. I have no words for her.

Romasha gives me a weak smile as if to say, *He chose you. What is there to say?* Then with a small nod, she disappears behind Kaushika.

I pull myself to my full height. *Enough.* It is time for a decision.

I DO NOT BOTHER RETURNING TO THE CLIFFTOP.

This time when I call for an emissary, Rambha materializes a few feet away from me by the obelisk statue. She has been waiting for my summons. Perhaps she was in the mortal realm already. Her beauty still staggers me, and I cannot help but note the sensuous green sari tightened around her waist, the spicy star-anise of her skin, the large doe eyes that watch me even as she moves closer. Still, it is sobering to realize that she does not affect me the way she once did. Only a few weeks earlier, we were on the path to becoming something more. What I have with Kaushika, and what I've learned about myself, seems to have obliterated any possibility of that.

A part of me feels sorrow at this, and my forehead creases as she glimmers with the blessings of heaven. Yet it is a sorrow not of a thing lost but of understanding finally how unrealistic my dream with her had always been. Suddenly I can see why I never made a clear suggestion to her despite all the opportunities. Did my mind always know what my heart refused to believe—that Rambha and I were ill-fated? I watch her as she approaches, noticing a beaded parcel slung around her waist like a belt, but I do not embrace her.

She does not attempt to touch me either. Light coats her like armor, and her eyes are unreadable, almost cold, like she senses the change in me. "Well, Meneka?" she asks quietly.

I raise my chin. "I know why Kaushika hates Indra. I know the manner of his challenge."

As clearly as I can, I tell Rambha everything this time about Kaushika's history as a prince, his vow to send King Satyavrat to heaven, the incident with the halahala, even the events at the Mahasabha. I try to be as dispassionate as a sage, reporting only the facts, but I wonder how much of my true feelings regarding Kaushika I am hiding from her. I cannot come to tell her about my intimacy with him—not her who, despite her decree that I should do exactly that, would never understand *why* I did it. My voice is hoarse by the time I finish, but Rambha simply stares into the water, not saying a word. I stiffen my resolve and speak without flinching.

"If Indra wants to end this," I say, "then all he has to do is allow this mortal king's soul into heaven. I am certain Kaushika will stop if the lord only relents, and we can put this behind us. It will all be over, and we can achieve this without any escalation. Lord Indra would not be in any danger, nor would Amaravati, and nor would Kaushika. The sages of the Mahasabha will be pleased—and for all we know, grow more favorable towards Indra in their own hearts."

At that, Rambha jerks toward me. The rest of my words wither in my throat. I don't move a muscle as she begins to circle me, as though seeing me for the first time. I try hard not to move or show my discomfort, even though the aura around her grows spiky, menacing. It is ironic that in this moment of uncertainty I am relying on my training from the hermitage.

She finally stops in front of me, her face inscrutable. "You kissed him. I feel his touch on you."

I nod once. Tightly.

"And what changed your mind, after all these years of abstaining with a mark? Surely not my instruction, if you make such utterances."

I still don't reply, but a muscle in my jaw ticks and it is enough for her. She knows my expressions too well.

Her mouth thins into a smile, and her brow arches cruelly. "Ah," she says, breathing out a humorless laugh. "So you would not break your foolish rule for the lord, but you would do it for your own desires. Is this also why you think the lord should debase himself to this Kaushika, negotiating with this odious mortal, letting *him* decide who should enter the lord's own home? How easily you have forgotten who you owe your devotion to."

I straighten myself, sudden anger cascading in me. "I have forgotten nothing. My devotion has kept me believing in Indra's innocence regarding the halahala. It is my devotion that demands I find a solution, that I speak the truth."

"The truth?" Rambha's laughter rings out, sharp and pitiless. "You know nothing of the truth, foolish girl. You were sent here to do your duty, not to question the very deva that gives you your magic. Look at what can occur—what is already occurring—in Amaravati because of your precious Kaushika."

Her wrists curl into unknown mudras, and suddenly I am back in the City of Immortals. Planets churn and stars glow over and under me. A wave of homecoming washes through me, and I blink, my love for the city taking over any other thought, but before I can truly inhale, the air turns to ash. The great mansions of the city wither, and the golden sparking dust turns gray, fizzling into smoke before righting itself again. In the change of the dust's nature, I see its effort. Amaravati is dying, and with it so is Indra. I stare in horror around me, spinning in small circles. I am in his throne room again, and instead of a lord hale and handsome, there is only a terrified deity, contemplating his own demise. Queen Shachi raves, growing incandescent and bitter, and Indra becomes more desperate, the wine flowing freely as he and the other devas attend one conference after another to discuss the growing irreverence in the mortal realm.

Above, the stars whirl in a passage of days, of months threatening to become merciless years, their alignment falling into that of the Vajrayudh, when Indra will become weaker. For millennia, Indra has survived, an essence of water evolving into a god. Will this next Vajrayudh destroy him completely? I hear this thought, and it is my own, but it is Rambha's, too, and I blink, Amaravati whirling around me, chaos in my heart.

I know that this is an illusion. That Rambha is carving all this just so I can feel what I'm feeling. Yet I know, too, that there is no artifice to this. The images are pulled from Rambha's memories and her fears of what will come to pass. Not all of them are true—not yet—but angry though she is, she is not lying; she is merely afraid of what will occur should Kaushika not be annihilated.

I sway on my feet, unable to breathe, willing my knees not to buckle. The images of Amaravati rush one into another, damning me, punishing me, weakening me. The orchards, the dance halls, the festival grounds, all of them decay and burn. I cannot think straight; Amaravati merges with the hermitage in my mind, and my will crumbles in the face of Rambha's magic. Nausea rises in me at witnessing the destruction of my city so clearly when I have been so bereft of it, when my desire to save it and return to it one day has not diminished, no matter what I share with Kaushika.

I can look no more, and my hands come up to cover my eyes. "This cannot be," I whisper. "I—I—Kaushika cannot do this. I will make him see reason."

I feel Rambha dispelling the illusion with a subsiding of her power. "Reason?" she scoffs. "You have other tools at your disposal, and you would waste time with reason when I have just shown you what will occur?"

I shake my head, denying her words. "It *has* to be reason," I stammer. "With Kaushika—he is a sage—reason is the jnani's path, an *intellect*'s path, and that is what he responds to—" My voice chokes. I look up at her through tear-filled eyes. "What about the halahala?" I ask desperately. "Surely you must want to know who has done it?"

"It is enough for me that *Indra* has not," she replies. "*That* is the mission. *That* is devotion. To quote a sage's path at me—" Rambha's mouth twists with disgust. "You truly have forgotten who you are. Your sisters are *dead* because of this man. Have you forgotten that too?"

"We—we do not know this for sure," I stammer. "The Kaushika I have come to know . . . I cannot believe he did that to Nanda and Magadhi and Sundari. Just like I cannot believe that Indra was behind the halahala. Rambha, they must follow the same reasoning."

"Then you truly have strayed far beyond redemption," she spits out. "If you think the two are the same, then you are lost to all sense, dancing around the truth."

My mouth trembles in hurt and anger. "And what *is* the truth?"

"That you care for this Kaushika," she says. "That you have fallen in love with him."

The blunt declaration is so bizarre that I am shocked into speechlessness. My tears dry. A denial bursts to my lips. *I am not in love. I simply understand the mortals better now.* I want to hurl this at her with coldness and certainty.

Instead, I freeze.

Because I cannot lie to Rambha.

And I cannot lie to myself.

She's right. It's ridiculous that her icy words have finally made me see it when there was so much other evidence, but this finally is the truth I have been looking for.

I've come to care for Kaushika.

I've fallen in love with him.

My eyes grow wide, and a dozen questions flood in me. Is it truly love when I am sent here on a mission from Indra, with little choice about what I am to do? Is it love when Kaushika has responded to my despair, when he doesn't even know who I truly am? When *I* do not know all of *him*? Freedom pounds in me with her declaration, a secret finally out in the open. A prison clutches that freedom, at what this love means and what it is showing me about myself.

Rambha watches the churn of emotions on my face—the horror, confusion, and sorrow. Her own expression grows pitying. "I knew you weren't prepared for this," she mutters. "This is why I volunteered to do this mission instead of having you sent. You are too young. Too inexperienced. Too naïve. Meneka, sages have intrinsic power. This is why they are such daunting enemies to seduce. It is not just their magic that rivals ours, it is their ability to veer us from our own path that truly makes them treacherous. I thought I warned you. I thought you were stronger. That I gave you enough reason to want to return."

Her last words are nearly a whisper. I glance up at her, and just for a second, I catch a flash of deep hurt on her face. It sends a pang through me. I have seen that expression on her before. I caused it when I accepted the mission.

Her lips tremble, and in my mind's eye I remember the shade of a promise she gave me. I feel the brush of her lips against mine. All the emotions it stirred in me had kept me hopeful for days, but was she simply being Indra's most devoted apsara even then? During our last meeting, when she told me to lay with Kaushika . . . Did she seduce *me*?

"Was it real?" I ask quietly.

"Does it matter?" she shoots back. "For heaven's sake, Meneka, I told you to sleep with him, not love him. I thought you were wise enough to see the difference. I thought you were an *apsara*."

Her words score my skin like blades. My heart clenches in tight pain. I move slowly like I am taking ill. With effort, I curl my hand into a mudra: Heart's Desire, an attempt to know what shape it will take, to see if it will tell me my own mind. A faltering illusion forms at my fingertips, a broken butterfly that dissipates. I catch a sob in my throat, seeing my own longing for freedom in the creature, seeing how I am not ready for it, not *worthy* of it.

Rambha's mouth thins, watching the cracked illusion. "Your celestial magic is already suffering. You do not see that Kaushika is simply another seduction of the mortal realm. You have fallen for a man who would destroy you if he learnt of your true nature. You have said yourself how Kaushika is attempting to rile other sages against Indra, attempting to usurp Indra's rule in the lord's own city. You have his admission from his own lips. I thought you would be clearheaded, *rejoicing* that he is smitten by you and that you have nearly finished your mission, yet you stand there talking of *reason* when a single dance, a final few illusions, could cinch everything. You could get your freedom from future missions. You could come home, honored as a devi. You could become Indra's most celebrated apsara. Why do these things not matter more than this childish love?"

I lift my eyes to study hers. "Then your advice to me is to deceive Kaushika?"

Rambha meets my gaze levelly. "My advice is to think of what will happen should you disobey Indra."

Tears blur my sight. If I refuse to dance for Kaushika, Indra will exile me from Amaravati. He will force me from my home, my power no longer fueled by the city except in inconsequential drips that would barely make a full illusion. Without my magic, I would become a wraith, neither of the mortal realm nor of the immortal, a wisp on the wind, an unheard whisper, forgotten until I can prove my devotion to the lord again. For such an egregious blunder . . . what form would my redemption need to take?

And what if I do dance for Kaushika? My mission with Tara drove me to desperation. Knowing I have destroyed Kaushika, this man I now understand I love, will ruin me.

Rambha glitters at the edge of my vision, and I look up at her wretchedly.

"If you want peace," she says quietly, "you will seduce Kaushika using your magic the way you were meant to. I will have to report to the lord everything you have told me, and he might consider Kaushika's very actions at the Mahasabha an act of war. He will be compelled to attack him. Who do you think will win in such a battle?"

I do not have to think. I know the answer. Indra would win any battle if it occurred now. Kaushika is powerful, but he has no support from the other sages. He has only his hermitage, and after the halahala, everyone is sorely depleted, including Kaushika himself. He could renew his magic again, it's true, but that would take months of tapasya, if not years. What havoc would the lord of heaven wreak in that time? Already, Indra has tried to flood the hermitage, if Kaushika's account is true. The sage would not be able to keep himself safe, let alone any of the others. Sobs lock in my throat, and Rambha nods as though I have said all this aloud.

"If you want Kaushika to live," she says, her voice soft, "then you will use the full force of your power. You will carve such a deep illusion for him that it will last through his lifetime, that he never again thinks to trouble Indra. You will avert a battle from happening, and you will save both your lord and the man you love. And then you will come home to your freedom."

I stare at my hands, but they shake through the prism of my own tears. My mission, my emotion, my very identity trap me. I love this man, but what does that make me when he is so wrong? I cannot help but be devoted to Indra in my own way, a compulsion even I fail to fully understand. What does that make me, when my lord is cruel and unjust?

The truth is that regardless of Indra's injunction, I *want* to dance for Kaushika. I've wanted to since the first time I saw him. I want to control his desire, but more than that, I want to test it—to see if he *is* as strong as I am made to believe. What does that make *me*?

My hands tremble, the mudras I want to create unborn so far. The last time I was in Amaravati, I bent under the kalpavriksh in Indra's garden, seeking to stay true to myself. This is who I am, then. A fool, caught in this trap of my own making.

Rambha moves, and I blink rapidly. Tears fall down my cheeks and I watch her as she removes the beaded parcel belt from around her waist. She holds it out to me wordlessly, and I take it out of habit. I open the silk packages contained within only to see that she has brought me the same things she gave me when I first embarked on this mission: clothes I buried near the hermitage, which I told her about the last time, the jewels I disguised by the forest floor, and among them, a crown unlike any I have seen before sparkling on a small cushion.

I do not have the will to question her. She brought these to me before hearing my latest report. Whether she did this in order to please me, bearing me gifts, or to remind me of my duty matters little. She gives them to me now for only one reason—to *use* them.

My fingers brush over the crown, the only jewelry within these packages that did not accompany me from Amaravati. It is a simple crown wrought with the most delicate gold. It is too big for me, but even as I watch, it begins to shrink until it becomes exactly my size, a headpiece that would sit like a deva's halo, like sunlight made molten. The gold membranes of the crown feel liquid to the touch. They glint in a thousand colors, catching the moonlight and Rambha's jewelry, turning gold into turquoise, emerald to sapphire.

More power than I have ever felt before radiates from the ornament, filling me. The tug behind my navel grows into a sharp pull, telling me this is no ordinary circlet. This belongs to Indra.

I look up at Rambha, bitterness entering my mouth.

It is the same crown she once said she wanted to see on me.

"I won't tell you what to do," she says quietly. "But for your own sake, think of what you can live with for the rest of your immortal life, and what will haunt you forever. I will be back at dawn tomorrow to see how you have fared. Make the right choice, Meneka. Once I tell the lord everything you have told me, he will wish to act. He has been waiting to use his vajra to behead this mortal. This could be your last chance. *Kaushika's* last chance."

I open my mouth to speak, but she has already faded away on Amaravati's wind, and I am alone again in the forest.

For a long moment, I stare at the package in my hands, the circlet winking innocuously, bidding me to obey her and my lord. I close my eyes, trying to block its power, but the tug behind my navel is too strong, a tether and leash tying me to Indra.

Make my choice? There is no choice.

A shudder passes through me.

As though in a dream, I approach the pond and begin to undress, carefully folding my garments from the hermitage and stowing them behind the stone obelisk. I walk into the water, the coldness bringing goose bumps to my skin. A small part of me hopes that the chill will wake me up from the horror of what I am about to do, that it will clear my mind. But everything seems to occur in a frozen shard of nightmare. I bathe in the manner of the apsaras, praying to Lord Indra, cupping the water in my hands and pouring it over my head as I murmur, but the prayer is by rote; the words do not incite any devotion—not right now when I act out of coercion. Instead, my heart beats rapidly in terror and shame. The instant I create my first illusion, Kaushika will see me for who I am. He will despise me, he will destroy me, and I will be unable to do anything about it, lost in my chaos. And if I do not go through with this . . . if I do not attempt to seduce Kaushika now . . .

A choked sob builds in my throat as I imagine the vajra slicing his head from his body. Isn't life—even life as a thrall—better than no life at all? If I truly love him, isn't this the only way to save him? My face grows warm with tears, and I feel paralyzed, unable to think of an alternative.

Slowly, I emerge from the pond, my skin glistening. From the package Rambha brought, I remove the oils and the perfumes. I massage them into my hair and skin, each action slow, knowing that no matter what occurs, I will never do this again. A small mirror accompanies the cosmetics, but I cannot bear to look at myself, so without its assistance I line my eyes with kohl and paint my lips red with creamy hibiscus dye. I do not need the mirror; I can do these things in my sleep. The sob finally escapes me, for I know that what should be a move of empowerment is really just evidence of my shame.

When I remove the clothes from the package, my hands tremble hard enough to almost lose my grip on the silk. I don my blouse, and it hugs my breasts tightly, constricting me. I wrap the glinting silver sari around my waist, and though it is trapped moonlight, its texture delicate, I cannot breathe. Indra's presence chokes me, tightening with every ornament I place on myself. The pearl necklaces. The crystal armbands. The light-as-air jhumkas. At one time these reminders of Indra's own power would have given me joy and peace. Now everything is a leash, pulling me toward inevitability. Amaravati's power burgeons in me and my heart shrinks.

Celestial magic sparkles on my fingertips. It electrifies my skin.

I am a prisoner of my own making. I am a stream of starlight. I am ethereal, otherworldly, dreamlike.

The woods churn around me, responding to all the magic in the jewels. Leaves stir, the trees themselves creating their own music. Indra's circlet glimmers on my head, sinking into my hair. Kaushika's wooden comb presses against the circlet, and though my celestial magic is too powerful to compare with my prana magic, the wild prana waits too.

I use it now, uttering first a whispered call to Kaushika, then the chant for strength and movement. I draw the runes, and fallen logs lift silently from around the pond. They create a bridge that leads me to the center, where water solidifies into shining ice.

I do not feel the cold under my bare feet. I kneel at the center like an offering, breathing the forest in, bathed in moonbeams. I am a gleaming figure in the middle of this silent pond. I am a dream, a secret. Mudras tingle on my fingertips, wanting to form, but I hold them back. Not yet—I won't start my illusion yet.

Kaushika will be here soon. My call to him demanded urgency and privacy. Desperation beats its wings inside me, needing him to be close to me, but there is fear there too—for the both of us and our lives. At least, there will be no more deceptions. I will finally let him in on my secrets, with all my shame and glory. He will do what he will, just as I will do what I must.

I close my eyes, listening to my own heartbeat. I wait.

# CHAPTER 20

My eyes fly open when I scent the rosewood in the air. I know it is him; I would recognize Kaushika anywhere. Only a couple months, and he has already become as familiar to me as the rhythms of my own breath.

Still, I scan the trees when I do not see him—and I stare in shock at the silent transformation of the forest. The trees circling the pond are aglow with beams of light, resembling berries of golden dust, luscious fruit ripe and ready to be picked. Soft music rims the air—not a true melody but a *hum*, like the one that always exists at the hermitage. The breeze, the water lapping, the chirping of a distant animal . . . all are like notes to this silent song.

My own beauty enhances this strange magic. Rainbows glimmer off my jewelry, catching the moonshine, the chips of ice, the light of my own aura. They splay around me, their angles falling on my eyelashes and throat, illuminating my waist and my slightly parted mouth.

Slowly, I stand. Is this my doing? I have not begun any illusions, nor curled any mudras. I have not made any runes either, but I search inside me, and I see the golden tether of Amaravati braiding with my prana. Both my powers harmonize in a strange enchantment, and I realize that whatever has done this, it is not any simple combination of the two magics. In this moment of danger and destruction, power itself has made up its mind on what it must be. It is the same as what I used with the halahala, the mirrored force that reflected Kaushika back to me, a magic that exists far beyond my own ken.

Then I see him.

Standing on the shore opposite me, still dressed in the clothes from only a few hours ago.

Even from this distance I can tell that his face is unreadable.

The mission, Rambha's words, the chant I used to call him here— all come crashing back to me, weighing me down. The moment of wonder surrounding the magic evaporates. I stare at him, unable to say anything, unable even to move, terror making my heart pound. How long before he ends me? How long before I betray him? I should begin my dance, create my mudras, but I stand there, frozen, a statue made of silver and shimmer, watching him come closer.

He approaches the bridge I built. His own power and grace, his fluidity as he comes closer, overwhelm me, making my breathing uneven. He is almost upon me, and belatedly I raise my chin, trying hard not to tremble. He is only a whisper away, curiosity in his eyes, eyes that are clear of seduced lust, not a speck of the hollowness in them that I have come to expect from my marks.

"Meneka," he murmurs, and glances around us at the beams of light ricocheting off the trees. "Did you do this?"

I nod but say nothing.

"How?"

My eyes dart to the incandescent forest. "I—I don't know," I whisper. "I—I didn't do it deliberately."

Kaushika nods slowly as though in secret understanding of something, then utters a small, rueful smile. "I should know better than to ask you," he says quietly. "You are power incarnate. You are magic made flesh. You are glorious."

His words are everything I have wanted to hear, and though his gaze is clear, there is deep admiration there too, just as if he were a mark. He studies me, drinking all of me in, and I inhale deeply, trying to hold on to my path, my hands loose by my side, waiting to curl into mudras.

Kaushika rubs one end of my sari between a thumb and forefinger. "Where did you find such clothes?" he asks softly.

"You are not the only one to come from royalty," I choke out.

His mouth curves in an amused smile, but then his head snaps back up to meet my eyes and he finally notices me quivering. "You're cold," he says, frowning.

I shake my head. It is not the cold making my body shudder, but he is already clicking his fingers. Warmth swirls around us in spirals of steam, and suddenly we are cocooned in a comfortable heat. Through the eddying strands, I still see the forest beyond, glowing, but I know instinctively that we are ensconced in privacy, protected by his magic.

He tips my chin up with a knuckle. "Is all this for me?"

"Yes," I whisper.

"Why?"

*To save your life*, I think. *To save my city. To prove my devotion.* The words crash in my head in a haze of storm, so close to coming out, but in that instant as I stare into his eyes, another truth emerges, and I blurt out, "Because I want you. I have wanted you for a long time." *Because I love you*, I add silently, cutting myself off before I say something I cannot take back.

He is silent for so long that my fear returns again, making my heart pound.

What am I doing? I should be *dancing*. But the jewels from heaven weigh me down, and my own intentions blur in my mind, and he is still so unreadable, everything too much, and I can't breathe, I can't *breathe*—

Kaushika leans forward and captures my mouth in a kiss. He cradles my head in his hands, and a whimper escapes me as his tongue savages my mouth. He tastes of heat and desire and pure hunger, and suddenly nothing exists outside of this moment. No Rambha. No Indra. No mission. Nothing matters except that we live in this instant, and that he never stops. His tongue punishes and soothes me equally, one second ravaging me with harsh strokes, the next smoothing over my lips, his mouth kissing mine in soft whispers. My hands reach to encircle his neck, my nails digging into the smooth skin, and I begin to pant, chasing each kiss of his with my own, claiming his mouth when he pauses to catch his breath. Desire strokes my belly at the familiarity of his taste, at how much I need him now in this moment of combined honesty and deception, and I skim his lips with my teeth, nipping back even as he chastises me with bold lashes of his tongue, hungering.

I don't want us to stop. I don't want this to end. I don't want to wake up from this dream, where this kiss is pure and untainted with anything but our greed for each other. Where I can simply lose myself and don't have to think of anything else but *now*.

With a groan against my mouth, Kaushika steps back. I am trembling again, but this time it is neither from cold nor from fear. I watch him, and his chest rises and falls.

"You want me," he says, and I nod, my breathing uneven.

I want him. It is the one truth I know in this moment.

He smiles, a half-tilted smile that reveals his dimples, and reaches up to my neck to unlock the chains from swarga. One by one, he detaches them all. They are some of the most precious amulets from Amaravati, filled with enormous magic, but he drops them, the pearls and sapphires cast aside like so many stones. They clink when they fall on ice, but neither Kaushika nor I take our eyes off each other. I watch him, breathless, as his fingers graze my bare neck to the earrings, which he removes too. He pulls the pins free of my braid, combing out my hair with his thick fingers until even Indra's circlet and his own crescent comb join the pile on the ground. My scalp prickles with his touch, and a husky sigh falls from my lips.

He watches my mouth like it is the tastiest fruit, deep desire in his eyes.

"Powerful though these amulets are," Kaushika whispers, "you do not need them. You never have. Not for me."

I shiver where I stand, chills erupting over me. His touch is like a tingling breeze, and his fingers skim over my neck and my jaw. He leans down and nuzzles me, trailing kisses along my cheek, along the corner of my mouth, and the soft spot by my ear. Kaushika inhales deeply, and the sound almost undoes me. I writhe in his grasp, but he keeps me steady, his teeth grazing along my neck as he sucks slowly, leisurely, at the delicate skin. A gasp wrenches from me, and I squirm harder, growing uncomfortably damp. My eyes flutter shut in exquisite agony. If he weren't holding me up, I would fall.

Lust grows in me, hot and heavy, and I want to lean forward and kiss him. I want to take him in my arms, have him pressed hard against me, but instinct tells me I must not rush this. Kaushika is doing this not just for me but for himself. My hair falls thick and heavy down my shoulders, released from my apsara braid, and his one hand weighs it, a growl in his throat, tugging it ever so slightly before relinquishing it. A half sob escapes me as my belly churns with fire.

Slowly, ever so slowly, he reaches to pull the ends of my sari from around my shoulders. The pallu drops, sashaying around my waist in a train. I do not sense him doing it, so consuming is my own lust, but before I know it he has unbuttoned my blouse. He removes my arms from it, discarding the clothing so I am standing in a river of sari, my breasts bare.

Kaushika steps back then, and his gaze flares as he studies me. "You are beautiful," he says softly. "Beyond what you can know."

I have heard words like this before, but I tremble regardless, because for the first time these words are said not just for my body. Kaushika alone has seen of me what no one else has. My nipples harden in the bare air, and Kaushika captures one breast, brushing the nipple back and forth with his thumb until it is almost painful. I suppress a cry, and my head drops back, just as he dips his head and sucks the other nipple. My mind blurs. I hold on to him as my legs almost buckle, but he continues to suck, bringing me to a peak of pleasure before turning to lavish his attention on the other breast.

The sounds escaping me are part whimper, part sob. When Kaushika stops, my eyes fly open and I reach for him, but he is only dropping to his knees in front of me. I stare at him, amazed and heavy-lidded, as he unravels the rest of my sari, pooling it away in a glistening stream. The rest of my jewels come off too, and he tugs at my silk underclothes. I step out of them as though in a daze, and he tosses them all away.

And then I stand there, utterly naked as Kaushika kneels in front of me. His hands rest on my waist, thumbs pressing hard on my hip-bones. His whole body shudders, his head bowed. He is still fully clothed, his hair still in a sage's topknot.

"You want me," he repeats softly, and it is almost as though he is talking to himself. "But you have had me since the first moment we saw each other. You have me now, and for as long as you desire, in any way you desire. And I"—Kaushika finally lifts his head, and his eyes glitter—"I would have you free. I would have you unbound. I would have you powerful."

My eyes widen. I see myself through his mind. Invincible. Exquisite. A goddess. Through the cocoon of warmth Kaushika has conjured, the magic in the forest roars at me, sensing my own acknowledgment of myself. I do not understand it, but I am here, and so is he, and perhaps it is because I am not weighed with Indra's jewels anymore, perhaps it is because I am finally here as *me*. Magic explodes out of me in a burst of radiance in recognition of my own nature, and the both of us gasp, alive and glorious and hungry.

Kaushika grabs me around the waist and lays me down. I have only a moment to wonder that he has somehow conjured a bed of heather, that I lie not on hard ice but on soft, cushioned moss. His hands push my knees wide, and a gasp twists from me as he bends low and drags his tongue across my entrance. My back arches, and I cry out his name. Pleasure rushes through me as his tongue finds my sensitive spot, and my fingers dig deep into his skin even as my hips rise for more.

"I—I—" Words stutter out, but he gives me no time to think. His hands push my legs wider, locking my ankles on his shoulders. His tongue nips and teases at that bud within me, licking, smoothing, circling until I am insensate, my body writhing. A spiral of heat grows within me, tighter and tighter, and my eyes fly open, my vision blurry with endless pleasure. Magic whips inside me like a cord, and my legs tremble uncontrollably. I have no questions in me, no doubts, no plans, nothing but pure pleasure. Kaushika pulls back and inserts one finger inside of me and I cry out in sweet relief, needing more.

It is too much. It is not enough. My hands scrabble at the heather, feeling the ice underneath. They reach for him, and he inserts another finger, pressing into the sensitive walls, alternating between his mouth and his hand. The double assault unmoors me.

Hot, terrifying pleasure jolts through me, and my back arches. My cry is throaty and raw as Kaushika licks me toward the waves of my orgasm, his tongue raspy and hungry.

And then I finally cannot take any more.

Ecstasy rips through me, taking all of me away with it, and nothing exists but that sensation. The white-hot agony of it spears through my back, my skull, my very bones, and power braids within me, raw and alive. Waves of infinite pleasure rush through me, one after another, until I am soaked below. I shatter in a thousand pieces of light, my mind blanking.

I am shivering as I come down from the precipice. My eyes drift open to moonlight, and I cannot believe that I brought *him* here to be seduced. That this was meant to go differently. That everything about it was somehow perfect.

I sit up and find him watching me, still at my knees. It irks me to see him fully clothed, but there is nothing like victory in his eyes. There is only humility and a wariness, like he cannot believe that he is here with me, that *he* is amazed by his good fortune.

"Meneka?" he asks carefully.

I lean forward and grab the collar of his kurta in my fist. "Take your clothes off," I command.

He arches an eyebrow at that. "We don't have to—"

"I want to," I interrupt. "Do you?"

Kaushika smiles. "More than anything."

I nod. "Then take your clothes off."

He does not argue this time. Kaushika obeys and whips his kurta off, baring his muscled chest. The trousers come off too, and he kneels above me, tall and handsome and powerful. I stroke his hardness from root to tip, and he groans, his hands burying themselves in my hair as I lean forward to kiss him—but then I pull him down in a swift movement, pushing him to his back.

Kaushika's eyes flare as I sit astride him, my legs wrapped around his. He doesn't say anything and neither do I as I guide his length inside me, but the moment we make contact, the both of us gasp. He grips my thighs and pushes into me until he is buried fully inside. His eyes flare and a groan rips from the both of us in how amazing he feels there, how perfect.

"Am I hurting you—" he begins, but I don't let him finish. I move my body, and he moves his in response. It is our first time together, but it is neither gentle nor tender. It is hard and fast and *rough*, and Kaushika's moans tear out of him, both our bodies sweaty as he thrusts. I place one hand on his muscled stomach, and my other grips his leg. His hands are tight enough on my waist to leave imprints.

And before the oblivion of my pleasure takes me once more, I have one final thought. I am no closer to my goals of seducing him like an apsara. I have always been lost with him. Yet tonight, I am found.

WE DO IT AGAIN. SO MANY TIMES THAT I LOSE COUNT.

It is sweet. It is painful. It is intoxicating. We explore each other's bodies. We learn what makes us gasp, what makes us laugh, what makes us senseless. We slap each other's hands away and press each other deeper. He holds me down, thrusting into me from behind, pulling my hair back and growling that he is not done when I make to move. I ride him again, and beneath me his eyes gleam, his breathing savage. His fingers crook into me, one then another, stroking, pushing until I am mindless over and over again. My mouth relieves him, sucking and lapping, taking him deep within my throat, and his back arcs, holding my head down, guiding me up and down the way he needs me.

The magic dissipates around us slowly. When he rests, eyes closed and breathing easy, I take all my discarded jewelry, even the precious crown from Indra, and toss it into the lake. I stand over it, disrobed, my hair free, staring into the water's depths as the moon travels across the night sky and gives way to a chest of treasure. I stare at myself in the water, my reflection blurry with the ripples. My body chills, goose bumps erupting over me, but I do not shiver.

A clarity descends on me. It is not a clarity of knowledge—for I still cannot fully fathom what I have done. No. This is a clarity of being certain without knowledge. Of being certain of myself. I know its fragility and foolishness. But it is love, and what is more foolish than love? Shiva himself nearly destroyed the universe when he lost Sati.

I used magic, so strong and unfathomable that even I don't understand it. Kaushika and I lay together. I did what Rambha asked me to do, but did I do it for her? Kaushika's eyes are clear, burning with intelligence and kindness like they usually do. Rambha will be back soon, wanting to know how I have fared. What will I tell her?

She flickers in my mind, faded and colorless, the star-anise scent of her just a memory. I stare at my naked reflection in the pond and see how she and I could never have been. We were just marks to each other. The shape of Kaushika's seduction, however, has always been my own. He has given me permission to love him the way I need. I have given him permission to live in my heart. And now, when I have finally been honest with myself, I can be honest with him. I can tell him who I am, and trust that he will believe my intentions.

Kaushika calls out my name, and I turn and smile.

He rises and dons his pajamas again. Bare-chested, he offers me his kurta. My sari, along with my jewels, is at the bottom of the lake. I carefully wear his shirt and tie my hair using the wooden crescent comb. I gaze at him questioningly.

"This thing you did," he begins, then pauses, shaking his head. His hand rests idly on my waist, but his gaze takes in the forest around us, studying the golden hues of the residual magic. "Meneka, you are powerful beyond anything I can contemplate. You do not even know the extents of your limits, let alone the shape of them. If you truly allowed yourself to unleash them . . ."

I don't know what to say. I follow his gaze and try to dissect what he is seeing. The golden, twinkling lights on the trees still resemble beads of fruit. I have made illusions more powerful than that, but then again, I don't know how I did this magic now. I simply closed my eyes, waiting for Kaushika, and magic poured out of me.

"I think it is similar to what we did with the halahala," I say softly. "A kind of combination of certain magics."

"I think so too," Kaushika agrees, though I know he understands *combination* as the power of his magic and mine, when I mean it to be Amaravati's golden power and the wild prana in me. "I have been thinking about how you assisted me with the halahala," he says. "I have questioned it, even looked into ancient texts, trying to understand—but all I know is that it was power braided in a rare manner. Still, it has told me another thing."

I tilt my head at him, noticing the serious look in his eyes. "What is that?"

"It is past time for me to show you something you have been owed ever since the incident with the halahala," he replies. "Past time I shared a truth about myself."

I move closer to him. "Kaushika," I whisper, my heart racing. "I must share a truth with you too."

"Allow me first," he says, and a ghost of a smile flashes across his features.

I want to insist that mine is more important. That what I say might change things. Here it is, finally, the truth I have been wanting to tell him for so long—of who I really am.

But still holding me, Kaushika closes his eyes, and a chant emerges from his lips. I have heard it before, and the hairs on the back of my neck rise. In front of us, air ripples as though a stone has been thrown into water. It parts, and a summer breeze drifts toward us.

My eyes widen.

All thoughts of sharing my true identity flee my mind in the face of what I see.

This is the meadow. *His* meadow.

Kaushika removes his hand from my waist but holds it out to me in offering. Wonderingly, I take it.

We step through together.

# CHAPTER 21

T he meadow assaults me at once, powerful, potent, mortal.

It stretches for miles around us, tall grass glinting like gold. The buzz of insects and bees fills my ears. Hills rise in the distance, blue and shadowy, and somewhere a stream clinks. Dawn breaks over the horizon, and though I remember that Rambha will return soon to the pond to seek my report, I am hypnotized by this meadow. It spreads as far as I can see, mountains growing in the distance. Kaushika created this? It is a kingdom worthy of a god.

The beauty is exquisite, yet somehow I cannot fully appreciate it. Dread begins to writhe beneath my skin almost as soon as we enter. Something is telling me to look behind the veil of this beauty, as though to unmask a terrible truth. As though all of this is an *illusion*. I try to take a deep breath, but my chest feels hollow despite the sweetness of the air. My tether to heaven flails, panicked, trying to escape back through the portal we came. I am disconnected from the City of Immortals here, and I cannot understand why. No matter where I have gone, no matter my missions, Amaravati has lived in my heart. Even exile cannot do this, for as long as Amaravati exists, *I* do, and—

My eyes widen in understanding. *Crime against nature*, Agastya said of this meadow. *An abomination*, Vashishta declared.

It is because we are no longer within the three realms. This is no mere kingdom. Kaushika has built another realm, one that does not acknowledge Amaravati. One where nothing of my home exists. My own power shifts, waves crashing in a sea storm, a beast unleashed, uncertain, afraid. The rays of the sun still shine in this place. Does that mean Lord Surya himself has been replicated? Could Kaushika make another Indra with his power if he wished to?

Suddenly I cannot see past my horror into the beauty of this place. I clutch Kaushika's hand in terror. He presses my fingers in comfort.

We stop walking and the portal glints behind us, still accessible. I want to run to it, to leave this place, but I hold steady against my better judgment. Golden grass surrounds us, brushing my bare knees, making my skin crawl now that I know how alien it is. Kaushika turns me toward him, his hands pressed to my shoulders. He has been watching my reaction. He knows I understand.

"What is this place?" I whisper.

"The meadow where I sent the halahala," he replies. "It was my only choice, to send it to this realm, removed as this place is from the three lokas. Otherwise, it would have poisoned all of creation eventually. Yet the action came at a terrible cost. Look, the halahala spreads here even now. We cannot linger too long."

My gaze follows where he points. In the far distance, clouds gather, dark and mirrorlike, bubbles rising from them like a volcano about to erupt. They swirl in the air, and I understand that those are no ordinary storm clouds. That is halahala, trapped here but attempting to escape as is its nature.

Is it because of the halahala that I feel such wrongness? I find it hard to think, still too shaken by my missing tether to Amaravati, but this alone tells me the halahala, although horrifying, is not the reason for my disquiet. This place is a violation *despite* it. Halahala is a disastrous poison, but it is natural, created of prakriti. This place is not.

I turn to Kaushika, unable to speak. His jaw tightens as he regards the cloud of poison, and he squeezes my hand almost painfully as though not realizing what he is doing.

"Everything I tried has failed," he says, anger lacing his voice.

"Once I sent the halahala here, I followed immediately, trying to capture it within a mountain, within the trees, even within the consecrated amulets I keep in the meadow." His eyes shine with repressed rage. "The halahala escaped all my attempts to trap it—weak as I was. The best I could do was allow it to pollute the skies while keeping the earth free. Now it roils and churns, descecrating this realm inch by inch. I made this place to be a haven, and Indra has ruined it even without knowing of it, because of his attack. That is another one of his crimes he will have to pay for."

"Kaushika," I say softly. "Please—please listen to me. Indra could not have done this. He is not allowed to, by his accord with Shiva. There are stories of this in my kingdom."

But Kaushika only shakes his head, and his hand grips mine. His eyes rove over the meadow, and his face grows serious, a line creasing between his brows. The darkness bubbles again, the halahala sparking its venom through this realm.

"Stories are not enough proof, Meneka," he says quietly. "The very fact that the poison was trapped in the bracelet Kalyani wore tells me it was no ordinary creature who designed this snare. Only someone as powerful as the lord of heaven could do this. It is how I *know* that Indra is to blame. I have thought about it ceaselessly since that day. His actions almost killed Kalyani—and he nearly killed the people I gathered here too. One reason I hurried here from the hermitage after the poisoning was to evacuate them. Until I can get rid of the halahala, this realm is not safe, and those who are loyal to me and need sanctuary cannot return."

"People you gathered," I say, dazed. "What do you mean?"

He waves at something in the distance and I let my vision sharpen. A mess of huts dot the landscape, too many to be a mere village but too far away to know. At first, I wonder if it is another hermitage, but something about the lines of the tents is too uniform, the tracks too firm, and then I see what could only be fighting grounds for warriors.

"An army," I breathe. "Not just people. You collected an *army* here."

"I did," he confirms. "All of them await my instruction, sheltered for now with a royal I trust. I will make ready to attack Indra soon. He forced my hand with the halahala. I only waited until the Mahasabha to see if the sages would aid me, but they have made their choice, and it does not matter. I have made my choice too."

I turn to him, horrified, knowing any objections will only anger him further. Now, when I am so cut off from my own power, I dare not rile him. So I shake my head and choke out, "How? How did you create this?"

"Let me show you," he says.

Kaushika's eyes flutter shut and his lips part. A chant flows from him. Unlike the ones before, this one sounds raw. Unmade.

His voice is as beautiful as ever, but where his other mantras have a practiced quality to them, this one is carefully sung, as though Kaushika himself is unsure of it and needs to focus on every syllable and how it is intoned.

Even as I watch, the grass around us grows taller. The breeze cools, ruffling my hair against my cheek. The tips of my fingers and toes tingle, and a sweet taste enters my mouth. The air behind us wrinkles with his song, and waves of it tumble away from Kaushika. Far from us, a hill erupts, silent dust ballooning and puffing, like the ground itself is breathing. Further away, air currents come up against an invisible wall, waves lapping against an unseen dome. Everything *ripples*, the sky, the earth, even the two of us.

My vision shakes. I know that beyond the wall is unmade reality, waiting to be molded. All magic changes reality to some extent, but how long will this endure? Will this place fall apart if Kaushika himself does? Is this realm dependent on him the way Amaravati is dependent on Indra? How does this make Kaushika any different from the deva he challenges?

Kaushika stops singing and opens his eyes. For a long moment, neither of us speaks. We watch as the ripples of air slowly dissipate, and the blur of unmade reality softens, a gap closing. Our gazes find each other. The reverberations of the chant still echo in my heart. They curl in my stomach like a quiet flame. I expect the chant to have only horrified me further, but this is where the beauty of the place comes from—from Kaushika himself. Yet the darkness comes from him too.

"What is this mantra?" I whisper.

"A chant to all the deities of nature," Kaushika says. "To the sun, the moon, the stars. A chant to the earthly, celestial, and atmospheric spheres. To petal and song, to wave and soil, to a single diffused particle of light and to our own immortal souls. A chant to everything manifested and unmanifested. This one chant is my greatest triumph, Meneka. It is an invitation to all the powers that exist, big or small. This is a chant to create and nourish a universe itself."

My voice is small. "I—I don't understand."

"Indra rules his swarga, and he rules it with tyranny. I promised King Satyavrat peace, and if Indra cannot grant it, then I must grant it myself." Kaushika smiles and throws out his hand. "I have created another heaven, my dear. One that will be ruled with righteousness. One that will *replace* Amaravati."

My eyes widen in shock. I shake my head, trying to deny his words, but the evidence of his power confronts me. I have done everything now, but though I myself have changed from the start of my mission, I could never have imagined this. Beautiful or not, this chant . . . this place . . . it is evil. The sages are right. Kaushika has gone too far. I swallow, trying to form words. It takes me three attempts.

"Why do you make your own heaven?" I croak. "Even if Indra has abandoned humanity, swarga is still pure."

"Is it?" Kaushika says. "When Amaravati and swarga are so tied to a corrupt god? No, my war cannot stop with Indra. I seek to usurp him and place someone more worthy on his throne, but even I understand Indra and Amaravati are irrevocably tied to each other. Indra built the city with his bare hands, laying every brick, planting every seed. Amaravati will lose her power without him. Righteous souls might never find a path into the city without him. That is why I created this meadow—to allow these souls sanctuary before they are released into a new birth. For now, my meadow is fragile, and it cannot hold souls for eternity. I do not yet have the power to churn a soul into rebirth, but I will learn. I will find it to fulfill my vow."

"No one has that power," I say, alarmed. "Not even Shiva. To allow rebirth is the nature of the *universe* itself, which dies and is re-born every second. Even swarga exists as a temporary abode for souls, holding them until it is their time to be reincarnated."

"Then that is the knowledge I need," Kaushika says, and there is a note of frustration in his voice. "It is why I must keep on my path as a rishi, perhaps until I can become the greatest rishi possible. For all its beauty and power, this place is yet dead—unconnected to prana. I can perform my magic here, and this meadow makes *me* stronger just like Amaravati makes Indra strong. But the meadow is useless to others, who must return to the other realm to replenish their life force. That is its weakness."

"The other sages will not allow you to do this," I say desperately. "They will not help you find this secret."

"The other sages have already tried to stop me, but they have no power here. They follow Shiva's path, Meneka; they will not interfere. To do so would deplete their own tapasya, and they are too intent on their desire for enlightenment. By the time they pay attention . . ." He shrugs. "By then I will be successful, and they will see that there never was any need to stop me."

My words fail me. I can only stare at him.

Kaushika grasps my hand. "Come," he says. "The army has left, and it is all I can do to not let the poison rip this place apart. The other sages will call Shiva to take it away, or I must, but until then the meadow is not safe for us."

We step back through the portal into the mortal realm. The *real* mortal realm.

I take a deep breath as we arrive, leaves and soil and magic bursting in me, awakening and reconnecting me to Amaravati. My knees shake slightly, and a great relief floods me. Kaushika's heaven was impressive, but the realm was a figment of his power, finite in its existence. My prana shrank there, as though enclosed in a vacuum. I am grateful to be back, to feel the warmth of a real dawn caressing my skin. Still, I shiver with dread, staring around me.

Nothing remains of the night of intimacy Kaushika and I spent here. No ice, no magic, nothing but a memory. With the morning, all has dissolved, but he is still here, watching me dress in my clothes from the hermitage. He does not interrupt me, but I know he is waiting for me to speak. My mind roils with everything he has told me. I try to sort my own thinking out. My intention has changed since the start of the mission. Kaushika's actions were immoral to me once, but I have come to understand them. He was nothing but a mark, but now he is everything. Still, what he has done with the meadow is too much. I need him to see this. Despite what Rambha said, I can make him see reason. I *have* to.

I turn to him. "If there is another way to fulfill your vow, will you abandon this war with Indra and Amaravati?"

He frowns. "Agastya asked me this too. To think of other means to give King Satyavrat's soul peace rather than the meadow. But after what Indra has done with the halahala, there can be no parley with the deva king. And Indra cannot stay in his swarga, Meneka, nor can swarga exist without him. This is the only way. We cannot have two heavens."

I remember the gandharva ambassadors Indra sent. "You have not even tried to speak with him," I say.

"Because I know it is futile," Kaushika says, adamant. "You yourself said he won't allow me to dictate who resides within swarga. Besides, I left my kingdom because I could see what damage his reign is doing. The prayers unanswered. The very circle of birth and rebirth broken. Indra allows only the pious into his home, but he determines who is pious. In a world that is changing . . ." His eyes harden, and he shakes his head.

"If Indra learns of this meadow—" I protest.

"He will not know. Very few people are aware of it. The sages know. They sensed the magic I was doing in the many years it took to create it. Anirudh and Romasha were told of it too, but they are loyal to me." Kaushika comes closer to me. "You are the only other person I've trusted with this."

I feel Amaravati's tether inside me, alive and golden. "Why?" I whisper. "We do not even know each other fully yet."

"I want you to join me," he replies. "I want you by my side. I cannot do that without trusting you."

I shake my head. His reaction does not surprise me, but Kaushika thinks he has the element of surprise. He does not know the lord is already preparing for battle.

"Indra will destroy you," I say. "I can't watch that happen."

"He will destroy me easier if you are not with me."

"And what of the halahala?" I ask desperately. "I still don't believe that was Indra."

"Meneka," he says, seizing my shoulders, "I cannot do this without you."

I hold his gaze, panic in my own. "You were going to before."

"Yes. But now . . ." His expression wavers, and a shudder passes through him. He grips my waist and leans in, and his mouth brushes over my lips. He doesn't kiss me. Simply closes his eyes and leans his forehead on mine. His breath feels like a prayer.

"I fear I will forget my way without you," he whispers. "I did once, and I am atoning for my sins every day. Tapasya gives me power, Meneka, but when I exhaust every bit of it, I still have power because of love. You reminded me of it, and you continue to remind me simply because of who you are. And I need the power desperately. To absolve myself of my greatest shame." He lets go of me and approaches the stone obelisk hidden in the trees.

I watch him curiously, not understanding. Kaushika brushes the low-lying branches off the obelisk. His eyes grow sad.

"Everything is tied to Indra," he says quietly. "My past, my vows. Even my mistakes."

He opens his mouth and sings a soft and melodious song. It is a melody of repentance. A lament, a eulogy, a dirge. It is only a few syllables, but it glimmers around the obelisk like a living thing, and stone begins to move, cascading into shape.

"You asked me once how I knew Queen Tara was seduced by an apsara," he says. "An apsara was sent to seduce me. I was deep in meditation, consecrating the meadow. The portal was open when she arrived in front of me and began to dance. The power she wielded frightened and angered me, and I—I turned the weight of my magic onto her in self-defense. My curse took hold before I could stop it. Anirudh has taught you the way mantras work. Once they are unleashed, they cannot be altered. The best I could do was lay a condition on what I did, that she remain in this form until she is released by a purehearted sage."

I remain immobile. His words and my own realization come to me as if from a distance, separated by an ocean of horror. I know what he is saying. I understand what is occurring. Still, I cannot accept it. I wish it to be untrue. For him to take back his words, his actions, and for me never to have learned this. I want him to stop speaking, but it is clear that after all the admissions and our night together, he wishes to keep no more secrets from me. His voice grows quieter, sadder.

"I have tried so many times," Kaushika says. "That very day you and I met in the forest by the hermitage, I was returning from yet another unsuccessful attempt at freeing this woman. Yet I will never be able to help her because *I* am not purehearted. It is why I was so angry that day, my own failure staring at me despite my tapasya. This is why I must deal with Indra first. Until I have fulfilled my vow to King Satyavrat, until I have balanced the karma that binds me so strongly, I can never know purity. And she will remain trapped."

The mantra seeps into the stone. Rock shifts, no longer in an arbitrary obelisk shape but resembling a dancer, her face terrified, arms raised in defense over her head, stone tears glistening in her eyes. Nanda, who taught me some of my earliest dance forms. Nanda, who could sing like a nightingale. Nanda, who was rowdy for an apsara, her jokes always slightly irreverent, her smile always a bit wicked, and who could make me laugh even while giving me the most arduous exercises to do.

I cannot take it. It is too much. The fight with Rambha, the pleasure I felt with Kaushika, the meadow and his heaven, and this pond where my terror and his danger bore witness to our lovemaking—they break my stunned moment of numbness. A horrified cry falls from me and I stagger forward to the statue, tears rushing down my face.

"No, no, no," I whisper. "What did you do? What did you *do*?" My hand touches Nanda's stone one. I turn around to face him, uncaring of the danger I am in. "Where are the others? Where are Sundari and Magadhi? Did you curse them too, Kaushika? Where are my sisters?"

He looks bewildered for a long moment, his brow creasing. "Your sisters?" he chokes out. "No, it cannot be. That must mean you are—"

He cuts himself off.

His eyes widen in pain and denial and understanding.

"It is not possible," he whispers, as if he is speaking to himself. "I warded the forest after Indra sent his gandharvas, knowing he would try again, but I shielded myself from apsaras after I encountered *her*. I did not think Indra would dare send another one, not with her missing. And you . . . you can do tapasvin magic like a yogi. No immortal is capable of it. I couldn't have been this wrong. It's not possible."

"Indra *allowed* me that power," I lash out. "Indra did it because I was sent—I am here—you may not have believed it, but I am an *apsara*, Kaushika! I always have been!"

I hurl out these last words, too upset to contain my shock and anger to soften them. Kaushika stares at me, his face caught in the horror of my confession, shaded by the vulnerability of his own admission about Nanda—and it is *this* expression which abruptly washes out my own rage, in how this moment between us has twisted.

Confusion and chaos pummel me, and grief weeps within me. This is not how I meant to tell him. I wanted to be tactful, show him that it doesn't matter anymore why I came here in the first place. My reasons changed because of him, and I want to tell him that he is my antithesis and my mirror, the destruction to my maya and the completion to it as well. My anger leaches out of me along with my horror, and all I feel in this moment is a deep sadness, for the sheer waste of what has occurred in his pride and my confusion. My hand touches Nanda's face, and my heart breaks into a million pieces because she shows me, in her smooth stone and stillness, just how wretched this mission has been from the start, and how everything has led to this moment of truth and collapse.

My voice is a croak as I stare at Kaushika. "Will you turn me into stone now too?" I ask.

Kaushika's eyes flash. His fists clench, and I read his fury, his pain, in that one movement. I wait, too heartbroken to care if he is going to lash out.

But Kaushika only nods once, as if to himself. Then he turns away, his movements wooden.

I stumble forward and grasp his arm before he can leave. I know he will not curse me like he did Nanda, but the prospect of losing him in this manner stirs me more than his danger. "Don't go," I say, desperately. "We can fix this. Let me explain."

"What is there to explain?" he replies, his eyes piercing into me. "I underestimated the storm lord badly. He won this round. He will not win again."

"He did not win. I haven't told . . ." But I cannot complete my sentence. Because I *have* told. I told Rambha everything Kaushika ever said to me, and she reported it back to Indra. Undoubtedly, the devas conferred, going over every bit of my information, seeing how to manipulate it. Even now, according to Rambha, Indra prepares for war. Based on *my* information.

Kaushika's eyes glint. "Why stop yourself from telling another lie, Meneka?"

His voice is flat, emotionless. The sheer pain and hurt in it, masked behind a cold indifference, break my heart.

"Did you breach my shield too?" he asks. "Did you look into my lusts and plant your own image? If Indra dares to send me another apsara, I would like not to be such an easy puppet."

He asks the question coldly, as though not truly expecting a response, but I see behind it the fear of what I did to him, in forcing him to lie with me.

"I—I didn't plant any lusts in you," I whisper. "I didn't ever use my magic on you, Kaushika. I saw your lust, and I saw myself, and it shocked me too. It means only one thing. That your lust for me was pure. Uncontaminated by any magic. That you desired me, plain and simple."

He says nothing, merely continues to stand there, frowning. I take courage from this and move my hand over his arm, trying to ease the tension from his bicep.

"You must have known," I whisper. "Somewhere in your heart, you must have known who I was. After all my defense of Indra, you must have suspected it, you must have accepted it."

Anger flares in his eyes. "Then it is my shortcoming? Even if that is true, then all you have done is subterfuge, when I hid *nothing* from you—I gave you *everything* of me. You were my goddess, my devi. If you truly believed my lust was my own, you could have *told* me you were an apsara, without any confusion and pretense. You could have trusted me to take all of you. Did I show you I was too weak for your desires? For you?"

"You cursed her—" I begin, pointing to the statue.

"Because she tried to desecrate my meditation, my power, and my free will! Is that what you did too?" His mouth twists, and the revulsion in him shakes me. "I cannot believe I have been so foolish. Of course, all your wisdom about the path of the Goddess, about the devi. Those were simply to thwart me, were they not? My trust, my *arrogance*, blinded me into believing that if you could do rune magic, you could not be an immortal. From that first day I saw you, I assumed your immense beauty could only mean one thing, but I fell for you against my better judgment, against all the warnings in my head, *seduced* by your mask of sincerity, giving you the benefit of the doubt.

I forgot myself. And is that not what your kind does? Make a mark forget their own will? Everything you've said has been a lie."

I shake my head in protest. "It wasn't a lie." I raise my hand to cup his face. "Kaushika, I—I made a mistake—surely you understand that. You've made them too—with her—"

I caress his face, but he wrenches me away from him, painfully, as though only just realizing I am so close to him. "Do not touch me," he snarls. "These are excuses. You did what was in your nature. Lies and deception and illusions. That is what an apsara does. You violate. That's your entire existence, and I foolishly thought it was love."

"It *was* love," I say. "It *is* love. Kaushika. I love—I am in love—"

"No," he says, and now the heat leaves his voice. He takes another step back. "I was a mark. A mission. You were sent here by Indra to deceive me. Deny it, Meneka. I dare you." A staggered breath escapes him. "I *beg* you," he whispers. "Please. Deny it."

I stare at him, and the words of explanation die in my mouth. Suddenly, I am sick to my stomach. Have I not thought the very same things he is saying to me now? Never with such brutality, never with such precision—but I have questioned my own nature the same way he is. I have been ashamed of being an apsara, knowing in the depths of my soul that I am a creature of poison and danger, forcing my marks to feel what they feel, forcing them to do things they would never do. I even questioned if *Kaushika*, despite never behaving like a typical mark, admitted the things he did to me because of my celestial power. I questioned it . . . but I did not stop.

A silence breathes between us.

Tears tremble and fall. I dash them away. I try to focus, be methodical, be clear. I take a deep breath to calm myself, relying on my training from the hermitage. From *his* hermitage.

"I can't deny it," I whisper. "It *was* a mission. You *were* a mark. But then you became so much more. I couldn't tell you because I thought you'd killed my sisters. Telling you would be a betrayal of the lord. I am his apsara, compelled to obey him and bound to Amaravati in a profound way. Please . . . I never wanted to deceive you."

"What you want matters little," Kaushika says quietly. "It is what you have *done* that must be judged. And your compulsion to obey is another thing Indra must answer for. Just like I will answer for what I've done to her. Is that not fair? That all of us pay for our mistakes?"

I can say nothing to this. He has trapped me with his reason, ever a sage's weapon.

Kaushika's mouth trembles, and his hand rises. For a second, I think that despite what he has said, he can forgive me. That we can face this together. I think he is going to touch me, my hair, my cheek, my lips. Almost, I lean into him, hoping.

When he speaks this time, his voice is low. Wondering.

"I worshiped you," he whispers. "When we lay together, when we kissed." His eyes drop to my mouth, and his own mouth hardens. His hand falls again. "Nothing you have said changes that you did everything intentionally."

"I love you," I say quietly. "Please believe me."

"How can I?" he says, just as quietly. "How do I know this isn't just another deception? That you haven't simply taken away my choice? Even if I believe you, how can I trust *myself* now, when it comes to you? When *I* have been so blind?"

We stare at each other.

His question sharpens the distance between us. Because in that moment, I don't know how to answer. I don't know if I know the answer at all.

Is this love at all? Am I even capable of it? I took away the choices of my other marks before, Tara, Ranjani, Nirjar, and countless other mortals. I broke my own sacred rule with Kaushika. I had so many chances to utter the truth to him—words of clarity, beyond the turmoil of emotion. Words that would show him who I was without a doubt, beyond the smoke of my power. He did not lie to me. He withheld and took his time trusting me, but what I did was a clear deception. Each time I chose to keep silent, I behaved like an apsara. And an apsara has always been a creature of illusions. Of duplicity and lust. Not love.

My hand rises in horror. My lips tremble.

He nods again. He understands.

Resignation covers his face. Kaushika's voice is quiet. Sad. It breaks me. "Never return to the hermitage again if you value your life, Meneka," he says.

Then he's gone, and I am alone, my loneliness showing me who I really am.

# CHAPTER 22

I don't know how long I stand there, stunned and grieving, unable to make sense of what has just occurred. Twice I attempt to move, to follow him and beg him to see my point of view, to *talk* to me, but any explanation I want to make seems hollow. I stand there as though *I* am the one cursed to become stone, my mind turbulent, reliving everything about the meadow, about Nanda's fate and Kaushika's words never to return, everything I've learned about myself.

It seems like hours pass. Perhaps it is only a few seconds.

My tether to Amaravati flames, and light grows in front of my eyes, and suddenly Rambha is back, just as she promised. I stagger, staring, momentarily forgetting my grief.

Rambha glows so luminous that she is almost blurry. I receive a startling sense that she is trying to hold her form. That she is so powerful her own body cannot contain her.

Then I blink, and the impression is gone. Rambha stands there, poised and beautiful, looking the same as she always has.

Still. Something is different. She has always been lovely—one of the most beautiful and seductive apsaras of Indra's court. Now a whole different power radiates off her. Her onyx skin glows golden, a glitter that reminds me of Amaravati's dust. Her sari, though wrapped around her sensuously, is no longer its usual green—a color Rambha prefers. Instead, it is bright blue, a favorite color of Lord Indra, reminiscent of the sky itself. The hues shift on it, clouds weaving in and out, each thread reminding me of a different mood of the lord. Even her jewelry is not part of an apsara's attire. Her emerald bangles, the sapphire rings, the ruby nose pin—all of those are from Indra's collection. The power in them sings to my own celestial magic, awakening it, even though I am not the one wearing them.

My heart sinks. These clothes are a sign. She has given herself over completely to Indra. No longer my friend but a handler. *His* agent.

A part of me still wants to go to her despite this, to search her eyes and beg her to make matters all right. I remain rooted to the spot instead, her magnificent power washing over me. There is an aloofness on her face I have never seen before. Her scent bewilders me. Once it was light, its star-anise delicate and insidious, the kind of scent that could carve a place in one's heart without their knowledge. Now it is sharp, with a fire edging it, like lightning in a storm. It attacks me, and my palms grow sweaty. I try to take a deep breath.

"Meneka," Rambha says, and her voice echoes. "Did you do as you were asked?"

I swallow. The timbre is as melodious as ever, but the words burrow under my skin. I want to submit to her. Please her. The compulsion grows in me, and I become slightly dizzy, the forest spinning in my vision. What is happening? What is she doing?

My voice comes out a croak. "Yes. I . . . I lay with him," I whisper.

At this, Rambha's mouth thins into a smile. "Then I must commend you. Though would it not have been better to do so from the very beginning, Meneka? If you did not think yourself better than your sisters?"

So much cruelty is laden into those questions that a spark of indignance flickers inside me. Kaushika and I lay together by this very pond. We worshiped each other. We loved. It was pure and sweet and true. I will not allow her to sully the memory.

I open my mouth to retort, but she is already shaking her head, past it. "Very well, then. You lay with him. What did that achieve?"

"No, it wasn't—I didn't—it was not for the mission—I wanted to—"

"You wanted to."

"Yes. For devotion—not like yours for Indra—but—" My words catch in my throat, bony and brittle.

The heartache of the last few hours pounds inside my head. I try to inhale and clear it, but Rambha's scent comes to me again, overpowering me, her magic so strong that I am slow in her presence. Her power is a subtle reminder. This is what Indra's blessing can do for me too.

"For devotion," Rambha says. "Then he is in love with you too? He is seduced?"

I stare at Rambha and try to remember her the way I saw her the last time. The ache for Amaravati, to finally return home after such a long internment in the mortal realm, blooms in me. Memories flash in my head—fruit-laden apsara groves, laughter and song, gandharvas with their music, and the sweet scent of cinnamon. Endless dance and gold mansions. Skies underneath my feet, chasing my footsteps. Hymns and solace and luxury. If I close my eyes, I can see it, the swarga where I belong, where I will live my immortal life. That is all I wanted.

But that was *before*.

Before Kaushika.

"Meneka?" Rambha presses. "Answer me."

My thoughts constantly pull away. I am in the middle of the ocean, a storm raging around me. My hold on lucidity is loose, and in desperation I lift my wrist, the motion slow. I carve a rune in the air, one Kaushika taught me. A rune for clarity. My wooden comb tingles in my hair, and even as the rune completes and dissolves, a burst of light suffuses me, clearing the fog in my head. I inhale sharply, blinking.

Rambha is still waiting for my reply. I see the revulsion in her eyes that I've used mortal magic instead of my own celestial one.

"Meneka," she says, and this time it is a command, "*is Kaushika seduced?*"

"No," I whisper. "He is not seduced and he will never be. Not through the methods of Amaravati. Not in the way we apsaras perform. Nothing I do will influence him."

Rambha smiles. It's a glint, so satisfied and malicious that a small gasp escapes me. "Then you have failed. I will report it to Indra, and he will decide your punishment." She turns, her mouth already opening to form the prayer that will take her back to the City of Immortals.

I move forward hastily. This is my one chance to set things right between swarga and the mortal realm. To save Kaushika. *He* did not listen to me, but Rambha will. She *has* to. She loved me once. She was my friend. The words pour out of me in panic.

"Rambha, wait. He knows I am an apsara. I—I told him. I *had* to, in order to prevent him from doing anything drastic. But he is furious, wanting to bring the battle to Indra with his army—and he will be destroyed. Rambha, you have to stop the lord, you have to make him understand—"

Somewhere thunder cracks, loud enough to drown out the rest of my speech.

The afternoon grows darker. Quieter.

Rambha trembles, her body still half-turned from me.

I think of what I must sound like to her. She and the lord are bound to each other in a way I don't understand. Did he feel her reaction to what I said? I look up at the sky, and dark storm clouds gather above, visible through the gaps in the leaves. I shiver.

"An army?" she says. "You have seen this army?"

I look back at her. "Kaushika has told me of it. But it is all a misunderstanding. If the lord only listens, if the two of them negotiate— Rambha, you can make the lord see reason. It is for the lord's own benefit, *please*. The mortal realm is already turning away from Indra, believing him to be the enemy. If Indra made peace with Kaushika, it would turn favor toward the lord again. Everyone would see him for his greatness and magnanimity. The lord only needs to ask forgiveness from Kaushika. He has done this with other sages before, and if he gives Kaushika the respect that is his due, then Kaushika will retreat, I know he will—"

Rambha spins around. Her eyes flash, and lightning cracks above. "This is blasphemy."

"No—I—"

"You think the lord should ask for forgiveness? You would defy Indra? To whom you owe *everything*, even your magic? For this one mortal man?"

I raise my chin. "I love him."

Her laughter is almost a shriek. "*Love?* This isn't love. It is a passing fancy. You are a child. What do you know about love? You may be an immortal, but you haven't lived more than a few years. Live longer, and then talk about love."

Her power sharpens, radiating around me, but I hold my ground. It is easier now that I've begun. "Maybe I don't understand true love," I say. "Maybe as an apsara I never can. It does not mean my feelings are insincere. Take my message to Indra, please. Or to Queen Shachi. She will listen, she didn't want apsaras to go to this mission, she will not want this battle—*you* do not want this battle, surely—"

She cuts across me. "Where is this army? Where did you see it assembled?"

"I—I didn't—I didn't *see* it, but—"

"Do not lie to me," Rambha snaps. "You are trying to protect him.

This creature you love is a threat to your lord, and yet you defend him at every turn."

"Because I finally understand. I've wanted my freedom from being Indra's weapon for so long, and what these people are asking—it is the same thing. Kaushika says he will not rest until Indra abdicates his hold on heaven. Rambha, living under Indra's rule, being sent for these missions because he has decided that is my nature—this is what I wanted freedom from. Maybe Kaushika is not entirely wrong. Maybe this is what we need, Indra not as the master of swarga, but its guardian—"

"How dare you?" Rambha rasps.

The skies open in a flood. Lightning flashes over and over again. I cry out, shielding my eyes, staring up.

The afternoon has turned wholly gray. A storm rains down, and I am drenched in seconds. Thick black clouds cover every inch of the skies, and thunder roils deafeningly with the wrath of heaven. My knees shake.

I glance at Rambha—but it isn't Rambha. Her face is changing, a veil slipping off. Everything around her blurs—

And then the illusion *explodes*.

My throat grows dry.

In Rambha's place stands Indra, tall and magnificent. His crown is so bright, I blink rapidly, dazed.

Shorn of his illusion, all his power smashes into me, and I crumple to my knees. The skies still rain, and the air grows heavy, making it hard to breathe.

"My—my lord," I whimper, confused and horrified.

It was never Rambha. I was speaking to Indra himself.

Lord Indra, who is the king of all the devas, ruler of Amaravati and swarga.

Lord Indra, who is storm lord, battle king, the destroyer of a thousand demons.

Lord Indra, who has never looked as furious as he does now, and who points his vajra, the sizzling lightning bolt, straight at my heart.

The vajra spits, sparks of fury burning off it. In Indra's contemptuous eyes, there is not a single hint of the drunken lord I saw last.

"Beg for mercy, child," he says coldly, the vajra thrumming in his hand. "And give me Kaushika."

# CHAPTER 23

I am stunned. I am terrified. I can't think.

The vajra hisses by my neck, the heat of it burning my skin. It blinds me, and I close my eyes, but tears slide down my cheek. *Drip, drip*, I hear them, or perhaps it is the torrential rain echoing in my ears. It all sounds like a terrified keening.

My mind feels fuzzy. It was Indra all along. Of course it was. The way my thoughts blurred. The way my tongue slipped. It was because of his aura and power. I should have seen it before. Why is he here instead of Rambha? Was it him earlier too? Does Rambha know the lord is impersonating her? What happened in Amaravati to account for this deception? To require it?

These thoughts form and die in my mind like mortal lives.

I start to shiver. The rain is a hailstorm of arrows, each drop sharp on my skin. It is Indra's wrath, too powerful. Surely every realm must sense it. My trickle of tears becomes a downpour. I hear a choked sound, and it is coming from my own throat. I realize I am sobbing.

The vajra twitches and vibrates in anger, sparks searing my cheek. I am already on my knees. My hands are already folded in prayer, begging for mercy. Indra does not repeat himself, but his command screams in my ears, and the words fold around my tongue, both a plea for mercy and the information he has asked for. Kaushika's whereabouts. Kaushika's plans. When he will attack, and in what manner.

I do not know the answers to these questions, but I see what Indra will do if he finds out. Images of Kaushika, Anirudh, Romasha, Kalyani, and all the other mortals flicker in my head, their bodies charred by lightning. My own exile looms, seconds away. I open my mouth to beg again, to ask for mercy and forgiveness.

Yet instead of the plea, a single word escapes me. "No."

It is soft and tremulous. For a second, I think that I did not utter it. Rain thunders around me, soaking me but leaving no mark on the lord. I wonder if maybe Indra has not heard. I wonder what possessed me to say this. I wonder if it will be my last word.

Then Indra shifts in a rain-filled blur of light. The vajra cuts into my throat, scorching my skin.

"What did you say?" he snarls.

I touch the vajra with one hand, and pain shoots through my body, burning. It is like touching the lord himself. A part of me is shocked at what I am doing. What *am* I doing?

Still, the fingers of my other hand quickly form the rune for strength. With terrible effort, I push the heavy lightning bolt aside enough to move it a few inches away from my neck.

I stumble to my feet and stand. Streaks of mud cover me. In my clothes from the hermitage, I look nothing like an apsara. Disgust curls Indra's lips as he studies me, and fury shines in his eyes. I am humiliated to be seen like this, but the brave, foolish, shocking word resounds over us. *No. No, I cannot let you do this.*

I don't repeat it. I take a few steps back, my fingers already carving other runes I learned at the hermitage. The rune for understanding, for patience, for forgiveness. They form and disappear, but their qualities pour into me and color the damp air around us. Indra watches me perform this mortal magic, and my cheeks heat in shame. I had hoped for the runes to affect him too, but he is a deva and I am unpracticed in prana magic. If I want to appease him, this is not the way.

I recall what Rambha did once.

Immediately, I change the movements of my fingers from carving runes into forming dance sigils. "My lord, please," I begin. "I didn't use the right words. If I only knew I was talking to you—"

An illusion forms from the tips of my fingers, and even as I make it, I know it is not going to be enough. Rambha—the *real* Rambha—is Indra's beloved apsara. Who knows what illusion she showed him? My fingers twist desperately, and an image of Indra's throne room forms. Maybe if I remind him of the palace he loves, he will calm himself. But terror makes my hands shake, and the illusion flickers without my permission. It changes into the apsaras' grove, then flickers again to become the buildings and homes of Amaravati, to the rock pools, the devas' harem, the hermitage.

"Please, my lord," I say as the image changes rapidly, uncontrolled. "I only meant—"

Indra makes a slicing motion.

The vajra cuts through the air.

I duck, uttering a choked cry, but the vajra is nowhere close to me. I blink and it is back in Indra's hand. His eyes gleam.

At first, I don't understand. Something has happened, something terrible. A deep horror seizes me, tasting of bitterness and bile. Everything looks much the same. The lord standing opposite me, his vajra glinting, rainstorm pouring around us. The illusion of the hermitage still glimmering. The isolation of my own good sense.

Then a hollowness grows behind my navel. It creeps its way deep into my heart, deeper into my soul. A whimper trickles from my mouth. The illusion I made turns gray.

My fingers are still curled into dance mudras, but an aching sense of loneliness yawns within me, my tether from Amaravati fraying, whiplashing. The illusion flickers, all color draining from it. It becomes weaker.

Within me, a flame dies.

I fall to my knees in the same instant the illusion vanishes.

"No," I whisper, knowing, feeling, not understanding. "No, please, no."

Indra's cold voice washes over me as though from a distance. "You have such a fondness for the mortals that you would betray your own king. You no longer need Amaravati and her power. You can live and die as one of them."

"NO!" I scream, grief making me raw. "My lord, please, I beg you, *I beg you.*"

"Stop blubbering, child. It is already done."

But I can't think. I can't stop.

It is not possible. He has taken away my magic. Nothing could have prepared me for this—it has not happened to any apsara in memory. What will become of me? There is no return to Amaravati anymore. No home. No illusions or dance. This is not merely exile. This is a death sentence.

In desperation, I curl my trembling fingers into a mudra as though to deny it all, but no magic emerges from me. In the place within me where my tether to Amaravati once lay is a burned cord, a severed thread. I am on my knees, keening, rocking back and forth.

"Please," I whisper, cold. "Please don't do this. I—I am an apsara of your court, my lord. I—I don't know who else to be. I don't—"

Light shifts, and Indra crouches to his knees in front of me. His hands settle on my shoulders, and I hear the command in my head to look at him.

His eyes are sorrowful. Kind. There is anger there, certainly, simmering underneath the impatience and coolness—but he is sad too. My eyes brim with tears. What have I done?

"Oh, daughter," Indra says softly. "You have failed me at every turn. You will never dance again. Should you survive the next few hours without your magic, you must find a way to atone for your sins. But you are finished here in this mission, never again to return to Amaravati."

It is the kindness in his voice that undoes me. I reach for the slimmest hope, searching inside me for the prana magic I learned at the hermitage. Kaushika's crescent comb burns at my scalp, and I try to focus on it. I imagine the dewdrops of my prana within my own breath. I think of the instructions of the yogis from the hermitage. A part of me always hoped it was not Indra who gave me the power—that it was mine and mine alone, learned through my own tapasya.

Yet there is emptiness within me when I hunt for my wild prana. A sickening feeling grows.

My eyes lift to Indra, who stands, his resolve clear on his face to destroy Kaushika. I see my own destiny sealed, and a tidal wave of grief smashes into me. Here is the truth, then, one I have been too afraid to accept.

Rambha had been right all along.

All my magic, celestial or mortal, came from Indra.

I truly am nothing without the lord.

# CHAPTER 24

**B**attle looms in the skies.

I watch it happen, in the storm clouds that race, the rain that thunders, the winds that churn. I stumble through the forest, trying to find my way back to the hermitage. To warn Kaushika that Indra is coming for him. To beg for his forgiveness for everything I did.

Yet with Amaravati cut away from me, my vision sways. I fall and stumble, a repelling in my stomach like a swallowed poison. I do not know if this is what occurs when an apsara is cut away from her magic and the city. I did not even know it was possible. Exiled apsaras are not spoken of in swarga. Their punishment is to remain forgotten until they can prove their devotion to Indra and become worthy of acknowledgment again. Am I dying? Only desperate hate and powerful magic can destroy an immortal, but Indra implied I might not survive the next few hours. It is too difficult to piece together these thoughts.

Pain seizes me with every movement as I stagger from tree to tree. Leaves, stem, bark. They touch me, caress me, stab me. Sometimes my vision clears, and I turn this way or that, thinking I see something familiar. Other times, everything is a haze, and I move only through sheer will and by rote. Do hours pass? Do days? I sleep, but I do not remember waking. I look at my hands, trembling, and I see Kaushika's fingers interlocking with mine, weaving in and out curiously, restlessly. I cannot remember his face from when he loved me. I can only remember his revulsion.

In my mind, the loss of my magic and the loss of him merge. My choices, my confusion, my betrayals. Where else were they to lead me if not here, in this forest so close to him yet all alone? Even my own reason abandoned me, by the end of it. Maybe the kalpavriksh tried to fulfill my wish. Maybe I didn't let it.

I wander deeper. The trees grow thicker, and darkness falls faster. Time loses meaning. I see Amaravati in dreams and nightmares. The apsaras' grove where I grew up. The gardens and gilded fountains of the city. The glittering performances during Indra's harvest festivals. Memory taunts me with what I cannot have.

Sometimes I think I see the sun shining above, but I do not know if it is truly daylight. What if this is simply the devas preparing for war, confusing the lands? It is their right. I falter and begin a prayer to Lord Surya, or to Vayu, or Agni—they are lords in their own right. They bear me no grudge, no ill will. I am nothing to them, just a devotee. They will hear me if I call.

My prayers turn to dust in my mouth. Even if they hear me, they will not cross Indra. I see them, arrayed around him in his throne room, all of them dazzling, magnificent, yet none more so than the king. Clouds churn, dimming the sunlight.

I catch my reflection in a passing stream. I blink at it, barely recognizing myself. My eyes are haunted, gold scratches on my face, tears streaked with mud. Once I had danced for the gods themselves. I would crook a finger and kings and queens would fall at my feet. This is what I have become.

My hands brush against Kaushika's wooden crescent. It weighs me down, useless when I am cut off from my own prana. Once or twice, I try to use the mantras I learned at the hermitage. My voice is a croak and I hear *him* in my mind, the beauty of his songs, the magnetism. My fingers tremble, trying to form a rune instead. To give me clarity or bravery or peace. It does not work.

Indra's intent burns in my heart. A dull sort of horror grows in me, urgent and quiescent at the same time, as I watch my own inevitable destruction come closer. It is a raging storm of rain and fire, and my cut tether to Amaravati flails inside me, whipping in a dark, hollow wind, looking for completion and connection. The sickness spreads from my stomach to my limbs. I fall every few steps, then crawl, before I can take a breath. I move again, dragging myself on the forest floor.

Urgency claws at me, even as I scrabble at the earth to force myself to stand. I think again of Indra and Kaushika, and the hateful intent in both of them. The war will be fought. Perhaps it has begun already. Will Indra kill Kaushika with the vajra? Will Kaushika overthrow Indra? I glance at the skies, and Indra's incandescent rage flashes in the clouds, threatening hail and lightning. I imagine him consulting his devas, all of them in battle raiment. I imagine Kaushika, along with Anirudh and the rest, doing the same.

I abruptly chance upon the cliff where I'd spoken to Rambha. My feet are bloodied. The sickness has reached my heart. I breathe hard, swaying. Moonlight glints over the jewel-like water below, waves susurrating. How easy it would be to simply fall. I think of whether that would be better than what is happening to me now.

My throat begins to close, and I choke. I stumble to the closest knot of trees, the river visible only as a shining ribbon. I collapse in the copse.

My mind grows sluggish.

A prayer escapes me, a song to an indifferent god. To neither Indra nor one of his devas but to one who exists far beyond the petty squabbles of the mortal and immortal realms. The prayer is merely his name, a call if I were intentioned so, but to call him is not my intention. I do not presume. There is comfort in knowing he is indifferent. What I have done, and what I am . . . it does not matter to him. There is peace in that.

I only realize my eyes have been closed when I open them.

I breathe for long minutes, noticing the pain in my body subside. The sickness is still there, but I feel detached from it, as though I am simply watching it take me over. This must be what death feels like for an immortal. It is not so bad.

Then I realize the quiet of the trees has changed. A thrum of energy pulses through them, slow and silent, like a universe breathing.

It takes me a long time to rise to my feet.

I move as though hypnotized, by instinct alone. My heart skips a beat as I see a man sitting in a small clearing a few feet away, his back to me. Was there a clearing here before? I cannot remember. At first, I think it is Kaushika; there is a surge of energy around this man I have only seen before with him.

But it is not Kaushika, and disappointment stabs me, as does relief.

Curiosity weaves through it, and I approach quietly at an angle, so as not to draw attention. The man is dressed in a tiger skin wrapped loosely around his waist. A mass of beads covers his arms, but as I look closer, I notice they are not beads but seeds, strung together in a childlike fashion to mimic jewelry. He must be a deva, but he is not of Indra's court, not dressed this way. Indra's devas are resplendent, which means he is a minor nature deity, perhaps the one this forest belongs to. A necklace coils around him, moving sinuously—

*Not a necklace.* I startle.

A cobra, twining around his neck lovingly, its head erect, its eyes glittering with awareness. I pause, my heartbeat slowing. I am mesmerized by the snake and how it moves around the man, as though they are friends. As though it is tame, even if everything about it screams of wildness and poison.

The man seems oblivious to any danger. His eyes are closed, hands extended to an emerald-green fire that changes colors even as I watch. His skin is so dark, it looks like an inky blue. If it weren't for his aura, shining with a dark light, I would hardly know he is there. It outlines him, both within him and beyond him, illuminating all of the woods with a dusky, radiant glow. Its scent eludes me, as though scent itself is a limited perception. Wiry and slim, he is no taller than I am, but I blink and he is as tall as an asura, his head and shoulders towering into the heavens. I blink again, and he is unmoving, seated by the strange fire.

His muscles gleam in quiet strength. Apart from the tiger skin around his waist, he is naked, but the effect is not sensual. It is . . . spiritual. His hair is matted, a tangle of long, thick curls. Twinkling within it is a crescent similar to the one I wear in my own hair, except mine is made of wood. His looks like it is the moon itself—

My eyes grow wide.

They flicker upward, where a minute ago the moon was gleaming.

It is gone now.

It is in his hair, tangled among the locks, pearly, luminous.

I am suddenly aware of my every inhalation. My every exhalation.

This is no mortal man. That fire is no ordinary fire.

It is spontaneous, self-contained, its presence a fuel to itself. Tapasvin fire.

I am looking at neither a deva nor a sage.

*He* is here.

Shiva.

## CHAPTER 25

I remain frozen.

Fear and shock coil inside me, panic close to spilling over.

The stories rush through my head.

Shiva is here. He who with a single glance burned Kandarpa, god of desire, to ashes for disturbing his meditation. Shiva, who forced Vishnu, the Great Lord of Preservation, to shed his incarnation in the mortal realm when the time came to return to his abode. Shiva, who in his form as Nataraj once danced the violent dance tandava, and shattered maya, the greatest illusion of nature that incessantly separates each soul from the infinite cosmos.

He is here.

Shiva is here.

My breath resounds in my ears. Disbelief paralyzes me.

Lord of Destruction. Lord of Yoga. Lord of Dance.

Lord of *Dance*.

Tears fill my eyes, and though the trees and the forest become mere blurs, he reflects in my sight unblinkingly. I am crying, because although I did not call him through prayer or devotion, he has come for me, to rescue me, to absolve me. He is here in the flesh, even though I have never been worthy, and I do not know now what to ask him, or what to say at all.

Shiva opens his eyes.

He smiles, and there is so much kindness, so much understanding and compassion in his gaze that suddenly, I forget my every worry. My tears warm my skin. They splash on my hands and my bare arms, and the gold scratches I have endured heal as though there is still magic inside me.

I don't realize I am sobbing, my cries soft.

I don't realize that I stumble toward him and sit by the tapasvin fire.

I only know that I am finally bleeding all my pain out, healing myself because of his very presence. I only know that I am no longer alone, for he has come for me when he would not come even for his most ardent followers. My own devotion to him is nothing compared to the other disciples' arduous calls. I can recall my distraction at the hermitage during my prayers to him. I can recall asking others to deviate from his path.

A part of me thinks that I should offer him prayers, or ritual, or flowers. If I had my magic, I would create those, transforming the woody clearing into a rich garden.

Another part of me thinks, what will Shiva care for any offering I can make? He is the Innocent One. He transcends division. He does not distinguish between pain or pleasure, between an orchard or a crematory. It is because he saw no difference between poison and elixir that the devas propitiated him to drink the halahala during the Churning of the Oceans. They knew that of all beings it would do Shiva alone no harm.

Through the blur of my tears, I see his throat now, the poison swallowed millennia ago still caught in it, turning his dark skin a deep blue. Halahala that he holds in his throat, neither swallowing it fully lest it poison him nor spitting it out lest it poison the world. Halahala that even now is in Kaushika's meadow, existing as a few uncaught droplets, a danger to all the realms. It reminds me of Kaushika and my friends. It reminds me of all I've lost.

Fresh tears tremble in my eyes.

"Lord," I whisper. "Om Namaha Shivaya." *I bow down to Shiva.*

Shiva smiles again. "Child of gods. Meneka. Daughter."

*Daughter.*

His voice is quiet, calm. It rustles like the softest wind. It coils its way into my heart, comforting me. My tears stop of their own accord.

"I am lost," I say.

Shiva shakes his head. "Never lost, as long as you have yourself."

I think whether I have myself at all. Pieces of it. Shards only. That is all I am left with.

"Indra. Amaravati. The war . . ."

"Evanescent. The only permanence is the truth of yourself. Only that which is real. Child of illusions," he adds softly, "understand the power of the greatest magic there is, which tries to convince you that you are alone."

We sit in silence. I expect no other response from Shiva, but breath by breath I reach for understanding. A creature of maya, I do not have the power to slice illusion from reality, but I am familiar with the legends. I am a being of legends myself. Shiva himself is here.

I listen. I try.

After a time, I am calmer. Perhaps it is his presence. Perhaps I have reached for something within me. My tears dry. My trembling body quietens. The pain of everything I have endured still crashes inside me, but it is distant, like the roar of a faraway ocean. The sickness from being cut off from Amaravati reduces to a seed. I watch it, in grief and sorrow. I feel my burned tether, regretful still, but this time the pain does not immobilize me.

"Where did I go wrong?" I ask quietly.

"*Did* you go wrong?" Shiva answers gently.

"Indra cut me away from Amaravati. Kaushika hates me. I have lost everything."

Shiva's face is tender, compassionate. "Pain is not always a consequence of doing the wrong thing. Hate is not always the opposite of love."

I think of how unfair that is. How obvious it is. I think of the army Kaushika has collected and the alternate heaven that he is creating.

Shiva leans forward. "The universes are much larger than you can imagine, daughter." His fingers hover between my brows, and my eyes grow large.

My breath seizes. Within my eyes, infinite galaxies form and die. The universe rushes, extending into every direction. Not one universe but a thousand, a million, infinite and continuous. I glimpse creation, the birth of everything; it occurs over and over again. I glimpse destruction, and they are the same thing, for what is birth without death? One leads into the other, a continuum, their divisibility itself an illusion.

The image shifts, and infinite Indras sparkle in my mind within infinite Amaravatis. Billions of Menekas and Kaushikas exist, both with and without each other. I see then that Kaushika's attempt at an alternate heaven isn't ambitious. It is useless, ridiculous, unnecessary. Infinite heavens already exist with so many possibilities. For an instant, the cosmic power, the absolute total eternity of Shiva's knowledge seizes me. I gasp at the sheer scope of it, knowing he has shown me but a speck of what he himself sees when he meditates. Infinity both contains and does not contain parts.

I blink, and the image dissipates, and I am here again, seated by the Lord, the tapasvin fire burning in front of us.

It takes me a long time to recover.

My breath is deep, but it is fast and shallow too—in another world, in a different universe. I pull myself back to my own existence sharply.

This time when I search for the lingering pain inside me, I hold it desperately, as though it is a log in a tempestuous ocean. My pain glimmers, and I lurch toward its heat and sharpness. The one thing I can call my own even now.

When I am steady, I speak, and my voice is low.

"This heaven he wishes to create. It cannot be." I swallow. "It would be unnatural. It would break the cosmic order of birth and rebirth. Amaravati is where mortal souls are meant to rest. I still believe this."

Shiva does not reply. He has no need to. This is not his affair to worry about. He transcends this, and I am still mystified at why he is here at all.

I wonder if I should ask him about the halahala and the conspiracy I suspect lurking there. About Kaushika's vow and his battle with Indra. I wonder if I should ask about the Vajrayudh, and how Shiva himself extracted a vow from the storm lord, or about ancient Indra and his evolution, or the deepest pains in my own heart and if I will ever heal.

Shiva answers me before I can speak. He decides for himself what question he wishes to answer.

"Kaushika is destined for greatness. There is pride in him, but there is purity too."

Kaushika's intense gaze burns my forehead. The way his mouth moves when he chants a mantra. The power of his magic, and the sincerity of his beliefs. Despite the distance between us, I feel it—the mirror I saw in him, the darkness that reflected itself back to me.

*And purity too*, I think.

"Does that mean you will help him achieve his goal?" I whisper. The thought terrifies me, even now, when I am severed from my magic. The wrongness of Kaushika's meadow and the consequences of war are too horrible to be real. My friends and kin may have abandoned me, but I have not abandoned them.

Shiva does not reply for a long time. I wonder if I have presumed too much. I begin to grow abashed, but then he speaks, finally, and there is weariness in his answer.

"I will take the halahala from his meadow. For it is part of my ancient promise."

His throat glistens a sharp bright blue. Poison roils inside, fumes and darkness that he holds at bay for himself and the world. His entire body darkens for an instant before it settles, the poison once again under control. In my mind, Indra's song resounds, one that he sang so long ago lamenting the power of halahala. The gandharvas say halahala is the embodiment of all vices, anger, pride, every dark hedonistic pursuit. What must it be for Shiva to hold it in and never swallow or release it?

Shiva's gaze falls on me as if he has heard my question. "Do you know why I do not swallow it?"

"It will kill you."

"If I swallow it, I will destroy it. It will burn to nothing with the tapasvin magic inside me."

"Then . . . why won't you?" I dare.

"Because the Goddess commands me not to," he says, and I know he speaks of his Shakti.

I am aghast. The three realms could be rid of this terrible thing. Halahala is the one thing that could destroy all of existence. Shiva does not distinguish between poison and elixir, but this could save the order of the universe.

I cannot help my impertinent question. "Why would she ask you to do this?"

"She is ambrosia and poison," he says, smiling fondly. "She is terrifying Kali and nourishing Gauri. She is everything, and everything more. She tells me that without pain, there is no pleasure.

And without either, there is no life. That is why I hold it, child. Because she is right."

Shakti flashes in my mind, astride Shiva, dominating him. The image changes to how Kaushika and I were, and I blink.

Shiva rises. In his gesture I recognize an end to our conversation. He wishes to return to his eternal meditation. Already, his form is dwindling.

The words burst out of me without thought. I am fearful of how he might answer, but the question has been circling me. I need to know if it's true.

My voice is a whisper. "Am I even capable of love?"

At this, Shiva's gaze turns sad, sorrowful.

"Oh, my child," he says. "You *are* love."

He fades, his voice a murmur on the wind.

I STAND UP.

All that remains are bael leaves fluttering. Vaguely, I think how there are no bael trees around.

It is Shiva's power, but is it magic at all? Magic seems dull around him. As the Destroyer, he decimates the illusion of any magic.

I make my way to the cliff.

I stand at its edge, and below, the river winds in a ribbon of blue. The moon has returned to the sky now that Shiva is back at Mount Kailash. Did Indra notice the moon's absence in his skies? I imagine the lord of heaven alarmed while he is in conference with his devas. I imagine him, worrying and rash, thinking that it is Kaushika whom Shiva responded to.

I stare at the heavens. Amaravati glints in my eyes, its halls and pathways forming in the constellations, beckoning me. Indra took away my magic. I thought I was nothing without it.

Bathed in moonlight, blessed by the Great Lord himself, I close my eyes.

I dance.

FOR THE FIRST TIME, MY DANCE IS FOR NO ONE ELSE BUT ME.

The mudras spin out of me without preparation. Strength of a Diamond. Spark of Agni. Flame of the Heart.

I feel them burning where my tether to Amaravati was cut away. Even though I breathe deeply, I can no longer sense the flow of my prana as I once did. Indra's gifts, both of those.

This dance is not augmented by any magic. Instead, the mudras come from a place of creation within my heart. No illusions flow out of me; I do not need them. My dance is expression enough.

My feet spin, arms thrown up to the sky. Dark green echoes in my vision, the circling of the trees, the night sky, the sliver of a returned moon. I close my eyes, aware I may trip and fall. I am too close to the edge of the cliff. This is dangerous.

I dance.

I tell a story. It is of a time before the Churning of the Oceans, a story of how apsaras were created. There are gaps in my knowledge, but it doesn't matter. My movements fill the gaps, making any spaces of loss meaningless.

Here we are, born as creatures of the water, when the three realms were nothing more than a congealed mess of swirling oceans. When Indra, Surya, Vayu, and all the other devas were nothing more than amorphous, barely sentient creatures themselves.

The world evolves. Indra and the other devas grow in shape and power. Apsaras, who were once barely more than fish, become water nymphs. My mothers and sisters from a different age transform, and their beauty is like the dawn of a new day—innocent, shining, full of possibilities.

Indra evolves. He takes the form of a man. He arrays his devas. He builds Amaravati with his bare hands and rules the city. He promises to follow the cosmic order of birth and rebirth. Promises to keep safe those who are pious before it is their time to return to the mortal form.

The three realms take shape. Rules develop, change, and die. Busy, busy, life goes on in all of them in some form. Indra approaches the apsaras—the most beautiful creatures of all the three realms, who flit from stars and clouds to rivers and streams, free. He offers them a home. "Bind yourself to me," he says, "and I will give you permanence."

We agree. We choose to serve him in return for a home in his beautiful city. We dance for Indra. We fall in love with the devas. We lie with them and the gandharvas. We bear children, always another apsara, whom we train into our art. Dance was always our form. We have only perfected it now, when before it was mere movement in water and dust.

Our devotion to Amaravati is rewarded, and the city succors us with each dance. Illusions drip from us, an enchantment even Indra did not know would occur. We are forever young, forever beautiful. We do not know the meaning of promiscuity—it is an ugly word. For us, our dance, our very bodies, are instruments of love.

My feet spin, and there is joy in my steps. Freedom, ecstasy, peace.

I tell my story, and I allow Shiva's wisdom to flood me. Everything I felt for Kaushika, all that I've felt for my friends, Anirudh, Kalyani, Rambha, even Indra and the city of Amaravati. I inhale that love, letting it soak my body, letting it soak *me*. My tether awakens, snaps around, and Shiva smiles.

And I understand what he means.

Mortal and immortal magic do not matter.

Love is a form of magic too.

Something sparks with this realization. Awareness flaps its wings inside me like a vivid butterfly. I dance, gasping, unable to stop—and Amaravati's force floods into me, a golden power, a dam that has been bursting to receive me. My own wild prana slams into my heart, tapasvin power I cannot be denied. Power is power, and I—*I* am a creature of power too.

My eyes snap open. Around me is the legend I told myself. Illusions of devas glimmering. The Churning of the Oceans as asuras try to take the amrit that was once promised to them. The world before the three realms, water and fluid coagulating. The legend of the apsaras and how we came to be. The legend of Indra and how he built Amaravati. And finally, embedded within all of these stories, the one I care about the most.

The legend of Meneka.

She is there, amidst it all, watching, understanding. She is immortal but young, and she finally understands herself and her history. She sees where she came from and her own choices. Kaushika kisses her. Anirudh wraps his arm around her. Rambha tips her chin up. Meneka is here, surrounded by her friends and her mentors. She is in Kaushika's hermitage, studying the mortals, and at Amaravati too, among the devas. She is alone, but she is never alone. For I am here too.

I fall to my knees, but the illusion still glimmers, powered by my sheer emotion. Indra, Amaravati, and all the other apsaras shine in the distance, but Meneka walks up to me. She kneels in front of me and lifts my chin. Her touch is as light as air. She smells like morning's fresh hope.

Meneka smiles.

I smile back.

*I see you*, we think. We blink—

And she's gone.

The rest of the illusion glimmers, fading into golden dust. Within me, my tether to Amaravati blooms rich and fluid, still bursting with power. I breathe deeply, and my own prana floods me, alongside the tether, both powers that I understand now were never gifted to me by Indra.

Wood and dust and heat create their own mirage. I breathe, and my body lights up, my own aura visible to me for the first time. Within me, my chakras glow, not merely the seven everyone can name but thousands of smaller ones. Prana flows in a rainbow river of radiance, and I watch it twining through my blood and bones, indistinguishable from any other part of me. *Give yourself permission*, Kaushika's voice says to me from a lifetime ago, and I unlock the chakras as though I have always known how to do so.

Mortal and immortal magic braid together, consuming me.

Strands of prana seep into my very soul, water meandering and finding its path to the most concealed parts of me.

My back arcs, and my breath slows.

I twist my wrist, and before the mudra is complete, an illusion shoots out, rich with Amaravati's gold. The heavens roar, a crack of thunder, and I look up. Lightning flashes again and again, and dark clouds storm the sky, gathering right above me in response to my magic. Rain begins to pour, in punishment and rage, and I know Indra can see me. Despite everything, he is my sire, and I am his devotee. This place is not warded from his view. I have taken back Amaravati's power despite my exile. I have disobeyed him again. He is coming.

*Let him come.*

I stand and shake my arms out, dispelling stormwater.

I am intoxicated by my own power. I am more clearheaded than I've ever been. A chant threads through me, one I did not know I had learned. It is a similar chant to the one Kaushika used to open a portal, and the air in front of me ripples.

I stare at Nanda in her stone form. She undulates, the stone raining, howling. The portal brought her here, closer to me, and runes escape from the ends of my fingers, the circle of freedom, the lingam of Shiva and Shakti, the sickle of healing. I press the force of my braided magic into the stone, and it weeps.

Then the obelisk bursts.

Tiny splinters of stone explode but do not harm me, turning into airy dust even as they touch me.

Nanda staggers from the dust and falls to her knees, a sob tearing from her chest. I lean down and lift her up, and I see the words in her eyes. *Purehearted sage.*

"Sister," I whisper, and she places her head on my shoulder, sobbing uncontrollably, unable even to form my name. Tears flood my eyes too, not just for releasing her but because *I* have been the one to do it. Both of us grip each other like we are in a stormy ocean, powerful and free for water is in our nature, but terrified too because of its freedom and danger.

I stroke her hair again and again, careful of the jewels she is wearing, sensing the magic in them. I want to ask her about Magadhi and Sundari, the two other apsaras besides us who were sent to seduce Kaushika. But she would not know; they were sent after her. Did Kaushika turn them into stones too? Why, then, would he not mention it when he spoke of his mistake with Nanda?

I say none of these things. I simply hold her, murmuring to her that she is safe. That I am here now, and I will let no harm come to her. Nanda quivers in my arms, sobbing quietly, and I think of the horrors she has experienced. Was she aware of herself the entire time she was trapped there? I hope not. I hope it was simply like an enchanted sleep and this is an awakening. I know it is an awakening for *me*.

The trees rustle, and we hear voices raised in argument. Someone else is here. The downpour has lessened into a faint drizzle but Indra has likely sent his minions already. A wry smile grows on my lips. Nanda draws back from me, still too overwhelmed to speak, but a quiet resolve buds in her eyes. She dashes her tears from her face and nods to me once, magic already curling around her fingertips. She is an apsara, a soldier. She knows what we must do in the face of any kind of danger, whether sent from the lord or otherwise. She was abandoned by those who should have protected her. Just like I was. We are ready.

We exchange one final glance, magic glinting over our bodies.

Silently, we approach the sounds.

## CHAPTER 26

I stop when I see shapes clustered in the clearing where I sat with Shiva. Nanda and I are hidden from view, still behind the trees. I hesitate as voices murmur and rise.

At first, I cannot see who is talking. The sheer magic of the clearing overwhelms me.

It is startling in its intensity. Vivid colors smash into me, blurring everything into a swirling mass of many-hued waves, battling one another. I have to close my eyes so the force of it mutes.

My other senses flare as soon as my eyes shut. Different rhythms ebb and rise in my ears, like the same note being repeated in several different octaves. Scents share the same base but manifest as different aromas. Mortal or immortal, all magic is really the same, part of the same universal song. These are auras I'm sensing, crystal clear for the first time, after my own conversation with myself.

Goose bumps erupt on my skin. Never before have auras revealed themselves to me in this fashion, as though I can see their connection to all of the universes and realms. Vaguely I question what auras really are. I have no true understanding of them, but Kaushika would know.

I try not to think of him. I breathe in slowly, trying to capture the freedom and power of my dance. Then I approach, careful not to make a sound. Nanda follows me silently, her footfalls even more practiced in subterfuge than my own.

The closer we get, the more I can distinguish each flavor of magic. This one feels like a long-held breath. This one crackles like fire over wet earth. Some are fleeting, too fluid to catch. Others flicker, in a whiff of perfume. All of them are familiar. Friends or foes?

Another few steps, and the voices become clearer.

"—has to be here," a man murmurs.

*Anirudh*, I think, as I glimpse him through the trees. His aura burns silver-bright, his fast fingers creating runes in the air. The rune of confusion, of fear, of cowardliness, of defeat. He is muttering what can only be mantras under his breath. The chants are deeply powerful; his aura whiplashes like mercury, trying to keep up with his magic. He is calling the raw and potent power of the celestials themselves, of devas like Surya, Vayu, and even Indra in their most natural forms. He is preparing to attack and weaken an enemy. Am *I* that enemy?

My other mortal friends array behind him, but they don't move. Parasara, Eka, even Romasha—

My breath catches. Kalyani is among them. Her round face looks wan, and though she needs to be supported by Eka, her expression is resolute and mutinous. A sharp grief burrows within me, seeking my shame. She must hate me. I have lied to all of them, but most of all to her. With a pang I realize that Kaushika is not with this group. If he sent them here to destroy me, then he could not have picked a stronger team. My friends from the hermitage are formidable in their own right.

I am wondering whether I should reveal myself at all when shadows and foliage rustle ahead of the mortals. They turn abruptly, raising their hands to unleash their magic.

Rambha emerges, all alone, and leans casually on a tree.

The effect is immediate.

My mortal friends blink, and all their gazes move to her.

She is lovelier and more deadly than I've ever seen. Her kohl-lined eyes are flecked with gold. Her hair is tied in an intricate braid that falls well below her waist, night jasmines threaded through it, intoxicating. The dark green sari wrapped around her is deceptively simple, with gold and diamond embroidery so subtle it is as though she is wearing the stars themselves. It tightens around her waist and chest as she moves. The gold dusting of her skin sparkles from the jewels woven into her clothes. She wears no ornaments, not even a nose pin, but Amaravati's power shines from her clothes. This isn't apsara raiment. This is battle armor. The blouse she wears is sheer enough that she might as well not be wearing anything at all. It hugs her breasts, an illusion in itself, the same color as her skin, shimmering.

Nanda stirs next to me, recognizing her danger too, and I quieten her with a touch. I watch as Anirudh's eyes grow wide. He blinks and shakes his head as though to clear it. Romasha's mouth falls open. Rambha smiles, radiant, and her wrists move like a melody, fingers lightly tapping the air.

Her eyes are cold. Calculating. Watchful. A shiver climbs my spine as it hits me how lethal she really is. I'm not sure how I can tell— perhaps it is the clarity I have gained from Shiva—but I know this is the real Rambha, not Indra in disguise again.

"No one needs to get hurt," she says, soft and seductive. Lazily, her wrists curl vapor into the air. It takes the form of a doe. "Just tell me where she is and what he has done with her. I sensed a surge of power. I know she is here."

"*She*," Anirudh says, blinking, "was betrayed by Indra. Are you here to finally kill her?"

I can scarcely believe Anirudh would speak to her that way, that he is not already bewitched. Suddenly I do not know who will win in this standoff.

Rambha smiles a slow smile. Kalyani leans forward, her face serious. Parasara straightens, resigned, and Romasha and Eka begin to spin fire.

*Enough*, I think.

I hurry from behind the trees, in full view. "Stop," I command.

A dozen eyes swivel to me and Nanda, magic and illusions aimed toward us, ready to be unleashed. Everyone's mouths fall open.

Rambha is the first to recover. She leaps forward, grace and poise forgotten. "Meneka!"

I am engulfed in her arms. I don't return her embrace, and behind her the others exchange glances but do not stop their mantras and runes from pointing at me even as Rambha turns to Nanda, nearly sobbing in relief. The two apsaras grip each other, shuddering, Rambha stroking Nanda's hair over and over again while Nanda assures her in murmurs that she is unhurt. Rambha is already inquiring about the other missing apsaras, but Anirudh stares at me.

"*Are* you Meneka?" he says. "I almost think we should ask you to prove it."

Rambha swivels, frowning at him as though to indicate she would know me from an imposter. I flinch, remembering how easily I was taken in when Indra was pretending to be her.

"Would you like me to make an imperfect rune," I ask dryly. "You can deny me any knowledge of Kaushika, then, and it will be just like old times."

At that, Anirudh grins. Behind him there is a murmur as the rest of the mortals relax too. They drop their magic, their half-formed mantras slowly dying, the tension receding. Smiles grow on their faces. Kalyani opens her mouth, glancing from me to Rambha to Nanda, no doubt noticing the same patterns in our beauty.

I nod in understanding. "Perhaps we better sit down. I think we need to explain."


RAMBHA SITS CLOSE TO ME.

She doesn't touch me, but she is there, just a breath away. She fills the corner of my vision. Her magic, her delicate perfume, swim in my head. I see us on the brink of my mission, Rambha brushing her soft lips against mine, and my urge to pull her to me, free her hair with my hand, kiss her senseless. The memory tosses in my head, a dead fruit, the heat and passion of it gone. I do not know if it was Rambha all those times when I made my report or if it was always Indra—but I do know it was her when the two of us walked out of the lord's throne room before I left for my mission. The Rambha then and the one now . . . It is hard to reconcile how far away from each other we have drifted, though we sit beside each other now, for all purposes finally on the same side.

I try to keep my thoughts lucid. I must learn certain things from her. Until then I cannot allow myself to get distracted. I don't look at her, not even when her fingers graze my arm accidentally.

No accidents with her, I remind myself. She is the best of apsaras. She knows exactly what she is doing. Her voice echoes in my head from before.

*You are too young. Too inexperienced. Too naïve.*

*Not that naïve anymore*, I think. The thought makes me cold.

Perhaps she senses my mood. Her aura stutters, subduing. Star-anise decays and quietens. She diminishes in the corner of my vision, a result of her own heartache. I take no pleasure from it; it saddens me. She is responding to *my* power now. This is not what I wanted, but I will take it regardless.

The others sit down haphazardly, though the mortals and the apsaras keep their distance. Someone builds a fire resistant to the rain. Suspicion still hovers heavy over us all, and the mortals look from me to Rambha and Nanda, their bodies still on alert. But Kalyani settles on the other side of me, her brows furrowed in concern. Unlike Rambha, who has quietly been asking for attention, Kalyani merely gazes at me.

I give her a watery smile, and she returns it. Relief bursts in me at her response, and her health. She seems weak, but no longer in danger. I saw Shiva take the halahala. Maybe that healed Kalyani too. Did Kaushika even register it happening, concerned as he was with what to do with the poison?

Though I do not touch her, I lean forward to ask her how she is. Rambha speaks first.

"Indra is coming," she says softly. "He detected the surge of power here too. This is where the lord will bring his battle." There is an iron edge to her voice, and she doesn't look at me. She stares at the ground in front of her, the dust and earth muddying her beautiful clothes.

Mortals and celestials all look at the sky. Thunder rumbles and lightning flashes again. The night darkens further, the drizzle continuing to lash. It is the slow anger of the gods, and Nanda murmurs in worry. She recognizes it.

Only *I* don't study the heavens. I finally turn to Rambha, the shape of her next to me, the curve of her body, the shell-like ear. Loose strands from her braid wave in the slight breeze, and an urge grows in me to tuck them behind her ear. I don't move.

Does she know what I endured? Does she understand how much of a part she played in it?

"Coming for me?" I ask, a foolish question.

"And Kaushika." Rambha looks at me then, and real pain flickers in her eyes. It reminds me of the woman I once loved. I wonder if she is remembering it too, the possibility we had before the choices she made. Before the ones I did.

The mortals from the hermitage exchange uncomfortable glances. It is the perfect opening to ask about Kaushika and where he is, but I cannot bring myself to take it. His absence lingers heavy, filled with the gravity of a hundred planets. It stares at me, and my own power flashes in retaliation and pain. I wrap my arms around myself and look away from Rambha into the fire.

"He is at the meadow," Anirudh says quietly. "Readying *his* army. Meneka, he will come here too—I am certain he felt the same surge of celestial magic we did."

Sadness pierces me, tinged with regret and slow horror. Of course.

"He is at the meadow, preparing," I say. "Yet *you* are here?"

"Yes," Nanda says, speaking for the first time. "Why *are* you here?"

Anirudh throws her a cautious glance. She smiles, a charming, guileless grin, and I stiffen. The mortals do not know it, but there is rage in her smile, and the promise of retribution. I reach out a hand to still her, shaking my head subtly. These mortals are not her enemies, as much as I can understand her fury.

It is Kalyani who answers. "He told us who you are, Meneka. An apsara."

I have been waiting for this, and I flinch out of expectation, but there is no heat or anger in her voice. Only curiosity. Still, I close my eyes. I imagine the conversation. Kaushika leaving me by the pond, walking away. Making his way to the hermitage, and to the meadow. Telling everyone who and what I am and how I was sent to seduce him. How I lay with him, loved him, lied to him.

"What did he say?" I whisper.

I open my eyes to see my mortal friends exchange a bewildered glance. "Just that," Anirudh says. "That you are an apsara."

"But you said I was betrayed by Indra . . ."

"It's what he told us," Romasha says softly. I tremble, remembering how she caught me and Kaushika in a compromising position mere nights ago. Kaushika was unashamed then. Have I shamed him now? "He said that by sending you to the hermitage, Indra betrayed your devotion in him. He said that about the other apsara who was sent for him too. We know what he did to her now, but it was not rage or revenge that made him curse her. Kaushika could have killed her had he wanted to. He just wanted to convince Indra to stop."

"And I should feel grateful that he did not, should I?" Nanda answers coldly. "What a heroic figure he is, indeed. To be so kind as to simply curse me for ten thousand years instead of outright killing me."

She makes a disgusted sound in her throat, her fingers sizzling with gold dust that is close to being unleashed. Romasha blanches, realizing finally that it was Nanda herself trapped in stone. I can see the question on her face, wondering how Nanda is free, but Romasha withdraws into herself and averts her gaze.

I say nothing, my mind whirling. Anger still courses through me at Kaushika's dismissal of me, but what Romasha said about Indra betraying me is too true to deny. The lord has punished his own devotees before. *I* have been the harbinger of that punishment. Does this mean Kaushika has forgiven me? Or simply that he pities me?

"You still haven't explained why you're here," Rambha says to the mortals.

"Neither have you," Kalyani snaps. "Did Indra send you?"

"Please," I say quietly, strained. There is no love lost between the mortals and celestials, especially after the damage Amaravati has undoubtedly already suffered and the events in Thumri and with the halahala. But I cannot have these people fight now, not when war itself looms between our realms. I give my friends from the hermitage a desperate glance, and Kalyani throws up her hands like it's the most obvious answer in the world.

"Why do you think, Meneka?" she says, exasperated. "We came here because we care about you. We were worried!"

"But I am an apsara. Mortals despise my kind. I—I deceived you."

"Did you?" she says, shrugging. "I think you were completely yourself when you were with us. Even if we didn't know you were a celestial. Your defense of Indra, for one thing . . . It should have tipped your hand, but of course, you could do rune magic. We didn't think it could be so."

"How *can* you do rune magic?" Parasara asks, leaning forward. "As an immortal, it should not be possible."

I shake my head. I owe them an explanation, but it is not safe to share with anyone yet. I always wondered if the wild prana was my own, unlocked by my own tapasya. I never considered that *Amaravati's* power had been my own too. Even though Indra cut me off from both of those, he could not deny me what is mine. He has been hoarding the city's magic, having us believe it is him we rely on. He has been keeping wild prana hostage, too, from all the celestials, likely for millennia. He must have considered me a threat from the time Rambha reported my rune-making to him; perhaps he sought to cut me off from both the magics, even then. If I shared the return of my magic, it would create a riot, swarga itself falling apart even as the Vajrayudh approaches. I cannot let such dangerous information out, not even to my friends, not when it can destroy my city. So even though my actions inevitably protect Indra's secret, I hold the explanation within.

"Power is power," I say simply, a line I have heard often enough at the hermitage. "When the rune magic came to me, it surprised me too. I did not mean to deceive you."

Parasara's forehead crinkles. I wonder if even that hint is enough for him; he has always been the wisest when it comes to understanding how magic works.

"It should not have been possible," Anirudh says, nodding, "though you have always been strong in magic. Yet we have magic too, Meneka. You would never have found yogis easy prey. Kalyani is right—we believe you showed us as much of yourself as you could, no matter the mission you were sent on. Kaushika left you in the forest, never to return to the hermitage, but Kalyani fought with him over it, censuring him for his callous actions—that he could simply abandon you even though he acknowledges it was Indra who betrayed you. It was because of her that we are here, for no matter what he thinks, *we* agree that Kaushika behaved thoughtlessly. What kind of friends would we be to him—to *you*—if we let you both drift away when we can see how you empower each other? We have been searching for days, but we have not been able to track you. We thought you returned to Amaravati, but when we sensed the magic here . . ." He shrugs. "We are here. We found you. You are not alone."

I am so taken aback by this little speech that tears flood my eyes. They argued with Kaushika for me. They came to find me, despite his power and hold over them. Despite the beliefs they shared with him and their loyalty to him. Despite the fact that I am a celestial who lied to them about who I was.

Kaushika may have forsaken me, but my friends did not.

I turn to Kalyani and she smiles at me, and there is such love and loyalty and understanding in her look that tears finally trickle down my cheeks. She shakes her head and envelops me in her arms, and I utter a half laugh and cling to her, desperately relieved that she is here, that she is all right, and she has not abandoned me.

"I thought you were going to die," I whisper, and my shoulders shake with all the terror I have held on to since her poisoning. "I thought—I thought—"

"Shh," she says softly, and her own voice shudders. "I am fine, my friend. I owe you more than my life, yet that is not why I am here. Oh, Meneka. No matter who you pretended to be, I cannot hold it against you. You taught me so much. Before you, I questioned little of what my teachers would tell me to do, but you taught me to be brave, to stand up for what I believe to be right. And in this quarrel between you and Kaushika, *you* are right. That is why I am here."

I can say nothing to that. I only hug her tighter.

When we release each other, she has tears in her eyes too. She laughs ruefully and brushes them away, and I give her a small smile.

She pats my hand and the two of us turn back to the others, composing ourselves.

I take a deep breath, trying to sort my emotions. I look at Rambha. "Does Indra know you're here?"

She glances at the sky and grimaces when a drop of rain plonks on her nose. "I did not tell him when I came to investigate the surge of power. But he has been raving in his court for days, working himself up into a frenzy. Only Surya and Agni have managed to stay his hand in doing something he would regret. Queen Shachi is furious with the lord. She has not forgiven him for sending you on this mission, but that has only made him angrier, with you and with Kaushika. Indra has wished to destroy the sage for some time now. With what you told him about the army . . . The Vajrayudh is still some months away, and the lord is too strong. He is going to annihilate any who oppose him."

"Kaushika is ready too," Anirudh says in turn. "When Indra arrives, Kaushika will be able to sense it. He will open a portal to the deva king, and his army will pour out. The deva king should not underestimate Kaushika or his army."

"He has placed wards around the hermitage," Romasha adds. "And he will bring battle far away from it."

"A battle that you once supported," I remind her softly. I trust my mortal friends, I *must*, but there are still things to clear up, and I will not move forward unless I understand all of it.

Romasha's gaze does not waver from mine. "Yes," she says dispassionately. "It was a battle we once supported. Anirudh and I have known about the meadow, and what it really is. But never before has Kaushika acted out of sheer rage. Oh, he has been angry but there has always been a righteous reason behind it. His abandonment of you now, however, shows he has a wounded heart. It is affecting his choices." Romasha shrugs, and though the gesture is casual, I detect pain and grief in it. "This war is an action of a spoiled prince, not a wise sage, and one must question if everything thus far has been guided by a similar sentiment." Romasha meets my eyes, and I see no lies in them. "The sages of the Mahasabha always did say that Kaushika was bound by his past karma. Perhaps we have been wrong to follow him so blindly. Perhaps he never would have chosen the peaceful path. You have revealed to us . . . a different side of him."

My brows rise. One by one the other mortals nod, agreeing with Romasha's words, and I think back to what they said after Thumri, and how they behaved at the Mahasabha. How Kaushika himself considered Anirudh and Romasha his most loyal followers.

"Do you no longer think Indra needs to be taught a lesson?" I ask softly.

"The storm lord has much to answer for," Romasha says. "But war . . ." She shakes her head, once, tightly. "We must think of another way."

My gaze takes in the other yogis huddled together. Under their brave expressions, their fear ripples. I realize how the words spoken by them before were always bold words, easy words. Which one of us save Rambha has ever experienced *war*? We only know the stories, and even Rambha does not speak of it, ugly as it is.

These mortals rebelled against Kaushika to come for me, but perhaps my disappearance broke them out of an enchantment they didn't know they were under. Kaushika would not have done so deliberately, but his very intensity and charisma collected a whole army. My mortal friends absorbed his anger for Indra as their own. They were bewitched by Kaushika's power. *Seduced*.

A bone-deep tiredness threads through me with this realization. How curious that I was sent here to seduce Kaushika, but what I've done instead is break the others from his seduction. He and Indra are so similar, out for blood and war, in the name of loyalty and power.

Yet I am the one who has somehow betrayed them both. Is this where I belong—fighting between each of their pulls on me?

*No.*

I refuse.

I stand up. "Indra is coming, and so is Kaushika. Soon this forest will become a battleground. We need to stop this battle we are all being manipulated into."

"How?" Nanda asks.

I pause, looking to the others for suggestions.

Anirudh comes to my rescue. "We can begin with creating wards here. Anything to prevent bloodshed. Anything to incite peace." He cracks his fingers together, then draws a few runes in the air. Harmony. Tolerance. Prayer.

They begin planning then, the mortals from the hermitage and Nanda, a move that surprises me, given they were nearly at arms earlier. Nanda begins to sing as she casts her illusions. Eka and Parasara murmur to each other, their mantras melding with her song. Magic ripples out from all of them, golden from Amaravati, and a thousand earthy hues from the mortals, blending and weaving, unleashed into the forest beyond the clearing.

I move to help, but Rambha is next to me, reaching out a hand.

"Please, Meneka," she says. "Let us talk."

I hesitate. I don't know what I will say to her.

Her eyes are large and liquid. She doesn't ask again. I glance at Anirudh and Kalyani, who are busy with the other mortals, and I think of how they came for me even though I deceived them. Do I not owe Rambha the same?

Sighing, I nod. Rambha leads us away from the clearing toward the clifftop.

# CHAPTER 27

We stand next to each other at the precipice of the cliff.

Below us, the tributary of River Alaknanda cascades like a stormy ocean, preparing for battle too. Waves rise and fall in the wind, the usual chinking babble now crashing violently over stones. Despite this, so strong is my sense of peace around Rambha, so familiar is her star-anise scent, that if I close my eyes I can almost believe I am back in Amaravati.

I do not close my eyes.

I stare ahead and will myself into stillness, forcing myself to see this moment for what it is.

Rambha swallows, the sound soft in her throat. Out of the corner of my eye, I notice the curve of her neck. The golden luminosity of her skin. The sari that hugs her and the blouse that is very nearly not there.

She is exquisite, but for once her beauty does nothing for me. Instead, I find myself thinking back to when I first met her all those years ago. I was an apsara of fifteen, and she was my new handler. I wanted to be like her from that first instance. Look where that brought us. If she encouraged me to become my own creature, would our destinies be different? Even Kaushika only ever wanted me to stay true to myself. I failed him when I failed to do this, never understanding my own nature—but Rambha, she only wanted me to become someone else, and I traveled that path into confusion and despair. What does she possibly have to say to me now? I turn to her, my mouth tightening, a question in my face.

She stirs. "I didn't know the lord was going to do it," she begins.

I wait. Do what? Impersonate her? Cut me off from Amaravati? Promise retribution? Which of these did she not know as his favorite apsara?

"When the lord told me that he exiled you . . ." Unexpected tears spring into her eyes, and Rambha brushes them away.

Instinct makes me want to move, hold her in my arms, and soothe her. If I only relent, the walls between us will break. I do not listen to that part of me. I remain frozen.

Rambha's gaze falls. "I begged him to spare you. I told him I did not want you harmed. But he is furious and frightened. The threat to his power and to Amaravati is greater than ever. This is why he comes for Kaushika, now before the Vajrayudh fully arrives, while he still can. There was a time when the lord was more open-minded, but he is weakened now, beginning to fear the doubt people have in him. Queen Shachi questions him in front of his devas, showing them how fallible he is. He would not countenance it from you, Meneka. He would punish you if I told him of your failing devotion to him. And I cannot lie to him—I do not *want* to. This is why I tried to dissuade you from your questions, why I tried to make you focus on your missions. To be involved in court intrigue is not something anyone should endure. You can be asked to make choices you will never be ready for." Her voice becomes a whisper by the very end.

I imagine it. Indra has just cut me off from Amaravati. A full court awaits him in his palace, and his fury lashes out at all the immortals. He slouches on his throne, frowning, wishing to be entertained and distracted. The apsaras perform for him, showing him illusions of his own greatness. And later, when the court has cleared, Indra remains on his throne, moody and sulking. Rambha is at his feet, a supplicant. Rambha, who has been thrust into court intrigue, or perhaps chooses to participate. Rambha, who has been asked to make difficult choices, between the lord she loves . . . and me.

The images pour into my head easily, too vivid for my own imagination. I am instantly suspicious. Rambha's aura shines, no longer subdued, and though her fingers do not twist into mudras, I think, *She has always been more skilled.*

"Why are you here?" I ask bluntly.

"I am here for you," she replies.

I raise an eyebrow. "Not for Indra?"

"For him, too—always. And Amaravati."

There is no guile in her response. She loves the City of Immortals just like I do. She has never been coy about it; in her mind, the city is inseparable from the lord. She has always worried about what Kaushika could do to it, from the very first time she told me about him.

"You kissed me before I left for the mission," I say, and this time I cannot keep the hurt from my voice. "Why?"

Rambha lifts her eyes to meet mine. "I was trying to protect you. I placed a charm on you, one that would shield you from the lord's wrath. I couldn't save you from Kaushika's unknown magic, but Indra's temper I know well." She smiles, and it is sad. "I know you, too, Meneka, and I knew this mission would test you. It would make you question the lord further, especially after the form your own boon took. My kiss was a transference of my own aura, to remind Indra in his time of rage that you are precious to me."

I stare at her for signs of duplicity, but all I see is grief in the bend of her shoulders. My anger leaves me in a wave of tiredness.

Rambha did not ask me before placing the charm on me, her kiss only clouding my mind. Yet it was because of this transference that Indra chose to exile me instead of killing me. He cut me off from my power, an action that might have killed me anyway with the sickness of being removed from Amaravati's magic, but he could have simply beheaded me with the vajra—and he did not. I reclaimed my power because I still lived. I should thank Rambha for this small protection, but my gratitude fades within the sorrowful chasm of what I endured. Nothing is left behind except ashes of pity for the both of us. Is this to be an apsara's lot? To love and protect but always do so without permission?

"So it didn't mean anything," I say. My voice is raw.

"It meant enough," she whispers, and moves closer to me.

I do not move away, but I recognize the answer for what it is. An evasion.

"Did Indra know about this charm?" I ask.

"No, but when the charm took effect, he understood what I did. He remembered my love for you."

I recall the expression of sadness in Indra's eyes, even as he told me of my exile. "Did he punish you?" I ask.

Rambha hesitates for a second. Then she shakes her head. "He would not. Not me."

I say nothing to this. I simply watch her.

She shivers under my scrutiny. "Meneka, it is complicated. We are immortals, you and I. We do not age like mortals do. Yet I am much older than you are. I was born during the Churning of the Oceans. I have been by the lord's side, his dancer, his muse, his devotee, for millennia. Indra and I have lived through a thousand battles, a hundred heroics, a million manipulations. He has taken my form before, to test me and to test others, especially apsaras who threaten to go rogue. I have held his hand, planned his wars and missions for him, comforted him. We have always been more than lord and apsara."

"Lovers," I say dully, and she nods.

Little wonder he refused to endanger her on such a dangerous mission. I suppose I have known all along. I try to work up resentment, but in my heart I understand. Would I endanger Kaushika if I had a chance to save him? I shudder, unable to contemplate such a position.

"Does Queen Shachi approve?" I ask instead.

"She knows," Rambha answers. "She has not objected. She understands Indra and his desires."

I think of the queen. Proud, beautiful, kind. A goddess who raised the apsara girls in her own grove, bearing gifts and sweetmeats for the little ones, sitting among the flowers, encouraging our dance. I recall her fury in the throne room, and how she challenged Indra. I cannot reconcile the image of that devi with what Rambha is saying to me. Would Shachi truly not care about Rambha with her own husband? Rambha was never part of Shachi's grove. If Rambha were truly born during the Churning of the Oceans, then she is as old as Shachi herself. Yet Indra is known as Shachindra. *Shachi's* Indra. Whether the queen understands Indra's desires or not, she is possessive of the lord.

Rambha reads my mind, and her smile is resigned. "Do not confuse faith with monogamy, Meneka," she says softly. "Monogamy is the invention of mortals. I have seen it come and go. I am not the lord's only lover, and the queen has her own harem. But I am a free agent, and my heart is to do with as I wish. Just because I love Indra, it does not mean I cannot love someone else. And what I feel for you—"

"What *do* you feel for me?" I interrupt, finally asking a question that has hovered between us from the beginning. "That kiss, and everything you have asked me to say or do for this mission . . . has it been for the lord? Or has it been for me?"

"It has been for both of you," Rambha says, though her face falls. "My love for the two of you is not different, Meneka. The lord will not want me here, but even if he wins it and destroys Kaushika, this war will only weaken him further. It will be a mistake Indra might never recover from, to kill a sage devoted to Shiva. Tell me," she says, and a cold edge enters her soft voice. "Why do *you* do this? Why did *you* make the choices you did during your mission?"

I pull away from her. Yet I cannot deny that the very same questions I have asked of her, Kaushika has asked of me. I understand her explanation, but pain still lances through me, cutting me fresh. Is this what Kaushika felt with my betrayal? With my explanation?

"Indra exiled me from Amaravati," I say quietly. "He took everything from me when he did so, unwilling to hear me out, and maybe that is what devotion is, the fact that I cannot help but still retain a measure of love and loyalty towards him, no matter his actions. But I do not forget what he did, Rambha. I do not forgive. I can balance both these emotions in me—just like Shiva holds both poison and freedom within himself. Do you understand what I am saying?"

She is silent for a very long while. Under the moonlight, her cheeks look pale. I wonder if she has ever been rejected.

"I understand," she says finally, and her voice is emotionless. "But if it is your objective to stop this war, then you need me."

A breeze ruffles my hair, heavy with the scent of storm. My mind swims with everything she has told me.

I shake myself. "Then help us in any way you can," I say. "The others are waiting, and we don't have time."

I leave without checking to see if she follows.


I RETURN TO A CLEARING OVERFLOWING WITH MAGIC.

Rambha and I were not away long, but already the mortals and Nanda are working together, albeit begrudgingly. Anirudh's rune of accord glitters with Amaravati's gold dust as Nanda spins a lazy circle around it. They push it out together, and it rises, enlarging, into the dusky sky above us, similar to how I once created a rune over the hermitage. I imagine it shielding the forest.

The braided magic works on me as well, almost as soon as I arrive. My muscles relax, and my head empties of its confusing thoughts. I join Nanda, and we mold illusions of Amaravati, its delicate sculptures that peek through the trees, its arches reaching over the clouds. The mortals clear the woods, and we fashion it to resemble Indra's own personal garden. *Do not war here*, I add silently, a prayer to the lord of heaven. *This realm is not so different from the one you love.*

My request to an invisible Indra is simple, but when I think of a mirror one for Kaushika, the peace I've acquired grows unsteady. What can I say that will convince him? I know his reasons for battle, and I have not been able to persuade him yet. Even his closest counselors have failed in this, as have his teachers from the Mahasabha. His dimpled smile flashes in my eyes. The heat and camphor of his aura. The softness of his skin. The kindness that fills his heart. I cannot bear it, the thought that he could be destroyed soon.

We stop to rest when the rain has completely let up, and the moon is high. My mortal allies settle around the fire in their bedrolls. Rambha and Nanda, of course, do not need to sleep as celestials. The two disappear into the woods, murmuring in low voices.

I lie on the ground beside Kalyani and Eka as the night climbs. Magic shimmers around us, in dimly lit illusory lanterns on trees, and runes that flicker just out of sight. A low hum of mantras circles us, providing a soothing cadence, and the fresh scent of petrichor sings in my heart. The mortals fall asleep almost instantly, but I lie awake, thinking. Only a few hours ago, Shiva was speaking to me in this clearing. Only a few hours ago these people were ready to attack one another. We are peaceful now, but what will the morning bring? Could I change Indra's and Kaushika's minds the way I changed the minds of these people here? I cradle my head in my hands, while I stare up at the star-studded sky. I imagine myself back in Amaravati, but I do not know if I will find relief there, not unless my friends and I succeed at what we intend tomorrow.

I should rest, yet all of Amaravati's magic around me keeps me alert. Rambha's laughter through the trees heats my cheeks. She and Nanda are comforting each other in the way apsaras often do. The celestials are not loud, and my mortal friends sleep deeply, undisturbed, but of course, they would not have a celestial's sensitivity to such pleasures. Unlike the mortals, we are made for song and dance and love. I can hear the two women release their fear and worry, the slight pants, the playful tones. Yet there is no one here who can help relieve me.

My hands twitch, and I rest them lightly on my belly. My eyes fill with stars, but all I see is Kaushika and the night we spent together. The length of him. The rosewood scent of his skin. The way he would move me just so, for the satisfaction he could give me. The way he would demand his own pleasure, rough and gentle and breathless. My breathing turns shallow, and my eyes start to close, drifting, drifting, so easy to forget that he might never forgive me—

"Meneka? Are you awake?"

I snatch my hands away from my belly.

I open my eyes to see a shadowy shape sitting up across the fire where the other yogis are. "Yes," I reply, my voice a croak. "I'm awake, Romasha."

She wriggles out of her bedroll. Her shadow moves, then she sits beside me, staring into the fire. She throws a few twigs in, biting her lip.

"You are worried," I say, sitting up too.

"I don't like this waiting. I hated it even when Kaushika was making all *his* preparation. Before Kalyani convinced Anirudh and me that we needed to find you."

"We've done all we can," I say. "This will work." *It has to.*

She does not reply, but her posture grows more tense. She is uncomfortable about something unrelated, wanting to unburden her-self to me. I wonder if she is about to declare her love for me too, like Kaushika once did, and then Rambha. It is such a ridiculous thought that I smile to myself in the darkness.

"Meneka," she blurts out, "he was distraught."

It takes me a second to understand.

Kaushika.

My heart begins to race. I want to ask a hundred questions, but my tongue is heavy in my mouth. I swallow.

"I have never seen him like this," she continues. "You have changed him."

My eyes close. Romasha's words are a balm to my soul, but I can-not accept them. Kaushika's face flashes at me, the way I saw him last, cold and emotionless, repulsed by me.

"He loves you," she says, her voice quiet.

"You don't know that," I whisper, tears pressing at the back of my eyes. I shake my head, wanting to change the subject, but Romasha looks into the fire, and her voice hardens.

"I *do* know that," she says vehemently. "I know *him*. He returned to us weeping after he left you. Oh, he blustered and raged while telling us what had occurred between you two. Criticized you and himself and all the betrayals. But you and I both know he is too strong to simply be seduced by a celestial. He was never as innocent of the seduction as he claims to be. He suspected you were lying from the very start; he even asked Anirudh and me to watch you while he was away from the hermitage, to see if you exhibited any suspicious behavior, to see if you attempted to attack him in any way. He began warding his home after you arrived, and he told us to trap you if you were found inside so he may deal with you. He never confided why, never telling us he thought you were an apsara. It was too close to his own shameful act with Nanda, I suppose. But he tried to trick you as much as you did

him, and now he is in love with you, even if he is too blind to acknowledge it yet. The pain from what happened between you two . . . I believe
this is what drove him to finally call his followers to arms."

Embers of hurt, indignation, and anger spark in me, flashing too
fast to keep track. Keeping them threaded is an animalistic thrill.
That he was hunting me all the while I was hunting him. That he
knew, he suspected, and yet here we are . . . I want to acknowledge
everything Romasha has said, but it is too raw. I latch on to the easiest
thing I can.

"So this war is my fault?" I say. "Kaushika is just like Indra, then.
Neither of them wanting to take responsibility for their own actions.
Neither of them—"

"Meneka," Romasha interrupts, "he is in pain. This war is for
you, not because of what you did, but because of what you were
made to do."

My anger melts away. I remember him saying, *Your compulsion to
obey is another thing Indra must answer for.* "Why are you telling me
all this?" I ask Romasha quietly.

She turns to me, surprised. "Do you not know? I thought it was
obvious. I am telling you because I love him."

I stare at her, and Romasha lets out a bitter laugh, turning back
to the fire. "Do not mistake me," she says. "I wish with every living
breath that he would see me the way he sees you. But I am a yogi, wise
enough to know what is simple desire and what is more. He loves *you*,
not me. He does not even know I care for him in this way, but I do not
need him to. When I look at Kaushika, I see Shiva. But he sees Shakti
when he looks at *you*. Who am I to stand in the path of his devotion?"

Words fail me. I open my mouth—to say what? Tell her I am
sorry? That I understand it is unfair? Romasha does not need my explanation or my apologies. Suddenly, I feel small and humbled.

I say nothing for a long time.

Stars glimmer above, beginning to fade. In the east, the pale-pink flush of Surya's first light colors the sky. Within the hermitage, they will be starting prayers. In Amaravati, the apsaras will be bathing, splashing water on one another.

"I have hurt him too much," I say finally.

"Who among mortals or immortals does not hurt the ones they love?" Romasha says, shrugging. "Love is hurt. But it is forgiveness too."

Her tone is indifferent, but this is wisdom. Indra would ask me to atone for my sins in order to gain forgiveness. Is this what Kaushika will want too? I open my mouth to ask Romasha, but she sits up abruptly, gazing behind me.

I turn toward the east to follow her line of sight.

Dawn comes faster than usual, flooding across the sky, the sun's rays burning my skin in seconds. Romasha and I stand up. My heart begins to race. The other yogis from the hermitage awaken as though this is an alarm, and when I blink, Rambha and Nanda are there too, beside me. Everyone is grim, and we can all see it now—chariots appearing in the sky, drawn by the massive steeds of heaven.

Devas glitter on them, Surya with his brilliant light-rayed crown, and Vayu, lord of wind, around whom the very air shimmers. Agni, with orange fire sparking over his body, and Samudra, lord of river and ocean, who can command the tributary of the Alaknanda, which lies behind us.

On and on they come, a hundred devas both great and minor, and Lord Indra rides amidst them, the most magnificent of them all. Indra's armor shines a brilliant silver, like the edges of a storm cloud, glinting with the combined power of all the gods he commands. His crown gleams so sharply that I can almost not tell it is made of thousands of tiny lightning bolts. Atop his armored war elephant, Airavat, Indra towers over all the lords, dark-gray clouds crackling in malevolent thunderheads above him. Celestial magic sings to me, and I know the devas are accompanied by apsaras, gandharvas, danavas, and uragas—all of them denizens of Amaravati, and each a warrior in their own right.

Indra has brought his full army to this fight, though there are no devis with him, and Queen Shachi is absent too. The goddesses have been left behind to protect Amaravati, their power meant to shield the real jewel while the devas bring havoc to the sage.

Terror laces through my heart. Lightning flashes and thunder rumbles long and loud, thrumming painfully in my chest.

Next to me, Kalyani cries out and points. To the west, a ripple appears in the sky. My eyes widen as a portal cleaves the air, wider than any I've seen before. Through the tear, Kaushika's army waits arrayed, and even from so far away, his aura shines as bright as Surya himself, a lone figure of light within the crowd. I cannot hear him sing, but he is certainly chanting. The army pours out onto the sky itself, sustained by Kaushika's power alone.

The devas shine brighter, and a long, drawn-out roar of thunder covers the forest, making the earth shake. Indra stares at the rip in the air, toward Kaushika. Agni glints, fire igniting his entire body, a smile of relish on his face.

None of them have noticed us, but I wait no longer.

Uttering a chant myself, I levitate into the air.

Next to me, Rambha ascends as well, two figures flying before war breaks out. I glimpse the others of my alliance as they spin runes, mudras, and mantras. I sense Kaushika's gaze as it flickers to me from a distance.

And then we are in front of Lord Indra himself, and I blink, my throat closing. Gone is the debauched lord of the throne room and bed sport. The Indra who watches me is all warrior, his armor dazzling enough to be a weapon in itself. His dhoti flaps in the wind, swirling with magic. His eyes are shards of crystal. The lightning-bolt crown on his head is interspersed with a wreath of bael leaves, seeking Shiva's strength for himself, and his magnificent vajra shines in one hand, blinding me, searing me with its heat and anger. He is surrounded by devas, each of them incandescent. Yet he is the most ominous, and I remember he has been king of heaven through a thousand mutinies, a hundred betrayals, longer than a million years.

My words curdle in my stomach.

I tighten my grip on my courage, praying to Shiva for protection.

"My lord," I say, and I am proud that my voice does not shake. "I would ask you for a blessing."

INDRA DOESN'T EVEN LOOK AT ME.

His eyes are only for Rambha, burning with outrage and hurt.

"Rambha," he intones, voice like the rumble of thunder. "You are here? I looked for you."

Rambha floats forward, palms joined, eyes downcast. "My lord, please do not be angry. I beg of you."

Images flash in my head, of Indra pacing his garden, bereft, seeking Rambha. Of visiting the apsaras' grove, calling out for her. Of looking into his own heart and finding her here in the forest, with me. I am so close to the lord, and his own mind is churning with so much turmoil, that his memories spill into me, showing me what occurred since Rambha left Amaravati to find me. She offered me her love; a free agent, she said. Somehow, I do not think Indra would have been pleased had I accepted her.

His next words tell me I'm right. "You would betray me? For this . . . this *child*?"

"Lord, this is a misunderstanding," Rambha says hurriedly. "Please—"

"She did not betray you," I say at the same time. "Neither did I—"

Thunder cracks, drowning out both our voices. Indra's face darkens, either at my insolence to speak to him or at Rambha's objection. The clouds kept at bay thus far by Surya's radiance break through the sky.

Instantly, we are drenched, devas and mortals alike, as a terrible thunderstorm pours over us all. Rambha cries out and covers her face. I mutter a swift mantra, drawing a secret rune to keep myself dry. None of the devas are truly affected either. Agni and Surya still glitter. Samudra, lord of the oceans, looks bored.

Yet Indra's anger is an act of aggression. I glance behind me, and Kaushika's army raises its many royal banners. With a start, I recognize the anvil of Queen Tara's country. Magic burns there, seconds away from being unleashed.

I close my eyes.

*Vayu*, I beg. *Hear my call. Help me now, deva. Help them hear me.*

I risk looking at the lord of wind. He is staring at me, his head cocked, amused. Vayu loves mischief and chaos. I have intrigued him.

He smiles, and a depth builds in my throat. The power sings in me, and I float a little higher. "Hear me, devas and sages. Hear me, mortals and immortals. Hear me, all of you who have assembled here for blood."

With the power of Vayu coursing through me, my voice rises even above Indra's thunderstorm, echoing all over the landscape. Indra throws Vayu an irritated look, but Vayu merely smiles again and shrugs, as though to say, *She prayed to me. What would you have me do?*

"Sages and devas, apsaras and gandharvas, scholars and kings and queens, listen to me. This is not your battle. Peace can be achieved if we only sit down to parley."

In the forest, Anirudh, Kalyani, and the others spin runes of concord, unleashing them into the air. The magic glimmers, aided by the power of Amaravati, strengthened by Nanda's illusions and amulets. My friends are aiding my desire for peace with their own magic, releasing strains of accord and wellness to amplify my words. Gratitude burgeons in me for their quick thinking.

"Send your ambassadors and speak with each other," I beseech. My heart races, thinking of what I will say if that occurs. Both the lord and Kaushika are too set in their pride to relent to the other. I will have to negotiate between them. Am I capable of that? "Lay down your astras," I continue. "Come with the peace of Shiva, and—"

Something whizzes past my ear. An arrow soaked in mortal magic. My eyes widen. It is only because of Vayu's power running through me that I have not been hurt.

But the arrow was not aimed for me.

It finds its mark.

Rambha gasps, and I turn back to the devas to see Indra holding the arrow in his hand. It vibrates there, inches from his skin, thirsty for his golden blood. Only his deva power has allowed him to stop it, soaked as it is with magic.

Terror overtakes me as Indra's eyes glint. A thin smile twists his mouth.

He burns the arrow with a thought, and thunder *ROARS*, drowning every other sound. His lips move, and I recognize his words amidst the snarls of lightning. My heart thuds painfully, about to break through my chest.

A conch rings, high and clear.

Heaven's war command.

# CHAPTER 28

I t is mayhem from there.

I am thrust out of the sky. The next thing I know, I am back in the forest. I blink, and lightning crashes above me, so close that I am dizzied.

Blurs appear everywhere, arrows and discs, magic flung indiscriminately. Celestial horses raze through the ranks of mortals, chariots with blades that injure and maim. Airavat, Indra's elephant, is berserk, the sound of his trumpeting bloodcurdling. Vayu is unseen, but great gusts of wind cyclone across the land and sky, throwing up mortals in Kaushika's army, churning trees in the forest.

Vaguely, I register that Rambha was thrown from the sky too. I have only landed safely in the forest because of the protection she has from Indra, extended to me by being near her.

Agni and Surya work together, burning and igniting with the power of fire and sun. Bodies hurtle, explosions in the sky like fireworks. Smoke climbs my nose. Glimpses come to me, apsara magic deluding the mortals into traps laid by gandharvas. Consecrated arrows hurtle through the sky, piercing illusions of seduction. Apsaras fall, blinking away into ashes.

Indra roars, and for an instant, his rage overtakes everything else. His vajra sizzles through the air, cutting tree and forest, to spin through the mortal army. Lightning strikes blind me. Beside me, Rambha cries out. My heart leaps, terrified—

But in a blink the army is gone. Kaushika's magic.

It appears in the valley, atop a hill, safe for a second on hard terrain instead of in the skies. Kaushika stands at the front, blazing with such strong magic that his body shines like a deva's. He thrusts his hands out, chanting, and the streak of Indra racing toward him twists in the sky, momentarily thwarted.

Horror and terror grip me.

Kaushika and Indra will destroy each other. Amaravati—and any hope for reconciliation—will be gone with an arrow's speed.

I try to ascend once more into the sky, but Rambha pulls me back, and both Indra and Kaushika disappear from view, battling elsewhere. Rambha gestures wildly to me, and I see that the forest is loud with cries of death. We huddle together, racing through the trees. A sword avoids us. We are nearly trampled by a runaway horse. I shriek as lightning crashes inches from me, and for a second, Surya shines above, blinding us further with his light. Then I blink and he is gone, pursuing an adversary, and we stumble again, scratching ourselves on trees and magic.

Splinters burst in front of us, and I shade my eyes. Rambha prays next to me, and I draw a rune of obscurity to hide us. I draw a second rune, this one for clarity, embedding it with the intent to see, and the trees explode around us, soaked in golden magic.

In the sky, devas split themselves. Agni is everywhere, fires popping all over the forest, heat lashing my face, cries echoing from the army that is so far away. Islands rise in the tributary of Alaknanda as magic takes unexpected forms.

I can't focus. There is too much chaos, flares of Surya's sun, shards of Indra's lightning, blood everywhere, golden and red.

Rambha screams in my ear, a question. She wants to know the plan.

I have no plan. Only faith. Shiva shines in my mind. I repeat his name over and over again.

Through dust and swirling leaf, I see a motley crew. My friends stand in a small circle of protection under a tree. Rambha and I stagger to Nanda and Anirudh and Kalyani and the others. Anirudh spins runes and chants, and I recognize the call to the innate form of devas. His eyes dart from sky to forest, where the battle is thickest, and even as I watch, Eka and Parasara unleash magic toward a knot of mortals in the distance. A tree trunk crumbles to dust before it smashes into the mortals. My friends have averted Vayu's aim by calling on his own power.

Next to them, Kalyani and Romasha are just blurs, darting in and out of the protection of the circle. They sprint into battle, carrying injured mortals, one time even a minor deva I don't recognize, then lay them to rest near us, where Anirudh performs healing chants. Nanda dances, her mudras increasingly desperate, casting illusions of peace around us, maintaining the shield that protects everyone. The illusion stutters, threaded with her panic, watery.

I shake Rambha off and stumble over to Nanda. I grab her arm.

Alarmed eyes question me, but Nanda does not stop. Though she is not looking, her aim is true. The illusion she creates blinds an archer. His arrow redirects over the cliff, saving the life of an unwary celestial. Her next illusion protects several mortal soldiers, making them appear like harmless rocks, while Vayu himself rages, fooled by her power. Nanda's mouth never stops moving in chants, consecrating her illusions even as she unleashes them. We are protecting one or two people. It is not enough.

"Sing," I command.

Golden blood trickles down her forehead. She breaks her chant long enough to give me a withering look, as though to ask, *What do you think I'm doing?*

It exacts a cost. Agni's fire climbs up a mortal, their flesh burning.

"No," I say urgently. "For me. Nanda, sing for *me*. So I can dance."

Amaravati's magic floods into me. It pushes against me. My prana surges, all my chakras activated. Is this a mistake? It is our only chance.

Her eyes widen. She understands.

In a blink, the half-formed illusions she has created disappear and are replaced with a mridangam. An earthly instrument made from clay. A mortal instrument, but an instrument of Shiva, one that accompanied his own maya-splitting dance, the tandava, thus making the mridangam an instrument of the devas too.

Nanda begins to beat against it, the sound thundering in my ears. Around us, mortals and immortals fall, but her eyes blaze. She throws her head back, and a robust song emerges from her mouth, clear, high, cutting through the noise like a sword. It is an illusion, but one that ensnares every being, so strong is she in her magic. *Dance*, I hear her command.

I close my eyes, curl my wrists, and rise into a sky that is thick with weapons.

I dance.


I FORGET THE BATTLE. I TUNE OUT THE SCREAMS.

*Am I even capable of love?* I ask Shiva. He gazes at me sadly.

*You violate*, Kaushika says. *That's your entire existence.*

Rain lashes me and I embrace it.

A vision of the universe. Infinite. Peaceful. Indifferent.

I throw my head back, unaware that I am dancing. What is dance but an expression of who I am? And who am I if not what Shiva himself has declared for me?

I spin, and Amaravati floods me. It gushes like a river, collecting my doubts, submerging them, elevating my own prana. The illusion carves around me, and even though my eyes remain closed, I can see it.

Kaushika holds me, telling me of his vow and his childhood. Indra tills the land of the mortal realm a millennium ago. I dance for Tara, and she falls for my seduction, sick with love. The apsaras weep for their fallen comrades and lost sisters while Indra sits on his throne, watching Amaravati's power die, helpless and defeated.

Devas need the mortals, but mortals need the devas too. What is Surya without the fields he warms? Who is Indra without the rain for crops? Merely objects, and dead things. Essences, formless and alone.

I dance, and around me my illusions swell. War and war and war, I show them. Who does it benefit? Everyone has a side. Everyone has reasons. Pointless, all of it.

Nanda's song becomes a litany of her own grief. Others begin to join her, gandharvas—singers of heaven—peeling away from Indra's own army. All their voices rise, reaching into swarga itself.

Arrows and astras fling past me, missing me through sheer luck. They escape under my wrist, pass my ankle, sizzle by my neck. I am a light of my own in the sky, dancing between clouds. I am a shield of my own making, protected by my conviction.

Amaravati's power rises in me and my mudras become runes. Lotus Blossom merges with the rune of patience. Rise of the Dancer melds into the rune of harmony. I open my eyes, breathless, and see then that I am not alone.

Rambha has joined me. She mimics my movements, and a thrill passes over me. Rambha is following *me*?

The awe lasts only a second, and I grip my peace even as I feel the emotion from her. Her pain and sadness, for me and for Indra, and even for Kaushika. Her understanding for what I have been put through, and her distress for Nanda. This dance is revenge against our loss. The peace we seek is vengeance. We are weapons but not of destruction. Illusionists, but the breakers of illusions too. Creatures of lust, but those of love too.

We dance, and create, and hope.

Mudra by mudra, the weapons start to distance from us. Lightning cracks but does not pierce us. Indra's gaze burns on me as he pauses to see what we are doing. His eyes rove over Rambha, and I see his rage as the storm circles us. We are in the eye of it, cradled by him, punished and pushed by him.

We mold the illusion, and it spreads, cutting through the seduction of hate and power, which are the reasons behind this battle. I tug at the emotions of all of us assembled here, the fear of the devas, the determination of the mortals, the desperation as we stagger, unable to understand how we balance one another.

We spin, and in our dance is life, and peace, and love.

Devas blink, seeing the devis manifested in our enchantment. Prithvi, the goddess of earth, shimmers as we apsaras create her form. She is naked, but it is not sensual. It is grief—look what war has done to her. Surya, her consort, averts his eyes in shame. He flashes, visible over a knot of mortals, then he is gone away from the battlefield. He has had enough.

I rejoice silently but do not stop dancing.

I call upon Aditi, the goddess of order. It is Vayu who relents to her. Made of mischief as he is, he recognizes stability. He sees her and grows abashed. A whirlwind of emotion flutters on his face, and then he leaves the battlefield too.

Raka, Parendi, Mahi, other devis emerge from our mirage, and one by one the devas grow shamefaced. They flicker, then leave. A deep breath, and I see tired mortals returning to their ranks, stumbling away as the attack abates. The most powerful of them, Kaushika, forms a ward and shield around his straggling army, while the sky clears.

Last of all, I create an image of Shachi herself for Indra. Her beauty, kindness, fierceness glow from my illusion. She is taller than either me or Rambha, her beauty more than both of ours combined. Her skin is golden brown. She is the queen of swarga, a daughter of an asura, married to the lord of heaven.

*Look at her*, I urge. *Would she want this? She has not joined your battle. Why do you think?*

High above me, Indra blinks, his hand around the vajra tightening.

He is a distant dot, yet clear to our celestial eyes nonetheless. His gaze cuts across the illusion back at us. He stares at Rambha, and her nervousness pounds at me through our apsara bond.

It is between them now.

I leave the illusion in her hands.

Amaravati tugs at me, and I spy Kaushika on the ground. He stands with his army again, blazing, all the chakras glowing within his body. He is coated in magic, watching me warily, seeing the illusions I carved. I float toward him, and suddenly he is there, rising to meet me. I hear his voice, golden and beautiful, across the barrier. He sings his mantras to maintain his shield from the devas and celestials. To maintain it from me. He watches me but does not stop.

*Let me in*. I know he can hear me.

He blinks, but the shield does not give.

*Let me in*, I say again.

Kaushika's mouth pinches in pain. We stare at each other across the divide, his defense pulsing against me. My prana flows in waves of illumination, drenching me from head to toe. I can break his magic if I want, so great is my power. He knows this. He can see it.

*Who are you?* He asks.

*Find out*, I challenge.

Kaushika blinks again. A wry, humorless smile forms on his lips.

He opens the barrier.

I SHOW HIM.

The second the shield drops, I shoot toward him.

I take him in my arms, and his shock radiates to me. Whatever he expected, this was not it. Magic whirls around us, raising us, cocooning us. He is still singing, chanting, protecting his people from the imminent onslaught of the devas. His eyes widen in question and confusion, even as shlokas and mantras pour out of him. His arms encircle my waist, and he pulls me closer.

It surprises the both of us.

His mantra stumbles, a mistake as he drops a note, then hastily picks it up. He looks at me, startled, both at his mistake and at his desire. I press my body to his. I interlace his fingers with mine. I stare into his wary eyes.

Holding him, I move.

It is a dance like no other, his body rigid and unmoving against mine. My body sways, ever so slightly. He sings—and I do what I do best. I dance.

Our magic entangles together. Note by note, twist by twist, it merges.

With our bodies so close, touching, our fingers entwined, a vision of love overtakes us.

He is carried away, both with his control and without. He is horrified, and curious, as I show him who I am, and who he is. Who *we* are, together.

A mirror forms between our very beings, like the time it did when we saved Kalyani. I will him to see within me, laying my heart bare. He dips himself into me, a touch in a pond, a hesitant exploration. *Look inside*, I say. *What do you see?*

*I see you*, he responds from a lifetime ago, and the memory grows alive in both of us. *A vision of beauty, sacred and deep.*

Kaushika shakes his head, pulling away, face distraught.

*Stay*, I whisper, and the illusion magnetizes with my emotion. Stolen kisses. That night on the pond. The words of devotion we said.

*Real*, I tell him. *All of it was real.*

Rainbow colors surround us, and in every direction we look we see only ourselves. Hand in hand, laughing. Me astride him, riding him. Him kissing my wrists with reverence. Our foreheads touching, like we are praying to what is between us.

*Who are you?* he gasps.

I sway.

*Who* are *you?* he pleads.

The mirror shows him.

The image rises above the both of us, clear for every mortal and celestial to see. It is a vision of me as I crouch in prayer by the kalpavriksh to make my wish. My voice echoes across the battlefield. *Help me find devotion.*

My story, my own legend, shines in waves. The journey to the mortal realm. The seduction of mortals. Falling in love with Kaushika. Exile and losing myself. I stare at my own lore, shocked with my power, and how it has always resided within me, waiting. It is there, laid naked, for everyone else to see as well—and beyond it, the kalpavriksh blooms, fruit forming with every step of my own journey. Fruits that are the realization of my own incoherent, vulnerable, honest, foolish wish. To stay true to myself.

In swarga, the kalpavriksh flowers.

Its leaves rain down along with Indra's rain. Forest and sky swirl, receiving its blessing.

And in that moment, I understand. The kalpavriksh never needed to fulfill that wish of mine. In the acceptance of myself is my reward, the fulfillment of my wish.

I sought devotion. I searched for it in Indra, in Kaushika, in Shiva.

I found it in myself.

My mistakes, my confusion, my indecision, my faith and my doubt—they have always been mine. A part of who I am. And at their foundation, something more, something unmoving exists. Something that shines with the power of a hundred universes, in that space between illusion and reality, between anger and righteousness. It is there, in that space between me and Kaushika. *That* is who I am.

Kaushika's pulse stutters.

*Love*, he says.

*Love*, I confirm.

Tears fill his eyes as he understands, as he accepts.

His chant wavers, then changes shape. The Chant to the Goddess. The Mantra of Devotion. Magic spins from him, but this time it does not hold the heat of battle. Instead, it holds the balm of care, of comfort.

Power spreads from us through the forest and the skies. It coats the army he has brought with him. It instructs them and guides them. It carries the magic of my friends and the illusion I have built with the apsaras. Mortal magic becomes stronger, calmer. It pushes gently and firmly against the devas. Indra, who is still staring at Rambha as she dances, blinks again. Storm and glory coat him, the vajra golden and sharp in his hand.

Rambha pushes the magic with her power and my illusion. She dances, leading other apsaras, changing the illusion, molding it from the vision of Shachi into a vision of herself. Now I see what she is showing Indra. The love he bears for her, hurt but ever-patient. The love he has borne for the world and all his devotees, forgotten, jaded, but present nevertheless. The love he has always felt for the mortals, even if it has cooled in recent times.

Indra's eyes widen in shock.

He glances at the devas in formation, their own warring paused.

Agni, the last of the titans still on the battlefield, gives Indra a small nod. The lord of fire clicks his fingers, and the celestial army returns to where they started, apsaras, gandharvas, and all the other survivors of the battle arrayed again behind the other devas.

Indra lingers in the sky, vajra still spinning. A beat, where my heart claws up to my throat and he joins his devas, at the lead. Then he relents, ending the fighting now that Kaushika has ended it too. Airavat trumpets once, the great elephant swinging its trunk. Everything stills with suddenness, as though battle has not occurred at all.

Rambha is already floating toward the lord, but this time instead of watching her, Indra's eyes are on me. The vajra still glitters in his hand, aimed for me and Kaushika. It singes me in memory, from when the lord placed it at my neck.

I peel myself away from Kaushika, but he squeezes my hands, arresting me.

*Don't go*, he says.

*Wait for me*, I reply.

For a heartbeat, he holds on to me. Then he lets go.

I approach Indra.


BEHIND INDRA, THE DEVAS AWAIT HIS COMMAND. AGNI'S ARmor still radiates fire, smoke curling from his fingertips. Surya is gone, but the rays of his sun are still sharp, the heat sizzling my skin.

Yet Samudra, lord of the oceans, nods at me in a sign of respect. He exhales a whisper, and a wave of dampness washes over my skin, cooling me as I levitate toward Indra.

Next to me, Rambha ascends as well. I press my palms together. I do not bow my head.

For a long moment, Indra studies me, his eyes like lightning shards. The lord does not look even remotely tired. I think of how close we came to the end. I think of how the mortals, and Kaushika, and so many celestials—apsaras, gandharvas, and kinaras alike— still dangle on the precipice. My tongue twists in my mouth, Indra's power potent and dangerous.

Perhaps I should incline my head, but instinct tells me it would be a mistake.

*Please*, I think. Indra's eyes flicker to the devastation below. To the skies still raining down storm. His chest rises and falls, the vajra still spinning.

Then he glances at Rambha next to me. Her head is bowed. She is submissive, powerful, beautiful.

Indra sighs, a quiet sound. The vajra disappears without warning.

"I will allow a pause to this battle today, daughter," he says to me coldly. "See to your injured."

I don't reply. Questions trouble me. Is this enough? Will Kaushika begin this war again? Was this merely first blood? Nothing has been resolved. Kaushika is still bound by his vow. Indra still has not agreed to change his laws. We could be here again, perhaps tomorrow, perhaps in a few years.

I open my mouth to ask again for a parley, but Rambha shakes her head in a very subtle movement. I understand. Now is not the time. I will have another opportunity.

Indra watches this exchange, his eyes missing nothing. He frowns.

"Come, Rambha," he says.

Rambha glances at me, a quick, searching look. Her hand accepts Indra's extended one, and he pulls her to him. The both of them gaze back at me, and in Indra's face I see the calculation that Rambha has made. The choice.

The devas, apsaras, and other celestials are already disappearing, blinking out of sight. My heart seizes to see Rambha go, as both her and Indra's lips move to call to Amaravati.

I speak before they are gone, my words slow and careful. "My lord. Amaravati is my home. You are still my king. I intend to return there."

Indra's brows draw together. I have issued neither a challenge nor a relinquishing of my own control. I do not demand. I do not beg.

It is still audacious. Lightning flashes near me once in warning.

Indra glances at the disappearing forms of his other devas. I know that now that the heat of the battle has passed, the very same questions must circle him. Who sent the halahala? How is he to survive the Vajrayudh with unrest in his own court? The mortal realm is losing its reverence for him—what will happen to his power? I have no answers, but Indra's eyes meet mine and he sees that I will not rest until I know. Not after my mission and life were embroiled in this without my say-so. The lord knows that I share his secret too—that he has been hoarding magic. Amaravati's power returned to me without his explicit permission, just like my wild prana did. Indra might have cut me off from both of them—but I am a *celestial* with or without him. My words now are a threat but they are an offer too, rolled into one perilous move that can make *me* a mark. My intention is clear to him. *I can be an ally, or I can be your nemesis. The choice is yours, my lord.*

A strange moment of understanding passes between us.

Indra gives me a curt nod.

Then they are gone, all the celestials winking out of the sky.

## CHAPTER 29

I float back to the ground.

My friends wait, having watched this exchange in the skies.

Nanda leaps forward to embrace me. Her chest heaves up and down in gasps. She is wrung out with the magic she performed; she is relieved like I am. Pain and sorrow will follow soon for both of us, for the fallen sisters who were forced into this battle. We do not yet know their names, but apsara fighting apsara has never happened before. She strokes my hair, and in the absence of Rambha I lean on her, tears filling my eyes for all that we have endured.

More bodies surround us, of the mortals who defended us. Anirudh squeezes me to him, and his eyes are blurred too. Kalyani's lips press my forehead. I clasp her to me, relieved she is alive. All of us embrace one another. Shock is written on everyone's faces, but laughter comes too, first from Nanda, then Anirudh.

Slowly, we untangle. Bit by bit, we clean the area around us, picking up stray arrows, vanquishing errant magic still remaining from the battle, creating funeral pyres for the dead. The mortals stop for food, but Nanda and I continue until the mortals join us again. I lose myself in the work. It is as though I am in the hermitage again, undertaking chores that silence my mind.

Noon rises, and I realize that we have been joined by someone else.

He comes to the camp silently, and next to me Nanda stiffens, part in terror and part in rage. I follow her gaze, and my heart skips a beat as Kaushika enters.

The other mortals stop what they're doing, wariness in their eyes, but none of them speak. Kaushika makes for Anirudh and they speak quietly. Anirudh glances at me, then shrugs. He points Kaushika to where the earth lies ruptured. Without a word, Kaushika approaches it and begins to smooth it with his own magic. It ripples, dust and root flaking, until grass begins to grow.

"Why is he here?" Nanda asks me angrily, but I don't respond.

I turn away, back to our own task, but my concentration and fragile peace are gone.

Kaushika stays with the group for the next two days. We do not speak to each other, though I am aware of his presence. Like planets orbiting the same sun, like lovers star-crossed, we move around each other, always in each other's line of sight yet never acknowledging each other. Camphor and rosewood make my throat dry. I want to go to him, to ask him questions and to answer any he has, but grief from the battle holds me back. How many bodies have we discovered already? So many mortals, but so many immortals too. I have even clutched the remains of apsara sisters, their forms dissipated into golden dust, returning to pure celestial power as soon as I touched them. I cannot forgive Kaushika what he has done. But why doesn't *he* come to me seeking forgiveness? We came to an understanding of each other during the battle, but it was never a full understanding. I wonder if any of it will ever be enough.

I do not seek him, and Kaushika doesn't relent either. In the daytime, he goes where Anirudh directs him. He never takes the lead but works silently in the background, never looking at me, but never consciously avoiding me either. I catch Nanda's hardening gaze. She does not speak to him, but her movements grow wooden when he is around. I suggest to her gently that she should return to swarga, but she shakes her head. She and I watch, our hands full of wood that can never go back to growing while the others build a hut as a symbol of a war sanctuary. I study the long lines of Kaushika's body, and the top-knot on his head. His simple clothes still never quite hide the muscle of his kshatriya build. Does he feel no remorse? Or is this work now a gesture of regret? I do not know what to make of him.

Anirudh and Parasara step back from the pile of rocks, and after a moment, Kaushika joins them. All three of them begin chanting, and their voices reverberate around us all. Nanda pauses next to me, and the other mortals stop their work on the hut, mesmerized. The voices of the men are tragic, beautiful. All of us watch as the pile of rocks begins to glow. It takes shape, becomes of one piece, almost fluid for an instant.

Then it solidifies into black marble, resembling an obelisk. Eka hurries forward and hands some tools over to Kaushika, who kneels and begins carving the dark rock. The marble begins to take shape under his touch. It is an apology. A regret. A shrine.

I stare at him for a moment longer, contemplating the stiff lines of his back. Only when Kalyani pulls me back to work do I blink and look away from Kaushika.

On the fifth day, when it becomes clear that Kaushika does not intend to leave, and instead help with setting things aright, Nanda corners him. I am surprised. Though she has so far given him dark, hateful glances, she has kept out of his way. But she has been growing incandescent with rage ever since the appearance of the marble obelisk, and now she marches up to him.

Tears glow in her eyes, and her face trembles. "Mortal," she says without preamble, "you desecrated me."

Kaushika straightens slowly from easing the earth back from the ruptures the war has caused. His hands drop by his sides. His mantras cease. He looks like he has been expecting this. He looks tired.

"It was done in error," he says in a low voice. "I ask for forgiveness."

Nanda spits at his feet. "Forgiveness?" she demands. "Ten thousand years you cursed me. To become inanimate rock for ten *thousand* years, trapped within my own mind. If Meneka had not released me, I would be nothing. I would be less than nothing."

"Yes," Kaushika says. His gaze locks on mine. "But what would have happened to me, apsara, if I had not defended myself? If I had simply let you command me without my permission? Would *I* have been less than nothing?"

For the space of a second, I can't breathe.

I stare at him, my mouth dry. His gaze burns like hot coals, full of promises. Full of danger and hunger.

Nanda screams and shouts, but I barely register it, and neither does Kaushika. Our eyes are only for each other, and within his regard, I sense turmoil, and confusion, and sincerity. It is only when Nanda pushes his chest in anger that his gaze flickers away from mine. I take a breath, thinking to calm her, but the moment has passed. Spitting and cursing, she disappears, carried by the wind of Amaravati.

The other mortals begin muttering, but Kaushika simply returns to his task, easing the earth into place again in undulating waves. His fingers move in front of him as though he is playing an instrument. I turn back to my own work, my mind confused, my chest hollow.

I stay away for the rest of the day, wandering through the forest, collecting firewood and berries. I cannot stop thinking about what Nanda said, and how Kaushika responded. I cannot get the image of Kaushika out of my mind. The way we held each other. The way he pleaded, asking me who I was. The way he watched me, not a few hours ago. What is he thinking? I only need to ask. I understand his silence is not to punish me. It is in daring not to presume. Command and consent. Is this the true seduction?

When I finally return, it is dusk. I hope to sneak into camp, but I arrive to see everything cleared and put away. The hut we have been making is complete. Anirudh, Kalyani, and the other mortals linger at the threshold, watching as Kaushika carves the marble sculpture with his tools. Anirudh spies me first, and his face breaks into a smile.

"Meneka," he says, and beyond him, Kaushika stills. "You're back, finally. We didn't want to go without saying goodbye."

My heart sinks. "You're leaving too?"

"We must," Kalyani says, hugging me. "We have duties at the hermitage. A life we must return to."

"You could come with us," Romasha adds. "There are still things you can learn from us, and teach us too."

I glance at her face. My heart breaks in that moment as I think of my friends and their laughter. They accepted me, despite myself, *as* myself.

I shake my head. I cannot go back there. I am not done here in this forest. I have not decided my path forward. It would not be the right thing.

Anirudh and Romasha exchange a look, though Kalyani looks saddened and unsurprised. "We understand," she says quietly. "But know that you will always be welcome there. No matter what."

I hug each of them in turn and watch as they collect their bedrolls and strap them to their backs. A lump grows in my throat, and I swallow it, watching their shadows disappear.

Then there is no avoiding it.

I turn to Kaushika, who stands up from his sculpture and glances up at me warily.

"You are not going back to your hermitage," I say.

"You are not returning to your city," he points out.

"I have unfinished business here."

"As do I."

I don't reply but merely stare at him, my chin lifted. Kaushika turns back to the sculpture, and I see then that it is not a shrine to the fallen. It is a statue of a dancer, her head thrown back, arms raised to the sky.

It is more than I can take.

Eyes filling with tears, I enter the hut to escape him.

He does not follow.


WE FALL INTO A STRANGE RHYTHM.

Every morning Kaushika tends the fire, or cleans the area around the hut, or makes a meal, similar to the fare we ate at the hermitage. I wander into the forest, collecting herbs and berries, one time finding wild potatoes, bringing them back to this place that we share.

We rarely speak, except in constrained politeness, the air between us thick with unspoken feelings, unanswered questions.

I dare not disturb this uneasy peace. What will I say? Where will I begin? Is it not better to delay? Kaushika is deliberate too. His aura still forces my attention, but there is something subdued about it after the battle. A thoughtfulness I am surprised to see.

He has never been volatile, but a steadiness accompanies him now, and for the first time since we met I understand how he is truly a sage. The steadfastness and solidity that tapasya requires, the long hours of meditation . . . Before this, I had only seen him performing magic or leading other students. I had only seen the prince and the warrior. This quiet economy and unobtrusiveness of existence is a whole new side of him, yet new only to me. It is a kind of trust, I realize. To let me see him this way.

It is slow—this return to trust.

It appears in fleeting moments.

One time I arrive at the small pool near the hut to bathe, and Kaushika is already there. He is submerged to the waist, his dark skin glistening, performing prayers while in the water. I hesitate, then re-move my clothes to enter the same pool. So what if he is praying? The pool is mine as much as his.

He knows I am there, but he does not open his eyes as he pours the water from cupped hands onto his hair and into the pool again. It is trust, again, a measure of it. To not interrupt him. To not be interrupted.

I gaze upon his muscular body, filled out like a warrior. He does not open his eyes, but his throat moves in a swallow, and my stomach stirs in anticipation. *You are a sage*, I think. *And I am an apsara. That will never change.*

I linger, watching his chest beaded with water, his neck open to the skies in offering, his lips that murmur a prayer. When he is done, he rises, unashamed of his nakedness. He gives no indication of noticing me, but after he puts his clothes back on he gives me a brief nod before disappearing into the trees. Trust, again. For more than the lust I feel within me.

Things begin appearing in the hut, day by day. Furniture, clothes, plates and cutlery. I return from the forest to see them there, Kaushika tending quietly to them, making this a place of comfort. At first, I resist the pull of my curiosity, but when there is no sign of him breaking first, I cannot help but ask. I sit opposite him, by an evening fire. I have been folding laundry, but my fingers stop and I clear my throat.

"Where is this coming from? The hermitage?"

Kaushika pauses as he unpacks a set of plain kurta and pajamas. He shakes his head. "The meadow," he answers. "When my army abandoned it, we did not take everything from there."

*Of course.* I try not to flinch. "What has become of your army?" I ask.

"They have returned to where they came from. I have sent the survivors home."

"But the meadow still exists," I remark.

"It does," he says softly. "The army will return when I ask them to. They have only returned to a realm that is more sustainable than the meadow, even though the halahala has disappeared."

He gives me a knowing look, as though he understands *I* had something to do with the removal of the poison, but I just laugh humorlessly, hands tightening on the sheet I fold. "Is that your unfinished business then? You retain your army and your meadow because you prepare for a second battle?"

His eyes meet mine across the distance. I feel my cheeks warming. It is a cruel question, a foolish one. I do not think he will reply, but he surprises me.

"No," he says quietly. "The battle is finished for now."

*But not forever*, I think. Still, I cannot help the lightness in my heart. He is here. He has not left. It must mean something.

He hesitates a long moment, then his eyes rest on mine. "I never lied to you, Meneka."

"Did I?" I retort.

"By omission, don't you think?" he says quietly.

It is true, and perhaps I should feel shame for it, but I do not. I raise my chin in silent defiance. Kaushika shakes his head as though to deny any need for a challenge.

"It is only a thought," he says mildly. "It is not an accusation." His eyes flit away from me, back into the woods, toward where the hermitage lies. "I will leave if you want. From here. From your forest."

An ache grows in me, sharp and confusing. "Why are you here at all?"

Kaushika blinks and his gaze finds mine. He swallows as though the words are difficult to say. His fingers move restlessly and a haunted look enters his eyes before he masters himself.

"Do you not know?" he murmurs. "I am here because I must atone, Meneka. You tried to tell me to stop. To find another way. But caught in my own pride, I did not listen to you. I do not expect you to forgive me, not after the way I abandoned you. Not after what I did to your own sisters. But I hope that you will allow me to apologize. That is what this is."

I say nothing for a long time. He does not rush me but merely goes back to arranging the clothes he has brought. Soon he begins to make a meal while I sit lost in my own mind. I know that the words he has spoken are more than an apology. They are both a reckoning for him and a path forward. How am *I* to proceed?

"I should have told you," I say finally. "That I am an apsara."

"Perhaps I was a coward too," he replies. His gaze flickers to me. "To blame you. To leave you when you could not tell me your reasons."

My heart seizes with his admission. It is one I never expected. I am disarmed beyond my own doubts. My fingers knot within the sheet I fold, creating wrinkles.

Kaushika's own hands still from the meal he is making. "Nanda came to me to deceive me," he says. "But perhaps you did not. I should have understood this before. I should have trusted myself to see, to know. Trusted you. Looking back, I can see how you even tried to tell me who you were, but perhaps I did not make it safe for you to do so. For that I am truly sorry."

Here it is, the apology that should make things better, but can I forgive so easily? What about my own mistakes? I have owned up to them, paid for them several times over—but too much has come between us already, and not all of it is resolved.

Yet there can be no moving forward without clarity about my intentions. If I am to salvage anything with him, I have to be honest, no matter how much it will hurt. I corral my courage and lift my chin again.

"I do not want to lie anymore," I say. "Know that I intend to return to Amaravati one day. My words to Indra were a promise. The battle may be over for now, but Amaravati still needs protection during the

Vajrayudh, and the city is my home. I will do whatever I can to safeguard it, even if I must do so from you."

My words are like stones in my mouth, but Kaushika only nods like he has been expecting it.

"I must keep my vow too," he says. "The souls of many are denied entry into swarga. Including that of King Satyavrat. Indra will have to relent, no matter his laws."

My brows rise at that. "Does that mean you expect me to relent too, regarding Indra? It might not make sense to you, after all the wrongs he has done me, but my devotion cannot be erased so easily, Kaushika. It runs in my blood. It is in the stories I grew up with. The beauty and luxuries of Amaravati, the peace I have felt there—these are not compulsions in the way you see them, but embedded within my heritage, my very *culture*, sustaining my devotion to the lord, even if he has behaved arrogantly."

He tilts his head and gives me a speculative look. A sliver of challenge flickers in his gaze, but he nods. "I understand. I don't expect you to love him any less, Meneka. But my own purpose burns within me, too, despite everything."

"Then this peace itself is an illusion," I counter. "We have resolved nothing."

At that, Kaushika's gaze turns quiet, searing. "I wonder," he says softly.

And I think of how I began this journey on my knees in Indra's court. How I faced the lord and won after my exile. How Kaushika and I are still here together despite everything, and how we shared a vision of love in the skies in the heat of the battle. Too many things have occurred to dismiss. His tears and mine. His causes and my betrayals. The journey we have taken, to be here now, in this quiet forest, by this intimate hut. Both of us are still bound by what we need to do, yet transformed beyond our dreams, holding two opposing purposes within ourselves even as we stay true to who we are. Kaushika and Indra have done so much wrong, yet I love them both despite their enmity, despite their flaws. I finally understand that my devotion for them has little to do with them, but everything to do with me. Is nothing truly resolved? I wonder too.

After that, it is easier between us.

LATER THAT NIGHT A VISITOR COMES TO THE HUT. I HAVE fallen into a fitful sleep, my head full of dreams of Kaushika, scented by camphor and rosewood. I open my eyes, and there she is, a luminescent glow emanating from her. Her aura fills the one-chambered home. My eyes widen and I stumble off the bed. I fall to my knees, aware that I am dressed in only my shift. My hair tumbles down my back. My knees and shoulders are bare. This is no way to appear in front of the goddess. No way to appear before the mother of heaven.

"Queen S-Shachi," I stutter.

I cannot breathe properly, too entranced by her loveliness. I have not seen her since that time in Indra's throne room when I accepted this fateful mission, but I have not spoken to her in *years*. Does she know my name? She must. She is here. Why *is* she here? My thoughts confuse me, the same way they once did with Indra. I dare not look upon her too intently, but even in my sleep-befuddled state, I can tell she is studying me. Shadows fall across the walls, and I see her tilt her head. The sari she wears hugs her curves, and unlike in the throne room when it was a fiery red, this time it is a sheer black, like she is a shadow of the night. The black shifts, sometimes edged with a shining silver, other times with stars caught within it, a mirage in itself.

Vaguely, I wonder why Kaushika has not sensed her, with so much of her magic pouring into the hut. Either he has left like all the others while I stay here in the indecisiveness of my own mind, or—a horrible thought—*she* has done something to him.

"He is still here," Shachi says, amused as though hearing me. "Asleep under my enchantment. He is a powerful man. But he is a man. And I am a goddess."

"Devi," I whisper, unable to say anything else.

"Rise, apsara," she says, flickering her fingers. "Sit."

I obey. Tentatively, I seat myself at the edge of my cot. It is then that I notice that she has arrived with two other figures. I blink at the two women standing on either side of her, watching me silently. No, not just two women. Two *apsaras*. The same two who were sent before me to this very mission to seduce Kaushika. Magadhi and Sundari both wear deep inky-blue saris, each of them as beautiful as the other, yet neither more than Shachi. A thousand questions pour into me, and a croak of disbelief escapes me before I can control myself. Goose bumps erupt on my skin. I know somehow that I am in terrible danger.

Queen Shachi studies me for a long moment, then sits down next to me. The bed does not shift with her weight. *Goddess*, I think. Is this an illusion?

"You called on the devis during the battle," she says softly. "Where do you think we were?"

"Protecting Amaravati," I whisper. "In case the war came to the city's doorstep."

Shachi shakes her head. "We were angry."

She is quiet for a long moment. I think of what Rambha told me about Shachi and her questioning of Indra.

"We have been angry a long time," Shachi says finally. "I think you are familiar with such anger towards the lord. Did you not feel it when you were sent for this mission? *I* did, when I learned you had been manipulated into it. Oh, Indra tried to tell me you *volunteered*, as though that should appease me, but I came for you to the mortal forest by Kaushika's hermitage, only to learn I was too late. It was I who triggered the sage's warding, though I did not intend to. I was unable to protect you, but you did well enough on your own, did you not?"

My eyes widen. I don't know how to respond. Kaushika's ward was triggered by one who meant to harm him or the hermitage. Is that Shachi's intent? It is all I can do to keep my face still, to not show her how much this scares me.

"When Indra sent Nanda the first time, we were all unaware of Kaushika's danger, his *capability*. When she did not return, I knew Indra had wasted her. He insisted on sending Magadhi and Sundari, but them I could keep safe. You, on the other hand . . ." Shachi reaches forward and lifts my chin. "I thought you lost, but you provided a fine opportunity."

Her luscious lips curve into a smile. A chill goes down my spine.

"The halahala," I cannot help whispering. "That was you."

The goddess laughs, a rich, tinkling sound. "Surely you did not believe it was Indra? The lord is not capable of it, he has vowed not to touch it. He made the promise to Shiva. Indra is too much of a coward to break the promise."

"But—but he is the only one who can access those vaults," I stutter. "The stories—"

"Forget so often about us women, do they not?" Shachi says in a whisper. "Tell me, apsara. What is my name?"

I blink, not understanding, then my tongue flashes out to coat my suddenly dry mouth with moisture. Shachi, she is called, but also Indrani, the goddess who *belongs* with Indra, who is a *part* of Indra, his other half, just like Shiva and Shakti are two halves of the same whole. If Indra can access the halahala, so can she. Why did the stories never sing of her? Why did even the gandharvas forget?

"Why?" I croak. "Why send such a poison to the hermitage?"

"Because I needed this battle to occur before the Vajrayudh," Shachi replies, eyes glinting. "Because I needed Indra weakened and defeated if possible. Rambha told us of your questioning nature, and I understood that Kaushika's hate for Indra is deep and enduring. All the sage needed was a push, but it would need to be a significant one. Sending halahala showed me not only Kaushika's power, unrivaled by any other mortal in this realm, but also his ambition. It unspooled his own actions, forcing him to deny the other sages in the Mahasabha, in preparing his army for battle." Shachi shrugs her lovely shoulders and strokes her thick, flower-filled braid carelessly. "Indra is not fit to rule swarga, and I have long sought someone more worthy. Who better than this sage who seeks to usurp the lord? Who better than a powerful being like Kaushika by my side, sharing my throne? I will still be married to Indra—to be together is our destiny. But perhaps this time *he* will serve me and become my concubine, while I rule swarga."

"Kaushika does not wish for heaven's throne," I whisper. "He will not want to take Indra's place."

"Does he not wish for the Goddess either?" Shachi says, amused. "You yourself taught him that wisdom, did you not? And who am I if not a part of divine Shakti herself?"

I see her power, her beauty, her ambition. My throat feels choked, filled with tears. I swallow, and it is a loud sound in the silence of the hut.

"Why are you telling me this?" I breathe.

"Indra has Rambha as his loyal servant, one who tells him everything about the apsaras. It is time I have my own agent too. And one who barely tolerates the lord, who has seduced Kaushika, even gotten him to fall in love with her?" Shachi's smile is wide. She reaches forward to stroke my cheek with a glittering, bloodred nail. "Daughter. You belong to me."

The implication is clear.

*Her* weapon. Not Indra's.

Shachi lets go of my face. I feel her nail marks burn my skin. Dread pools in my belly, and I touch my cheeks but there is no scarring. She has left her mark *within* me somehow, claiming me for her own.

The queen stands up, but leaves behind a package on the cot. Apsara raiment, glorious and magical—and upon it a celestial blade. It is carved and jagged, shaped like a lightning bolt. A weapon from heaven, perhaps from Indra's own quiver. I tremble as I remember the manner in which the halahala released like a blade of lightning. Is this one tipped with poison too?

"The clothes are for when you return to heaven," Shachi says. "And the blade should you need it before that. Indra sent you on a task to stop the sage from attacking him before the Vajrayudh. Your job now is to *encourage* him to do so within that time. Only a few months remain, daughter. Do not fail me."

A thousand questions bubble within me, but my tongue feels heavy. It doesn't matter. A reply is not expected. With another sharp smile, Shachi and the two apsaras blink out and I am left alone. I gasp as though a weight has disappeared from my chest with the queen gone.

The clothes and jewelry shine at me from my cot, but it is the lightning shard I pick up as if hypnotized. It is powerful, but it is not tainted with halahala—I would sense it were it so. Still, it is as threatening to me as that poison.

Once it was Indra who commanded me, but now it is Shachi, and I dare not disobey her either. *She* was the one who sent halahala to Kaushika, something that could have ripped him from the cycle of rebirth altogether, all as a test of his mettle, of his worth by her side. Shachi had no way of knowing if Kaushika would survive it. He almost didn't—it was only my magic that saved him. What if she finds another way to harm him? The blade feels heavy in my hand, giving me the answers.

She wishes to rein Kaushika, the two of them together ruling heaven, but if I fail to obey her, she will kill Kaushika herself. She will either have him by her side or destroy him. Perhaps she will force me to destroy him with my own hand—in her own capriciousness and pride.

As for me . . . I have already made an enemy of Indra. If I make an enemy of Shachi too, I will never be able to return home, no matter who has the throne. Shachi has shown me how unpredictable she truly is. She is born of the asuras, her father a king of the hellish realm. Her marriage to Indra has always been shrouded in mystery, but though she is as heavenly as I am now, once she resided in the demonic realm. I cannot imagine what she would have in store for me. Between Shachi and Indra, how will Amaravati be safe? And am I to choose between the lord and his queen, when they are so inseparable?

My mission has not ended. It never will.

My heart grows cold. I leave the hut, clutching the blade to me in a daze. Outside, the air is clear and Kaushika stirs by the fire, waking now that Shachi's spell has lifted. His voice is weary, thick with sleep. He makes to rise.

"Meneka? What is it?"

I am upon him in an instant, the blade to his throat. Immediately his eyes sharpen, glinting with firelight. He is wide-awake now, alert and on his knees.

My voice is a warning. "You said you will keep your vow to King Satyavrat. That Indra will need to relent. Do you intend to war again?"

Kaushika watches me without a hint of fear. "I intend to do what I must. But I will not lie to you or hide things from you. That I can promise."

"It is not good enough," I hiss. I push the blade into his skin. A trickle of blood appears and I stare at it, but Kaushika does not seem to notice.

"What kind of promise would you have me make, then?" he asks quietly.

"One you will not break. One as deep as your deepest vows. I cannot have you harming my sisters anymore. Nor my home. The creatures who live within Amaravati are innocent, and we cannot be casualties to your purpose. I will not allow it."

Kaushika nods slowly. "I promise you. I will find a way to fulfill my vow that will bring no harm to your city or your kin. I will not harm your sisters. On Shiva's own name, I vow this."

He looks at me expectantly, and I do not know what I will do with Shachi's instruction, but a weight in my heart releases. Still, I do not pull back the blade. I will have another truth from him, this one for myself.

"You speak of Shiva," I say softly. "He told me I was a creature of love, but Indra has always called my kind creatures of lust. Within the groves, we are treated like soldiers, dancers of heaven's army, trained for one purpose alone."

Kaushika frowns. "You are more than any of those," he says gruffly.

"And what is that?"

His eyes meet mine. "You are whoever you wish to be, Meneka."

The blade trembles in my hand. He doesn't flinch.

"And if I *am* a creature of lust? If I am an instrument of power? If I am everything I dread?"

"Then you are still Meneka," he says angrily. "And you are still mine."

He pushes the blade of lightning away like it means nothing. He stands up, towering over me, staring at me. "If you will have me," he says quietly, "I am yours too."

The lightning shard falls from my hand. I reach for him, heart blazing. His hands encircle my waist, and Kaushika bends his head to me. I close my eyes as our lips meet. Our tongues collide in a hungry assault, our pain and loss and desire all rolled into one heated kiss. His mouth punishes me, and I punish his in return, clinging to him as his tongue swirls and teases me. I know the kiss is more than lust. It is curiosity about who we are, now that we see each other in our honesty and reality. It is a promise to attempt love, to *fight* for it, even if the three realms themselves keep us from each other, pulling us away.

Kaushika angles my head, kissing deeper, and a satisfied sigh builds in me. I think with a rush of emotion and peace and fragility that this is how it always will be. We are immortal souls, all of us caught in the conspiracies of life. If it is not Indra, it is the goddess, and if it is neither of them, it is us, ourselves. We can choose to belong to ourselves. We can choose to belong to each other.

For now, I make the easy choice. I choose to trust in my love for this man, and in his love for me. I thread my hands through Kaushika's hair and let him take me.

# AUTHOR'S NOTE

I first learned the story of Meneka when I was a child, reading stories of Hindu culture in the Amar Chitra Katha comics, watching Telegu and Kannada serials, and growing up in a household where prayers and mantras were regularly recited. Yet my introduction did not start with the apsara herself, but with Sage Vishwamitra—Kaushika, as he is known in *The Legend of Meneka*.

Ask any Hindu household, and they'll know who Vishwamitra is. He is one of the most revered sages, not only credited with writing the Gayatri Mantra—arguably the most powerful mantra in Hinduism, and one I practice regularly myself—but also one of the brahmarishis, the highest order of seers, powerful beyond compare. His influence permeates Hinduism from the time of the Rigveda—a text so ancient that its roots are lost to academic discussion.

Yet, while there is a lot of information about Vishwamitra the sage, there is little information about Kaushika the man. It is known that he was a king, that he lusted so deeply for power he finally sought the greatest cosmic power there is, thus beginning his training to become a sage. This pursuit of knowledge led to his own spiritual revolution into a great seer, but for me a true indication of his enlightenment and devotion came from the story of Meneka, the apsara who was sent to seduce him.

Meneka and Kaushika famously fell in love. She clearly had a tremendous impact on Kaushika's life, yet she is often relegated to a footnote. I found myself fascinated with her. Why was it that, though Meneka and Kaushika's story is one of the most beloved love ballads of Hindu culture, so little is known of Meneka herself? Why is she consigned to obscurity, known only through her interaction with the great sage and her service to Indra? When I began writing *The Legend of Meneka*, I wanted to retain all that I knew of her while also giving her a chance to become her own woman. Doing so meant discovering her, understanding her, and staying true to who she has always been—an apsara.

Apsaras, of course, have always been epitomes of lust. Whether you find them in Hinduism or Buddhism, in India or Thailand or Cambodia, through the Rigveda or the Mahabharata, their dance and seduction have always been a central part of their identity. That they were routinely sent to seduce sages is also known. They were virgin, whore, devotee, and prostitute, all at once, performing their duties with enthusiasm, then returning to the celestial plane where they belonged.

Lust—in religion, too—is not a sin. Hinduism is rife with sexual imagery. Our gods, our temples, our philosophies are wildly rooted in sexuality, both heterosexual and queer. Shiva is represented through his phallus. Temple architecture, Konark being a favorite example, often depicts scenes of deep and graphic intimacy. *Kamasutra*—which everyone knows perhaps more than any other ancient source on sex—is a historical Hindu text that is a guide into the nature of love and pleasure, sexuality and eroticism.

My Meneka was always going to be a sensual being, this much I knew. She would enjoy her own power and seductive beauty. What she'd struggle with is understanding the contradictory nature of her own identity and the path that Kaushika was on. If seduction was coercive, could any feelings that emerge from it ever be true? *Did* Meneka actually deceive Kaushika? If seduction was her very nature, what path could Meneka choose while being true to herself? These questions guided me as I wrote her story. I found her devotion an interesting counterpoint to Kaushika's own journey to becoming a brahmarishi.

This is a matter that has leanings in the four-thousand-plus-year history of Hinduism, and in the rise of the Bhakti school of thought within the Upanishads that considers devotion the sweetest path to nirvana or moksha, the absolute freedom of the self. Several people will draw a distinction between Bhakti as godly emotional devotion and Kama as sensual erotic devotion. Both can be paths to enlightenment, but they are inherently different, some will say. There is room for argument in that, just as there is for *anything* in true Hinduism. Yet for my Meneka, both Bhakti and Kama become the same thing when it comes to Kaushika. Meneka's lust for Kaushika *becomes* love. And Kaushika's love and lust, by the end of it, merge into a spiritual devotion for Meneka too. After his encounter with Meneka, Kaushika realizes that the way of the Goddess is not in competition with Shiva's way. The two are strands of the same helix—interconnected, interdependent, complementary.

Yet in several versions of the love story, Kaushika abandons Meneka once he realizes she is an apsara. In one famous retelling, he curses her to be separated from him, knowing that Meneka truly loves him and that this would be the greatest punishment she could endure. *The Legend of Meneka* deliberately departs from this. I wanted to give them a second chance to become their own people. I wanted them to discover their own minds. At its heart, the story of Meneka and Kaushika is always about love. It is about understanding the shape and depth of love. It is about questioning what love means.

# GLOSSARY

**AMARAVATI:** The City of Immortals, and the capital of swarga, heaven.

**AMRIT:** The golden nectar that appeared during the Churning of the Oceans, which gives celestials their immortality.

**APSARA:** A celestial dancer of Lord Indra's court and heaven.

**ASURA:** A creature of the hellish realm, akin to a demon.

**CHURNING OF THE OCEANS:** An ancient event where the oceans were churned by creatures of both heaven and hell, in order to release amrit. Other substances emerged from this churning too.

**DEVA:** A male deity, though collectively this often is gender neutral.

**DEVI:** A female deity.

**GANDHARVA:** A celestial musician.

**GODDESS VS GODDESS:** *Goddess* (capitalized) usually refers to the one power of the feminine energy, Shakti, as she is known; *goddess* (lowercase) is an individual representation of that power.

**HALAHALA:** The most dangerous poison that exists, which appeared during the Churning of the Oceans.

**KALPAVRIKSH:** A wish-fulfilling tree that grows in Lord Indra's garden.

**LINGAM:** A representation of Lord Shiva, which is similar to a cylindrical shaft sitting inside an oval-shaped basin.

**MAHASABHA:** A sage's gathering, where decisions about yogis and hermitages are made.

**MANTRA:** Chants of great power, consecrated through meditation.

**MUDRA:** A dance sigil that mimics different shapes and unleashes an apsara's magic.

**NARAKA:** The hellish realm.

**PRAKRITI:** Nature in its most fundamental essence.

**PRANA:** Magic of the universe. All magic can be traced to prana, and mortal yogis yoke this directly through a process called tapasya. Immortals only have access to it through elemental deities such as Lord Indra, who harnesses it to provide it to the rest of the population of Amaravati.

**RAKSHASA:** A creature of the hellish realm, akin to a monster.

**RISHI:** A yogi of great power, a sage. This is a self-proclaimed title, though assessed by other sages.

**SOMA:** A celestial alcohol.

**SWARGA:** Indra's heaven.

**TAPASVIN:** One who does tapasya. Also refers to the kind of magic that tapasya unleashes.

**TAPASYA:** Arduous meditation that yogis undertake, which allows them to access the power of the universal prana.

**THUMRI:** A village in the mortal realm.

**VAJRA:** Lord Indra's lightning bolt, a weapon of great power.

**VAJRAYUDH:** A cosmic event that occurs every thousand years or so, when the beings of heaven grow weaker.

**VEDAS:** Ancient texts that discuss rituals, philosophy, and a variety of spiritual knowledge.

**YOGI:** A practitioner of yoga, one who often undertakes arduous meditation in order to gain enlightenment.

# ACKNOWLEDGMENTS

For a variety of reasons, this book was a challenge to write. How do you take a beloved myth and do it justice, finding your own story concealed within it while keeping true to a mighty shared tradition? It raises a hundred questions for an artist—and those questions did not leave me when I wrote *The Legend of Meneka*. I am fortunate that I was surrounded by such competent, kind, and brilliant people while on this journey, without whom I could never have discovered the story I wished to tell.

Massive thanks to my amazing editor, Julia Elliott, for everything you did for this book—championing it at every stage, providing such incisive edits that it made my heart sing, believing in my skills as an author to pull this off, and always being available. Thank you for our chats and your continued passion, warmth, and professionalism.

Thanks also to my editors in the UK, Natasha Bardon and Aje Roberts, for all the work they put in. Hours and hours go into any book, and anyone in the industry will tell you that the first thing you need for success is an invested, excited team—and I couldn't have gotten luckier with the hardworking people at Harper Voyager and William Morrow, who have shown up for this book with such fervor. There are so many of you I wish I could name—you know who you are, and I hope you know I am grateful.

Deep thanks also to my agent, Lucienne Diver, and The Knight Agency. You took this project at a stage when one truly needs a wonderful agent in their corner to usher a book into completion. You advised me with much kindness and sincerity, always keeping my best interests at heart. It is wonderful to have you be a part of this.

Deep thanks to my cover artists. Truly, look at this beauty. I have gotten so lucky to be working with such talented people—and this book will have a special place in my heart, in no small part because of you and the gorgeous rendition of this world and character.

To all my author friends, from the early beta readers who read versions of this manuscript I would be mortified to show most people to the ones who heard me vent and sob about everything in between. Special mention to friends without whose advice this book literally would not have happened: Shannon Chakraborty, Hannah Long, Elyse John, Essa Hansen, and Sunyi Dean. A lot occurred when this story was in the works, in both my personal and professional life, and you guys kept me grounded, never wavering in your care and insight.

Thanks also to my *non*-author friends, who reminded me that there is so much more beyond writing—a fact I seem to forget all too often—and who rescued me from terrible burnout. Community—both within and outside of publishing—is a beautiful, precious thing, and I am so grateful to have found it in both places. Special thanks to Amu, Santosh, and Sam-Sam, in whose house my family and I parked ourselves for so long, and where I did my copyedits amidst a hectic cross-country move. I started writing this section at your kitchen table, while you plied me with chocolates and love.

Thank you also to every reader who is picking this book up and talking about it with such grace; to all those who have followed me from my other works and those who have found me here. I hope you continue to stay with me—there is a lot in the future, and I cannot wait to watch us grow together. To every bookseller who is shouting about *The Legend of Meneka*, and book bloggers, reviewers, podcasters, Instagrammers, BookTokers, and everyone else who is recommending this to someone else—whether online or offline.

Your unflagging enthusiasm never fails to astonish and humble me. I hope it never does.

As always, thanks to my family—Tate and little Rohan and the even littler one, whose name is still a secret but who will arrive long before this book is out. I have never known love in the way you give it. Your patience, generosity, and gentleness with me while I write mean the world to me. You are the anchors of my mind, the ones who matter the most, the true gifts of my life. I love you in every reality and in every universe.